D0228521

MOLLY GREEN has travelled the world, unpacking her suitcase in a score of countries. On returning to England, Molly decided to pursue her life-long passion for writing. She now writes in a cabin in her garden on the outskirts of Tunbridge Wells, Kent, ably assisted by her white rescued cat, Dougie.

Also by Molly Green

An Orphan in the Snow
An Orphan's War
An Orphan's Wish

A Sister's Courage

MOLLY GREEN

avon.

Published by AVON
A division of HarperCollins*Publishers* Ltd
1 London Bridge Street
London SE1 9GF

www.harpercollins.co.uk

A Paperback Original 2019

A catalogue copy of this book is available from the British Library.

ISBN: 978-0-00-833244-0

Typeset in Minion by Palimpsest Book Production Limited, Falkirk, Stirlingshire
Printed and bound in UK by CPI Group (UK) Ltd, Croydon CR0 4YY

MIX
Paper from
responsible sources
FSC **FSC C007454**
www.fsc.org

This book is produced from independently certified FSC™ paper to ensure responsible forest management.
For more information visit: www.harpercollins.co.uk/green

To all those remarkable women in the Air Transport Auxiliary who risked their lives every day to make sure their male counterparts had the planes they urgently needed for training and combat. There were 168 female pilots including four female engineers who joined the ATA during the war years, along with their male counterparts – sadly, there were a number of fatalities.

I would like to make a special dedication to Pauline Gower, a qualified pilot before the war with her own aviation business, who successfully fought for the right of female pilots to be allowed to join the Air Transport Auxiliary along with the men, and was appointed Senior Commander of the women's section.

Before the war it was unheard of for women to have equal pay in any job whatsoever, but in May 1943 Miss Gower was the first person in any company or organisation to obtain equal pay for the women pilots in the Air Transport Auxiliary. She pushed home the point that her pilots were doing exactly the same job and taking exactly the same risks every day as the men. She refused to take no for an answer – a truly outstanding achievement.

Unfortunately, after the war, the gap between male and female pilots' pay was once again firmly in place.

Tragically, in 1947 Pauline Gower died at only 36 having just given birth to twin sons who thankfully survived. Who knows what more she might have achieved if she'd had a longer life?

Before . . .

'Can I go up, Daddy? *Please.*'

'Your mother said I was not to let you.' Raine's father looked down at his daughter, taller than most fourteen-year-olds, with long, spindly arms and legs. He couldn't help smiling at the set of her chin, her clear violet eyes, just like her mother's, the long dark wavy hair lifting slightly in the breeze. Yes, she was a beautiful girl – everyone said so. Which was why her mother was determined to protect her.

'I don't know why you want her to go and see such a dangerous performance,' Simone said when he'd told her he was taking their daughter to watch Cobham's Flying Circus perform at West Malling. 'But if you insist to go against my wishes you must not allow her into one of those contraptions.'

'You should come with us.' Robert gazed at his wife fondly. She was French, twenty-one years younger than him, and she tried hard during their marriage to keep him in line. Sometimes it worked. But not today. He intended to keep his promise to his daughter to at least take her to watch the spectacle.

'You think I want my shoes muddy, my coat splashed in some 'orrible field?' she'd said, her eyes flashing.

Simone didn't know how seductive she looked when she was annoyed, Robert thought, his mouth curling in amusement. And how delightful her accent, which she was so sure she'd lost ten years ago.

'I shall find out if she goes up,' Simone had warned.

Now, looking at his daughter's pleading expression, Robert relented. 'If I let you, Raine, you must promise faithfully not to tell your mother. We would both be in terrible trouble.' He looked down at his daughter with affection. 'You know, you do rather take after your mother in your determination when you've made up your mind about something.'

Raine beamed. 'That's a good thing, isn't it, Daddy?'

He laughed. 'Yes, I suppose it is. It might carry you through life. On the other hand, you might be in for some huge disappointments.'

Raine gave a theatrical sigh. 'I promise I won't say anything, Daddy.'

'Good girl. Now let's find out how long we'll have to wait in the queue.'

Robert strolled across the field to collect his daughter as the biplane touched down. He had to admit his heart had thumped in his ears as he'd watched every second of the plane's progress, knowing his precious daughter was strapped into the 'flimsy contraption', as Simone had called it. But when his eyes alighted on his daughter's shining face as she ran light-footed over the grass towards him, he smiled to himself that he hadn't tried to clip her wings.

'It was wonderful, Daddy. I didn't feel sick at all.' The words tumbled from her lips in her exhilaration. 'The pilot – he said I could call him Jim . . .' She took in a quick noisy breath. 'He thought I was scared when I called out, but it was only 'cos I was so excited. I felt like a bird . . . or a kite.'

2

She laughed. 'I wish you could have come with me, Daddy. You'd have loved it. And guess what . . .?'

'I couldn't possibly.' But he knew without guessing.

'One day I'm going to be a pilot!'

'I'm not so sure about that.'

She stared at him, a defiant expression crossing her face.

'I'm *very* sure, Daddy, and you and Maman won't be able to stop me!'

Chapter One

'I'm so proud of you, darling.'

Raine's father removed his spectacles and regarded her. She was sitting opposite him in his study, a room stuffed with books, papers and files. Blotting paper, pens and pencils littered his desk, and his beloved wireless set perched on a bookcase. He was holding the paper with the results of Raine's test, the one that would give an indication as to what she might expect when she took her Higher National Certificate in the summer. He glanced at the paper again.

'You're up for top marks in mathematics.' He looked up and caught her eye. 'I'm not surprised. You gained a distinction in your School Certificate.' He continued reading. 'A pass in history and scripture, and credits in English, science and geography . . . even French. You'll be able to converse with your mother in her native language at long last.' His eyes twinkled as he looked at her and Raine gave a ghost of a smile.

Her father was well aware her mother was an impatient woman who couldn't stand more than a couple of minutes' French conversation with Raine without criticising her. Everyone in Raine's French class envied her having a French mother she could practise with and who helped with her pronunciation and grammar.

If only they knew.

'Well, there's no question why you've got these results,' her father broke into her thoughts, 'being the brains of the family.'

Raine shrugged. 'It's only an indication, Dad. Who knows what the results will be when I take the proper exam. I'm not banking on anything in case I disappoint you. And I don't want to be known as the brains in the family, either. Look at Suzanne with her music. She's incredible the way she follows all those music scores and can play two instruments beautifully – the only one in the family who's musical.'

Her father paused to pull out a packet of cigarettes. 'Don't know where she gets it from. Certainly not from me,' he said, shaking one out. 'But it's marvellous, all the same.'

Raine noticed his hand was a little unsteady as he flicked the lighter. She noticed his hair was thinning and his eyes had heavy bags under them. She saw the deepening lines from his nose to his mouth. Maman had encouraged him to go into partnership with two other accountants eighteen months ago and Raine feared the extra responsibility was taking its toll on his health. Come to think of it, her father didn't look very happy these days, either. She supposed he was getting old. She always forgot he was so much older than her mother.

'But that doesn't take away *your* achievement,' her father continued, drawing on his cigarette and blowing out the smoke in a long stream through his nose.

She waited. She knew exactly what was coming, but today she had her answer prepared . . . and her request.

Her father took in another long drag and exhaled. Raine felt her eyes stinging but knew better than to say anything.

6

Her father's study was his haven. Even her mother wasn't allowed in unless invited, and very definitely not Doreen, the cleaning lady, unless he was present. He always said he knew exactly where everything was, even though the papers and books piled on his desk were in danger of cascading any minute.

'We've touched on the subject before, Raine. Maybe a little too soon when you were hardly old enough to make a decision, but I hope with these excellent marks – especially the one in mathematics – you'll take up my offer to start a career in the company.' She remained silent. 'I know it will be harder for you to be accepted as a girl, but I can help overcome any problems on that front.'

Raine bristled. 'Dad, I intend to fight my *own* battles. It would be awful if you interfered like that. Can you imagine what would it look like, one of the partners giving his daughter a shove up the ladder? They'd resent me and there'd be nothing you could do to stop it.'

Her father's voice hardened a fraction. 'What are you saying, Lorraine?'

'That I'm not going to work in the company. I'm sorry, Dad, but I'm not interested in accounting – I've told you before – so I wouldn't be any good at the job.'

'Raine, I'm offering you a proper career – you'll thank me one day. Then when the time comes and you decide to marry – though I'm not sure who would put up with you, you're such an independent miss – at least you'll have something solid behind you, should you ever need it.'

'Thank you, Dad, but no. I'm not doing it. And as for getting married, I've no intention of doing that, either – not for a very long time, if ever. I want to see something of the world. Live a little. Not be stuck in some deadly office doing deadly figures with deadly people.'

Frustration rose in her chest as she sprang up to leave, but her father put his hand on her shoulder and firmly pressed her down in the chair again.

'Not so fast, Lorraine,' he said, his voice stern.

As though I'm a little girl, Raine thought, annoyed. She sat in sulky silence.

'Didn't they teach you better manners at that expensive school we sent you to? Your mother is very upset with your outbursts lately.'

He never called Raine by her full name unless he was displeased with her. It was the first time he'd ever used the cost of her school to make a point. Inwardly, Raine cringed. She'd always adored her father, but these days he rarely stuck up for her against her mother, who used every feminine trick to twist him round her little finger. Raine swallowed her scorn. Batting her eyelashes and looking up adoringly to some man to get her own way was not something she could ever contemplate. If she didn't stand firm now, he and Maman would take over her life. She looked unwaveringly back at him.

'You're very stubborn,' her father went on when she remained silent, 'and that's not always something to be proud of. You remind me so much of your mother.' His face softened as he gave a rueful smile. 'And I wouldn't be saying this if I didn't think the world of you both.'

She threw off his words with a laugh as if they were of no consequence to her, but deep inside she knew her father was right. She *was* stubborn. No matter how hard she tried to be tolerant, if someone couldn't see things the way she did, she lost all patience.

'Don't you see, Raine, it's because we love you and want the best for you.'

'I want more from life than what you and Maman seem

to have mapped out for me,' she fairly snapped back. 'A trainee accountant, for however long that lasts. And all I'd have at the end of it would be my name on a brass plate on the door. Can you imagine?' She pulled a face.

'You'd be a partner in time.'

Raine snorted. 'Me? A woman?' She rolled her eyes. 'I doubt it. But it's not what I want, anyway.'

'Well, what *do* you want?'

Raine shook her head, her mouth tight. She knew she was letting her father down. That his dream had always been that she'd join his company one day and become a full-blown accountant. All because mathematics came easy to her. She wished she'd failed her mathematics test now. If she had, she might not be sitting here, facing her father, fighting for her future.

'Didn't you get any career advice at school?'

'Oh, heaps.' Raine rolled her eyes. 'Nursing . . . teaching . . . secretary . . . vet's assistant. Why didn't they tell us to aim higher – become a doctor . . . or headmistress . . . or go into politics, now we have the vote? No, not that, on second thoughts,' she added hastily, in case her father took her up on it. 'Actually, I'd hate that.'

'Strangely enough, you'd probably be good at it,' he said. 'You certainly wouldn't let the opposition get a word in.' He drew in another lungful of smoke, blew it out in a stream, some escaping through his nose, then ground the stub in his ashtray. 'Well, I have to say, Lorraine, I'm disappointed. It would've been good to know when the day comes you'll be there to carry on the name.'

Her heart squeezed as she studied her father. What was he hinting at? Now she thought about it, he was suddenly looking a lot older. Not just tired but exhausted. She felt a flash of sympathy for him. However hard he worked she

9

knew it was never quite enough to keep Maman satisfied. But if she caved in, *she'd* be the one to be unhappy. She drew in a deep breath.

'I want to do something exciting with my life. Something challenging – learning new skills.' She gazed at her father, imploring him to understand. 'Dad, have you forgotten what I told you I wanted to be that day at the flying circus?'

Her father momentarily closed his eyes and shook his head. 'No, Raine, I haven't. But if you won't come into the business and you don't have any other sound ideas, I think you'd better concentrate on getting a distinction in your Higher Certificate. That would make your mother proud that her faith in you is justified.'

'But will you let me take flying lessons on weekends? I don't want to put it off any longer. Please, Dad, say I can. You know it's what I want to do more than anything in the world. I've never changed my mind. I'll never be happy unless I can learn to fly.' She held her breath.

He gave her a look she couldn't fathom.

'You're not yet eighteen. Far too young to take flying lessons, and I know your mother will say the same.'

'Boys no older than me are pilots.' Raine held her father's gaze. 'If I'd been a boy, you wouldn't have said that,' she flashed. 'Would you?'

'I don't know, love. I'm not used to sons. I've only got three lovely daughters.'

He smiled and she knew he was trying to soften the blow. But she wouldn't allow herself to be softened. This was too important.

Her father lit another cigarette. 'Well, Raine, I'll have a word with your mother, but I don't think it'll get you anywhere.'

Raine frowned. 'Why can't you stand up to her for a change?

Why does she always have to have the last word? She'll never agree. She's too French. All she wants is for me to look pretty and dress like a Frenchwoman and marry a rich man. Preferably on the other side of the Channel so she has an excuse to visit France. And that's not what I want at all. What's right for her is not right for me, but she'll never see it.'

Her father patted her hand. 'Enough, Raine. I've told you I'll speak to her.'

'No, I will *not* permit Lorraine to take lessons for flying.' Simone's voice rose.

When Raine had decided to go by the name she called herself when she was little – she couldn't pronounce 'Lorraine' – her father had immediately humoured her, except when he was displeased. But her mother had simply ignored her request, telling her she was quite ridiculous to give up her lovely French name. And no amount of foot-stamping by the little girl would alter her mother's attitude.

Now, in the sitting room, her parents were talking about her as though she wasn't there. Raine pressed her lips together. She was old enough to be treated as an adult. She could make her own decisions. They *must* see how important it was for her.

'Why won't you?' Raine demanded.

Her mother swung round, her eyes darkening with anger. 'Because I say so.'

'That's not good enough, Maman,' Raine said, pushing down her fury and speaking in a measured tone. If she showed any childish sign, her mother would leap on it. She knew that from past experience.

'You had better explain to her, Robert.' Simone gave a theatrical sigh and turned on her husband, her tone cool. 'I'm going to take a headache pill and have a lie-down.'

'I know we can afford it,' Raine said when her mother had left the room. 'And I'll scream if Maman says one more time how dangerous it is. It's no more dangerous than skiing and everyone does that without even thinking about it.'

'Sit down, Raine. I'm afraid I have something to tell you, which your mother and I have tried to keep to ourselves rather than upset you girls.'

Raine perched on one of the leather armchairs, leaning forward. What on earth was coming? Her father drew his eyebrows together as he did when he had something important to say. She braced herself.

'I'm glad we were able to give you and Suzanne a good education, darling, but we won't be able to do the same for Ronnie.'

What's he talking about? Oh, of course.

She breathed out. 'Ronnie's the first to admit she's not brainy,' Raine said, 'so it would probably be wasted on her anyway.'

'No education is ever wasted,' her father reprimanded. 'It's not that at all. Ronnie deserves the same education as her sisters. But I won't beat about the bush. You're old enough to know the truth.' He looked directly at Raine. 'I'm afraid I've lost quite a lot of money.'

Raine gazed at her father in horror.

'How?'

Her father wouldn't meet her eye.

'I don't want to go into it at the moment,' he said flatly. 'Just take it from me that flying lessons are out of the question for the time being. So please don't mention it again.'

'What about Maman . . .?' Raine said desperately. 'Hasn't she got some money of her own?'

'She has a little tucked away and that's what I was hoping she might use. I've tried hard to persuade her on your behalf, but she's completely against women flying . . . especially her daughter. She maintains it's not feminine. That it's too dangerous. She's terrified something bad will happen to you. It's a man's job, she says. I must say I don't totally disagree, though I think you'd probably be an exception.'

Rage stuck in Raine's throat. Anger for her father for being foolish enough to lose his money and not strong enough to stand up to his adored wife who had independent means. Fury with her mother for being so narrow-minded and not understanding how learning to fly meant everything in the world to her.

She had a sudden thought and managed to swallow before she spoke. 'Are we going bankrupt?'

Her father sighed. 'No. Your mother won't allow that to happen. But we're going to have to move to a smaller house.'

The shock almost sent her reeling.

'But I like living here.'

She couldn't bear the idea of leaving. Leaving their beautiful Edwardian house in the enormous garden full of trees and flowers with lawn stretching for what seemed like miles when they were children. Where she and her sisters had played hide-and-seek, where they'd kept chickens for years until one day the fox got them. Tender-hearted Suzanne, who refused to eat the chicken Maman had subsequently served, had cried for days until her father built a stronger coop and bought another clutch of hens from the local farmer.

Raine's heart beat furiously.

'I'm afraid it's not up to you, Raine.'

'It sounds like you and Maman have everything already planned,' Raine said, not bothering to disguise the bitter edge to her words. 'Where will we go . . . and when do we have to leave here?'

'A family have been to see the house and made an offer. It's a fair one and will get us out of debt. But there won't be much over – we'll have to rent somewhere.'

'And then what will happen to us?'

'We'll be all right so long as we're careful. You might have to share a bedroom with your sister. And flying lessons, I'm afraid, can't come into it. You're nearly an adult.' He regarded her as though he still couldn't believe it and shook his head. 'You should seriously be thinking about a vocation.'

'What if there's a war? Everyone talks about it all the time. Another one with Germany. They said as much on Pathé News last night when Sally and I went to the cinema.'

'I don't think it will happen,' her father said, his eyes sad. 'People haven't forgotten the last war, a war to end all wars, and Mr Chamberlain secured the current peace treaty when he went to Munich last year.'

'But a piece of paper doesn't necessarily mean anything if Hitler's mad enough,' Raine argued, 'and if I was a pilot—'

'They'd never allow girls . . . women . . . to fly,' her father interrupted. 'Look at the RAF. They don't even have a women's section, let alone women pilots. You're wasting your time. And you wouldn't be able to take the discipline, even if they did. Believe me, Raine, I know you better than you know yourself.' He paused. 'But I also know something else about you. You're a very determined young woman. If it's your heart's desire and you *really* want to learn to fly, you'll find a way to pay for the lessons yourself.'

Raine threw him a long hard look and without another word, leapt up and marched out of the door, slamming it behind her, ignoring his order to come back. She went up to her room, the room she'd had to herself since she was twelve. Her mother had actually allowed her to choose the paint colour and curtain material and even the rug. Would

14

she miss all that? No. She wasn't sentimental about the house. Not like Suzanne. Raine loved changes, challenges, variety. No, it was because she couldn't bear the thought of the humiliation. Her father's humiliation and the family's.

She sat on the edge of the bed and put her hands to her face. Simply being in her room gave her the privacy she craved. Sharing with one of her sisters? Unthinkable. Her chest coiled as tight as a jack-in-the-box and she was ready to lash out at anyone.

She went over every word of the conversation with her father. Why wouldn't he tell her how he'd lost a load of money? She supposed he was too embarrassed to talk about it. Or her mother had forbidden him to tell her the truth. And there were two other questions he hadn't answered: when they were moving and where.

Beaten, she burst into tears.

Chapter Two

March 1939

The night before the move Raine heard Suzanne crying through the wall of her bedroom next door. She sprang out of bed and rushed into her sister's room.

'Come on, Suzy.' She put her arm around the shaking shoulders. 'Come on – don't take on so.'

'I can't bear to leave,' Suzanne sobbed, the words muffled in her pillow.

'We've got to put up with it,' Raine said. 'Dad will get his bills paid off.' She smiled at her sister, though she didn't particularly feel like smiling. 'It won't be all bad.'

'But we're moving miles away . . . to some village I've hardly heard of . . . away from everyone we know.'

'You haven't been concentrating in your history lessons.' Raine gave her sister's shoulders a little shake. 'Downe is where Charles Darwin lived. It might be interesting to see his house. And if you look on the map you'll see that Bromley isn't far. There'll be a bus from the village, so there's no need to worry about your music lessons—'

'I'll have to give them up,' Suzanne interrupted as she sat up on the bed and sniffed.

'Why do you say that?'

'How can Maman and Dad afford them?'

'They can because Maman has her own money. She won't let you go without your lessons. That comes before food on the table as far as she's concerned.'

Suzanne narrowed her eyes. 'Why would she do that when you're not allowed to have flying lessons – and you're the eldest?'

'There's only enough for one luxury and you're the favourite.'

'Course I'm not.'

'You are. Always have been. And you're jolly lucky Ronnie and I don't hate you for it.' Suzanne opened her mouth to protest but Raine stopped her. 'You're the one who's really talented. You know Maman's mania for culture.' She caught her sister's eye. 'Not that we don't all appreciate your pathetic squeakings on the violin, over and over and over . . .' She chuckled and Suzanne giggled.

'Do I really sound that bad?'

'Yes,' Raine said, still laughing, 'but we're willing to put up with it because you'll be famous one day, and we'll come and watch you perform – and brag to anyone who'll listen how clever you are.'

Suzanne's eyes shone with tears. 'If only that dream would happen one day, but it's like you wanting to be a pilot. Professional orchestras still refuse to take women – unless you're a harpist. And even when *that* miracle happens, you're kept out of sight in the wings. They don't even put your name on the programme.'

Raine grimaced. 'Same old story.' She looked at her sister. 'But it doesn't mean to say it's impossible, Suzy. We'll both have to work extra hard to show the men we're as good, if not *better*, than they are. We have to keep badgering those in charge until they can't refuse us. Until then you need to buck up. The sooner we get moved, the sooner we can get on with our lives.'

'It's all right for *you*. You're much braver than me. I could never argue like you.'

'You have to learn to do it with a smile,' Raine said seriously. 'Act like mad. Be as charming as you can. It's the only way.' She looked at her sister. 'You've got just as much determination as me, Suzy, with the way you focus on your music. You're stronger than you realise.' Raine gave her sister a hug.

Suzanne reached for her handkerchief underneath her pillow and blew her nose.

'That's better,' Raine said. 'We have to make the best of it. Look, I don't want to go any more than *you* do.'

She knew she wasn't being entirely truthful with her sister. At first she hadn't wanted to leave her familiar home, but the moment her father had told her they were moving to Downe her heart had leapt. Not only was it a short bus ride into Bromley, but she'd also discovered it was just a hop and a skip to Biggin Hill where there was a major aerodrome. According to the scale of the map, she'd quickly worked out that the house they were to rent was a mere four-mile cycle ride away. Perhaps *her* dream was closer to coming true.

A fortnight later . . .

Every Saturday morning before her mother had risen, Raine cycled from her new home, a semi-detached cottage in Downe, to Biggin Hill. She hung around the aerodrome watching, breathing in the atmosphere, loving every minute. In the early morning all was silent except for an occasional plane coming in to land or taking off, muffling any birdsong. She could think herself into another world, concentrate on its sound, the thrum of the engine, the glamour of the pilot when he stepped down from the open cockpit in his flying suit and whipped off his helmet.

One day that will be me, she told herself.

She'd been a member of the library in Bromley since she was a child, and on her last visit she'd found a book with photographs and descriptions of different aircraft, devouring it with far more enthusiasm than she'd ever done with her homework. Now, standing at the edge of the aerodrome, looking over the gate, she took great delight in recognising them and ticking them off in her notebook, committing them to memory.

This morning she was here particularly early when a man pulled up in his car. He leaned out of the window and smiled. She noticed his eyes, as blue as a summer sky.

'Hello, there. Want a lift over there so you can see the planes closer up?'

Her heart soared. 'Oh, yes, please . . . if you're sure it's no trouble.'

'None whatsoever.' He smiled again. 'Jump in, then. Name's Douglas White. You can call me Doug.'

'Raine Linfoot.' She held out her hand and he shook it.

She looked at him with interest. Chestnut hair, nice open face, and wore his uniform with an air of sophistication. Maybe mid-twenties. Too bad he was too old for her. She hid a smile.

'I've seen you hanging around,' he said as he put the gear into first. 'Do you fancy having a spin in my plane?' He turned to her and grinned.

'Oh, yes, please,' she said again. 'Is it really your own aeroplane?'

'Well, I rent it. I shouldn't really be doing this,' he added as they strolled towards the Tiger Moth, Raine's heart threatening to burst out of her chest. 'But no one's here this early except Bob, one of the mechanics. We need him to swing the prop. We'll just give it twenty minutes, all right?' He tilted his head. She noted he was actually very good-looking. 'How old are you, anyway?'

'Eighteen.' *Only a small fib.*

'Ever been up?'

'Only once, a few years ago – at Cobham's Flying Circus.'

'Were you sick?'

'No.'

Doug chuckled. 'Long as you're not sick in my plane. If you are, you'll have to clear it up.' He turned as one of the ground crew called to him.

'Having an early morning spin, sir?'

'Morning, Bob. Thought I'd take her up for a few minutes to show this young lady who wants to learn about planes.'

Bob looked doubtful as he lifted his cap to Raine. 'Righto, sir . . . miss. I'll get you started.'

Doug strapped her into the seat of the open cockpit and she felt him take the seat behind her. He handed her a very worn leather flying helmet, but she was so nervous she couldn't find the strap.

Feeling an idiot, she twisted round to face him. 'I can't seem to get this on.'

In seconds her helmet was secure, which did nothing to still her heart, pulsing madly against her ribs. She'd soon be up in the clouds again. It felt a long time since that first flight.

'Put these on as well.' He handed her a pair of goggles.

Almost before she'd adjusted them, Doug called out, 'Contact,' and Bob swung the propeller.

The engine burst into life and after waiting a few moments, presumably to warm it, Doug signalled to Bob and shouted, 'Chocks away.'

She saw Bob grab two lengths of rope and jerk the wedges out from under the wheels, then jump smartly out of the way.

A short run and they were airborne, the shock of the cold early morning slapping her face. She was in heaven. She giggled at the thought. She was probably about as close to heaven as she'd ever get. And when she saw the clouds floating above her, looking like candyfloss, and the sun just beginning to show on the horizon, she shouted with joy. She looked this way and that, noticing how the fields below reminded her of Grandma Linfoot's patchwork quilts, interspersed with doll's houses – at least that's what they looked like from her view. Raine pinched herself, happier than she'd ever been since that first flight with Cobham's Circus.

Without warning, there was a terrific lurch and suddenly she was hanging upside down, only the safety harness keeping her in place. But before she had time to react, the aeroplane righted itself. All too soon Doug brought it down on the grassy field with a couple of gentle bumps.

'How did you like the slow roll?' he asked as he helped her from the cockpit.

'I was too scared to scream. But then I wanted you to do it again.'

'Didn't think I'd better under the circumstances,' Doug chuckled. 'Maybe next time.'

There'd be a next time. Her heart, which had just settled back to normal, began to pound again.

He was looking at her. She liked the way his blue eyes twinkled.

'Do you want to go up again?'

'What, *now*?'

He laughed. 'I don't mean now. I've got work to do. But if I see you hanging around again and it's early enough, we'll see. For now, let's get you back.'

This was her chance to tell someone who would understand, she thought, as they approached the gate.

'What I *really* want to do is to train to be a pilot . . . but my parents can't afford lessons.' Oh, how she hated admitting that. 'I need a job,' she added quickly, hoping he would see she was trying to be independent.

She was gratified that Doug didn't roll his eyes when she'd mentioned being a pilot.

'What are you intending to do now, then?' he said.

'My dad wants me to be an accountant. Just because I'm good at mathematics and because he's one, he's decided it's a natural choice.'

'And your mother? What does *she* say?'

'Maman?' Raine grimaced. 'All she wants is for me to make a good marriage.'

'Hmm. But you don't want that.'

'Definitely not. I want to see something of the world first. But until then I only want to learn to fly. And if there's a war—'

'We won't mention any war,' he cut in. He looked at her thoughtfully. 'What about if I put in a word for you? Maybe get you a job over here. Clerk or general dogsbody or something. Nothing glamorous but the good thing is, you wouldn't be far from Hart's Flying Club. They rent a small airfield and stick mainly to biplanes, but that'd be perfect for you . . . and I'm one of their instructors.'

'I thought you were in the RAF.'

'I am – but as a volunteer. It's called the RAFVR. The VR bit means Volunteer Reserve. So when war is declared – and I'm sure it's going to happen sooner or later – I'll automatically join the RAF.'

Raine's heart raced. 'How far away is the flying club?'

'About five miles.' He glanced at her bicycle. 'No distance on a bike.'

'Maybe, but I couldn't afford to be a member of anything like that.'

'Not in normal circumstances, you probably couldn't,' Doug replied, grinning. 'But the Civil Air Guard are preparing pilots for war. They're offering subsidised flying lessons at five bob a go. That's dirt cheap, so you should be able to manage one a week.'

Five shillings. Maybe it was dirt cheap for a flying lesson, but she knew Maman would never give her the money for them. Her mouth tightened with determination as she remembered her father's words to her in the study that day. She'd pay for them somehow.

'And who knows' – Doug was smiling – 'you might even get me as your instructor. In fact, I'll put a word in for you at Hart's and tell them I'd like to teach you if I'm not at Biggin Hill that day.'

'Oh, Doug, that would be wonderful.' Raine felt her chest would burst. 'And do you really think you could get me a job here?'

'Leave it to me.' He winked. 'When are you coming again?'

'Tomorrow?'

'No, tomorrow's Sunday. But I think Tuesday would be okay – say, ten o'clock?'

Thankful the school term had ended and it was the start of the Easter holidays, she said, 'Yes, please, Doug.' If she had her way and something turned up, she wouldn't be going back to school.

'Okay. I'll meet you at the gate.' He looked at her and she nodded. 'Meanwhile, I'll see what I can do.'

Chapter Three

The hours dragged by until Tuesday. When it finally dawned, with raindrops splashing down her bedroom window, Raine hopped out of bed and quickly washed and dressed without disturbing Suzanne. She'd become used to sharing a room now, and Suzy would never betray her.

Would Doug have any news about a job for her? It would be so wonderful if he had. She wouldn't even cycle over to Hart's Flying Club and speak to anyone about taking lessons until she knew she could definitely pay for them.

'Tea, Maman?' she said as her mother waltzed into the kitchen in her satin dressing gown, looking for all the world like a glamorous film star. How her mother was going to tighten her belt, heaven knew.

'Thank you, *chérie*.'

Raine hummed as she poured a cup for herself.

'You sound very happy today, Lorraine.' Her mother gave her a sharp look before glancing out of the window at the grey clouds. 'And on such a morning where it looks as if it will storm.' She turned round. 'So why are you so cheerful?'

Raine knew that tone in her mother's voice. She tried to laugh it off.

'I'm always happy when I go to the library,' she said, 'and that's where I'm off to.'

'But you went Saturday.'

Careful, Raine. Maman is already suspicious.

'I know. I didn't like what I'd chosen, after all.'

Her mother regarded her thoughtfully, her forehead creasing into a frown.

'Your hair needs cutting,' she said finally. 'It looks most untidy. I will cut it for you this morning since we cannot afford the 'airdresser.'

Alarm rose in Raine's throat. 'Maman, I want to go to the library this morning before it gets busy, so you can cut it this afternoon, if you like.'

'Yes, I *do* like,' her mother said. 'But I like to do it this morning. Until then I will return to my bed. I did not sleep well. Please wake me at half past ten with coffee. This tea tastes 'orrible.' She swept out.

Raine gazed after her mother. She was sure Maman suspected she was up to something. Well, she was not going to sit docilely while her mother, who had never cut anyone's hair in her life, hacked at hers this morning. She liked her hair long. She could tie it back from her face or put it up out of the way. She wasn't going to have Maman's experimental haircut. No. She had an appointment at Biggin Hill aerodrome and no one – not even Maman – was going to stop her from keeping it.

Raine wasn't concentrating as her feet automatically pedalled along the lane. A steady drizzle seeped under the collar of her jacket. Her mind was far above in the dark clouds when a rabbit shot in front of her. Swerving across the road to avoid it she landed in a ditch, mud and water clinging to her and the bicycle.

Damn. That's all I need.

She managed to push the handlebars to one side and climb

out, then hauled the bike up. On inspection, she noticed the handlebars were at the wrong angle. She tugged them hard in the opposite direction, but they didn't budge. Disappointment flooded through her. She'd hardly slept all night, she'd been so excited when Doug had offered to put in a word for her about working at Biggin Hill. She'd be with other pilots – telling them how she longed to learn to fly. Fancy him being one of the instructors at the flying club. And now, when she didn't turn up, Doug would think she'd lost interest and not bother with her again. Tears sprang to her eyes.

I'll walk, she told herself fiercely. It can't take more than an hour, even wheeling the bicycle. But after twenty minutes of pushing the heavy bike she felt a sharp pain stabbing her right arm. She must have fallen more awkwardly than she'd realised. She paused for a minute and impatiently rubbed it, but it only gave her slight relief. She glanced at her watch. Already ten past nine. She would never make it by ten.

Well, it was no good bawling. She'd have to thumb a lift in a lorry or something that could take her bicycle as well.

She stood out on the road, but the only large vehicles were buses that carried on past her to their next scheduled stops. Biting her lip in frustration, her right arm beginning to throb, she made a pact with herself. If nothing suitable comes after five more cars, I'll stop the next one – whatever it is – even if I have to dump my bicycle.

It was a pony and trap. The driver doffed his cap as the pony clopped by. 'Morning, miss.'

'Oh, please stop,' Raine called desperately.

'Whoa, there, Matilda,' he called, pulling the reins as he addressed the horse. 'Let's 'ear what the young lady 'as to say for 'erself.'

'Are you going anywhere near the aerodrome?'

'Would that be Biggin Hill?'

'Yes.'

He looked at her. 'And what would you be doing on an aerodrome, miss?'

'I work there.' It wouldn't hurt to tell him such a fib. 'But I've had an accident on my bicycle and if I don't get there soon I'll be late.'

'You'll be telling me you're one of the pilots next.' He grinned, showing more gaps than teeth. 'I'm picking up our Ellie but you're welcome to climb in the back.'

'Can I bring my bike as well? It's a bit banged up.'

'Course you can.' He grinned again and jumped down. 'Hang on. I'd better give you a hand.'

He helped her climb in, then picked up the bike, grunting a little as he hoisted it in the air and heaved it into the trap. Raine steadied it against the side as he took up his position.

He turned round. 'All set?'

'Yes.'

'Righto. Off we go.' He cracked a whip and the pony set up a plodding pace.

It seemed as though they'd gone miles along country lanes before he eventually halted outside a row of terraced cottages and whistled. A woman of indeterminate age wearing a long black skirt and cardigan, slippers on her feet, came to the doorway of the first one.

'That's our Ellie.' He nodded towards the woman. 'Hey, Ellie,' he shouted. 'Get a move on. We've got a guest in the back who needs to get to the airfield – sharp!'

The woman nodded and disappeared. A couple of minutes later she came out with a basket on her arm and wearing a pair of scuffed lace-up shoes. She struggled up the step to the spare front seat and turned to look at the 'guest'.

Raine smiled and said hello, but the woman whispered something to the old man. He shook his head.

27

'She tells me she works over yonder at Biggin Hill – the airfield,' he explained to the woman. 'She's damaged her bike, so I'm giving her a lift.'

'But—'

'Be still, Ellie. We're giving her a lift and that's final.'

Raine's stomach fluttered with anxiety. Would the woman make her step down? Maybe the best tack would be to keep quiet. She peered at her watch again: seven minutes to ten. She swallowed. If the driver had diverted much to pick up Ellie, whoever she was, Raine knew she'd had it. She'd never get to the aerodrome on time.

She willed herself not to look at her watch any more, but to her relief it was only fourteen minutes past by the time the driver steered his horse off the road to the right, where her heart lifted as she saw the planes lined up at the far end, ready for take-off.

Surely Doug would wait a quarter of an hour before he gave up on her.

'I believe this is where you wanted to go, love,' the driver said, turning his head round to her.

'Yes, thank you.'

He nipped down and put his hand out to help her. Then in a flash he'd swung her bicycle out and set in on the ground.

'I'm really grateful for the lift,' Raine said.

'Always glad to give a lift to a pretty maiden,' he said as he doffed his cap. With another spring he was back in his seat and urging the horse forward.

The minutes ticked by as Doug failed to appear. Raine glanced at her watch every few seconds, willing him to come. Five minutes passed, then ten, now fifteen – it was gone half past ten. She began to worry, hoping nothing had happened to him. She remembered the way his eyes crinkled when he smiled and her pulse quickened. Enough of that. She doubted he'd ever give her the time of day, though if he'd take her up again, he'd be her hero forever.

Someone was loping towards the gate. The man came nearer but to her disappointment, she could see it wasn't Doug. This man, about the same age, she guessed, was nowhere near as handsome. Still, he was smiling as he ran up to her.

'Are you Raine?' he asked as he removed his cap.

She nodded.

'Andy Strong.' He paused and studied her. 'You look like you've been in the wars.'

Raine looked down at herself. She was splattered with mud. 'I fell off my bike,' she said, 'and I can't move the handlebars back.'

Andy glanced at it. 'Here, let me.' He took hold of the bicycle and put his legs either side of the front wheel. Then he pulled hard on the handlebars until they were straight. 'There you are,' he said. 'That ought to do it, though you should get that nut tightened up,' he tapped it to show her, 'as soon as you can.' He felt in his jacket pocket. 'Oh, nearly forgot the reason why I'm here. Doug gave me this to give to you.' He handed her an envelope marked 'Raine' and a long squiggle underneath.

'Thank you.' Her heart beat hard as she ripped open the envelope and pulled out a small sheet of paper and read Doug's scrawl.

Raine, I'm most awfully sorry not to be there this morning as I'd hoped. But I'm definitely on for Saturday morning, same time, if you can be there. Do hope so. There's a job going which I'm sure you could do. Doug

She read it quickly again then folded the note and tucked it back into the envelope.

'Any reply?' Andy asked as he gave her a curious glance.

'Yes,' she said breathlessly, the words 'there's a job going' running through her head, making her dizzy with excitement. 'Yes. Please tell him I'll be there.'

'Roger.' He set his cap back on and, giving her a cheerful wave, ambled off.

She stood staring after him, happy that Doug hadn't wanted to let her down. Something had turned up, but he hoped to see her again, maybe with some news. She'd discipline herself to be patient until Saturday. She'd even be patient with Maman. That was until she realised her mother would get hold of her as soon as she was home. Well, she'd go to the library, after all. Take her time. Then she wouldn't have to tell any lie, and with a bit of luck, Maman would have forgotten all about cutting her hair.

Raine propped her bicycle in the shed and walked nonchalantly through the door into the sitting room, carrying her library books, annoyed with herself for needing proof of where she'd been. Maybe Maman wouldn't let rip as she usually did while her sisters were there.

'I thought I told you—' her mother started, leaping up from the chair by the fire.

'I didn't want to wake you,' Raine said, trying to muster a concerned smile. 'So Ronnie said she'd bring you a coffee and I could change my books.'

'You will *not* go against my wishes again,' her mother said as she stood before her. 'Is that clear?' She gave Raine a critical glare. 'I have waited in to cut your hair.'

'Maman, I'll be eighteen in June. No longer a child. So please let me decide whether I want my hair cut or if I'd like to change my library books, or other normal things an adult chooses to do.'

'Not while you are under my roof and not until you are twenty-one,' her mother retorted.

'Then perhaps the best thing for all of us would be for me to pack up and leave.'

She heard Suzanne and Ronnie gasp.

'You will do nothing of the kind.' Her mother's eyes flashed with anger. 'But I will speak to your father when he is home about your insolence.'

'What's all this about not obeying your mother?' Raine's father asked her that evening when her sisters were in their rooms busy with their homework.

Her mother had gone to visit a woman she'd met in the village baker's who spoke French.

Raine told him as briefly as possible about her weekly visits to the aerodrome, without mentioning she'd been up in a plane again.

'One of the pilots, Doug White, said there might be a job going for me,' she finished.

'Doing what?'

'Just general . . . something clerical, I expect.' She didn't want to use the word 'dogsbody' or her mother would have another fit.

Her father paused to light his inevitable cigarette. Raine knew it was to give him time to think.

'I believe this is something we don't need to discuss with your mother,' he said finally, taking in a deep drag of the cigarette. 'But I'll come with you on Saturday to meet this chap.'

'Oh, Dad, don't come with me,' Raine said, horrified. 'He'll think I'm a complete baby.'

31

'No, he won't. If he's genuine, he'll know that I'm a concerned father who wants to make sure his daughter will be safe and happy . . . and not taken advantage of.'

Her father and Doug got along as though they'd known each other for months instead of having just met. Doug took them to meet Flight Lieutenant Hartman, in one of the administration buildings, who asked Raine many questions about her school subjects and what she enjoyed. She tried to reply as intelligently as she could.

'Hmm, you have impressive results for your School Certificate and your recent test,' he said, folding the paper and handing it back to Raine. 'But don't you want to finish school? Take your Higher Certificate?'

She shook her head.

'I wish she would,' her father said, to Raine's exasperation. 'And so does her mother. But she's bent on getting her pilot's licence, so she needs to work to pay for the lessons.'

Hartman looked straight at Raine. 'Well, there's nothing to stop you having flying lessons on the civilian side, but you know that as a female you'll never fly with the RAF as a pilot, even if they form a women's section.'

'Yes, I know that,' Raine said, fighting a bubble of irritation.

It was so unfair. But she refused to use the word 'never' in her vocabulary. Women used to think they'd never get the vote, but thank goodness a few women had been iron-willed in their fight to change the law. And after years of battling it had finally happened. So she could dream that things might change one day as far as women flying for the RAF was concerned.

'I can offer you the job of a pay clerk,' Hartman went on, 'which might or might not make use of your mathematic skills.' He looked at her. 'However, the pay isn't much –

nineteen shillings a week.' He leaned forward over his desk. 'How does that sound?'

To Raine it sounded a fortune and she had to will herself not to look too thrilled.

'It would be wonderful, sir,' Raine started, 'especially if you could make it a whole pound a week.'

That would pay for a weekly flying lesson, leaving fifteen shillings over – ten shillings a week to her mother and she'd still have a few shillings in her pocket.

Hartman gave her a startled look, then burst into laughter. 'A girl who's not afraid to speak up for herself,' he said, glancing at her father. 'Well, Mr Linfoot, have you any objections to this single-minded daughter of yours?'

Her father caught her eye and smiled. 'I think she's already made up her mind, and far be it from me to stand in her way.'

'Then the matter is settled.' He scribbled a note and glanced at the wall calendar.

'There is just one more thing, sir,' Raine said, desperately hoping he wouldn't consider she was trouble with so many requests. But this was the most important of all. 'What time would I finish each day?'

'Normally, half past five.' He looked at her. 'Is there a particular reason why you ask?'

'Yes. I intend to take weekly lessons at Hart's Flying Club,' she said. 'I'll need to cycle there but it'll be dark by then.'

'You'll have Saturdays off and I'm sure they offer lessons at weekends, as well.'

'It's just that my mother isn't keen for me to fly and she'd want to know where I was going every Saturday. I don't want to worry her unnecessarily, so long as Dad knows where I am.' Raine held her breath.

She noticed Hartman catch her father's eye. Her father nodded.

'We'll soon be changing the clocks,' Hartman said, 'so if we say you may leave once a week at half past two, would that suit? Without altering your pound a week,' he added with a twinkle.

Raine breathed out. 'Oh, thank you very much, sir. It's just that flying is what I want to do more than anything in the world . . .' She hesitated.

'Another question for me?'

'Only when can I start?'

'Soon as you like.'

She turned to her father with shining eyes. He sent her a wink.

'Would tomorrow be all right, sir?' Raine asked.

'Good to see someone who's keen.' Flight Lieutenant Hartman stood and shook hands with her father, then smiled again at Raine. 'We'll see you here at eight o'clock sharp tomorrow morning then, young lady.'

Chapter Four

Raine loved this new world she'd entered, loved hearing the thrum of planes taking off and landing as she rushed over the aerodrome taking messages, or set to tackling the bursting filing cabinet in between learning to be a pay clerk. She'd hoped to see a bit more of Doug, but he'd left a note to say he was taking some leave and would see her when he got back. Oh, and he hoped she was enjoying her new job.

The new job, if she was honest, didn't need much of a brain to do it, although there was plenty to keep her occupied. Sometimes she felt more like a tea lady after she'd made the dozens of cups of tea demanded by the people in both her section and two other sections every day. She wasn't ungrateful, not one bit, but she couldn't help wishing her work took her closer to the aircraft.

Thankfully, her father merely told Maman that Raine had found a job in a busy office in Biggin Hill with no mention of an aerodrome. Raine knew that name would mean nothing to Maman. She also knew her mother wouldn't bother to ask where the office was or any details about her work. This time, her mother's seeming indifference would work nicely in her favour. Raine couldn't help a wry smile.

The pilots all treated her in a friendly manner and would stop to have a word with her, or give her a flirtatious wink and a smile as they occasionally strolled by her desk, but her boss, Mrs Chilvers, never mentioned anything about her leaving early one day a week. Raine hadn't even had a chance on a Saturday to go to Hart's Flying Club to set up a schedule. Should she wait until Mrs Chilvers said something? All of a sudden she caught herself. What was she – a determined young woman who'd set herself a goal, or a meek little mouse waiting for someone else to speak on her behalf? She set her chin. *She* would be the one to take action. And it was no good going to Mrs Chilvers who might not even know about the arrangement.

Her chance came the following day. And it was with Flight Lieutenant Hartman himself. He stopped at her desk to ask for a file.

'Thank you, er, Miss—' he said.

'Lorraine Linfoot,' she replied with a smile.

'Ah, yes, Lorraine.' He looked at her. 'And how are you finding us?'

'I'm enjoying being here and there's plenty to learn.'

'Mmm. Well, I'm sure there's always someone to help with any questions.' He started to walk away.

She couldn't let him go.

'Sir, there is one thing . . .'

He turned.

Her heart racing, she steeled herself. 'You mentioned I could have time off once a week for flying lessons, but—'

'Ah, yes, indeed. But Mrs Chilvers tells me you have a lot to learn and it's impossible at the moment to let you off early with two clerks away.'

So he had *mentioned it to the woman.*

'Sir, if I remember correctly, you said it was part of my—'

36

Just then one of the senior clerks came rushing in.

'The new Hurricanes are arriving, sir. You said you wanted to be informed.'

'Good show,' Hartman said and hurried off.

Raine hesitated for a few seconds then shot to her feet. She'd dash out and have a look at the Hurricanes. But she'd make sure she kept out of Hartman's view. She flew out of the door and looked up to see six aeroplanes flying closely together, one after the other, coming in to land. She gasped. What a magnificent sight!

The six beaming pilots stepped out of the shining new aeroplanes. One in particular caught her eye. Tall with fair hair, and although some way away, his smile as he glanced in her direction looked as though it was on full beam.

A strand of her hair whipped across her face in the wind as she gulped and sent him a shy smile in return. Several pilots whom she now recognised gathered around the six men, excitedly firing questions, and one of them climbed on the wing to have a look in the cockpit. Raine wished with all her heart she could do the same. What would they say if she ran over the grass and asked if she, too, could have a look? Actually, thinking about it, they couldn't kill her for it.

In the next instant she was running towards Hartman who had his back to her, talking to the clerk who'd announced the Hurricanes' arrival.

She would tap him on the arm and ask his permission to have a closer look at the planes. But the pilot with the beaming smile broke away and strolled towards her, looking every inch a film star with his sun-streaked hair ruffling and his broad shoulders encased in a smart RAF tunic. She couldn't look away.

The moment was broken by one of the Hurricane pilots calling him.

'Marshall, over here. The chaps want to know if you're going to the mess and—' The rest of his words were caught by the wind.

So his name was Marshall. She supposed it was his surname. They all seemed to use each other's surnames or nicknames. Her heart picked up its beat again as he mouthed 'Sorry' and turned to the others. She stared after his retreating back, aching to belong – the way they did. All pals together. She sighed. It was just a dream.

With hunched shoulders she trudged back to the building, to her desk, to tackle the never-ending pile of dull paperwork.

Another week passed with Mrs Chilvers dumping as much as she could on Raine's desk. If she was honest, Raine was a little scared of the woman.

'I need this chart completed by noon,' Mrs Chilvers said, 'so please give it precedence.'

Now, Raine.

'Mrs Chilvers, may I speak to you about something?' Raine got to her feet. She was pleased to note she was several inches taller than the woman.

'What is it, Miss Linfoot? I'm very busy.'

'It's about leaving early one day a week.'

'What's that?' Mrs Chilvers barked. 'What are you talking about? You're here full time.'

Raine took a breath. 'Yes, that's right, but Flight Lieutenant Hartman said I could leave at half past two one day a week – a day to suit you, of course,' she added hastily.

'Yes, he mentioned something about it, but I told him it's not possible.'

'You see, he promised. It was part of my wages.'

Mrs Chilvers thrust her matronly chest out. 'And what is the reason, may I ask?'

'I want to take flying lessons.'

There was a deathly pause. Raine's heart beat fast.

'Do you realise we will probably be at war any day?' Mrs Chilvers began, her voice trembling with annoyance. 'We shall need all hands on deck to keep this section going smoothly, and all the other administration sections, for that matter, so the men who work here at the moment can be released for duty.' She stared up at Raine with expressionless eyes. 'It would be a complete waste of time. And anyway, we're far too busy to start letting you off early. You're still learning the job. What would be more use to us is if you could type.' Mrs Chilvers's mouth tightened. 'But you can't, so be grateful we've given you a job when you're not even trained for anything.' She smiled without it reaching her eyes. 'Now run along. I need that chart by noon.'

Raine stood. 'I *am* grateful, Mrs Chilvers, and you'll have the chart by noon.'

Cursing under her breath as Mrs Chilvers disappeared, Raine looked at the chart for the staff's work schedule for the month. It certainly wouldn't take her two hours to finish. She sat quietly and began to fill in the columns. As she worked, her lips curved into a smile. She knew what she was going to do. It might be the answer to getting a transfer. Something closer to aeroplanes than the pay section. But she would be careful not to let Mrs Chilvers know what she was planning.

Progress was slow. She daren't ask anyone to show her how to actually get the piece of paper in and roll it to its position as her secret would be out. But her mechanical mind soon picked up the basics. To her delight she'd found an instruction book with a clear diagram of a keyboard showing where to place her fingers. It sternly told her not to look down at the letters and even to stick little pieces of paper over the keys if she was tempted. Raine merely kept her eyes fixed on the sheet of paper in front of her. In a week she could type without looking at the keys. It was time to appeal to Flight Lieutenant Hartman. And she would make it official by typing the letter and putting URGENT on the envelope to make sure it got to him personally.

Her chance came when Mrs Chilvers telephoned in sick the following day. She began her letter, the tip of her tongue sticking out between her teeth as she concentrated.

> *Dear Flight Lieutenant Hartman,*
>
> *I know you are very busy, but I hope you will understand if I remind you again that you promised during my interview you would allow me to leave early one day a week so I would have time to cycle to Hart's for a flying lesson. I have kept up with all the work Mrs Chilvers has given me, but I have been here for nearly a month and am very keen indeed to start.*
>
> *I am very serious in my intentions to become a qualified pilot.*
>
> *Thank you in advance.*
>
> *Yours truly,*
>
> *Lorraine Linfoot*

Raine read the letter twice, then stuck it in an envelope. She put Hartman's name on the outside and wrote PERSONAL and URGENT.

She'd walk over to his building this very minute and leave it on his desk.

The following day Hartman found her as she was in the office kitchen boiling a kettle.

'Thank you for your letter, Lorraine,' he said.

40

She couldn't tell by his expression if he was annoyed or not. Then to her delight she saw the beginnings of a smile tilt his lips.

'I hope it was in order to write,' was the first thing that came to her.

'I'm glad you reminded me. I'm sorry we haven't kept to the arrangement. Lot going on at the moment.'

'I understand, sir, but I'm up to date with my work and Mrs Chilvers isn't in today, so I was wondering if I could leave early because I still haven't been to the flying club yet.'

Hartman looked at her. 'You're really keen, aren't you?'

'Yes, I am.'

'Then by all means pack up now and go and see them.'

Raine beamed. 'Oh, thank you, sir. Thank you very much. You never know. If there's a war my skills might come in handy.'

'As I told you before, not with the RAF,' he said. 'But it's still an excellent qualification to have, all the same.'

He swung away, leaving Raine in a pool of happiness.

It took Raine just short of half an hour to reach Hart's Flying Club. She set her bike in a rack near the entrance, enjoying being close enough to watch a few planes take off and land for a few moments before she turned into the entrance.

She swiftly told the very nice elderly man at the desk that she would like to sign up for flying lessons once a week under the Civil Air Guard scheme. He nodded and took her name and address.

'Are you on the telephone at home?' he asked, his pencil poised.

She hesitated a fraction of a second. No, better not. Her mother might answer.

'Afraid not,' she said.

Flicking through a large desk diary, he tapped his finger triumphantly on one of the pages.

'I have ten o'clock this Thursday, but only because of a cancellation.'

'I can't,' Raine said. 'I work at Biggin Hill but I can be here any afternoon from three o'clock onwards.'

He shook his head. 'Got nothing in the afternoons. I'll have to put you on the waiting list.'

She wasn't going to leave the club without an appointment booked.

'Oh, please. There must be something.'

He sucked air through his teeth and turned another page in the diary.

'Ah, this might help, but it's only half an hour on Fridays – three thirty. Would that do to begin with?'

'Yes, it would do very well,' Raine said, breathing out. 'Tomorrow's Friday. May I start then?'

'I've already put you down for it.' He looked up and smiled. 'You'll take a Tiger. And because it's only half an hour it will only cost you half a crown.'

'Put these on.' Doug handed her a flying helmet, a fleece-lined jacket and a pair of goggles the following afternoon.

Immediately, Raine felt as though she'd taken a whole step nearer to her dream as she fastened the strap under her chin.

'First of all, study your checklist and mentally tick off the items one by one.' He walked her round the Tiger Moth, pointing out things she must look out for, such as the tyres and oil or fuel leaks. 'And make sure the control surfaces are free and undamaged,' he added.

Raine noticed two men in overalls looking on, ready to turn the propeller and pull away the chocks. They were smirking. Were they talking about her, a girl, having the audacity to think she could learn to fly? She decided to ignore them.

'Doesn't the mechanic do the checks?' she asked.

'Yes, but it's always the final responsibility of the pilot,' Doug said. 'Now, use the cockpit checklist,' he instructed, tapping her on the shoulder and handing over a sheet of paper once they were strapped in. 'Make sure you've completed every one of them before take-off. This time I'll show you everything as I'm checking and saying the names aloud, and you follow them on your list.'

Raine's eyes dropped to the sheet of paper. She skimmed through it but it meant very little, so she quickly focused her attention on the instrument panel in front of her.

Doug leaned over her shoulder and pointed to the various controls. 'This is the rev counter, the air speed indicator, altimeter to see how high you are. Here's the oil pressure gauge, the control stick—' He broke off. 'Put your fingers round it to get the feel. It's very sensitive so it only needs a light touch.'

She took the stick in both hands, the skin stretching over her knuckles in her nervousness.

'No, not like that,' he remonstrated. 'You're gripping it – just use one finger and thumb . . . yes, that's better. Now, pull it gently towards you to rise up, then gently push away to descend, then move it to bank left . . . that's it . . . then the opposite to go right.'

She vaguely heard the word 'throttle' and a few other names, but she knew she wasn't taking any more in. Then she suddenly remembered something he hadn't mentioned.

'Where are the brakes?'

'The Tiger doesn't have them,' Doug said nonchalantly. 'You'll come to a natural stop when you land correctly.'

'That's what I wanted to ask you about,' Raine said. The 'no brakes' remark had made her chest tighten. 'I'm a bit scared of landing.'

'Don't be,' he came back. 'You won't be doing anything like taking off or landing on your first lesson – or your third. So don't worry.' He patted her back. 'Okay . . . are you ready?'

'Roger.' Raine's voice came out in a squeak of nerves, beads of perspiration gathering over her top lip.

This was it. No going back. She felt sick with fear and excitement as Doug's voice came over the speaking tube attached to her helmet.

'Okay. Switch on the ignition.'

She gave a satisfied smile as the engine flared. But her smile vanished when Doug shouted for her to open the throttle. She'd forgotten where it was. If he'd ever shown her, that was.

'Okay, I've got it,' Doug called. 'Don't do anything more . . .' He paused. 'Right. Off we go. Remember, always take off and land into the wind.'

When the plane was airborne Doug continued to shout various manoeuvres and instructions. Occasionally she understood, but often her mind went completely blank to the point where she didn't even know her left from her right. More than once she was too heavy with the control stick.

'You're banking too hard,' he shouted and she felt him adjust the plane. 'Now, hold it steady and we'll cruise for a couple of minutes.'

Her nerves frayed, she tried to straighten by jerking the control stick again. And again she felt him right it. She almost wept with frustration and fury with herself. She'd wanted to do so well, to show him what a good pupil she was.

'Right, I'm going to bring her down,' Doug called. 'I'll tell you what I'm doing at every stage.'

A few minutes later they had touched down and were taxiing along the grass landing strip.

She let out a long sigh. The flight had been a disaster. She squeezed her eyes shut to stop the tears. She'd never get the hang of it. He helped her from the cockpit without saying anything.

'I'm so sorry, Doug.'

'What for?'

'I was awful. I couldn't keep up with everything.'

'Don't fret,' Doug said. 'It wasn't that bad for a first time and there's a lot to learn.' He gave her arm a light squeeze. 'The main thing is, did you enjoy it?'

'I loved it more than anything, but I didn't think it was going to be that difficult.'

'It isn't. It just takes practice. And if you must know, I didn't expect any more from you, but . . .' he looked at her sternly, 'I *will* expect more the next time and you'd better have improved. And the third time you'll be flying without my help – except for the take-off and landing.'

Immediately, her heart lifted. She felt lighter. *Not that bad for a first time.* She turned to him. 'Do you think I'll really improve with practice?'

'No, you'll never make it.'

Her face crumpled.

'Don't be a goose,' he said, giving her a playful chuck under her chin. 'I was just teasing. You're going to make an excellent pilot one day – I'll make sure of it. But until then,' he looked at her, 'you need regular lessons. Hartman has suggested once a week, but I'll try to accelerate them and get you in a couple a week.'

Raine felt her face flood with joy. 'Will you really, Doug? Oh, that would be marvellous. How many lessons before I can go up on my own?'

'Solo?' He raised his eyebrows. 'You've had one lesson. One. With no take-off or landing practice. Don't run before you can walk. We'll take it a lesson at a time.'

'Will you always be my instructor, Doug?'

'That, I can't guarantee. Friday is quite a good day for me so I'll do my best. I'd love to know it was me who trained you.'

'So would I.'

Raine laughed out loud as she cycled home, her hands off the handlebars, her pedals feeling as light as wings.

Chapter Five

May 1939

Raine felt as though she was leading a double life. It shouldn't have to be like this, deceiving her mother. She was especially happy when it was her 'flying day'. But even when it wasn't and the work was monotonous, she was still blissfully content in her surroundings. It was only when she went home that she felt she didn't really belong. She only had to walk up the path and a feeling of gloom would sweep over her. But today was different. Today, she could barely contain her excitement.

She knocked on the door, wishing for the dozenth time that her parents would give her a key. *For goodness' sake, I'll be eighteen next month*, she thought. But her mother wouldn't budge. Maybe when she heard her news, Maman would finally regard her as an adult instead of a wayward child. Raine gave a rueful smile. She might not be twenty-one yet to legally acquire 'the key of the door', but surely her mother couldn't refuse her now.

'I've got something to tell you all,' Raine said as she glanced round the table at her parents and sisters. She took another bite of her meat pie and looked up to see she had their attention. 'I hope you'll be pleased for me, though I haven't mentioned anything about it before. I didn't want to until it was definite.'

'At last! You've met a nice young man.' Her mother's face was wreathed in smiles, her voice breathy with excitement. 'When are you going to bring him home? We can't wait to meet him, can we, Robert?'

'Why don't you give Raine a chance to answer?' her husband said, sending his wife his usual tender look.

'It's nothing like that,' Raine cut in before the conversation took a worse turn. She summoned a wide smile towards her parents and sisters. 'I went solo today.'

There was a sudden hush. Raine stole a glance at her mother whose fork was frozen in mid-air.

'What *are* you talking about?' her mother said, narrowing her eyes as she put down her fork, the small piece of meat still attached to the prongs.

'I went up in a Tiger Moth on my own today.'

'A what?' Her mother frowned.

'It's an aeroplane.' Raine glanced at her mother whose face was working as though she was trying to control herself.

'How *dare* you! You've been taking flying lessons without my knowledge.' Maman's voice was steel.

'I dared because I knew you wouldn't approve.'

'You were perfectly correct.' Her mother laid down her knife. 'How can you afford lessons with the pittance you earn in that office of yours – as a *clerk*?' She raised her eyes to the ceiling. 'Lorraine, who has her head in the clouds.' She swung back to Raine. 'Could you really not do something better with your School Certificate, Lorraine? I'm ashamed when people ask me what you are doing now you have left school. That you are a clerk in an office, wasting a fine education.'

'The work is actually very interesting,' Raine returned with as cool a smile as she could muster, her thrill at having gone

48

solo still overriding any pettiness from her mother. 'Especially as the office happens to be at Biggin Hill aerodrome.'

Her mother's face paled. 'I did not know that.'

'Simone,' her father interrupted, 'let's be happy for her. It's what she's always wanted to do. And she must be good if her instructor has let her go solo today.'

'You seem to know much about this, Robert.' Simone flashed him an accusing glare. 'You knew all the time. Both of you 'ave betrayed me.' She gave a sob. 'My own 'usband and daughter.'

'It's hardly a *betrayal*, Maman,' Raine said. 'And you never once asked me what I was doing in my job – you weren't interested, so I didn't have to tell you any lies. And I can tell you it's the best feeling in the world to have – what you call – my head in the clouds.'

Ronnie giggled.

'Véronique.' Simone swung round to Ronnie. 'I am not amused.'

'Doesn't Lorraine remind you of someone, darling?' her father said. 'If *you* make up your mind to do something, you always do it. So you can't be surprised that your eldest daughter has taken after you in that way.'

If it hadn't been so serious, Raine would have laughed.

Her mother rounded on her father. 'I *am* surprised that you encourage her, Robert,' she said, her mouth thinning in anger. 'And even more that you did not tell me what my own daughter was up to.'

'You would only have worried, darling,' he said soothingly.

It's not the whole reason, Raine longed to say to her father, but she knew it was useless. Her father would always adore his wife and continue to make excuses for her. Raine sighed.

He turned to her. 'Well done, Raine. I know you always wanted to be a pilot so I'm happy . . . we're *all* happy for you,' he added firmly. 'And to prove it, I'm going to open a bottle of champagne so we can make a toast. It's the last one but I think the occasion deserves it.'

'I'm not qualified yet, or anything.'

'No matter. I won't be a minute.'

Her father had always kept a few bottles of champagne on one of the slate shelves in the cool of the pantry at the old house – just in case. 'I like to be ready for any surprise celebration,' he'd say with a twinkle. Raine's heart warmed. It was typical of him to bring out his last bottle for her.

'It's wonderful news, Raine.' Suzanne rose from the table and gave her a hug.

'You *are* clever,' Ronnie said, eyes wide with delight. 'Isn't she, Maman?'

Raine looked her mother straight in the eye. Maman was leaning back in her chair as though she could no longer support herself. But in her eyes was an expression that made Raine recoil. She could only decipher it as a spark of envy.

'Here we are.' Her father came back into the room with the champagne. 'We'll have the best glasses, darling,' he said to her mother.

'I'll get them.' Suzanne jumped up – probably so she didn't get drawn into the argument, Raine guessed. She watched as her mother took in a deep breath, her chest rising.

Here we go.

'Lorraine, I have been thinking. *Écoute.* You remember Mrs Garland who is the proprietor of the beautiful dress shop in the arcade in Bromley? She said she would like to talk to you about working there. I told her you will soon be in your father's firm, but she said, "Lorraine's so tall and slim and so very attractive – just the right figure to be a model. She could earn more money than doing sums all day."' Her mother gave a tinkly laugh. 'She said she would be 'appy to train you.' She looked at Lorraine as though

50

seeing her for the first time and nodded approvingly. 'She is right, Lorraine, and I want you to think very serious . . . serious*ly* about it. And do not concern yourself with your father's wishes. I will persuade him.' Then immediately her expression hardened. 'Until then, I will hear no more about flying. You will *not* continue the lessons.'

'I don't think you quite understand, Maman. I'm not *interested* in selling dresses to dippy girls and vain women. I flew *solo* today. When I have enough flying hours I can take my test. Become a qualified pilot.' She rounded on her mother. 'Maman, can't you understand that flying means the world to me. It's the only thing I want to do with my life.'

Her mother's eyes bored into her. 'We will see about that.'

Raine realised it was not a bit of good getting on the wrong side of their mother. She held her mother's glare as many seconds as she could bear, then lowered her eyelids. Best to let her mother think she still had the upper hand.

Suzanne returned with the best champagne glasses, saved from the old house, and set them carefully on the table. Their father popped the cork and filled each glass, handing the first to Raine and the second to his wife. Simone shook her head.

'I have the 'eadache,' she said, rising to her feet. 'You must all celebrate – if that's what you want to call it – without me.' Her gaze swept over the table, then settled on Raine. 'If we go to war with Germany again, your lessons are pointless. As a *girl*' – she emphasised the word – 'you will *not* be allowed to fly planes in the *militaire*. Thank goodness there is some sense still in this world.'

Raine looked at her mother's rigid back as she left the table, then her eyes wandered to her father. He was staring after his wife, but to Raine's surprise he didn't follow her as he usually did. She was grateful for that small gesture of solidarity. Having her father's approval was more than enough.

51

Chapter Six

Raine opened her eyes. They stung, as she'd barely slept a wink while fretting about the morning. And now tomorrow had come and she'd never felt less like taking a plane up. Sighing, she pushed the covers aside and got to her feet. It was still early so with luck she'd have the bathroom to herself for a few minutes.

No sound. No one was up. She shot into the bathroom and splashed cold water on her face, grimacing at the blood-shot eyes, then ran a shallow bath. Swiftly, she put on her rayon briefs and brassière, then tied the cord of her dressing gown firmly around her slim waist and went downstairs.

'What *is* the matter, Lorraine?' her mother asked at the breakfast table. 'You look as though you have cried all night.'

'Suzanne kept me awake with her heavy breathing.'

Her mother's face softened. 'Poor child. I think she has the sinus problem. You must be patient with her.'

Raine had the grace to feel guilty at such a fib. Suzanne had been as quiet as a mouse. Raine badly wanted to tell her mother she would be taking her pilot's test this morning, but instead clamped her lips together. It never worked to be excited about anything if her mother wasn't involved or hadn't got some kind of control. And if she hoped for her mother to wish her good luck, she knew that was a wasted hope.

After breakfast Raine stepped into her overalls. She'd seen a lovely bright yellow flight suit on one of the other women at Hart's who was also having lessons and she'd immediately longed for one just like it. But try as she had, she'd never been able to save enough money. Giving her mother ten shillings a week had put a stop to any luxury.

She *had* to pass. She just had to. Flinging a raincoat over the overalls in case she came face to face with her mother, she slipped out of the door and cycled to Hart's.

'You took a gamble last time I watched you,' Doug reprimanded as they were walking over the airfield towards the planes. 'You deliberately went into that loop the loop. You were jolly lucky not to have come a cropper. The engine has a reputation of stalling with that manoeuvre. More than one pilot has lost his life by doing that. And you're even more lucky that I know you, and how good you are, and didn't send you to the Chief.' His eyes held a warning. 'You're not experienced enough yet to start doing fancy aerobatics, Raine, and the last thing we want is a fatal accident on our hands.

'These planes are bloody expensive to repair or replace.' He smiled wryly at her expression. 'The RAF worries almost as much about the loss of an aircraft as it does the loss of a pilot. So no more showing off in the air. I mean it. Put your own safety first. Stick to observing weather conditions and be sensible as to whether or not you even attempt a flight until bad weather clears, and thoroughly go through the checks. If you do that, you'll automatically keep both you *and* the aircraft safe.'

Doug was speaking to her now as though she was a wayward rebellious child. Maybe she was. She stuck out her chin. She'd often dreamed of doing the loop, but that day she'd dared, knowing it was against the rules but also sure that Doug wouldn't report her. She wouldn't have missed that feeling of pure liberation for all the world when she'd somersaulted.

'I promise I won't try it again,' she said, trying hard to sound contrite.

Doug threw her a suspicious glance and sighed. 'It'll only be a matter of weeks – maybe only days if dear Mr Hitler has his way – and we're in another world war, but at least *you* won't be called upon as a pilot. That should be a comfort to your mother . . . and to me,' he added unexpectedly.

'But it seems such a waste if I can't use my flying skills just because I'm a woman.' Raine's voice rose in indignation. 'And if the war starts I won't have a chance to keep up my hours.'

He studied her as though for the first time. 'You know what, Raine? Even for someone as obstinate as you, there's no future in flying until things settle down. But there is some news you might not have heard about. The RAF has just formed a section called the Women's Auxiliary Air Force. There'll be plenty of jobs to involve you in the various aircraft. I think you'd find something to interest you.'

'But they won't allow women pilots,' Raine said flatly.

'That's true.'

'Then I'm not interested.'

'I thought that's what you'd say,' Doug said. 'Well, forget it for the moment. I'll hand you over to the chief flying instructor for your test. In fact, there he is . . . walking towards us right now.' He bent his head and kissed her cheek. 'Good luck, Raine. You have the makings of an excellent pilot. You'll pass – I'm sure of it.'

* * *

Anxious that she had the eyes of the instructor tracing her every movement, Raine carefully carried out all the solo test manoeuvres to the book. Although her landing wasn't quite as perfect as she would have liked, she didn't think she'd performed too badly on the whole.

The instructor nodded to her without a hint of whether or not she had made a satisfactory test flight. Instead, he asked her to follow him to his office where he fired questions at her for half an hour, noting down her answers.

'I think that will be all, Miss Linfoot,' he said, rising from his desk as her indication to leave.

'Thank you very much, sir,' Raine said, willing him to give her an idea as to how she'd performed.

'You'll be hearing from the CAG in a fortnight or so.' He nodded his dismissal.

After what Raine considered was enough time for her licence to arrive – that is, if it was ever going to – she watched for the postman every day before anyone came downstairs.

On day eight she collected the post from the mat. There was one for her mother and one for her – from the Civil Air Guard. With shaking hands she opened it to find a short letter wrapped around her pilot's licence. This was it. No word of congratulation. But she didn't need any. She'd passed! Class C – whatever that meant. But whatever it meant, now she was truly a pilot.

Her heart pounded as she remembered Doug's words about being a comfort to her mother. She didn't want to be a comfort to anyone. She wanted to play her part if there really was going to be a war. And going by the headlines in her father's newspaper, the government was preparing for it to happen any day.

There *must* be some use for her as a pilot, even if she

wasn't allowed to fight Jerry. But she wouldn't tell anyone in the family just yet that she had her licence. She'd keep that delicious secret to herself until the time was right. And then she'd show them.

The following day, Friday, 1st September, Germany invaded Poland. Although everyone expected it, it was still a shock to hear such terrifying news. Raine's second shock was the unexpected announcement at Hart's that all civil flying had now stopped for the duration of the war. She wouldn't be able to add to her solo hours. She might even lose her skills. If that wasn't bad enough, the RAF took over the running of Biggin Hill. She prayed they would let her keep her job at the airfield as a civilian, and decided her best bet was to turn up every day and keep her head down.

Sunday, 3rd September 1939

Every morning and evening her father turned on the wireless to hear the news. Raine had begun to make it a habit to join him in the front room of the cottage. This morning she looked up from the crossword puzzle she was doing in yesterday's *Daily Telegraph*, her glance falling on Suzanne who sat nearby on a straight-backed chair clicking her knitting needles. She was making a scarf for Ronnie who refused to listen to the news and was out on her bicycle, even though they'd had thunderstorms in the night. Maman was in the kitchen so it was only Dad, Raine thought, who looked properly attentive. She bent her head over the crossword again, but with her ear cocked for the latest news.

'At eleven o'clock this morning, on the BBC, the Prime Minister has a serious announcement to make,' came the clipped tones of the newsreader, startling Raine from her concentration.

'That's it, then.' Her father threw his daughters a look of absolute despair.

'What is?' Suzanne stopped knitting, the stripy scarf falling in a heap on her lap.

'Announcement that we're at war, do you think, Dad?' Raine said, biting her lip. She couldn't believe they were even speculating such a horrifying event, but after Friday's shocking announcement on the wireless that the Nazis had invaded Poland, it was surely inevitable.

'I'm certain of it now.' Her father flung down the morning's newspaper in disgust. 'This will all be stale by the time we hear what Chamberlain's got to say.' He stood, his expression heavy. 'I hoped right up until we heard about Poland that it could be staved off, but that's it, now.' He blew out his cheeks. 'I'd better tell your mother to make sure she's here in two hours' time.'

He left the room, shaking his head in disbelief.

'Do you really think that's what the Prime Minister's going to announce?' Suzanne said, her face pale.

'I don't see what else it can be, now Germany's invaded Poland,' Raine said. 'We promised Poland if that ever happened, Great Britain and France would stick together against Germany. It's too serious a promise to break.'

At five minutes to eleven Raine's father switched on the wireless again to warm it up. As soon as the pips came, no one spoke. In the gravest tone, the Prime Minister began to speak.

'This morning the British Ambassador in Berlin handed the German Government a final note stating that unless we heard from them by eleven o'clock that they were prepared at once to withdraw their troops from Poland, a state of war would exist between us.

'I have to tell you now that no such undertaking has been

57

received, and that consequently this country is at war with Germany.

'You can imagine what a bitter blow it is to me that all my long struggle to win peace has failed.

'The Government have made plans under which it will be possible to carry on the work of the nation . . .'

Raine's mind was working furiously. She didn't hear much of the rest of Mr Chamberlain's speech until she heard him say:

'. . . in the days of stress and strain that may be ahead. But these plans need your help. You may be taking your part in the fighting services or as a volunteer in one of the branches of Civil Defence. If so, you will report for duty in accordance with the instructions you receive. You may be engaged in work essential to the prosecution of war for the maintenance of the life of the people – in factories, in transport, in public utility concerns or in the supply of other necessaries of life. If so, it is of vital importance that you should carry on with your jobs.

'Now may God bless you all and may He defend the right, for it is evil things that we shall be fighting against – brute force, bad faith, injustice, oppression and persecution – and against them I am certain that the right will prevail.'

There was a crackling noise, then the words 'air-raid siren.' Her father switched the wireless off.

Maman was the first to break the silence with a stifled sob. 'Where is my baby? Where is Véronique?'

'She'll come back any minute when she hears the siren,' Robert said. 'You know she doesn't like being hemmed in.'

'Does she dislike us so much?' Simone raised her eyes to her husband.

'Of course not, darling. She just loves being outside and you can't protect her forever.'

'I need to know she is back,' Simone said, her eyes beseeching him. 'You will have to go and find her.'

'I'll go,' Raine said, leaping up.

'Stay here.' Simone's tone was harsh. 'You will not leave the house.'

Taking no notice of her mother, Raine made towards the door. At the same moment Ronnie breezed in, soaked from head to foot, her face glowing from her cycle ride.

'What's the matter? Why are you all looking so serious?' She looked from one member of the family to another.

'Only that Mr Chamberlain has declared war on Germany,' her mother said in a tight voice. 'And we were worried about *you*, Véronique, *naturellement*.'

'*I'm* all right.' Ronnie shrugged off her light jacket and threw it on the back of a chair. 'Well, at least there'll be some excitement going on around here for a change.'

'How can you talk like that?' Simone snapped. She turned to her husband. 'Can't they understand anything, Robert?' she said, her voice imploring him. 'All those lives lost only twenty years ago. How many more will be erased before they all come to their senses?'

'We're not talking about anyone with common sense as far as the Nazis are concerned,' Robert answered. He got up to offer his wife a handkerchief which she practically snatched and held to her eyes.

'I can't bear this to 'appen again.' Simone's voice was muffled.

'Don't take on, darling. You must keep strong for all our sakes.'

Taking her handkerchief from her face, she looked up at him, tears streaming down her cheeks. 'I'm only thankful

I've got girls. All the poor mothers who have sons. It will be terrible for them.'

'We *all* have to play a part,' Raine said, gazing across at her mother. 'Just like Mr Chamberlain said. All of us means exactly that – girls and women as well as boys and men. And I intend to do my bit.'

'And just what do you intend to do, Lorraine?' her mother challenged.

This was the opportunity Raine had been waiting for. It was such a shock to hear they really were at war, that telling her mother she was now a qualified pilot would get everything over with in one go. But her answer to her mother's question was swallowed up in a wailing sound, which sent shivers across her shoulders. An air-raid siren.

Simone screamed and rushed to the window. 'They're bombing us already!' She began to sob. 'Oh, why did we have to leave our lovely house with the basement to keep us safe?'

Raine saw her father flinch at Maman's accusatory tone.

'It will only be a practice,' he said, 'though I'm afraid we'll have to get used to the sound. But it won't happen for a while, I'm sure, until the Germans decide how to respond now we've told them it's war. And the village shelters aren't far.'

Simone rounded on her husband. 'How do you know what that creature is thinking?' she demanded. 'And what is the use of a shelter in the village if we are trapped here and killed?'

'Calm down, my love. I imagine it was quite a surprise to the Germans. Hitler was always so sure that Britain would be persuaded to become one of his allies. How little does he know the British mind.'

Peace in our time. Would anyone ever forget the Prime Minister's triumphant words? Raine thought grimly. Neville

Chamberlain and Herr Hitler had signed an agreement to say the two countries would never go to war with one another again, when now, almost exactly a year later, Chamberlain had told the nation that war had been declared on Germany. It was too terrible to imagine. And yet she understood how Ronnie was feeling. At least we know for sure, she told herself, aware of a frisson of excitement. Surely now she'd be able to put her pilot's licence to good use.

Raine quietly left the room. She needed to get some air and think what to do next.

Mr Gray, the village air-raid warden, came to the house a few days later to announce that gas masks were being sent to the village hall, and families should come to be fitted and collect theirs the following week.

'I will not wear anything so ugly,' Simone declared when she saw the masks lined up on the trestle tables in the village hall next to a pile of cardboard boxes for each one to be carried in.

'It might save your life, Maman,' Raine said grimly, trying hers on.

Ugh. The rubber stank and there was a strong smell of disinfectant.

Simone wasn't the only one muttering. Most of the men seemed to accept that they were a sensible precaution, but several of their wives decided they didn't like the look of them at all.

'Keep it on for a few minutes, dear,' one of the ladies who was helping people with their size said to Raine. 'It'll get you used to it.'

Raine didn't think she could last that long. It was difficult to breathe and the smell was making her feel queasy. After a long minute, she pulled it off and went to the door, drawing in deep gulps of air.

Simone refused even to try it on. She simply took the size the woman recommended her and put it in its cardboard box.

'I will look at it when I am home,' she said, but Raine knew she would do nothing of the kind.

'How are you two getting on?' Raine asked her sisters.

There were muffled replies and both of them removed theirs.

'They're hateful,' Ronnie said. 'It'd take a catastrophe for me to wear mine.'

'That's the idea,' Raine said.

Suzanne promptly rushed to the cloakroom and came back white-faced.

'That was horrible,' she said. 'I felt I was suffocating.'

'Let's just hope we never have to use them,' Raine said.

When several weeks went by and still nothing happened, people began to call it a phoney war. They became more casual about keeping their gas masks with them at all times. But as far as Raine was concerned, there was one big difference. There were no more civilian pilots, no more flying clubs. Anyone who was a pilot was serving their country – and that, of course, didn't include female pilots. She gritted her teeth. Maybe she should join the WAAFs, after all. At least she'd be amongst people she respected and admired. But still something held her back.

She'd finally heard from Doug. He sent her a private letter care of Biggin Hill aerodrome.

28th October 1939
Dear Raine,
I'm so sorry I left so abruptly. You must have wondered what had happened to me. I had a crisis at home and then when I'd got myself back together again there was a war on!
I heard you got your pilot's licence so my heartiest

congratulations. You see I do know a bit of what's going on even though I'm quite a long way from you at the moment – can't say where. You've probably left Biggin Hill by now and joined the WAAFs. That's what I wanted to tell you – that I've joined up – RAF, of course.

Raine chewed her lip. So Doug was a fighter pilot doing his bit for his country. She prayed he hadn't been called on to do anything too dangerous. He'd become like a brother to her over the months he'd taught her to fly and she'd been hurt, then worried, when she hadn't heard anything from him for such a long time. She read on:

I think very fondly of you and I'm so proud of you. We're bound to meet sooner or later, particularly if you've joined the WAAFs as at least you'll be close to the action.

However I do have something interesting to tell you. A civilian organisation called the Air Transport Auxiliary (ATA for short) has just been formed and its function is to ferry aircraft to airfields around the country for the RAF. They're taking pilots who are too old this time around, or injured from the last war, so not fit for combat but they can still deliver a plane safely. And this is the real news – apparently they're planning to form a women's section of experienced pilots. I'll let you know when I hear anything more.

Write to me if you get the opportunity. Address at top and it will be forwarded to me.

With much affection,
Doug x

Raine read the last part of the letter about the ATA again, her heart practically leaping out of her chest. Here was the reason she hadn't joined the WAAFs. This ATA was going to admit women pilots! She'd try to find out more about it at work tomorrow. Because if she didn't get some regular air miles in her log book soon, she wouldn't stand a chance. She swallowed hard. All she had worked for, all she had dreamed, would be shattered. There *had* to be a way for this ATA organisation to take her. There simply had to.

Chapter Seven

October 1940

'Miss Linfoot, please come to my office right away.'

Raine jumped as her desk extension rang. She'd been in her usual reverie, looking out of the window watching planes landing and taking off, longing to be up there with them. At first it had been exciting peering up at the dogfights going on right over her head at Biggin Hill, seeing the RAF boys shooting down the Luftwaffe in what Winston Churchill called the Battle of Britain. But when she'd witnessed her first sight of a Spitfire spiralling down in flames, the pilot having had no chance of baling out, or surviving a ball of fire on impact, she'd immediately thought of Doug. He'd be up there somewhere. If it wasn't today, it would be tomorrow.

At least she and the family were far enough away not to have suffered like Londoners who had gone through night after night being bombed. Thankfully, Hitler now seemed to have turned his attention elsewhere. Heaven knew in what condition the Luftwaffe had left their beloved capital. And knowing what constant danger Londoners were living in, if anything, made her even more resolute to be part of the action.

Raine had been in the pay section for a year and had become more and more frustrated stuck in an office. Although she'd taken over the role of a fully-fledged pay clerk, she wished for the hundredth time that she'd been born a man. Then she would have been welcomed with open arms as a pilot. It was all so ridiculous. Women were every bit as good as the men. But even the ATA was cautious, it seemed. Doug told her they'd only taken eight very experienced female pilots a few months ago – all of them with several hundred flying hours or more. There was no point yet in applying with her few. He'd suggested she seriously think about joining the WAAFs, but she didn't want to. She'd have to sign up with them. Commit herself to however many years the war was going to last in a non-flying position and perhaps lose the opportunity of flying with the ATA – what she'd set her heart on. No, she wouldn't risk it.

But she'd go mad if something didn't turn up soon. Even Maman had joined the Women's Voluntary Service and was busy collecting aluminium utensils from friends and neighbours for the war effort. 'We will turn your pots and pans into Spitfires and Hurricanes, Blenheims and Wellingtons,' Lord Beaverbrook had recently announced on the wireless, and Maman had jumped up and told the family she would talk to the WVS immediately.

And she had. Raine couldn't help smiling at the memory of her mother approaching every single family in Downe. Almost every housewife had gladly handed her something aluminium for the war effort, not wanting to be thought of as unpatriotic, especially when faced with a Frenchwoman who was asking so delightfully for her help.

Sighing heavily, Raine picked up the huge aluminium teapot and poured yet another twenty mugs of tea, letting the liquid slosh over the rims without pause. She'd asked for a transfer to one of the other administration departments and was sent to Maintenance Command section under Flight Lieutenant Fox. It had been a bad mistake on her part.

'Miss Linfoot, are you there? Please answer.'

Foxy's tone was never a polite request but an order. He was of medium height, stockily built, dark hair slicked back with plenty of Brylcreem. His cocky swagger when he came into the office and his condescending attitude made it obvious that women had no place in the department unless they were behind a typewriter. At least once a day she berated herself for ever having learnt how to type. As for Foxy, she detested working for him. His handwriting was appalling and he always took umbrage when she gave him a letter for signing, having guessed the words and the gist of it as she'd gone along.

'I didn't write it like this,' he growled more than once.

She'd answer that it had read a little ambiguously, so she'd tried to make it clear.

'Hmm,' he would grunt, but to her surprise he never insisted she retype it.

That was by no means the worst thing. She'd only been at the job a week when he'd pounced as she was leaving his office. He'd barred her way as she had her hand on the door handle and grabbed her.

She'd twisted her neck away from his repulsive lips. 'Please don't.'

'Come on. You're no prude. You girls – prick-teasers, all of you, with your pouty red lips and your pussycat bows, forever tossing your hair—'

'What nonsense!' Raine's voice was ice as she pushed her hand hard against his chest. 'But I *am* here to do a job without any unpleasantness from anyone.' She glared at him.

67

'So don't ever touch me again, *sir*,' she emphasised with sarcasm, 'or I'll report you.'

'*You* report *me*?' He laughed in her face. 'The general dogsbody. Who do you think they'd believe – you or *me*?' His laugh became a sneer. 'Make one move in that direction and I'll have you removed . . . for good.'

She could only grit her teeth. She'd get nowhere if she threatened him. He was her superior and he could easily make her life a misery. She'd stepped back and made her exit as dignified as she could, knowing his eyes were on her. Since then, he'd always made a point of looking her up and down every time she had to speak to him, but he'd left her alone and she'd hoped that was the end of it.

Now, a fortnight later, he was asking to see her on her own again. With Foxy she realised she'd overstepped the mark in threatening him. But she hadn't been able to stop herself from trying to frighten the rat. She should have known that threatening such a bully would never have worked. Blowing out her cheeks, Raine picked up her notepad, hoping, praying he only wanted to dictate a letter, although Foxy dictating was as bad as deciphering his writing. He'd march back and forth across the floor, mumbling and gabbling, then would say nothing for a whole minute – just turn and stare at her. She wrinkled her nose as she knocked on his office door.

'Please, sit down.'

Something in his tone alerted her. He wasn't about to dictate any letter. He leaned back in his chair, steepling his fingers, and studied her. His gaze lowered to her legs, then back up her body to her face. She loathed everything about him – those pinprick cold grey eyes piercing through her, as though sucking out all her problems, laying them bare and grinning at them, but she would not be intimidated.

She tried to imagine him naked – she'd read somewhere that it helped when you were in such a situation – and almost giggled at the image dancing in front of her.

'Have I egg on my chin or something?'

'What?' She managed to recover herself. 'Oh, sorry, sir, I was—'

'Never mind that,' he said abruptly. 'I have something to discuss with you. I understand you're a qualified pilot.'

Her heart leapt.

'Yes, sir, I have my licence.' She couldn't stop the note of pride that pervaded her answer.

He nodded and picked up a sheet of paper from the top of a pile, his eyes flicking from one side to the other, taking his time.

As though he hasn't already read it.

'This letter . . . ' he waved it in the air, 'is from the ATA – that is, the Air Transport Auxiliary.'

'Yes, I've heard about it,' Raine said coolly, though inside her heart was beating fiercely, silently thanking God that Doug had explained who they were.

Foxy gazed at her as though he couldn't believe she was not some empty-headed slip of a girl. 'I'll give you the thrust of it,' he said, breaking off to wink at her. 'It's from a Miss Gower. Apparently, she's in charge of a ferry pool . . . ' he rolled his eyes that a woman should be in charge of something so important, 'and she urgently requires pilots. She's even asking for *women* as well as men.' He stared at Raine. 'My God, she *must* be desperate.'

Don't annoy him, Raine. Let him think he has the upper hand.

'She needs highly experienced pilots, of course.'

Raine's heart dropped. She hadn't flown for nearly a year. But at least this Miss Gower was asking for more women.

Those eight female pilots must be doing a good job. It gave her a sudden hope.

'Does she say how many flying hours . . . sir?'

Please let me have enough.

He sent her a steely gaze. 'How many hours do *you* have, Miss Linfoot?'

'Twenty-five.' It was actually nineteen, but she wasn't going to tell him that.

A smirk crossed his thick lips, but he said nothing.

Was her dream about to come true – or be smashed to pieces? He was deliberately keeping her in suspense.

'How many hours does Miss Gower require?' Raine asked, her heart beating hard.

Foxy glanced down at the letter again. 'I'm afraid Miss Gower requires pilots with two *hundred* and fifty . . . *minimum.*' He sent her a triumphant look. 'So you only have ten per cent of her requirements.' He paused to let that sink in. 'I'm afraid we will have to put that idea aside.' His mouth twisted.

'But with the war, surely—'

'I'm afraid there's no more to be said.'

She could see her chance slipping away before her.

'Please, sir, if I could—'

He held his hand palm upwards towards her. 'I'm sorry, but you simply don't have enough experience. And by the time you increase your hours the war will be over. Without any help from *women.*' Before she had time to react, he said, 'But there's something else I want to talk to you about.'

The tone had become ominous. Raine deliberately kept her eyes on him, trying to ignore her thudding heart.

'I'm afraid . . . ' he paused as though for effect (*dear God, if he said he was afraid one more time she would cheerfully throttle him*), 'we no longer require your services at Biggin Hill.'

Her jaw dropped. She hadn't been prepared for this. His eyes were narrowed in malice. What a nasty little man, enjoying the power he had over her. She could have kicked herself for threatening him. This was his moment of triumph. Her punishment for daring to stand up for herself. Well, she wasn't going to go down without a fight.

'Doesn't my time here count for anything?' she said in as reasonable a tone as she could muster. 'I'm showing the ropes to a new girl who's supposed to be helping me now we're busier, but she has a lot to learn before she can be left on her own. And she can't possibly do my job *and* hers.'

'Miss Rogers is perfectly capable of being left,' he said in a firm voice. 'And there is always someone around if she needs advice, or indeed any help. Me, for instance.' He gave her what passed for a smile. 'I'm sorry, Miss Linfoot, but I'm giving you notice. You have until the end of the week to hand over all your work to Miss Rogers and explain everything she needs to know. But for now, please give me your key to the filing cabinet. We wouldn't want any nosy parkers let loose in my office, would we?'

He held out a pasty hand.

Raine could barely hide her fury as she returned to her office. Only Linda Rogers was there, frowning over a stack of files on her desk. She looked up as Raine stormed in.

'Whatever's wrong?'

'Only everything,' Raine said, biting her lip hard to stop herself from bursting into tears of frustration and anger. She caught Linda's stare. 'Foxy's just given me notice to be out by the end of the week.'

Linda's eyes widened. 'Why? What are you supposed to have done?'

'It seems I'm no longer required. That you're perfectly capable of doing my job . . . as well as yours.'

As she was speaking she put the cover over her typewriter and retrieved her handbag that was tucked underneath the desk. She swung it on her shoulder and turned to Linda.

'Right, then, I'm off. Best of British and all that.'

'But you said the end of the week.' Linda came round from her desk. 'I can't do the job without your help. And anyway, I don't want to be stuck in this office on my own with hardly anyone around. When anyone *does* come in, they just dump stuff on the desk, give me a wink and a smile as though that's all that's needed to set me up for the day, then rush off.'

Raine felt sorry for Linda. She'd be leaving the girl on her own to face Foxy every day. But she couldn't stay in this place a moment longer. Hartman had been abrupt enough, but he wasn't unfair. And he didn't make obnoxious passes, either. That was something she wouldn't stand for.

There was no reason to stay to the end of the week, especially as Doug was no longer here. If only she knew where he'd been sent, but she'd drawn a blank with everyone she'd asked. Foxy would have known, she thought bitterly, but she wouldn't dream of asking anything of that creep.

'Sorry, Linda, I don't want to hang around any longer. I need to decide what to do now. But I've enjoyed working with you and wish you all the luck. I mean it.' She turned towards the door.

'Raine, wait a minute . . .'

There was an urgency in Linda's tone that made her stop.

'Can we go to the NAAFI and have a cuppa?' Linda said. 'I need to talk to you about something, and I also want to know the reason why Foxy has sacked you.'

Raine hesitated, the image of Foxy's eyes roving over her legs. Maybe she should warn Linda that he had a lecherous streak so the girl was prepared. Linda might only be seventeen but she was as well developed as any woman.

'All right,' Raine said. 'I could do with one – and maybe treat us to a bun,' she added with a thin smile.

They walked companionably but silently to the canteen and took their trays to a table in the corner.

'I detest that Foxy,' Linda blurted as soon as they sat down. Her eyes shone with indignation. 'Whenever you're out of the room he comes in and hangs over me when he asks me to type a letter. His hair oil stinks. It makes me feel sick. And yesterday when you went to the Ladies' he came up behind me and put his hands on my breasts and told me to keep quiet or he'd get rid of me. He's tried to touch me before but always pretended it was accidental. This time, there was no mistake – it was deliberate. With you not around he'll be even worse.' She looked at Raine, her eyes beseeching. 'I need my job, Raine, and he knows it.'

So this was what Foxy giving her notice was all about. He wanted full access to Linda without Raine curtailing him. What a pig! This was far more serious than she'd imagined.

'He tried it on with me when he first came to the section,' Raine said.

Linda's eyes were wide. 'What did you do?'

'Threatened to report him. And didn't I pay for it . . . with my job.' She looked at Linda. 'What did *you* say to him?'

Linda swallowed some tea. 'I asked him to please stop, but he gave them a quick pinch, which really hurt 'cos I had the curse, and just laughed.'

'The filthy beast. I wish you'd told me earlier.'

Linda shook her head 'What was the good? I wanted to forget it. But I feel sick every time I see him.'

'Let me think for a minute.' Raine spread some margarine on her bun and took a bite. 'Ugh. I'll never get used to marg. And now they've rationed that as well as butter.' She scraped it off, then took another bite, slowly chewing, savouring the spicy flavour, all the while with Linda's anxious face in front of her. Then she smiled. 'I always think better with a currant bun.'

She noticed Linda hadn't touched hers.

'Okay, Linda,' Raine said after a minute or two. 'I have a plan. I'll help you if you'll help me.'

'Anything,' Linda breathed.

'First of all, I'll stay until the end of the week. It's only four more days but we have things to do.'

The next morning when Flight Lieutenant Fox put his head in the door Raine was quietly at her desk working.

'I'm pleased you're conscientious about doing a proper day's work in light of our conversation, Miss Linfoot,' he said.

Raine looked up, keeping her expression neutral. 'I couldn't do anything else, sir.' As he turned to go she crossed her fingers that Linda was keeping a cool head.

Half an hour later Linda came in, a grin plastered over her face, her thumb up.

Raine stopped typing. 'You managed it, then?'

'Yes. I asked him if he had any letters to dictate. I could see the letter you're talking about already in the filing tray. So I picked up the files with the letter on the top and asked what I should write back. He told me to ignore it. "Not worth a reply," he said. "We don't have anyone here who would be suitable."'

Raine clenched her fists. 'Then what?'

'As soon as he went out I copied the address. I have it here.' She took a folded piece of scrap paper from her pocket and handed it to Raine. 'Then I filed everything in the tray, including the letter which I put in a new file I made up called ATA, as I would have done normally.'

'You don't know what this means to me, Linda.' Raine

opened her bag and quickly tucked the scrap of paper inside the little pocket where she kept her mirror. 'Miss Gower asked for a pilot with more experience than me, but I'm going to write to her anyway. Even if she puts me on a list. That way, if I can increase my hours I can approach her again.' She glanced at Linda. 'I can't thank you enough.'

'I enjoyed doing it,' Linda said. 'I felt like a spy.' She giggled.

Raine smiled. 'So that's the first part of the plan carried out successfully. The second part we'll do on Friday, my last day.'

'You know, I've been thinking a lot since yesterday,' Linda said. 'I don't even like office work but it's bearable when you're here. Now you're leaving I'm giving in my notice. So Foxy will lose both of us at the same time. Serve him right.'

'Are you sure you're doing the right thing, Linda?'

'I'm *very* sure,' Linda said mischievously. 'I'm old enough to join the ATS. And that's what I intend to do. Get in with some of the action.'

'That's a marvellous plan,' Raine said, smiling. 'I think you'll be a real asset. But we should still report the swine, as who knows what he might do to the next unsuspecting girl. So we'll keep our appointment this afternoon. Agreed?'

'Oh, yes.' Linda nodded enthusiastically. 'I can't wait.'

An hour before the time the two girls were due to leave, the phone rang. Raine picked it up.

'Flight Lieutenant Fox here. I'm ringing to tell you that appointment you and Miss Rogers have this afternoon with the CO has been cancelled.'

Anger swept through her body. What was going on? Why was *Foxy* giving her the message? Had he somehow got wind of the reason the two of them were about to talk to his senior with some problem? His behaviour, for instance?

'His secretary suggests Wednesday next week,' he continued,

'but of course you won't be here.' He gave a chuckle and the line went dead.

'That was Foxy,' Raine said to Linda who'd stopped typing to listen. 'Our appointment's been cancelled.' Fury coated her words.

'Why?'

'He didn't give a reason but I think he guessed.'

Linda chewed her lower lip. 'Raine, it's no good. It won't get us anywhere – and I'll be leaving anyway.'

Raine sighed heavily. 'Well, I suppose at least we tried. But I can't bear the idea that he'll get away with his disgusting behaviour.'

She finished the letter she was typing for him, not bothering to correct his grammar. Let them all think what an ignorant little— She stopped the bad word before it formed. She banged the lever of the carriage to the left, typed the valediction, rolled out the letter and for the last time shoved the cover over the machine.

'That's it,' she told Linda. 'I'm not doing any more for that rat.'

As though on cue, Foxy came in and pointedly looked at the covered typewriter.

'I see you've already packed up,' he said. 'But there *is* one more thing.'

Raine waited. *What now?*

'According to the rules, when someone leaves, their bag has to be inspected.' He smiled his oily smile. 'Just a precaution. I'm sure it's not necessary in your case, Miss Linfoot, but we'll do it anyway, just so I can make a note on the file that I carried out the correct procedure to the letter.'

Dear God, no. He knew. The incriminating evidence was there for him to find. She'd be in real trouble, but worse, so would Linda. Her heart thumping, Raine glanced at the

76

girl, who seemed to have frozen, her eyes wide with dismay. She opened her mouth but Raine quickly shot her a warning look.

'We won't wait until five thirty,' he said. 'We'll do it now and then you can go early. So just tip your things out of the bag where I can see them.' He thrust out his chest and folded his arms, his attention focused on Raine's handbag.

Cursing inwardly, Raine opened it, deliberately taking out the items one by one and laying them on the desk. The fountain pen her father had bought her for her eighteenth birthday, a notebook, her purse, a sanitary towel wrapped in a brown paper bag (*please don't let him look in there*), a small fabric bag she'd made at school to hold her comb and lipstick . . . everything except the mirror with Miss Gower's address tucked behind it.

'That's everything,' she said.

'What's in that paper bag?'

'A woman's item,' Raine said, choking with rage that he should put her through this.

He opened it and peered inside, made a grimace then dropped the paper bag back with the other items with a flick of his fingers as though it were something revolting. Just when she thought she'd got away with it, he put his hand out and jerked his head towards the bag.

'Give me the handbag.'

Pulse racing, she kept it open as she handed it to him.

Keep calm, Raine. Don't let him see you're at all anxious.

Her stomach growled in defiance as she watched him put his hand in the space, fingering all the corners.

'Ah, a secret pocket, no less . . .' He paused, his mouth twisting. Raine's stomach clenched. 'What have we got here?' A flash of disappointment crossed his face as he laid the mirror on the table with the other items. '*Now* I think we can say the bag is empty,' he sneered. 'All right, Miss Linfoot, you can be on your way.'

He marched out of the office, giving the door a slam.

'Phew,' Linda said. 'I couldn't have held my breath much longer.' She gave a weak smile. 'I really thought he'd find the note. Didn't I see you put it in your handbag?'

'I don't understand,' Raine said, shaking her head. She picked up her empty handbag and sat at what was her desk, running her fingers inside the mirror pocket. 'Why didn't he find it when he pulled out the mirror?' She looked up, appealing to Linda. 'I pushed the note behind it, but it's not here.'

'It must be.'

Raine turned her bag upside down but nothing fell out. Mystified, she peered inside, then searched the mirror pocket again. It *had* to be in here. And then one of her fingers felt a flap in the lining and she remembered. Triumphantly, she pulled out the tiny piece of paper.

'Here it is,' she said as she waved it towards Linda. 'There was a tear in the lining that it got caught behind. I keep meaning to ask Suzy if she'd stitch it. I'm glad I didn't.' Raine chuckled. 'It saved my life where Foxy is concerned.' She tossed the contents back into her bag. There'd be plenty of time to tidy it up later.

'You'd make a great spy,' Linda said, smiling now. 'Oh, Raine, I'm going to miss you. Will you leave me your address?'

Raine scribbled her address on a scrap of paper from Linda's wastepaper basket. 'You can get hold of me here,' she said. 'We'll keep in touch. I want to know how you get on in the ATS.'

Linda nodded. 'Now, where shall I put this?' she said, glancing at the address. 'I don't think I have a special slot for top-secret notes in *my* handbag.'

78

Raine grinned and gave the girl a quick hug. 'You'll find somewhere, I'm sure. Maybe down your bra. Wouldn't Foxy love to discover *that*?'

'He'd wish he hadn't,' Linda said fervently, then caught Raine's eye and they both burst out laughing.

'I hope I shan't be around for him to find out,' Linda said. 'Trouble is, I think I'll have to wait until I'm officially accepted in the ATS before I give my notice. I need the money to help Mum with the other kids or I'd follow you out of the door.' She rolled the carriage of her typewriter to pull out the last letter she'd typed. 'I want to know if you get into that air transport place.'

'The ATA?' Raine said grimly. 'If I don't, it won't be for want of trying.'

Chapter Eight

'I'm very content you have left that place,' Simone said when Raine told the family at supper that evening the news that her services were no longer required. 'Maybe you will now forget about flying and do something sensible.'

'Maman, you don't understand. I'd give anything to be up there, helping our boys.'

'Then I am glad you will never be allowed. The men must be left to get on with their job.'

Raine managed to stop herself from mentioning the possibility of joining the ATA. It would only lead to another argument, and anyway she might not ever be accepted.

'Maman, we all have to do something to help.' Her mother opened her mouth to interrupt but Raine continued. 'Look what's happened already in the Channel Islands. Poor innocent people. British subjects and we haven't sent anyone to help them. I bet anything Hitler will have his evil eyes on us next. They're always talking at work about his plans to invade us.'

'Well, you are no longer at work,' her mother flashed. 'Why do you not come and help me with collecting the aluminium for your precious aeroplanes?'

'I'm a qualified pilot,' Raine half rose from the table in frustration that her mother simply had no idea what drove her daughter, 'not a scrap metal collector.'

'Lorraine, sit down,' her father interrupted. 'And don't

demean your mother's efforts. Eat your meal – a feat in itself with all the rationing.'

Raine sat down, biting back a retort, knowing when her father called her 'Lorraine' he wasn't going to tolerate any more backchat, as he called it.

'There will be no further discussion on the subject of invasion in front of your sisters.' Maman popped a morsel of meat between her perfectly painted lips. 'I will not have it.'

How can her father ever have said she was like Maman? Raine gritted her teeth.

'Very nice stew, Simone,' her father said mildly as he placed his knife and fork neatly together. 'Did you have to queue very long for the meat?'

'You don't need to change the subject, Dad,' Ronnie spoke up. 'Suzy and I aren't babies. We do listen to the wireless.' She turned to Raine. 'What are you going to do now you've left Biggin Hill?'

'Find out if there's any way I can increase my flying hours,' Raine said without hesitating.

'You'll find the answer,' Ronnie said, ignoring their mother's glare. 'You always do.'

Later, Raine went upstairs to write her letter to Miss Gower in private before Suzanne came back from her music lesson. She sat on the edge of her bed with a sheet of writing paper and a book underneath to act as a desk. Uncapping her pen, she began to write.

Dear Miss Gower,

I understand you are seeking pilots, both male and female, to join your ferry pool at Hatfield and I would like to apply.

I have twenty hours with a 'C' pilot's licence – mostly in Tiger Moths at Hart's Flying Club near Biggin Hill in

Kent, but since the war started I haven't had much opportunity to increase the hours.

I would be very pleased to come for an interview any time at your convenience and in the meantime, I look forward to hearing from you.

Yours sincerely,

Lorraine Linfoot (Miss)

She read it through once, swiftly, and decided it couldn't be improved. The message was simple. She was a qualified pilot and would love to join the ATA. The only thing holding her back was that blasted two hundred and fifty hours minimum flying time.

She folded the letter and stuck it in an envelope, then licked the flap and pressed it firmly down. Using the note Linda had slipped her, she carefully copied the address. She'd go to the post office first thing in the morning. If only she could increase her flying hours . . . but with a war on, and the expense, and now no job to pay for them, and no civilian flying clubs open even if she could, she was seeing her dream slowly drift away.

'Maman said you were in our room.' Suzanne crept in. 'I hope I'm not disturbing you.'

'Course not. How did your lesson go?'

'Not so well today.' Suzanne flopped on her bed. 'I couldn't seem to concentrate.'

'Why not?'

Suzanne breathed out a long sigh. 'All this war stuff. And I'm old enough to do something towards it.' She looked at Raine. 'Like you, being a pilot. That ought to be really useful.'

'You would think,' Raine said, pulling a face. 'And there's an organisation called the ATA – the Air Transport Auxiliary – who will actually accept women pilots, but I haven't enough hours clocked up.'

Suzanne's eyes were warm with sympathy. 'Do you know who's in charge?'

'Yes, it's a Miss Pauline Gower. In fact, I've just finished writing a letter to her to apply.' Raine waved the envelope in front of her sister. 'But I don't hold out much hope. She wants girls . . . women with a lot more experience than I've got – even though I know damned well I could be trained to do the job.'

Suzanne gave her a hug. 'Well, at least you'll have tried. And you know what? I have a strong feeling this Miss Gower might make an exception for you.'

Raine hugged her back. 'You've always been my greatest fan,' she chuckled. 'But I'm concerned about you. Maman will go mad if you don't keep up your lessons. Which you would have to forego if you really wanted to do something worthwhile in the war.'

'It'd be worth it,' Suzanne said soberly. 'I can pick it up again when the war's over. People are saying it shouldn't last more than another year.'

'It's barely started as far as Great Britain is concerned,' Raine said. 'Our boys are still fighting off the Luftwaffe, so I think we're in for a long haul. They said at the start of the Great War that it would be over by Christmas, which was only a few months away . . . and look how long that one lasted – four terrible years for those poor soldiers in the trenches. Who knows how bad this one will get before Mr Hitler realises he'll never get the better of us.'

It was only five days later, on a crisp autumn morning, that the postman handed Raine a typed addressed envelope. She didn't dare think it might be from Miss Gower. She glanced at the postmark: Hatfield. She couldn't help her lips curving in a smile. This letter could change her life.

'Looks like it's good news,' he said, giving her a wink.

'I hope so.'

She stood outside the garden gate watching the postman cycle off whistling, and contrary to her father's instructions to always use a letter opener, she ripped the envelope open where she stood and withdrew a folded sheet.

Until I open it I can believe Miss Gower is inviting me for an interview, she thought, the letter trembling a little in her hand. *But if it's not – sorry, you haven't enough experience . . .* Raine momentarily shut her eyes. *But suppose it's good news . . . I'd then know . . .*

Dear Miss Linfoot,

Thank you for your letter. I was most interested to read that you are already a qualified pilot with a certain number of flying hours.

Raine's heart leapt with excitement. She read on.

It is urgent that we recruit more ferry pilots and we are able to take a certain number of experienced women pilots. Unfortunately, I'm afraid all the places were immediately filled. However, I have put your name on a waiting list and will contact you if the situation changes. In the meantime, I suggest you join the WAAFs, as at least you will be in your chosen environment.

Yours sincerely,

Pauline Gower (Commanding Officer)

Raine stumbled to the front door, tears pouring down her cheeks without a sound, and rushed up to her bedroom. She threw herself on the bed and sobbed. How ridiculous, now the country was at war, to turn qualified pilots away, whether they happened to be female or male. There must be hundreds of women like her who wanted to do their bit for their country.

After thumping her pillow and using a few choice words, she finally got up and found a handkerchief to blow her nose. Then she went to the bathroom to splash her face. She stared at herself in the mirror, her eyes pink and puffy. She actually looked beaten. What on earth was she going to do? If she'd never dreamed of being a pilot, she would have signed up to join the WAAFs like a shot. But it would be too frustrating for her to wear the uniform and talk to male pilots, all the while knowing she would never be allowed to fly, even though she was as qualified as they were.

'As though I'm some sort of inferior being,' she said aloud.

Sniffing and brushing away her tears, Raine pulled the letter from her coat pocket and reread it. Miss Gower promised – well, not promised, exactly – but said she would contact her if the situation changed. In other words, if Miss Gower was given permission to take on more women. Raine supposed at least that was something. A glimmer of hope.

What to do in the meantime?

She wasn't in the mood to think straight right now. The library. She'd cycle into Bromley and have a good look round. Libraries were full of information. She heard her mother in the kitchen so she put her head in the door.

'Maman, I'm just going to the library to change some books.'

Her mother was peeling potatoes for dinner.

'You'll be back by one?' she asked, looking up. 'Are you all right, Lorraine? You look as though you've been crying.'

'It's probably a cold coming on,' Raine said. 'And yes, I should be back by one.'

That would give her plenty of time to calm down. Try to think sensibly what to do.

* * *

85

Mrs Jones, the elderly library assistant, looked up as Raine walked in and put her three books on the library counter. She smiled as she recognised her customer.

'Hello, dear. Are you looking for anything in particular today?'

'Not really,' Raine answered. 'Um, that is, I don't suppose you have any information on the ATA, do you?'

Mrs Jones pushed her spectacles up her nose. 'The ATA? I'm afraid you'll have to enlighten me, dear.'

Raine explained, but Mrs Jones remained looking nonplussed.

'I've never heard of it,' she said. 'Perhaps the librarian will know. I'll have a word with her when she comes in later. But I have something that might interest you – if you're set on aeroplanes, that is.'

Raine followed her over to a table with a couple of daily newspapers and a few out-of-date magazines.

'Ah, here it is.' Mrs Jones pounced on a magazine displaying drawings of several different aeroplanes on the cover. 'A gentleman brought this in, in case one of our readers was interested.' She took off her steel-rimmed glasses and smiled at Raine. 'You're welcome to have it, dear.'

'Oh, thank you,' Raine said, taking the magazine and glancing at the name: *Flight*. 'I haven't seen this one in the newsagents'. How kind of you to think of me.' She gave Mrs Jones a beaming smile. 'I shall really enjoy reading this.'

'Is there anything else I can help you with?'

'No, thanks. I'll just have a look around the shelves.'

She passed a table where there were some pamphlets about a dance on at the Palais in Bromley. She picked one up and put it in her bag without looking at it. She hadn't been out for a long time. Perhaps that was just what was needed to cheer her up.

* * *

That evening, before supper, when Raine was in their shared room, she read Miss Gower's letter to Suzanne.

'Oh, Raine, how disappointing.' Her sister regarded her. 'What are you going to do?'

'Good question. I wish I knew.'

'Well, you must write to this Miss Gower and thank her,' Suzanne said firmly. 'Maman taught us that. Tell her how disappointed you are but thank her very much for putting you on her waiting list. And that you look forward to hearing further if things change. No, on second thoughts not "if", but *when* things change. Because they're bound to with so many of our soldiers losing their lives.' She blinked away a tear.

'I don't want to bother her when she's obviously busy.'

'I still think she'd appreciate a letter,' Suzanne said. 'At the very least, it will keep your name in front of her before anyone else who applies. You don't know, but you could hear in a few weeks' time.'

'You're such a wise owl,' Raine said, smiling for the first time all day. She hugged her. 'I'll do it straightaway. Oh, I nearly forgot. I picked up a leaflet in the library about a dance at the Palais. I haven't read it properly, but we've never had an evening out on our own, have we?' She pulled the leaflet from her bag and handed it to her sister.

'It's this Saturday,' Suzanne said, looking up excitedly. 'Oh, Raine, I'd love to. They've got a jazz band playing.' She glanced at the leaflet again. 'Richard Spicer is the bandleader – he's one of my favourites – and Sally Rivers is singing. She's becoming very popular on the wireless but I'd love to hear her in person, wouldn't you?'

'Yes, but you'll have to be the one to convince Maman,' Raine said. 'She's much more likely to agree than if *I* asked her.'

Chapter Nine

To Raine's astonishment her mother was actually amenable to the idea of her two daughters going to a dance together.

'How will you come home?' Simone asked.

'Same way we go – on the bus,' Raine answered.

'Well, you may go if you promise not to lose the last bus.'

'We promise, Maman,' Suzanne said.

'And to look after your sister at all times, Lorraine.'

'I will.'

Ronnie's face was a picture when Raine and Suzanne waltzed down the stairs on the evening of the dance.

'Look at you two – dressed up like a dog's dinner.'

Raine gently pulled one of Ronnie's pigtails. 'You're still a baby. I'm sure in a few years' time you'll have given up being a tomboy and will be just as excited to go off to a dance as we are.'

'I'm hardly a baby at fourteen,' Ronnie protested, 'but I just hate all that girl–boy stuff. Waiting on the edge of the floor to be asked to dance by some pimply boy with greasy hair. Ugh.' She made an ugly face.

'We don't intend to dance with pimply boys,' Suzanne said, laughing. 'There should be a few *slightly* more mature ones around, being so close to the aerodrome – if they're not all away fighting the Germans, that is. If there's no one we fancy we'll have a dance together, won't we, Raine?'

'Let's hope it doesn't come to that,' Raine chuckled. 'Come on, Suzy, we don't want to be late and miss all the fun.'

The dance hall was packed as the two sisters entered. Raine swiftly glanced around, wondering if there was anyone she knew from Biggin Hill, but it was difficult to see the faces clearly because of so much smoke. And as many of them were in uniform it was even harder to differentiate between them. She suddenly thought of Foxy and hoped to God he wouldn't be here or suddenly turn up.

The floor was already crowded with couples dancing to the small orchestra playing 'Crazy Rhythm' and Raine found herself tapping her foot to the infectious beat. She glanced at Suzanne, who was staring at the small stage, eyes half closed, mesmerised. Suzanne looked delightful in her new dress, Raine thought. Her sister had made it out of a length of bright flowered cotton that one of Maman's housewives had given her, saying she didn't have any spare saucepans but hoped the material would help the war effort.

Suzanne had altered one of Maman's gowns for Raine – a bright red silky affair with a short full skirt that flew above Raine's knees when she'd twirled in the mirror and a halter-neck top. What a marvel her sister was with a sewing machine.

'I'll get a drink for us at the bar,' Raine said, 'if you can find a table.'

Even though she was tall, and wearing her eye-catching red dress, Raine could *not* catch the barman's eye. Men who should have been behind her somehow edged their way in front and were served. Chewing her lip in frustration she finally elbowed her way forward and stood directly in front of one of the bartenders, then opened her mouth to give her order. Ignoring her, he nodded to the tall man who had suddenly appeared on her right. Raine sucked in a breath of irritation. What was so special about *him*?

She gave him a sideways glance. He was in RAF uniform, as were many of the other men – three or four years older than her, she decided. His fair hair was swept back from his forehead to show the world what a very good-looking bloke he was. He knew it, too, she thought scornfully, by the cocksure way he'd managed to get served before her. He had no manners. He jolly well knew she was at the bar before him.

As though he felt her staring, he turned to her. His eyes, the green of a blade of grass, held hers. And then he smiled. She gave a start. She'd seen that smile before. It lit up his face. But where? At this moment he was regarding her with open admiration, but it did nothing to thwart her temper.

'Excuse *me*, but I've been standing here for ten minutes.' She flashed him an angry look. 'But I realise I must be invisible.'

'Oh, no,' he chuckled. 'Believe me, you are *extremely* visible – particularly in that vampire's dress.'

'In that case, I'd like to put my order in before you,' she snapped.

'Be my guest.'

He shifted no more than an inch or two, supposedly giving her the impression he was letting her go in front. She noticed his wings and the two bars on the cuffs of his tunic. He was a pilot – and an officer. *He* wouldn't have had any trouble joining up. The RAF would have welcomed *him* with open arms. And because she was a woman she was not only denied getting into the ATA to do something worthwhile for the war effort through lack of solo air miles, but it was also as though this cocky pilot was rubbing her nose in it at the same time.

Common sense finally came to the rescue and aware that the bartender was enjoying the little scene, she said in as cool a tone as she could muster, 'Two lemonades, please.'

'Coming right up,' the barman said, and she saw a wink pass between the two of them.

They were laughing at her! In a split second she'd turned on her heel, but the pilot was too fast. He grabbed her arm.

'Hey, what's the matter? You've made your point. You're being served now.'

She shook his arm off. 'The trouble with you men in uniform,' she began, her voice trembling with anger, 'is that you all think you're God's gift. All I asked was for good manners, which I would've thought they'd have taught you in the RAF, even if your parents didn't, which doesn't mean sharing a joke at my expense with the bartender just because I made a *point*, as you call it.'

She stopped abruptly to take a breath, inwardly seething.

'I'm sorry,' he said, looking like a contrite schoolboy who didn't really mean it. 'I admit, it was rude of me. Come on back and I'll buy those drinks. Who are you with, anyway – a boyfriend who drinks lemonade?'

'You can't help the sarcasm, can you?' she said scathingly. 'If you must know, the other one's for my sister.'

'Ah, a sister. And is she as bad-tempered as you?'

How dare he!

And then he threw back his head and laughed. 'Sorry, I'm teasing you. Honest. Name's Alec . . . Alec Marshall.' He stuck out his hand. 'What's yours?'

Marshall? She hadn't forgotten that name. He was one of the six pilots who'd brought in the new Hurricanes that time. The one who'd smiled at her. Who'd begun walking towards her . . . until one of his mates had called him away. So his name was Alec. She needed to get away before he recognised her.

'I must get back to my sister,' she said, disregarding his outstretched hand.

'She'll be disappointed if you go back to her without her drink.'

Ignoring him, she quickly made her way over to the other side of the room, near the orchestra. Suzanne was bound to have grabbed somewhere close to the musicians so she could watch them playing.

'I was beginning to wonder where you were,' Suzanne said as Raine sat down at the table for four, across from a couple who couldn't keep their hands off one another.

Raine jerked her head towards them and rolled her eyes. Suzanne giggled.

'You didn't bring any drinks. Was the queue at the bar too long?'

'I got waylaid,' Raine said.

'By me!' A man's shadow fell over the table.

Oh, no. Raine parted her lips and blew out an exaggerated sigh. He'd followed her. And he was carrying a tray holding three drinks.

'May I join you?'

'There's no spare chair,' Raine said in an icy tone.

'Sorry, I didn't catch that.' Alec Marshall hunkered down by her chair, his face close to hers. 'The band's a bit loud.'

She knew he'd heard her. Not drawing back an inch, she said slowly and clearly, a few decibels louder, 'There's no chair.'

'Take this one,' an older woman from the table nearest called. She nudged an empty chair towards their table.

The pilot thanked her charmingly and squeezed in between the two girls.

He turned to look at Suzanne. 'I think you must be the lady's sister,' he said, 'though I haven't yet had the pleasure of knowing her name even though I've told her mine. I'm Alec Marshall.'

'That's easy,' Suzanne said immediately, ignoring Raine's glare. 'This is Lorraine, my sister, but she goes by the name of Raine. And I'm Suzanne.'

To Raine's intense irritation Suzanne put her hand out and shook Alec's hand.

'Pleased to meet you, Mr Marshall.'

'Do call me Alec.'

Suzanne smiled and nodded.

Alec Marshall turned to Raine. 'I must say I wouldn't have put you down as sisters . . . and it's not just the hair colour.'

Raine sucked in her breath. She knew he was having a dig at her.

Without pausing, he added, 'So now we've been officially introduced, perhaps I'll have the pleasure of a dance with *both* of you.' A smile hovered over his lips, then became a delighted grin. 'You know something, Raine? I've seen you before.'

'I can't imagine where.' She glared at him. 'And by the way, only people close to me use my nickname.'

She felt Suzanne give her a sly kick under the table but took no notice. *How dare he be so familiar.*

'Oh, so-*rry*,' he said, bowing his head in mock subservience. He looked up. 'I completely forgot my manners. Do forgive me, Miss Crosspatch.'

She wouldn't lower herself to answer, though she kept her eyes on him. He was too attractive for his own good. He held her gaze, causing her pulse to quicken. Why was she being so prickly with him? After all, he was right. She'd seen him, too. Well, she wasn't going to give him the satisfaction that she'd realised who he was.

He suddenly tapped his head. 'I've got it! You were the

93

kid at Biggin Hill. You caused quite a stir with the chaps when one of them told us you were learning to fly.'

She shook her head, pretending to recollect when and where it could possibly have been.

'How soon we forget.' He gave her a half-mocking smile. 'It was when we delivered the new Hurricanes that time – before the war even started. It was you, I'm sure, and if you gave me a little smile now as you did then, I'd know definitely.'

Yes, she had smiled back at him that day. Now, she would die before she gave him another.

'You saw me coming over to talk to you, but the chaps called me back. And it wasn't anything that couldn't have waited. But by the time I came to look for you, you'd vanished. I asked who you were, but no one knew your name, only that they thought you were one of the clerks. I kept hoping we might run into each other one day – and here we are.' He grinned then took a deep swallow of his beer without taking his eyes off her.

She hesitated as though she was thinking. 'Yes, I do remember the Hurricanes being delivered,' she said after some deliberation, 'but I can't say any one of the pilots caught my attention.'

Alec Marshall drained his glass. 'You know, if you weren't so prickly, *Lorraine*, I'd ask you to dance. But if I did, I'd be worried you'd pierce my heart with one of your barbs.'

'That is, if you *have* a heart.' She sent him a steely look.

'Raine, stop being so horrible,' Suzanne said, tapping her sister's arm. 'It's not like you.'

At that moment, the music changed from another jazzy piece to a slow foxtrot. It was 'Moonlight Serenade' – one Raine particularly loved. If she hadn't been so cutting with Alec he might have—

'May I have the pleasure?'

A well-built boy about her own age in a smart suit stood in front of Raine with a hesitant smile. Without a backward glance she nodded and rose, following him onto the floor, feeling Alec's eyes boring into her back. Her partner put an arm around her waist and took her hand in his.

A minute later she wished she hadn't been so keen. His hand became sweaty as he lowered his head, watching his feet and muttering in her ear, 'Slow, slow, quick, quick, slow.'

Raine knew she was a good dancer. She'd enjoyed learning at school and nothing would have given her greater pleasure than to glide around the dance floor with a partner who knew what he was doing. Unfortunately, this poor boy didn't.

'I'm sorry,' he said as he stepped on her foot for the second time.

'It's all right,' she said, not wanting to make him even more nervous.

After the band finished that particular piece, she made her excuses and walked back to her seat. The lovey-dovey couple had vanished and the two other chairs were empty. Presumably, Suzy was dancing with Alec Marshall. Well, her sister was welcome to his charms.

She picked up her glass and took a few sips of lemonade, irritated that he'd bought the drinks. The liquid soothed her hot, dry throat. She drank some more while scanning the dance floor. Yes, there they were, making a striking couple with Suzanne's gleaming blonde head resting on his shoulder. She could tell he was an accomplished dancer by the way he was holding her, taking the lead, his movements fluid and practised. She felt a trickle of envy as he bent his head to say something. Suzanne laughed and Raine cringed at the thought they were laughing at her. Then she told herself off. Of course they weren't. Suzanne would never do that. But the thought didn't make her feel any better towards Alec

Marshall. He was a conceited oaf and she hoped to God she wouldn't bump into him again.

'May I have this dance?'

A smiling man in uniform stood in front of her.

'You may.'

Raine rose to her feet and soon she was on the dance floor again, chatting to this very pleasant officer. But her thoughts were elsewhere. And she couldn't help looking over his shoulder every few moments – just to check her sister was all right, she told herself.

'Is anything wrong?' Suzanne asked as she and Raine were on the last bus back to Downe.

'What on earth makes you say that?' Raine said, inwardly battling with her annoyance at the whole evening.

It hadn't been as much fun as she'd thought. None of her partners had been good dancers.

'Because you've barely spoken since I danced with Alec.'

'I don't know what you're talking about.'

'Oh, I think you do.' Suzanne looked serious. 'And something else. I think you *have* met him before but won't admit it.'

'What makes you think that?'

'Because underneath it all you find him attractive but you won't admit that either, so you're trying to have the upper hand and put him in his place. But you've picked the wrong one. He's more than a match for you.'

Raine was silent.

'And when I happened to mention you were a qualified pilot—'

'You didn't!' Raine interrupted. 'I don't want him to know my business.'

'Why? He's really nice when you get to know him.'

'Well, you should know. You had enough dances with him.'

Suzanne's eyes clouded. 'Don't be so dog-in-the-manger, Raine. You made it clear you wanted nothing to do with him, so why shouldn't he ask me?'

Immediately, Raine felt guilty. Her sister had done nothing wrong and she was being perfectly horrible to her, spoiling her evening. She put her hand on Suzanne's arm.

'I'm sorry, Suzy. Don't take any notice of me. I expect it's the time of the month.'

'It's all right. I get irritable myself then.'

'I've never noticed.' Raine smiled. Then her smile faded. 'What did he say when you told him I was a pilot?'

'Tickets, please.' The bus conductress held out her hand.

The sisters gave her their tickets. She clipped them and handed them back, nodding her thanks.

'Where were we?' Raine said casually, as though any continuing conversation about Alec Marshall was of no consequence. 'Oh, yes . . . about being a pilot.'

'He was most impressed. He said again how you were watching the new Hurricanes land at Biggin Hill and that he'd immediately wanted to get to know you. He said he never forgot your face and regretted that you didn't properly meet.' Suzanne turned her head to Raine. 'They're the exact words he said.'

'Is he stationed at Biggin Hill, then?'

'No, he's usually stationed near Maidenhead, but he happened to be at Biggin Hill today with some friends, so they thought they'd go into Bromley – have a look in the Palais. Normally, we wouldn't have met him at all.'

'It would've been just as well,' Raine said shortly.

'He said for me to tell you that you should join the ATA,' Suzanne went on, ignoring the comment. 'It would be right up your street, he said. I told him you'd tried and hadn't got in because they were only taking a certain number of women at present. He said he would put in a word for you to that lady you wrote to – Miss . . . what was her name?'

'Miss Gower.'

'Oh, yes, that's the one. He knows her.'

He would. Prickles of irritation ran up Raine's spine.

'I don't want that man to put in any good word for me,' she said. 'I don't want to be beholden to anyone, least of all him. If I ever get into the ATA it will be from my own effort – not some cocky pilot's.'

'I think he really likes you.'

'If he does, he's got a strange way of showing it,' was all Raine said.

As far as she was concerned, the subject was closed.

Chapter Ten

June 1941

Dear Miss Linfoot,

 If you are still interested in joining the ATA, I should be very pleased to see you as soon as possible. Would you therefore come to Hatfield aerodrome on 21st June for an interview and bring your pilot's licence. Just go to the main building and ask for me and someone will take you to my office.

 I look forward to your confirmation that this is convenient.
 Yours sincerely,
 Pauline Gower (Commanding Officer)

Raine skimmed the letter again. She should be feeling elated with Miss Gower's letter asking to see her, but instead she was terrified. It was now eighteen months since she'd set foot in an aircraft and the thought worried her sick. There'd be a test even to get into the ATA. So much to face before she'd be accepted – that is, if she reached that stage. Not to mention the difficulty in convincing her mother that she wouldn't be happy unless she could take up her flying again.

She'd finally caved in to her mother and was working in the dress shop for Mrs Garland. But there wasn't enough custom to keep her occupied. It would be even less now the clothing ration had just been brought in. She dreaded the idea of listening to complaints from women who thought nothing of buying two or three couture outfits at a time, and who now had to monitor their clothing coupons carefully.

If it hadn't been for Mrs Jones in the library giving her that copy of *Flight*, which she'd thoroughly enjoyed, so much so that she'd asked the village newsagent to order it for her as a monthly treat, she would have gone crazy. Desperate to keep abreast as to what was happening – as much as the public were allowed to know, anyway – she soaked up the articles on the RAF pilots and the various aircraft.

She'd tried hard to be patient but had become more and more fed up and irritable with each month that passed. The war news had been consistently depressing, brought close to home when the beautiful little parish church in Bromley was ferociously bombed in April. The papers said more than two hundred bombs had dropped that night, making hundreds of people homeless. Maman had had hysterics, ordering everyone to go to the village shelter, but Dad and she and her sisters had refused to turn out at midnight, saying they would do so only when the sirens sounded in Downe itself.

Seeing the devastation in Bromley when Raine had cycled to the library one day soon after had made her stomach heave. How badly she wanted to help the war effort. How ridiculous that she wasn't allowed to use her skills. The worst thing about the wait was that she was no longer flying.

But Pauline Gower, whom she admired more than almost anyone, had asked to see her. She had to keep that in the front of her mind. And the twenty-first of June was her birthday. A wonderful coincidence. Well, it would be the best birthday present possible if Miss Gower liked her.

Raine glanced out of the window, noticing the postman

100

walk up the path to next door's, her mind reeling with possibilities. Only Maman was at home. And she was the last person Raine wanted to share the news with that Miss Gower was interested in talking to her. She hadn't forgotten how in January Maman had handed her a newspaper with an article about Amy Johnson, a highly experienced pilot who'd recently been reported as missing. It made chilling reading. They'd finally discovered her body in the Thames Estuary along with a crew member of a naval trawler, who had heard her cries for help and had tried to rescue her from drowning.

'Maybe when you read this you will understand why I do not want you to be a pilot in this terrible war,' her mother had said stiffly.

If only Maman had told her that she loved her and wanted her to keep safe – that she couldn't bear to lose her – instead of simply giving her an article to read. If only she'd given Raine a hug rather than that stern warning about ending up in the Thames like poor Amy Johnson. But 'if onlys' were a waste of time. Raine bit her lip. Maybe she was more like her mother than she cared to admit. She, too, found it difficult to tell anyone her innermost feelings.

In the end Raine didn't mention any interview with her parents or her sisters. It was simply too delicate a subject at the moment. She'd wait until after the interview, and if it led to nothing she wouldn't have upset her mother for no reason.

'Happy birthday, *chérie*,' her mother said as Raine was boiling the kettle for tea. Suzanne was still asleep and no one else was up.

She'd hoped to have a cup of tea quietly on her own before the big day. Not her birthday – she couldn't care less about that – but her interview with Miss Gower. This was going to make or break her future and she wanted to be on top form. She could only hope her mother wouldn't question her too closely about what she was planning to do. She'd already tried it last night at supper, mumbling that she might go and visit a friend in hospital in London. She knew it was a lie, but she needed to tell her mother she was going somewhere that wouldn't encourage Maman into insisting on accompanying her. Oh, why was everything so complicated?

'This friend of yours you're going to visit. Do I know her?'

'Hilary? No, I don't think you've met her.'

'What is the matter with her?'

'She fell in the blackout and hurt herself.'

Raine crossed her fingers behind her back. It wasn't a total lie. Her friend *had* fallen in the blackout, but she hadn't ended up in hospital.

'Hmm. If I didn't know you better, I would think you were doing something quite different,' her mother said, not taking her eyes from Raine's.

'And then I might have a look round Selfridges on the way back,' Raine said, ignoring her mother's insinuation and needing the excuse to be gone the whole day.

'There is nothing of worth in the shops,' Simone said triumphantly. 'Many have been bombed.' She looked directly at Raine. 'Besides, you do not love shopping.'

'I want to see how London's been affected,' Raine said. *Please, Maman, don't go on.*

'It's a fine thing when you cannot spare the time to be with your mother on your birthday,' Simone said unexpectedly. 'What time will you be home?'

Raine shook her head. 'I'm not sure. Just have supper without me. But I shouldn't be *too* late. If I am, I'll find the nearest phone box and let you know.'

*   *   *

'How did you find out about us?' Pauline Gower looked across her desk at Raine with a friendly smile.

Raine sat nervously on the hard office chair, mesmerised by Miss Gower's three gold stripes on her epaulette, glittering and winking at her. She'd rehearsed the next bit.

'The pilot who taught me to fly mentioned it,' Raine said, 'but at that time you'd only taken eight women who I was told had several hundred hours each. I was sure more women would be taken on eventually, so I resolved to stay at my job at Biggin Hill airfield rather than join the WAAFs and not be allowed to fly. Then one day a flight lieutenant I worked for . . . ' Raine forced the memory of Foxy's sneer to the back of her mind, 'knew I was a qualified pilot and he read out part of a letter from you, where you asked if there were any experienced pilots, including women, who would be interested in joining the ATA.

'I was so excited for a few moments, thinking my chance had come,' Raine continued, 'until he asked me how many flying hours I had. When I told him, he looked at your letter again and said you'd stipulated a minimum of two hundred and fifty hours.'

'He said that?' Pauline Gower's smile disappeared. A puzzled look crossed her face.

'Yes.' Raine suddenly had a thought. 'Would it be rude to ask if you actually said that in the letter, ma'am?'

'No, you wouldn't and I didn't,' Pauline said immediately. 'I remember exactly what I said, which was that I'd be delighted to see *any* qualified pilot who was not able to engage in flying for the RAF. And I specifically said, "which, of course, includes female pilots".' Pauline frowned. 'I wonder why he told you such a thing.' She caught Raine's eye. 'Did he dislike you for any reason?'

What should she say? She didn't want to get into the lecherous advances Foxy had made or Miss Gower would think she'd be trouble with any male pilots or other male staff around. It sounded so pathetic even to mention it. But should she lie?

'Your hesitation makes me think there was some kind of problem there,' Pauline said. She nodded to Raine, her sharp eyes missing nothing. 'What is this flight lieutenant's name?'

Raine hesitated, wishing she hadn't started this. It might scupper her chances of being accepted. Then Linda's face came before her. For her and any other girl who had the misfortune to work for him, she had to answer.

'Flight Lieutenant Fox.'

Pauline jotted something – his name, Raine supposed – on a pad, then looked up.

'The most important thing is – are you still keen to join us?'

'Oh, yes,' Raine breathed. 'It's what I want to do more than anything.'

'I'm sure you know the ATA is a civilian organisation, so there's no saluting or marching or drills and suchlike, but we are under the regulations of the RAF so far as secrecy is concerned. That means no chit-chat with friends and family about airfields where you deliver the aircraft, or what planes you're flying. It's common sense, really – but breaching their security would be a most serious offence. You'd be signing a letter along those lines.' She paused. 'I don't know if you realise, Lorraine, but the ferry pool at Hatfield is all female – official title is Ferry Pool Number 5. It's the first of its kind.'

Raine beamed. 'I didn't realise, but I think it's wonderful, ma'am. I'd be proud to be part of it.'

'Never forget, Lorraine, for a moment, that we women have to be whiter than white. We can't have accidents that are our fault or show any feminine weakness whatsoever. Only then will we be considered *nearly* as good as the men, even though we might individually be far more experienced and skilled.' She broke off and her gaze was stern. 'Totally unfair, but we have to buckle down and get on with the job as professionally as we possibly can. Is that understood?'

'Oh, yes, ma'am. Completely.'

Pauline's expression relaxed. 'By the way, you can call me Pauline. As I said, we're not in the military and we're all in this together. All right?'

'Yes, ma'am . . . I mean Pauline.'

Pauline smiled. 'Then I'll arrange for you to have a medical and an eye test. If you have time, we'll get it done while you're here.' She paused. 'Presumably you're in good health.'

'Oh, yes, as far as I know.'

'Remind me how old you are.'

Please don't let my age be the thing that stops me from getting in.

'Twenty . . . today, actually,' Raine began in as confident a voice as she could muster, 'and if you accept me, it will be the best birthday present I could wish for.'

A wide smile lit the neat features of Miss Gower. 'Oh, my dear, I do wish you a happy birthday.'

Raine hardly heard the words. Almost without knowing, she shifted to the edge of her chair, waiting for Miss Gower's next comment on whether she might be acceptable or not. As though she'd read her mind, Pauline leant across the desk.

'You're very young,' she said, 'but I have another twenty-year-old who's our youngest at the moment and she's doing an excellent job. And now the French have capitulated it's a sad day not only for them but for us as well.' She put her hand to her face and shook her head. 'So now we fight on alone and it's even more imperative that we keep our air cover in top form. It's us against the mighty Luftwaffe.'

Raine held her breath. So far Miss Gower had said nothing about needing parental approval. She felt a certain optimism as she looked into the warm eyes of the commanding officer.

Pauline glanced at Raine's notes.

'We'd give you full training on a number of different aircraft, but as you haven't flown for quite some time, you'll need to do a flying test for us.'

'Can you tell me what plane that would be in?'

Pauline smiled. 'So as not to complicate things, I think we'd better stick to the Tiger Moth, which I understand you're very familiar with.'

Raine, who'd been holding her breath without realising, breathed out slowly in a happy sigh.

The meeting was clearly at an end when the commanding officer rose to her feet. Raine hesitated. She immediately liked this woman and felt sure she could trust her.

'Pauline . . .' she started.

'Yes, Lorraine?'

'You asked me who the flight lieutenant was at Biggin Hill.'

'That's right.' She looked directly at Raine. 'Why do you ask?'

'Because I think if he found out I was here he would make trouble for me.'

'In what way?' Pauline's mouth tightened.

Raine hesitated. Linda had been emphatic about not taking it any further after all, and Raine had gone along with it. But she hadn't promised not to say what had happened to anyone else. And if she didn't tell this nice Miss Gower, or Pauline, as she'd been instructed to call her, she might think Raine had done something awful and not allow her to join the ATA. She looked at who she hoped would be her new boss, who nodded to her to continue.

'It's just that . . . well, he thinks young women who report to him for stenography are sometimes there to serve other purposes.'

Pauline grimaced. 'I understand perfectly, my dear. No

need to explain any further . . . so if you'd like to follow me, we'll get your medical done.'

It was late when Raine arrived home. Supper had already been cleared away. She guessed Maman and her father were in the sitting room, Dad reading his paper and Maman probably knitting a sock for an unknown soldier. Raine could hear her muttering in French as she often did when she was annoyed. Probably trying to turn the heel. Her mother hated that part of the war effort.

Raine gave a wry smile as she put her head round the kitchen door. Suzanne and Ronnie were washing-up, her youngest sister with soapy water up to her elbows and Suzanne drying. They both turned when they heard her come in.

'Hello, you two.' Raine dumped her bag on one of the kitchen chairs. 'Something smells nice. Is there anything left over for me?'

'Suzy saved you some macaroni cheese,' Ronnie said, 'though it's more macaroni than cheese since it was rationed. But don't tell Maman that.' She jerked her head towards the oven. 'And there's a bit of cabbage in the saucepan. Probably overcooked now, but finish it up and then I can wash the pan.'

'How did you get on?' Suzanne turned to her sister. Raine sent her a warning frown, but Suzanne said, 'It's all right. I've told Ronnie. She's not a baby and hasn't breathed a word.'

'Don't know what you're talking about,' Ronnie said, winking at Raine.

Raine laughed. The secret would have to come out sooner or later.

'As long as the medical test is okay and I do a perfect test flight, I should be in. And you'll never believe this, but the Hatfield ferry pool – where I'd be – they're all *women* pilots. Isn't that astonishing?'

'It's wonderful.' Suzanne hugged her. 'It's exactly what you've dreamed. Although I don't really like thinking about you up in the clouds with Germans flying around and shooting at you.'

'I don't think it's quite like that,' Raine smiled, remembering Doug's words, just as she was about to take her pilot's test. She spooned the last meagre portion of macaroni onto her plate. 'The aeroplanes are too precious to take any risks with mere human beings.'

A week later Raine received a letter from Pauline Gower.

Dear Miss Linfoot,

I am pleased to inform you that your medical has proved satisfactory and to that end, we would like you to join us on 15th July. You will immediately start your training on the various types of aircraft.

Please would you report to Hatfield at 10.30 a.m. on that day for further instructions on your flight test and your accommodation where you will be billeted from 15th July for the foreseeable future.

I should be grateful if you would confirm your acceptance, but in the meantime, if you have any further questions, please do not hesitate to ask.

Yours sincerely,

Pauline Gower (Commanding Officer)

This was it! What she'd dreamed for so long. Treated like the male pilots, doing the same job, earning . . .

Raine stopped. Miss Gower hadn't mentioned anything about wages. But even if she never earned a penny for her efforts, Raine would gladly have said she would still join them.

But now she had to break her news to Maman. Best get it over with while Dad was with her.

Chapter Eleven

Raine and her two sisters, Suzanne and Ronnie, stood together in their front garden, heads tilted upwards to a sky that was cloudless, for once – a real summer blue.

'We're so near Biggin Hill aerodrome, I bet it won't be long before the Germans have their eye on it and start bombing,' Raine said, looking grim-faced. 'We'll soon know about it, if so.'

'If that's the case, I'm glad you don't work there any more,' Suzanne said, shielding her eyes from the sun. 'We'd all be worried to death.'

'I'm already worried to death,' Ronnie said in an anxious voice, sounding older than her years. She turned to look at Raine. 'You'll be up there amongst it all soon.'

'Not in any fighting,' Raine assured her. 'My job will be to get the planes delivered so they don't have to use their pilots for routine work – they need every single one for our defence. The Germans are so sure their Messerschmitts are superior to our Hurricanes and Spitfires, but I reckon they're in for a nasty shock.'

She daren't let her sisters know, but inwardly Raine was sick with fear for the RAF boys in Fighter Command, especially since Doug had joined them, itching to do his bit to bring down Jerry, as he'd said in the last letter.

But don't worry about me, Raine, he'd written. *I'm doing what I love best and the chaps are first-rate. But thank God they don't allow women in combat or I'm sure you'd join up without a moment's hesitation.*

Raine swallowed. He was right. If she'd been allowed to, and had had the training, she didn't doubt she'd be up there giving those Germans what for. But that didn't stop her praying nothing bad would happen to Doug. So many times in the past she'd asked herself exactly how she felt about him. He'd never treated her any differently than he would a kid sister, being that much older, but when she was sixteen she'd had dreams that one day he might realise he really cared for her. Now she was older she realised that was all a schoolgirl crush. Now, she happily thought of him as a special friend she adored, and the one who'd made her dream of flying come true.

'You make it sound so simple,' Suzanne said.

'It's the only way. Once you start fretting you lose your nerve. But when I'm in the sky I feel more at home and relaxed than ever I do on the ground.' She suddenly realised how tactless she was being. 'Oh, I don't mean away from my sisters, or even Dad and Maman. It's just that I feel I'm alive – and free – and that I'm capable of doing anything I set my heart on.' She shrugged. 'It's hard to explain.'

'Well, rather you than me,' Ronnie said firmly. She gave the sky another cursory glance. 'I'm going for a walk with my feet firmly on the ground. That's always what helps *me* to relax. I just wish Maman would let me have a dog,' she flung over her shoulder as she strode off.

'It would be nice if Maman *would* allow her to have a

110

dog,' Suzanne said when Ronnie was out of earshot. 'She's crazy about animals, so it doesn't seem fair.'

'Maybe you should have a word with Maman, Suzy. She listens to you more than anyone.'

'I already have,' Suzanne said, the corners of her mouth turning down, 'and she said I wasn't to mention it again.'

Raine frowned as Ronnie disappeared from view. Her youngest sister was nearly always on her own. Ideally, at fifteen, she should have a girlfriend who also enjoyed messing about outside. But as an alternative, a dog would be the perfect companion.

'Well, I'll have a go with her,' Raine said resolutely, then grinned. 'Luckily, she hasn't given *me* the same order not to mention it again.'

She didn't hold out much hope with persuading her mother if Suzy hadn't got anywhere. Maman wasn't in the best of moods at the moment. She was barely speaking to Raine ever since she'd told her she'd been accepted in the ATA. No, she'd tackle her mother about the dog when things were more settled between them.

Once again Raine had slept badly, but this time it was barely concealed excitement that overrode tiredness. She'd done her best to keep her joy to herself that she was finally being admitted into a world she'd longed for. Today, she'd meet other women pilots like herself; until now, she'd never met one – except for Miss Gower, of course – which ought to help her stop feeling like an outsider as she did where the family was concerned.

She'd had her bath last night, so after a cursory wash she dressed in her only two-piece that she'd worn every day at Biggin Hill, not for the first time thankful it was navy and reasonably smart, and not a million miles from a picture of the ATA uniform Miss Gower had shown her.

111

I'm sure lots of things will be made clear today, she thought, as she swallowed the last of her toast and jam and finished her cup of tea. She glanced across at her suitcase, already packed and the lid fastened. Quickly she rinsed her cup and plate. The kitchen clock showed twenty minutes to seven. Her cab would be here in five minutes. She couldn't help smiling as she anticipated the day and where her head might rest tonight.

Suzanne and Ronnie were still in their nightdresses when they saw her off. Her dearest sisters. She'd miss them, but it wasn't enough to disturb her happiness that she was escaping Maman's clutches and beginning her new independent life. She only hoped Suzy and Ronnie would find their own paths during this awful time. *Please, God, let the war be over by the time Ronnie comes of age. And then* – Raine chewed her lip – *where would that leave her?* She'd never get a job as a female pilot in civilian times. But as long as the war continued she'd be needed for her beloved flying. Feeling guilty that she should think something so terrible for her own benefit, she shoved the thought away.

Raine couldn't see a vacant seat when the train finally pulled in. Once on board, she walked along the corridor, glancing through the windows of the compartments. Every single one was full, with soldiers standing – body shoved against body – between the two rows of seats. Finally spotting a vacant seat through the glass of the last compartment, she slid open the door to four adults and five boisterous children.

'I have to warn you,' what appeared to be the mother said as Raine sat down, 'they're a noisy bunch when they all get going.'

Raine gave a polite smile and sat down, then immediately wished she hadn't. Something was sticking to her skirt.

She jumped up and inspected the back of it. Ugh. A gluey

brown substance had attached itself to the material. Raine tried to pull it off but it clung on. A few threads of gold came away on her fingers. Toffee. The worst thing to clean off.

'I'm so sorry, dear.' The mother looked frazzled. 'It's not easy trying to control them without their dad.' She lowered her voice. 'He was killed at Dunkirk.'

'I'm so sorry,' Raine said, immediately contrite.

How awful. He'd left his young family behind and the mother had as much admitted that she couldn't cope.

It wasn't a particularly long journey, but only half an hour had passed before the first hold-up. Her heart sank. No one ever knew how long it might be and rarely were the passengers given any information. Thankfully, this time it was only a few minutes and then the train slowly moved off like some old man, grumbling away. Raine sighed with relief.

But only a few more minutes down the line they suddenly stopped again. Time dragged by and no guard came to explain the delay. By now Raine could feel the perspiration gather on her forehead. She'd left in plenty of time, allowing for these hold-ups, but two within such a short period was worrying. Sighing, she glanced at her watch for the umpteenth time: twenty-five to nine. 'Come on, start moving,' she muttered as she peered out of the window. The man in her carriage didn't even look up from his newspaper. He probably did this journey every day, Raine thought, and took it all for granted that these delays were normal. She needed to report for duty, she wanted to shout. At this rate she was going to be late. And she didn't think that would go down at all well with Miss Gower.

Raine pulled her book from her bag and tried desperately to read, but she was too anxious to concentrate. All she could do was keep looking at the hand on her watch inexorably turning.

When she'd reached the point of screaming, there was a sudden jolt and several jerks. The man peered over the top of his newspaper and gave her a sympathetic smile. She gave him a half-smile back then fixed her attention on her book.

At long last the engine roared into life and moved a few hundred yards, then slowly gathered speed, spewing out a cloud of steam.

She rose and opened the compartment door. A walk up the corridor would give her legs a stretch. But a cluster of uniformed young men and women inadvertently blocked her way. How she wished she was also wearing a uniform. It would have made her feel more self-assured, particularly when one young woman looked pointedly in her direction, then averted her eyes and whispered to the woman standing next to her.

Raine longed to say something, tell them she was a trained pilot and was off to do her bit, then laughed at herself for being so vain as she returned to her seat.

Oh, please let me get there on time.

But fate wasn't on her side. By the time she'd waited for a late-arriving train at Finsbury Park and was on the one to Hatfield, it was already five past ten.

Raine was almost in tears by the time she arrived at Hatfield aerodrome. The weather had changed in the last hours to a heavy mist. It was gone eleven when she stepped into the building where she'd first met Pauline Gower. Frantic, she asked a passing pilot where she should go to report that she'd arrived.

'Along the corridor and second door on the right. Someone will be there to show you where to go.'

Raine thanked her, envious of the woman's rank and her confident air, and furious with herself for not catching an earlier train. Arriving late wasn't going to make a good first impression.

She half ran down the corridor and stood outside the second door on the right for a few seconds to catch her breath. She was just about to knock when the door opened and a man – maybe in his thirties – in pilot's uniform came out. He glanced at her.

'Are you looking for someone?'

'I'm Lorraine Linfoot. This is my first day and I have to report to Miss Gower to—' She broke off as she saw the smile slip and a frown take its place.

He made a deliberate job of looking at his watch, then looked at her.

'You're very late, Miss Linfoot. We've been waiting for you.'

'I'm sorry, but the trains—'

'Well, never mind that. We'd better get going.'

'Where to?'

'Your flight check.'

Raine frowned. 'But Miss Gower didn't say anything about having one today. I've only just this minute arrived from Bromley, my home.'

'No matter,' he said, looking at his watch. 'I've got a busy schedule today, but I told Miss Gower I'd take you up for your flying check. She was short of instructors. Or should I say *instructresses* . . . if there is such a word.' His lip curled a fraction. He gave her a hard look. 'So we might as well get it over with.'

Oh, don't say he's going to do it.

'Is something wrong?' His tone was curt.

'No, nothing,' she said firmly. 'I was just wondering where I should leave my suitcase.'

He jerked his head towards the door he'd just come from. 'Leave it in the office.'

'Don't I have to sign anything that I've arrived?'

'As I said, you can do all that later.'

It wasn't the best beginning. She wasn't mentally prepared to fly today and she was still wearing her skirt suit, which made some of the manoeuvres difficult. Her nerves now shredded, she pushed her hair away from her face with a trembling hand. Dear God, don't let him have noticed. If he had, he wouldn't even allow her to climb into the plane.

'Right, follow me.'

Why was he so irritable? He hadn't even bothered to tell her his name. Was he another one who didn't approve of women pilots? He must hate having to work in an all-female ferry pool, even if it was only temporary. She unclenched her fists and followed the examiner onto the airfield.

He continued to march in front towards a small single-engine plane. But it wasn't a Tiger Moth. Her heart plummeted. She'd never flown a Puss Moth.

'Excuse me, sir, but Miss Gower agreed I should do the flying check in a Tiger Moth . . . the plane I'm more familiar with, as I haven't flown for a while.'

'Sorry, haven't got one available at the moment,' he said, his eyes piercing hers. 'Of course, if you want to make another time—'

'No, no, of course not,' she cut in. Like he said, she might as well get it over with.

The whole atmosphere felt strained. Aircraft were taking off and landing in regular intervals, but it had been too long since she'd last flown, and in her present state, nothing seemed familiar.

Furious for allowing her nerves to give way because of some grumpy instructor, she breathed in the smell of the airfield as she hurried after him, allowing the noise of the other planes' engines to pulse through her veins. When she somehow managed to hitch her skirt in an unladylike fashion, practically

116

falling into the cockpit, she strapped herself into the front seat and immediately felt the toffee stick to it. It really was too bad but she'd have to ignore it. Reaching for the little blue book of the Ferry Pilots Notes, she flipped over the pages to find the description and tips on this particular make.

Thank goodness it doesn't appear much different from the Tiger Moth.

Gazing at the controls, she forced herself to concentrate on this all-important flying check. She swallowed the lump in her throat. If she failed they could send her home. Aware of her instructor's clipped tones when he asked her if she was ready for take-off, she felt that going home was a distinct possibility.

Her scalp prickled with anxiety as she recited aloud everything she checked, both for her own verification and the nameless instructor. Her mind seethed with resentment that he seemed to want to put her under as much pressure as possible. What a horrible man. Well, she'd show him, if nothing else.

Minutes later they were in the air. She almost blew out her cheeks with relief, but didn't dare let him see how tense she'd been. So far, he hadn't made any comment, hadn't even spoken, and of that she was grateful.

'We'll go north . . . towards Welwyn Garden City. That way I can see how you perform in the country and the town.'

Now she was safely airborne she relaxed. She was once more in control. She'd worried unnecessarily; it didn't matter that she'd never flown a Puss Moth. It felt like only yesterday that she'd taken a plane up instead of getting on for two years. If she'd been flying solo she would have laughed out loud with the exhilaration she felt coursing through her body. Freedom in the skies. A different world. A world she loved.

They'd only been in the air for ten minutes before her mood gave way to concern. The light mist when she'd first arrived at Hatfield less than an hour ago suddenly turned into a bank of heavy cloud. Wishing she could zoom above them, she tried to keep the aircraft just below, but the ground was getting too near. She could barely discern the railway line and the town in the haze. The wind whipped into a storm, the rain beating against the windscreen. There was no word from the flight lieutenant. Clearly, he wasn't going to give her any kind of advice. She was on her own.

And then she saw something that made her blood curdle.

A line of barrage balloons. And her plane was heading straight for them.

Don't get tangled in the cables, Raine. For God's sake, don't get caught in those wires.

The words buzzed around her head like a mantra.

You can get out of this. You've been trained.

With sweating palms she quickly opened up the throttle and pulled back the control stick – her sole focus on getting out of danger. And if she had to go above the clouds, to hell with the rules.

The plane just missed the cables as it sailed up.

She didn't dare look round at the instructor, but she heard him curse under his breath.

'Bloody Nora, that was a close one.'

Raine's heart was hammering as she finally brought the plane back to a painfully jolting landing, almost entirely the result of her shattered nerves. She'd failed. It was as plain as if he'd told her to her face there and then. Visibility was poor in the low cloud and she hadn't seen the barrage balloons until it was too late. Excuses spun through her head. She'd been forced to obey the ATA rules and fly low and there they were. As a pilot you were supposed to be told where the balloons were in advance so you could steer clear of them. But the nameless instructor hadn't mentioned it, so he'd obviously not known about it either. And she'd bloody nearly cost both of them their lives, not to mention the breaking up of a perfectly good aeroplane.

Perspiration poured off her forehead and trickled over her lips. How could she face her family? How could she face Miss Gower, whom she'd let down most awfully? Miss Gower had taken a chance with her being so young and inexperienced, and it hadn't paid off.

Raine's legs felt so wobbly that she was inordinately grateful when the instructor actually helped her down from the cockpit, her jacket clinging to her back with cold sweat, and to her embarrassment, her skirt somehow riding up. Wishing she could make a dignified exit but knowing she had to face him, she made herself look him in the eye. His face was pale. She must look equally in shock. Her heart began to pump again. He'd make out the report and say she had not only endangered their lives but had also come close to losing an aircraft.

'I don't know what happened there,' she stuttered as he started walking away. 'I wasn't expecting something like that. But—'

'We'll have a chat later, Miss Linfoot.' He barely broke his stride.

Half running, she was intent upon keeping up with him, even though her humiliation made her want to crawl into a dark corner.

Without looking at her, he said, 'In the meantime I suggest you go to the NAAFI and have a mug of tea with two sugars. They're only supposed to give out one per cup, so tell them I said so.'

With no hint of any expression, he marched on ahead of her.

Chapter Twelve

To Raine's embarrassment, her name was on everyone's lips at lunchtime; the gossip had already made her into an unwilling heroine when the news had flown round that she'd almost had a fatal accident on her flight test.

'Do come and sit with us, Lorraine, and tell us what happened,' a girl with bright red hair beckoned her.

Reluctantly, she moved towards their table. There were five women, all young except a woman maybe in her late thirties. They were all chattering, but as soon as she pulled out a chair they fell silent.

'What a shock.'

'It must've been frightening.'

'Did you panic at all?'

'Did you think you were going to die?'

'So many questions.' Raine smiled thinly as she looked around at her fellow pilots. They all smiled back. 'Raine Linfoot.' She held out her hand to a girl with dark curly hair who reminded her of Ronnie.

'Joan Dawson. Pleased to meet you.'

Patricia Denman, Beth Phillips, Sandra Hardy, Audrey Parker . . . one by one, they introduced themselves.

'I'll try to remember your names,' Raine said, catching each girl's eye and nodding.

'Tell us exactly what happened,' Audrey, the older woman, demanded.

Raine told them as briefly as she could, then finished her mug of extra-sweet tea. 'I'm not sure what to do now,' she said. 'I suppose they'll want me to make a full report.'

'Your examiner will do that,' Audrey said with a grim face.

'They'll let you know when they want to see you,' said Beth. 'We don't get much time off, so take advantage of a half-hour to get over your shock.' She wiped her mouth with her napkin. 'By the way, where are you billeted?'

'I haven't a clue,' Raine admitted. 'But it doesn't matter, as I imagine I'll soon be going home once Miss Gower has seen me.' She rose to her feet and made herself smile. 'It was nice to meet you all, although I'm sorry it was so brief.'

'By the sounds of it, it wasn't your fault,' Audrey said. 'And from what I hear, you rose magnificently to the occasion – literally.'

The others chuckled.

'If the plane is still standing upright,' Audrey went on, 'that's all they worry about.' She gave a wry smile. 'Anyway, don't fret about it.'

'I'm all right, honestly,' Raine said. 'But I must know where I stand. So if you don't mind, I'm going to see if I can find Miss Gower and at least explain what happened.'

Pauline Gower was nowhere to be seen. Raine hesitated. She needed to know if she was going to be sent home or not. If so, she should make her way to the railway station right away. There was no point in hanging around once she'd located her suitcase. But who could she speak to who would know? There was so much toing and froing. Three women in uniform, parachutes slung over their shoulders, walked arm in arm across the grass to the Anson taxi waiting to pick them up. Oh, how she envied them. They'd all passed their flight test and were getting on with the job of delivering planes.

Just as she was about to knock on a door that seemed vaguely familiar, the pilot who'd tested her came out. He halted abruptly when he saw her.

'Ah, Miss Linfoot.'

'Yes, it is, sir. I'm looking for my suitcase.'

'It's where you left it – in the office. In fact, come in as I want to talk to you about the test flight.'

This was it. Swallowing hard, Raine followed him into the office.

'Please sit down.'

He looked serious. She shook with nerves again as she sat on one of the visitors' chairs, her eye on her suitcase she'd set down against the wall what seemed like hours ago.

'Where are you billeted?'

The question took her by surprise.

'I don't know,' she said flatly, not meeting his eye. 'But it doesn't matter now, because I'll soon be on my way home.'

He sent her a stern look. 'What, because of the test?'

She nodded.

'If we all felt like that when faced with an emergency, we'd have given up months ago. We can't let something like that interfere with stopping Jerry from invading.' He let that sink in before continuing. 'I don't usually work out of Hatfield, as I said, and I'm afraid I hadn't realised when we were over Welwyn Garden City that because they don't have any Anderson shelters, Balloon Command put barrage balloons up instead. And they hadn't done their job of warning us as they're supposed to.' He leant forwards in his chair. 'It wasn't your fault at all about the barrage balloons.'

'You mean—'

'Yes, Miss Linfoot, I've passed you. I have to admit I was

122

pretty worried when we first saw the bloody things, but you kept a cool head, so well done. I've explained to Pauline all the details and she's relieved you handled the situation so well. She said she'd be back at twelve noon and will give you the address of your digs.' He looked at his watch. 'She'll be here in exactly twelve minutes and thirty-three seconds. I'm sure you can hang on as long as that.' He actually smiled and nodded to her case. 'You may retrieve your case, Miss Linfoot. And wait here for Mrs Gower.'

She stared at him in disbelief. She'd done it! And apparently she'd done it with flying colours!

Pauline Gower smiled as she entered the room.

'I hear you've had rather a difficult flight test,' she said as she took a seat behind the desk where Raine sat. 'I'm so sorry, my dear. But Flight Lieutenant Stock was very impressed by the way you handled a potentially dangerous situation. So I'm delighted to say you may report for duty tomorrow. In the meantime you can settle into your billet this afternoon. It's in the village.' She glanced at a card. 'Mr and Mrs Adamson are expecting you. I think you'll be happy with them.

'It might pay you to get hold of a bicycle so you can cycle back and forth, but for now I'll get one of the chaps to give you a lift as you've got your suitcase. And tomorrow another pilot, Stephanie Lee-Jones, will be joining you.'

What did that mean? That she'd be in the same house, or actually sharing a room? It was bad enough sharing a room with her sister, let alone a stranger. Raine pulled herself up sharply. There was a war on. She couldn't expect a hotel suite. And this girl had as much right to be there as she did. And *she* probably wouldn't relish the idea of sharing a room with a stranger any more than herself.

'This is the address,' Pauline said, handing her the card. 'I would go now and make yourself known to them. Then we'll expect you in the morning at eight o'clock sharp when you'll start the first phase of your training. In between times you'll need to get some more solo hours under your belt.' She paused. 'Once you're fully trained you will be paid six pounds a week, although out of that you pay for your own billet. Until that time, we will see to it.'

It seemed like a fortune. 'Thank you, ma'am . . . I mean Pauline,' Raine added when Pauline raised her eyebrows. 'You've been most kind.'

'Let's hope you continue to feel that way when you finish a thirteen-day shift.' Her new commanding officer sent her a wry smile. 'It's not an easy job, but with every delivery, you'll know you're doing something vital for the war effort.'

The young lad who drove her to the Adamsons' house didn't stop talking. Raine knew he was being friendly, but she would have preferred to be quiet for a few minutes after her ordeal.

A mile or so later he dropped her outside one of a row of semi-detached Victorian houses along a busy street, swung her suitcase from the boot and placed it on the short path leading to the front door.

'Good luck, miss.' He waved and vanished.

Raine tilted her head to look up at the house before she knocked. It had a deep bay window on the first floor flanked by a smaller but equally decorative window. On the ground floor was a matching bay and a curved arch forming a porch to the front door, painted maroon. The small front garden was neat and well kept and Raine imagined it would be the same at the back. It felt like an inviting house which would give her some respite. She only hoped Mr and Mrs Adamson would be equally happy to have two women they'd never met sharing their home.

She took a breath and raised her hand to the knocker. There was loud barking from within and the door opened immediately. An elderly gentleman stood there, holding the door wide, a small brown-and-white terrier at his heels. He was in his seventies, Raine guessed, with silver hair and a moustache to match, and kind, twinkling eyes. Best of all, he was beaming at her.

'I'm Thomas Adamson. And you must be Lorraine. Come on in, love. We hoped you'd be early so you could settle in.' He stepped aside to let her pass, the dog still barking at her but wagging his tail. 'That's enough noise, Bobby. Miss Linfoot is going to be with us for a while so you'd better be friendly.' He bent to pat the dog, then rose up with a wince. 'Not so supple as I once was,' he said to Raine with a rueful expression. 'Do you like dogs?'

Immediately Raine thought of Ronnie.

'I'm not really used to them,' she said, but instinctively she bent and patted Bobby's head. 'Good boy,' she told him, and was rewarded with a lick on her hand.

'He's making friends with you already,' Mr Adamson said, pride in his voice. 'Come through, come through. My wife's in the front room. She's got arthritis, so she can't move about too easily.' His eyes fell on her case. 'Why don't I take that suitcase and show you your room first . . . then you can meet the missus.' He picked up her case before she could protest.

Raine followed the broad figure up a curved flight of stairs to the landing. He opened one of the doors, but instead of being a bedroom it was another flight of narrow steps.

'We're only three bedrooms on the first floor, so we've had to put you in one of the attic rooms,' he said over his shoulder. 'Both our sons are in the army, but they do manage

125

to get home occasionally. And recently Barry got engaged, so with you and your colleague we're going to be a full house.'

He opened a door to the left and entered, setting down the suitcase. It was a larger room than she'd expected, though only two-thirds would give her enough headroom. Nevertheless, a shaft of sunlight filtered through a dormer window, picking out the single bed. Inwardly, she sighed with relief.

Mr Adamson pulled open a door in the sloping wall to reveal the wardrobe.

'Bit short of coat hangers,' he said.

'It's absolutely fine,' she assured him. 'I haven't brought that much, so I'll quickly unpack and come down and meet Mrs Adamson, if that's all right.'

'Perfectly.' Her host looked round the room in a vague manner. 'Anything else you might need to know?' He raised his white eyebrows.

'Just where the bathroom is.'

'Ah, yes.' He glanced at the bed. 'My wife's put the towels out for you – on that chair.' He nodded towards a Lloyd Loom chair with two neatly folded towels. 'You and the other young lady – I forget her name – will have to share our bathroom. It's on the first floor. Door second on the right. There's a cloakroom downstairs and your colleague has a sink in her room. That does help. Anyway, my wife will sort those arrangements with you.'

How wonderful. Her own room. A bit of privacy.

'Thank you very much,' she said fervently.

'Come and find us whenever you're ready,' he said. 'No need to rush. I'll make us all some tea and we'll be in the sitting room. Don't bother to knock.'

When he'd disappeared Raine breathed out. She took stock of what would now be her new home. In spite of the sloping ceilings where she would have to duck, the main part was a good height and the room looked as though it had been recently decorated, though it was sparsely furnished. The floor was linoleum of an indistinguishable colour, cheered with a large, richly patterned dark red rug by the side of the bed. There was a heavy chest of drawers on the far side and a bedside table with a lamp. Lovely. She'd be able to read at night . . . something she hadn't been able to do since she'd shared a room with Suzanne who needed her sleep. At the thought of Suzy, she gulped. She knew she was going to miss her sisters terribly.

Raine stepped over to the dormer window to see people scurrying by, all seeming to have a purpose. Women were balancing shopping bags with children too young to go to school hanging on their arms, the kiddies stumbling and crying. She noticed a couple of businessmen walking on the other side of the road deep in conversation. A bus pulled up at a stop only a few yards from the Adamsons' house, where several people alighted.

She watched for a minute or two then opened the window. Immediately, it was noisier – a child's scream, a motorbike roaring past – and she could smell the fumes from the bus. There was only the odd motorcar since the petrol rationing, but a horse and milk cart slowly clip-clopped its way along the road. She smiled at the lack of urgency of the animal and its driver. They were obviously carrying on normally, war or no war.

The warm summer air fanned her cheek. This room would be her refuge. She only hoped the new pilot would be nice. With a light heart she hurried downstairs.

Voices came from behind one of the doors. She opened it and immediately Bobby ran towards her, giving little whines of delight.

'Come in, my dear,' called an elderly plump lady. She was sitting as upright as the straight-backed chair encouraged, her misshapen fingers gripping her knitting needles as she slowly proceeded along the row.

Raine's first impression was that she looked formidable in her dark grey plaid dress, her silver hair severely pulled back from her face in a bun, her lips devoid of colour. But as she tilted her head towards Raine and their eyes met, Raine saw that her smile was as wide and genuine as her husband's.

'Do come and sit down,' she said, gesturing for Raine to take one of the pair of leatherette armchairs. 'You must be tired with your journey.' Before Raine could answer, Mrs Adamson said, 'Tom's in the kitchen making tea for us all. I'm sure you could do with one.'

Her hosts were very similar in that they both talked nineteen to the dozen without waiting for any reply. Raine hid a grin. But they were making her welcome and that was heavenly. Bobby, the dog, was soon snoring softly in his basket.

'I think you girls are wonderful,' Mrs Adamson said, shaking her head as she took up her knitting again. 'Flying those great machines all on your own. They scare me to death. You wouldn't catch me up in one.'

Raine smiled. 'The training gives you everything you need to know and, besides, I've always wanted to fly.'

'Your poor mother must be worried sick with all those Germans in the sky trying to shoot down our boys.' Mrs Adamson heaved a sigh from her full bosom. 'It doesn't bear thinking about – but I suppose Mr Churchill knows what he's doing.'

'Tell me about your sons,' Raine said, desperate to change the subject from her mother.

Mrs Adamson's face clouded. 'Danny and Barry? I worry about them night and day, though they tell me not to,' she said. 'They're in the army – officers, both of them,' she finished on a note of pride.

'You must be so proud of them,' Raine said. 'And I hear Barry's just got engaged.'

'Yes.' Mrs Adamson beamed. 'To a sweet girl. Daphne. She'll make Barry a wonderful wife . . . and a lovely daughter-in-law.'

'Tea up.' Mr Adamson wheeled in a trolley. 'Shall I be mother?'

'Oh, yes, dear, you're better at it than me these days. My hands are so shaky.'

Mr Adamson poured a cup for Raine and handed one to his wife. As Mrs Adamson put out her hand to take it, the cup rattled in its saucer. Raine turned her head away, pretending not to notice. She took a sip of the warm weak tea.

There was a sudden loud knock at the door.

'Now who can that be?' Mrs Adamson said. 'We're not expecting anyone, are we, dear?' She looked at her husband for confirmation.

The knock was more impatient this time and Bobby leapt up and began to bark.

'Let me get it for you.' Raine sprang to her feet.

'Oh, how kind,' Mrs Adamson said, beginning another row of her knitting.

'Stay here, Bobby!' Mr Adamson ordered, as he struggled from his chair.

Bobby gave his master a reproachful look but lay down in his basket again, his ears on full alert.

Raine opened the door to a petite young woman, maybe two or three years older than herself, her strawberry blonde curls escaping from her pert straw hat, smiling in the way of a woman who is used to having men falling over themselves to rush to her aid. A suitcase, almost as tall as her, stood alongside. Raine glanced over the girl's shoulder and was just in time to see the rear end of a large cream car as it vanished down the road.

'Hello, I'm Stephanie Lee-Jones. And you must be Lorraine.' She stuck out a hand and Raine couldn't help noticing the long, manicured nails painted shocking pink.

'That's right.' Raine briefly shook her hand and stepped aside. 'Raine Linfoot. I don't believe the Adamsons are expecting you until tomorrow. But come in. I've only just arrived myself.'

'There's been a mix-up on the times,' Stephanie said, attempting to pick up her suitcase. She hesitated, then looked up at Raine. 'I can't lift this thing. The driver had to carry it to the door.' She looked down at her shoes. 'And these heels don't help,' she added.

'Here, let me have it,' Raine said automatically, then immediately wished she hadn't offered as she struggled to pick the case up under the watchful eye of Stephanie. She let it drop with a thud in the hallway. 'Come and meet our hosts.'

As soon as Raine opened the sitting room door, Bobby barked and shot out of his basket, his tail wagging hard. He jumped up at Stephanie, his front paws firmly pinned to her skirt, causing her to stumble backwards.

'Bobby! Naughty! Come here at once!' Mr Adamson got hold of Bobby's collar and pulled him away. 'Into your basket!' He looked at Stephanie. 'I'm so sorry, my dear. You're probably not used to dogs.'

'I'm not,' Stephanie said, white-faced. 'As a matter of fact, I'm scared of them.'

'Oh, don't worry. Our Bobby wouldn't hurt a fly,' Mrs Adamson said. 'He always pretends to be fierce with the tradesmen.' She squinted at Stephanie who looked visibly shaken. 'It's Hetty, isn't it? The baker's daughter. We haven't seen you for some time, but I thought you were fond of Bobby. No matter. Mrs Fuller said you were coming home on leave and would pop in and see us . . .'

'No, this isn't Hetty,' Raine said, biting her lip hard to stop herself from laughing aloud at Stephanie's shocked expression, 'it's Miss Stephanie Lee-Jones, your other pilot.'

Mrs Adamson gave a gasp of dismay. 'But you're not expected until tomorrow and I haven't made up the bed. I must—' She broke off as she tried to pull herself from the chair.

'Now, dear, don't upset yourself,' Mr Adamson said. 'I'm sure the girls are able to make up a bed.' He turned to Stephanie. 'Do forgive my wife. She hasn't got her glasses on and she's a little short-sighted. Come and sit down. I only made the tea ten minutes ago.'

'I'd prefer to see my room first, if you don't mind,' Stephanie said in a stiff tone. 'Get unpacked, et cetera.'

'I'll take your case upstairs, then.' Mr Adamson heaved it towards the door.

Raine couldn't allow him to struggle with it up two flights of stairs.

'It's all right, Mr Adamson,' she said. 'Stephanie and I will carry it between us.'

'If you're quite sure.' Mr Adamson retrieved his seat, panting a little.

'I'm sorry I can't help,' Stephanie said to Raine's disbelief. 'It's these heels.' She nodded towards them as though to convince Raine she wasn't exaggerating.

Managing to stop herself from giving the girl a piece of her mind, Raine half pushed, half pulled the suitcase up the first flight of stairs, Stephanie grumbling all the while about the long journey she'd had stuck in a motorcar and the driver refusing to stop so she could stretch her legs.

'I'm bursting to go to the lavatory,' Stephanie said as they stepped onto the first landing.

'Bathroom's the second door on the right,' Raine answered a little curtly as she began to haul the case up the second flight.

What on earth was the woman carrying? By the look of her it was probably full of lipsticks and nail varnish and high heels, she thought resentfully.

Her forehead perspiring with the exertion, Raine opened the bedroom door at the opposite end of hers and was about to shove the damned suitcase in the doorway and leave, when curiosity won. She dropped the case with relief for her aching arm and looked around.

It was a slightly bigger room, and the window at the far end was larger. She walked over and peered out. Mmm. Stephanie had definitely got the better view. Her eyes swept over the fields in the distance and the arrangements of allotments and little sheds close to the back of the house. She heard light footsteps up the stairs.

'What's the view like?' Stephanie stepped into the room, obviously recovered from Bobby's exuberance.

Raine turned. 'Very nice – a lot quieter than mine which faces the road. And you have a sink, no less.'

'Hmm.' Stephanie stared at Raine under thick black lashes. 'I'm used to having my own bathroom. Don't know what Mummy and Daddy would say to just a *handbasin.*' She looked about her. 'And it's so *small.*'

'I'm sure it will all work out and we'll get used to everything,' Raine said, becoming thoroughly annoyed with the woman for worrying about what her parents would say to such a primitive set-up. *We don't like to think of our child living in reduced circumstances*, they'd probably say to one another, she thought scornfully. She bit back a retort and instead politely asked, 'Have you come far today?'

'Kensington.'

How on earth did you manage to come all that way by car with petrol rationing? Raine almost blurted. But she supposed someone with a double-barrelled name would be used to travelling in style. Stephanie Lee-Jones oozed wealth, from the top of her shiny blonde hair to her expensive-looking high heels.

'Did you say your name was Raine?'

Raine nodded in response.

'I've never heard that name.' Stephanie studied her with baby-blue eyes.

'It's Lorraine, but I rarely use it.'

'Then I shall call you Lorraine,' Stephanie said as though that was the end of the matter. 'I think it's nicer.' She paused. 'And please don't ever *think* of calling me "Steph". Or even worse, "Stevie".'

'I wouldn't dream of it,' Raine said. 'And far as I'm concerned, it's only my friends who call me Raine, anyway.'

With that she swung out of the room, only just hearing Stephanie's murmured, 'Thank you for bringing up my case.'

Chapter Thirteen

Not a good start, Raine thought, annoyed with herself that she'd been overtly irritable, but really, Stephanie was too privileged for words. She would be from a big house in its own grounds and still have servants if they hadn't already volunteered to go off to war. What kind of pilot was she if she couldn't look after herself? Who couldn't even manage that damned tank she called a suitcase. Raine shrugged. It wasn't her concern and presumably she and Stephanie wouldn't see that much of one another. Even if they were on the same shift they'd be delivering to different airfields.

And at the back of it, wasn't she just a teensy bit jealous of Stephanie's upbringing where money was no object? Just then, the scene downstairs where Mrs Adamson thought Stephanie was Hetty, the baker's daughter, came to mind. Stephanie's horrified expression. Raine couldn't help breaking into a smile as she saw the funny side. Then laughter took hold as she sat on the edge of her bed, tears of mirth rolling down her face. Desperately she tried to control herself but it only ended in a snort.

Someone's voice pierced through her laughter. Stephanie. 'Lorraine! What is it?'

'N-n-nothing,' Raine stuttered, looking up at her and

breaking into a fresh peal of laughter. The next thing she felt was a hard slap on her cheek.

'Stop it at once!'

There was a harsh silence. What on earth was the matter with the stupid woman? Raine brought her hand up to her flaming cheek.

'Why the devil did you do that?'

'You were hysterical,' Stephanie accused, standing over her. 'I had to do something drastic.'

Raine blinked. 'How dare you! Of *course* I wasn't hysterical. In future, keep your hands to yourself.' And then an image of the barrage balloons flashed in front of her and she trembled.

'Are you *sure* you're all right, Lorraine?' Stephanie plonked herself on the bed beside her. 'I know I've only just met you but you seemed a bit out of control.'

Raine heaved a sigh. 'I was laughing because I suddenly saw the funny side of something, but it was probably just pure relief.' She paused and looked directly at Stephanie. 'I nearly had a fatal accident this morning and I don't know how I got out of it.'

'What on earth are you talking about?'

'On the test check,' Raine said in a dull tone. 'I was with the examiner. I couldn't see until the last moment because the weather was so awful. Thick cloud – I couldn't make out anything.'

'I know,' Stephanie said impatiently. 'My driver had to crawl along.' She studied Raine. 'So what happened to you?'

'We nearly got caught in the barrage balloons.'

Stephanie put her hands to either side of her face. 'Oh, God, I've always dreaded something like that happening.' She looked up. 'Aren't we supposed to be warned about that sort of thing?'

'The instructor said Balloon Command should have warned us, but they didn't,' Raine said, the terrible image of those balloons still floating in front of her. She swallowed as she relived those long few seconds.

'Where were you?'

'Over Welwyn Garden City.'

'I'll definitely remember that in future.' Stephanie paused. 'Well, look on the bright side,' she said. 'At least you missed them.'

'It was a fluke,' Raine said. 'We were upon them before I knew what was happening. All I could see were the balloons and I had no idea where I was, or where to land. The plane missed them by no more than a few feet.'

Stephanie shuddered. 'What plane was it?'

'A Puss Moth.'

'Well, at least that's a nippy little plane, though it's not particularly powerful,' Stephanie said. She was silent for a few moments. 'I don't know what I'd have done. I hope not panic.'

Raine said nothing, desperate for that to be the end of the conversation. She wanted to be left quietly on her own for a while.

As if she knew what Raine was thinking, Stephanie said, 'Well, I'll leave you to it then, and go and unpack. We're bound to have a big day ahead of us tomorrow.'

'Here you are, miss. Your boiler suits.'

The clerk handed her two blue boiler suits. Raine held one against her and bent her head to see how far up from her ankle they were – about the same as the depth of bathwater they were allowed: a full five inches. What should she do? Say anything? Or would everyone think what a fusspot she was when there were other matters far more important to deal with?

'Ah, I think you need the next size,' the clerk said, following her gaze. He reached behind him in a cupboard and brought out another suit. 'This might do. It'll be a bit big but longer in the length.'

Raine smiled her thanks. She needed to change swiftly and report for duty. Her training started in fifteen minutes and she couldn't wait to get cracking.

Now, wearing her boiler suit, Raine felt as if she belonged to the ferry pool. She discovered she was to be on the same training course as three of the pilots she'd had lunch with the day before – Joan, Sandra and Beth – plus Stephanie and five others.

The course was only six weeks but the instructor in charge, First Officer Peck, hardly drew breath. Raine felt every tiny space in her brain was crammed with information about technical matters such as engines, navigation using only maps and compass, meteorology (if the weather didn't look too good it was up to the individual to decide whether they should attempt the flight or not), which towns used barrage balloons and how to steer clear of them. She grimaced during that particular session, and quickly recounted what had happened to her above Welwyn Garden City as a warning to the other pilots, several of whom threw her sympathetic glances.

The various subjects went on and on, and if she took in anything more, Raine thought her head might burst. Annoyingly, Stephanie seemed to breeze through all the classes, almost treating the whole thing as a bit of a lark, but the others struggled at first, especially Joan, who constantly wore an expression of fierce concentration.

As the course drew to a close Raine realised just how excellent a trainer First Officer Peck was. Although he went at a breakneck speed he often stopped, his eyes landing on each pilot, to say, 'Are you all with me?' when a lecture was particularly technical. But he never gave any sign that he thought they were a bunch of women who shouldn't be there in the first place and would never understand the technical side of flying. He never minded when someone asked a question and would answer fully and seriously. She now felt much more confident to fly other aircraft beside the Moths that she and the others in her training class had already started delivering. And not only had she regained her confidence, but it had also stoked her enthusiasm to welcome the chance to fly larger and more powerful aircraft.

Next came the practical work of cross-country flying until they were familiar with the landscape, checking rivers, railway lines, aerodromes, factories – anything that might be a useful landmark – and recognising spaces to make the dreaded forced landings.

'You've been a first-class group of students,' First Officer Peck told them, 'so I wish you all the very best for the future.' He paused and glanced around at the pilots. 'And I'm pleased to tell you we've just heard the news that women are now allowed to fly fighter aircraft.' He smiled at the outbreak of cheering. 'I'm sure you're all aware that that includes the Hurricane and the Spitfire.'

Raine clapped with the others until her hands burned. This was what they'd all been hoping for. She was sure it was Pauline Gower's efforts that had instigated this change of heart.

The day finally came when everyone gathered in the lecture room waiting for their commander to tell them whether or not they had passed their course and could now proceed to train on the Class II aircraft – the fighters.

Raine stood with her fellow pilots, her stomach churning. Her biggest fear was that she'd be the only one to fail the course. If that happened she wouldn't be allowed to move up to the next class with the others.

'I'm delighted to tell you that you've all completed this first phase satisfactorily.' Pauline smiled at the cheer from Stephanie. 'You will be able to wear your first stripe as third officers, but first you may sew on your wings.'

She called out each girl's name and when that pilot stepped forward Pauline handed her the gold embroidered wings, saying, 'Well done,' to enthusiastic clapping.

'Lorraine Linfoot.' Pauline smiled as Raine accepted her wings. 'Lorraine, you've worked incredibly hard to achieve this as you have far fewer solo hours than anyone else here, so give yourself a pat on the back.'

Raine gave a modest smile to more cheering and clapping.

'I'm proud of you all,' Pauline continued when the clapping died down. 'I want you all to know you're already making a difference to exhausted pilots with your deliveries, but you'll certainly be even more valuable to us when you can start ferrying the fighter planes. And I will tell you now, nothing in the world is like flying a Spit. You've heard this many times from many pilots, but it only becomes reality when you're in that cockpit – it's a perfectly marvellous experience like no other.'

Raine hugged herself. Soon, soon, she'd be in that Spitfire.

Pauline glanced around the group of eager faces.

'Just remember, ladies, the most important thing of all – take good care of your plane with every delivery. Take no chances, no risks. Treat it as tenderly as you would your own child, and consequently the plane will take care of *you*.' Another pause. 'Are there any questions?'

'Just one,' Sandra, the tall, elegant pilot said. 'Where do we go to be fitted for our uniforms?'

'You'll be fitted next week for your basic uniform although

some girls choose to go to Moss Brothers or Austin Reed,' Pauline said. 'In fact, Winston Churchill is one of Austin Reed's regular customers.' She smiled at the small group.

'I'm ordering mine from Savile Row,' Stephanie put in, 'as in my opinion they're the best tailors – if one can afford them, that is.'

Raine wondered if the woman realised quite how tactless she sounded at times. She obviously came from a family with more money than sense, judging by today's flight suit. No overalls for Stephanie. Today she was in pale blue. Yesterday's had been cyclamen pink.

Pauline frowned at Stephanie's remark. 'We pay for your basic uniform and boots,' she said, 'but if you choose first-class tailoring, you would naturally pay the difference.'

Even Austin Reed was bound to be expensive if Mr Churchill shopped there, Raine thought, but if she only had to pay the difference, that's where she'd go. It was where her father had always had *his* suits made. He'd taken her there once before when she was a child, but since the crisis over his finances he'd had to look elsewhere. But he always maintained he'd never found another suit that came up to the same standard as an Austin Reed one.

She shrugged. That was then – this was now. She had two days' leave coming up and was determined to go to London. Even if she found an Austin Reed uniform to be beyond her purse, it would still be heavenly to have a proper break.

Chapter Fourteen

Raine squeezed between the standing soldiers in her compartment, all of them smoking and laughing and chatting together, to take the seat that one of them had given up for her. She thanked him profusely and opened her book. Apart from giving her admiring looks when she'd first set foot in the compartment, the soldiers went back to being absorbed in their conversation. Two middle-aged women opposite, both firmly holding a small child on their laps, gossiped and every so often hushed their children who were starting to whinge.

'You'd think she'd've joined up by now, wouldn't you?' Raine heard one of them mutter. 'We all have to do our bit. Look at us, practically bringing up our grandchildren while our girls are working themselves to death in the factory.' The woman stole a sly glance at Raine.

'Well, she looks old enough, don't she?' the other one said more loudly. 'Going to London to meet her fancy man, I shouldn't be surprised.'

Her temper flaring, Raine snapped her book closed. She looked across at them.

'Excuse me, ladies—' she started, her tone cool.

The two women's heads shot up and stared at her in surprise.

'I'm not sure whether you're discussing *me*, but I thought I'd tell you anyway that I'm going to London, not to meet any

141

fancy man, but to be fitted for my pilot's uniform.' She let that sink in, gratified to see their reddening faces. 'You see, I've already joined up and I'm serving in the Air Transport Auxiliary.'

'What does that mean, love?' the first woman bent towards her, her large stomach ready to squash her little grandson.

'It means I pick up aeroplanes and deliver them to our fighting boys wherever they are, so *they* don't have to waste time doing it.'

There. She'd said it, but it had probably fallen on deaf ears. She opened her book again and bent her head, pretending to read, but the words jumbled in front of her. Blasted women.

'Excuse me, dear . . .'

Oh, what now? Raine looked up, trying hard to hold back her impatience.

'You mean you *fly* them? You're the *pilot*?'

'Yes,' Raine said shortly, going back to her book, but she was quickly interrupted again.

'A *lady* pilot,' said the other. 'Well, I'm blowed. I never knew women could fly aeroplanes.' She looked at Raine with open admiration. 'It must take plenty of courage to go up in one of them things, let alone *fly* it.'

'It doesn't take courage or bravery,' Raine said coolly. 'It's simply doing a job that needs to be done, and I wouldn't do anything else in the world.' She sent them a pointed glance. 'There are quite a few lady pilots doing exactly the same as me. And believe it or not, we're every bit as good as the men.'

'Well I never.'

'I'm sure we didn't mean no 'arm, dear.'

Raine caught the heavy-set woman's eye. 'Maybe not, but it's probably not very wise to assume that any young man or woman not in uniform is avoiding the war effort.' She gave them a smile to signal the end of the conversation.

Why was she so worried about what a couple of strangers thought of her? An image of her mother's face floated into her mind. Disapproving, it seemed, no matter what she did, however hard she tried. Forget them, she told herself sternly. Not long now and I'll be in London.

At King's Cross it was pandemonium. It looked as though the whole of London had decided to descend upon the station. Shouldering her way through the crowds, dodging couples saying tearful goodbyes and trying not to choke in the belching steam of a nearby train that had just arrived, she was finally on the tube to Victoria. One of the station masters told her she could easily walk it from there and she relished the idea of stretching her legs.

Following the crowd Raine picked her way through scores of mattresses and blankets and pillows people had left in 'their' spot along the platform. That's where they would spend tonight and the next and the next . . . She shuddered, reminding herself how lucky she was to have a proper bed at night. As did her parents and sisters.

The stale smell invaded her nostrils as she mounted the subway steps, pushing along with dozens of people desperate to get out into the air. With relief she stepped onto the pavement, blinking in the summer morning sunshine, not quite prepared for the sight that met her. There seemed to be more rubble than buildings everywhere she looked.

Walking along Victoria Street her heart sank at the sight of so much destruction. A church was now a completely burnt-out ruin. It must have taken a full blast of several incendiary bombs. She swallowed. A pretty little church where people had gathered to pray, attend weddings and christenings and funerals was now the saddest echo of memories. Her eyes filled with tears.

143

She joined some office workers who were carefully picking their way through the debris as though it was quite normal. She supposed it was. It crossed her mind that Austin Reed might not have survived, but as she eventually turned into Regent Street, there it was. A handsome building with its enormous upper-storey Regency windows. Thank goodness it was still intact, although she noticed some glass panels above the entrance were smashed.

The interior was much larger than she'd remembered. All quiet elegance in Art Deco. Calmness itself. Except for one middle-aged gentleman, the other three assistants were all women, arranging their particular counter, polishing their glass tops. It was as though the staff were cocooned in their own little world, paying no attention to the war that was happening right outside their doors, their focus only to serve the customers in the traditional manner they always had. There was only a handful of customers, mainly elderly gentlemen wandering around the display cabinets eyeing the accessories. The male assistant stepped from behind his counter.

'Are you looking for anything in particular, miss?' He spoke quietly and almost reverently.

Raine smiled. *Act as though you do this every day.*

'Yes. I'm Lorraine Linfoot, a pilot in the Air Transport Auxiliary – and I understand I can be measured here for my uniform.'

'Yes, we have an account set up for the young ladies from that worthy organisation.' He gave a slight bow. 'Mr Duncan, at your service, though I do wonder sometimes about you all in those aeroplanes.' He cupped his chin in his hand and stroked his jaw. 'One of the young ladies told me you fly those aeroplanes on your own – without a man in the cockpit.'

'It's true.' Raine wanted to giggle. 'We fly them all by ourselves.'

144

The tailor blinked, without the trace of a smile. 'So you'd be wanting the skirt and tunic?'

'Yes, please, and also the trousers.'

Thank goodness Pauline had persuaded her superiors that the women should be allowed to wear trousers for flying – so much easier to deal with than a skirt that would ride up above the knee, making flying totally impractical and hadn't helped on her disastrous flight test. She made up her mind there and then only to wear the skirt when she wasn't on duty but in uniform.

'The ATA provides you with a forage cap,' Mr Duncan was saying as he went back behind his counter and took out a notebook.

He was a few minutes and Raine began to tap her feet. She just wanted to get herself measured up, then go and have a proper look around the city. See what further damage poor old London had succumbed to.

'Shall I have Miss Brown measure you right away?'

Raine nodded. 'Yes, please.'

'I'll show you the fitting room and send her in.'

Miss Brown was slow with her measuring. She was very serious, taking her time to be exact, and Raine had to bite her tongue to stop herself from asking if she could speed up. It wasn't as though she had to be anywhere, but she was longing for a cup of tea.

'There – all done.' Mrs Brown stretched up and rubbed her back. 'I'll give this to Mr Duncan. He's the one who cuts it out.'

Raine thanked her and pulled open the fitting-room curtains. She stepped out at exactly the same time as two young men in RAF officer's uniform came through the entrance.

She startled. One of the men was Alec Marshall, the cocky pilot. As soon as he caught sight of her he stopped in his tracks and removed his cap.

'Well, if it isn't Miss Crosspatch,' he said, his face wreathed in smiles.

The tailor glanced towards the other two assistants who were now busy. He frowned, then turned to the two prospective customers. 'I won't keep you,' he said.

'No trouble at all,' Alec replied, still smiling. 'I know this young lady, so perhaps when we're all done she'll allow us to take her for coffee.' He pulled his gaze away from Raine and glanced at the other officer. 'All right with you, Baxter?'

How dare he call her 'Miss Crosspatch' in public! She glared at him but he simply grinned back. He was trying to trap her in front of his friend. Mr Duncan stood looking bemused at the little group.

The pilot called Baxter shook his head. 'As you two already know one another I'll bow out. I want to go to the V and A. Maybe meet later at the RAF Club?'

'If you're sure . . .' Alec sent him a knowing grin.

The two of them were deliberately leaving the coast clear for Alec Marshall to spend time with her, with no one asking if *she* fancied that arrangement. A coil of anger unravelled as Baxter nodded to her, said goodbye and disappeared.

'I'm sorry, but—' Raine began in a firm voice.

'Are you having a uniform made?'

'That really isn't any of your business,' Raine said, trying to control her irritation.

'Oh, dear, you're still cross with me.' He studied her, his eyes gleaming with mischief.

She looked away and instead spoke to Mr Duncan, who was patiently waiting with a bolt of navy-blue material.

'This is our standard uniform material we use for the ATA,' the tailor said.

'Ah.' Alec was at her elbow, grinning with triumph. 'You

146

took my advice and joined the ATA. I was telling your sister that's what you ought to do.'

What an infuriating man.

'I'd made up my mind to join well before you said anything about it to Suzanne,' Raine said pointedly.

'Shame the uniform has to be such a dull blue,' he said, ignoring her remark. 'With your looks you should always wear bright colours.' He pointed to a roll of deep lavender-blue material. 'Is this lining?' He turned to Mr Duncan.

'Yes, it is, sir.'

'Could you please cut me a small piece?'

The tailor obliged and handed the strip to Alec. Alec touched Raine lightly on the shoulder so she was facing him.

'What are you doing?' She took a step back.

'Raise your chin a little,' he said, bunching up the material and tucking it under Raine's chin. 'Yes, I thought so,' he said. 'It matches your eyes to perfection – especially when you're cross, which is most of the time with *me*, it seems.' He turned to Mr Duncan. 'If the young lady gives you the order to make her uniform, would you consider lining the lady's tunic and include it in your price to the ATA?'

Raine opened her mouth to tell Alec Marshall to stop interfering, when Mr Duncan raised his eyebrows to Raine.

'I've allowed for the standard lining – but I could do that if the lady would like that particular colour,' he added, turning to Alec. 'Although I believe she would be going against regulations.'

Raine seethed. How dare the man, officer or no, interfere with her order. Who on earth did he think he was?

'Mr Duncan, would you please direct your attention to me and my order as I was here before this *gentleman*.' She emphasised the last word so Alec Marshall would have no question about where he stood with her.

The tips of Mr Duncan's ears turned red. 'I do apologise, Miss Linfoot. I thought you and the officer here—'

'I barely know him,' Raine said coldly. 'But I *would* like the tunic lined with something a little more bold, so may I see your complete range?'

'Of course. Come this way.'

Raine stepped past an amused-looking Alec to the next counter where there were a few bolts of satin on the shelves above.

'We only have a small range since the war started.' Mr Duncan's tone was regretful.

Raine's eyes flicked over the black, grey, navy, emerald green and the bright lavender-blue Alec had picked out, and landed on a dazzling red.

'I'd like that one,' she said, pointing to it.

'It's a real scarlet,' Mr Duncan said, pulling down the bolt and unrolling it a few feet. 'I think you will be the envy of your colleagues when you turn your tunic inside out. And I assure you no one else has chosen that colour.'

'I like to be different,' Raine said, smiling at him. 'And by the way, I wouldn't dream of asking you to include the extra in the price, so I'll be happy to pay the difference.'

She threw Alec another glare, but to her fury he sent her a wink.

'If you're done, then will you do me the honour of having coffee with me?' he said.

'May I take your address first, please, Miss Linfoot?' The tailor looked at Alec, then back to Raine.

Raine drew herself up. 'Yes, of course, Mr Duncan.' She wasn't going to risk saying it aloud with Alec standing there watching her, so she wrote it out for him.

'I will write to let you know when you can collect it,' he promised. 'It should be ready in four to six weeks. And may

I say it's been a pleasure to do business with you, Miss Linfoot.'

He moved towards the door but Alec was too quick for him and opened it, giving an exaggerated sweep of his arm to allow Raine through.

'Didn't you come here to buy something?' Raine's manner was curt as she stepped outside.

He was close behind her. She heard him draw a sharp intake of breath.

'Clever girl. I'd ordered a shirt and tie. Supposed to pick them up today.' He looked at her with an appreciative smile. 'Seeing you sent it right out of my head. Will you wait a minute? Promise you won't leave.' He shot back inside the store.

Her annoyance with him hadn't abated in the least. She didn't want to spend time in his company, or have him try to take control. She had enough of that with Maman. No, she wasn't having any of it. She was in London. Free to do whatever she wanted before setting off for Hatfield this afternoon. She might wander along the Thames enjoying the sunshine. But first, that cup of tea . . . though Alec's suggestion of coffee sounded even better.

She hesitated. No. Just because he had the most incredible green eyes and a mocking smile in them as well as on his mouth, that was no reason for her to kow-tow to his bidding.

Without a second thought or a backward glance, she hurried down the street. She thought she heard her name, faintly, in the distance, but it might just have been her imagination.

Alec mentioning coffee made her mouth water. Remembering how Maman had enjoyed the Lyons teashops when she'd first arrived in England, Raine decided to head for the nearest one. She turned the corner into Oxford Street. And there it was, next to one of the theatres showing a new

149

play. If there was a matinée she might even buy a ticket. She'd never been to a London show before.

Raine stepped back to admire the façade of the Lyons teashop with its extravagantly curled Art Nouveau lettering. And when she opened the door the bell tinkled; she caught her breath. It was a massive room with dozens of tables draped with immaculate white cloths and people, it seemed, occupying every single one. Waitresses flew round in their crisp aprons over dark frocks, their striking caps pulled low over their foreheads, trays held high over the diners.

One of the waitresses hurried over. 'For how many, miss?' Raine held up her forefinger. 'Just one.'

The waitress scanned the room. 'I think I can squeeze you onto a table with another couple. Would that suit you?'

'Perfectly,' Raine said, 'so long as they don't mind.'

She followed the waitress to a table towards the back of the room. The waitress said something to a middle-aged couple who nodded and smiled, and wished her good morning as she sat down. Before scurrying off, the waitress handed her a menu.

Raine suddenly realised she was hungry even though it wasn't yet noon. Quickly, she skimmed through the snacks menu and looked up.

'May I have Welsh rarebit and a coffee?' she said. 'If it's all right to order coffee in a teashop,' she added, smiling.

'Of course, miss.'

The door opened and three more people walked in. Automatically, she glanced over. *No*. She lowered her head, pretending to stare at the menu, her pulse racing. He couldn't have. There were other cafés to have a morning coffee. So how had he tracked her down? He was already striding towards her table. He gave a winning smile to the other couple and before she knew it, he'd had the nerve to bend down and kiss her cheek.

'Raine, I'm so sorry I kept you waiting, darling.'

Her cheek flamed under the warmth of his lips and the endearment. He was doing this on purpose, knowing she couldn't make a scene in front of this nice couple. The lady was gazing at them misty-eyed.

'Have you already ordered for me?' he asked.

'No,' she said so sharply she felt the lady beside her stiffen. 'I wasn't sure how long you'd be,' she added in a softer tone, 'or what you wanted . . . *darling*.' She could play at that game.

He gave her a sly grin. 'I'll have the same as you.' He looked up as the waitress bustled over. 'Could you bring me the same order as the young lady?'

'Right away, sir.'

'Have you planned what you'd like to do this afternoon?' Alec asked her.

'I thought possibly the theatre next door,' Raine said sweetly. 'I believe it's a new play called *A Royal Divorce*.' She emphasised the last word.

'As long as you don't get any ideas, my love,' Alec said with a chuckle, covering her hand with his own.

She forced herself not to snatch it away. Why spoil the other couple's enjoyment of sharing a nostalgic moment with a young pair who were obviously in love? A smile hovered over her lips. *It's going to be such fun bringing Alec down to earth as soon as we're outside*, she thought. But for now, she couldn't help being aware of his hand on hers. And as though he knew what she was thinking, he linked his fingers through her own, making each one tingle as he gazed at her with an expression she couldn't fathom.

Pretending she needed to brush her hair from her face, she removed her hand. But she could still feel the imprint of his warm skin.

Thankfully, the waitress was prompt with their order, so

151

she didn't have to force any further conversation, except to say how good the Welsh rarebit was and what a surprise to have 'real' coffee instead of Camp.

Alec led most of the conversation and even brought their table companions into it.

'We're very proud of our young fighting men,' the gentleman said as he wiped his mouth on the napkin. 'Wish I could join you all.'

'I'm sure you did your bit in the last war,' Alec said.

'Ah, that was a bad one.' The man's eyes half closed in memory. 'Lost so many of my friends – well, they were more like brothers. I can recall every one of them – every name, every face.' His eyes filled with tears.

'I think it's the intensity of it all,' Alec said in a sympathetic tone. 'It must have been a nightmare in those trenches.'

The man nodded. 'I don't ever talk about it,' he said, wiping his eyes with a pristine white handkerchief. 'No one wants to know now their heads are full of this one – and rightly so. This war is different altogether.' His eyes were full of sadness as he looked at Alec. 'I only hope you come through it, my boy. Our dear son didn't.'

'Oh, I'm so sorry,' Raine said immediately, looking at the lady whose eyes were swimming with tears. She reached for the lady's hand and gently held it for a few seconds. 'How terrible for you both.'

'It's war, unfortunately,' the man said. 'Happening all over the country.' He hesitated. 'May we know your name, dear boy?'

'Alec Marshall, sir.'

'Stan Holland and my wife, Edith. Delighted to meet you.' His eyes fixed on Raine and smiled. 'And your young lady?'

Alec gave Raine a tender smile – *all put on for their benefit*, Raine thought, thoroughly annoyed by now.

'This is my beautiful fiancé, Lorraine, though we haven't set the date yet, have we, darling?' he said, turning to her.

'Don't leave it too long, my boy,' Stan Holland said.

'We won't.'

'No, we won't,' Raine said, 'especially as I've only laid eyes on him twice,' she added. This time she couldn't help herself.

'I fell in love with my Stan on the very first meeting,' Edith Holland said, seemingly taking no notice of Raine's sarcastic tone and instead gazing fondly at her husband. 'He asked me for a dance and that was it.' She turned to Raine and smiled warmly. 'You don't have to know someone well to know he's exactly the right person for you, dear.'

Raine squirmed in her seat. Her stupid comment had backfired completely. Alec was looking at her and chuckling. The couple joined in and without warning it struck her as funny as well. Ten minutes later the four of them were laughing together like old friends.

'You looked so gorgeous when you were laughing in there,' Alec said as he closed the teashop door behind them. 'You should do it more often.'

'Maybe I would if you didn't irritate me so much,' Raine retorted.

'There you go again – getting cross for no reason.' Before she could stop him he drew her to him and lightly brushed her lips with his. 'Life's too short to be angry. Look at Stan and Edith losing their son. That message rings loud and clear these days when you're watching for the last plane to return and it doesn't come and you know another of your mates has bought it.'

His eyes darkened with pain. Suddenly Raine felt ashamed of herself. Her job was relatively safe whereas his . . . he'd be looking out for the enemy at every turn. Maybe carry out one operation too many. She'd never know about

153

it. A cold chill ran across her shoulders even though the sun was warm.

'I'd love to spend the rest of the day with you, Raine.' His eyes searched hers. 'It's been six months since I last saw you. Tell me you'd like it, too.'

Who knew from day to day, hour to hour, what this war would bring. That's what Stan had been trying to tell them. If anything happened to this man . . . She swallowed the lump in her throat. She would never forgive herself for not sharing one lovely summer day with him.

'All right,' she said. 'So long as we don't have to sit in a stuffy theatre to find out how we can get a divorce.'

He threw his head back and laughed. 'That's my girl.' He gazed at her, his face now serious. '*Will* you be my girl?'

Doug's image popped into her head. She'd loved him for a long time when she'd been far too young to know the real meaning of love. And what of Doug himself? She was like a kid sister, he'd always said, which was hardly conducive to romance. To be fair to Doug, he'd never given her any reason to think she could be anything more. But she couldn't simply switch Doug off and turn Alec on.

For one thing Alec never ceased to annoy her with his cocky attitude. So why did she make things worse by always rising to his bait and snapping something back? If she thought she was putting him in his place, she rarely succeeded. She frowned. She never had to act like that with Doug. But was that all part of it with Alec? A spark, if she were honest, she'd never felt with Doug? Embarrassed, she became aware of Alec watching her with a thoughtful expression.

'You've gone very quiet,' he said, fishing in his pocket and lighting a cigarette. 'Does that mean I have competition?'

'If you mean, do I have a boyfriend . . . not exactly.'

Alec inhaled deeply, then blew out a stream of smoke. 'It's

154

the "not exactly" bit I'm bothered about.' He stopped and looked at her. 'So there *is* someone?'

'I don't want to talk about it.'

'Point taken.' He flung the almost whole cigarette on the ground and stamped on it. 'Do you still want to spend the day with me?'

'So long as we have an understanding that I don't want you to read anything into it.'

'Oh, I wouldn't dream of it.'

They were back to their usual way of firing another shot at one another. Raine felt on edge. He was going too fast for her, almost as though he had a right, and she didn't like it at all.

To her surprise he suddenly chuckled. 'I shall never give up asking you that question.'

'Which one? You've asked so many.'

'The "Will you be my girl?" one.'

'As long as you remember I'm no Edith Holland,' Raine said, smiling, trying to lighten the tension.

'More's the pity.' He ducked as she pretended to swipe him.

'How's that lovely sister of yours?' he said as they strolled through Regent's Park, Raine feeling a little more comfortable with him. 'Suzy.'

'Did she tell you to call her that?'

'Yes. Why?'

'She normally only lets family and friends call her Suzy. And even then Maman hates it. The three of us use different names from the ones she gave us. She's French and takes it as a personal insult.'

Alec smiled. 'Mine's too short to muck about with. The parents said they did it on purpose.'

When they came to a bench he sat down, drawing her

close beside him. She inched a little further away so he didn't get any more ideas.

'This is nice,' he said, his face lifted towards the sun. 'You can make-believe there's no war on when you hear the birds singing and people going about their business. I'm just so sorry for the parents living here – they've had a rough time being bombed night after night, but my mother refused to leave Dad to go to her sister's in the country where she would have been much safer.' He looked at Raine with a wry smile. 'That's love for you, I suppose.' When she didn't answer, he said, 'Thankfully, the worst seems to be over, but we all worry what the next thing is that Mr Hitler might have up his sleeve.'

'What do your parents think about you way up in the sky, fighting the Germans?'

'Mum's worried, as all mothers are. Dad's okay about it. He fought in the last war so he understands.' He turned to her. 'Thing is, I'm not actually fighting.'

'Oh.' Pauline Gower's warning came to her mind. It might be verging on a security breach if she asked him anything more.

'I'm in photographic reconnaissance,' he continued, as though he'd read her thoughts. 'So in many ways I'm lucky. Though Jerry does come close sometimes. Good thing my Spit has the power to get me out of any trouble, because we're unarmed.'

Raine's eyes widened. 'I hadn't realised.'

'I like it better that way.' He gave her a wry smile. 'Let's get on to a happier subject – though I actually love the job I do, so don't go feeling sorry for me.'

'I don't. Not at all.'

She wasn't going to let him suspect anything different.

'Shall we go?' He held out his hand.

She nodded and took his hand as she jumped to her feet, once again feeling that electric tingling as his warm skin came into contact with hers.

They wandered alongside the Serpentine, hand in hand, admiring the swans, Raine wishing the day would never end. She sighed with contentment.

'I only wish I was coming back with you,' Alec said, almost reading her thoughts, 'but Baxter and I have a 48-hour pass, so after we've seen my parents we thought we'd go to a show this evening.' He regarded her with those unnerving green eyes. 'You'd be more than welcome to come with us.'

'It's kind of you to offer, but I have to get back,' Raine said, endeavouring to keep her voice steady.

She wondered how Doug would feel if he knew she was spending the day with another man. Probably wouldn't bother him at all.

'I'll see you onto the train at least,' Alec said.

The rest of the afternoon flew by. Walking, stopping for afternoon tea, and walking again. Raine swallowed hard whenever they came upon yet another street that had been hit. Even the department stores in Oxford Street hadn't escaped damage. John Lewis had built a wall of sandbags around its entrance and several shops had followed suit.

'Do you want to go in?' Alec said as she glanced in one of the windows, but she shook her head.

In no time they were on the platform waiting for the train to pull in. Alec stood, saying nothing. She gave him a sideways glance but he caught her looking.

'What is it?'

'I was just wondering what was the matter.'

As soon as she said the words she wished she hadn't. Why should she worry about what he was thinking?

'It's this damned war. It sweeps over you sometimes, doesn't it, how serious it is. How we don't know if we'll even be alive tomorrow.'

'Don't speak like that,' Raine said, her words half drowned in the whistle from one of the guards.

'But it's true. You know it is. That's why I didn't want to waste any more time arguing. I'd much rather spend the time getting to know you – as I have done today.' He studied her. 'Stan was right. You're very beautiful, you know. Although that smut on your nose . . .' He sent her a mocking grin as he drew out a freshly ironed handkerchief.

'Where?' Her hand flew up to her face.

'You don't know where it is, so let me.' He put a corner of his handkerchief between his lips to moisten it, then gently wiped the tip of her nose. 'There. Nothing now to mar your beauty.'

'It obviously doesn't take much to mar it,' Raine chuckled.

'Your face lights up when you laugh,' Alec said, 'and your eyes are the colour of violets in the rain.'

'You're being very poetic,' she said, her cheeks flushing with sudden embarrassment.

'I'm being serious, Raine. You're starting to become rather special to me.' His finger traced her jaw with a featherlight touch that set her senses reeling. 'When I first set eyes on you I never stopped hoping that one day we'd meet again.'

She didn't know what to say. She'd felt the same though she'd never admitted it to herself. And even now she couldn't tell him.

'I decided if it was meant to be, we would,' Alec went on. 'And whoever this chap is, I get the impression he hasn't made any proper commitment to you.'

'I don't want anyone to make a commitment to me and

I don't want to make a commitment to anyone either. It's fruitless in war. And anyway, I've got a job to do.'

'Maybe you're right.' A shadow passed across his face. 'I only know I don't want to wait another six months before I see you again, that's all.'

He fumbled in his jacket for his packet of cigarettes and Raine had the distinct feeling he was giving himself time to decide something, the way her father used to, though what was going through Alec's head, she couldn't imagine. He shook out a cigarette, lit it and inhaled deeply, then regarded her, tilting his head slightly to one side as he blew out a stream of smoke.

'I simply can't take my eyes off you – you're so lovely.'

'It's a wonder you can see me with that smokescreen in the way,' Raine quipped.

He gave a rueful smile, dropped the cigarette and ground it beneath his shoe. 'Point taken.' He paused. 'Am I allowed to ask if you're stationed at Hatfield?'

'How did you guess?'

'Most of the women pilots start their training there.' He paused, his eyes narrowing. 'Raine, would you at least allow me to write to you?'

Doug and now Alec. It seemed a long time since Doug had written. If she let Alec write to her there'd be someone else to worry about if she didn't hear from him regularly. She couldn't bear it if something happened . . . to either of them. She glanced at him. He was standing silently, waiting for her answer. She swallowed.

'I think it's maybe better if you don't,' she said, then could have bitten out her tongue.

Why had she said that? What would have been the harm to let him write to her? She wished she could take the words back and tell him she would love to have a letter from him

159

sometimes – to know he was safe. But it was too late; she'd seen his hurt expression.

'Okay. That's fine by me.'

His words were almost swallowed up by her train approaching the platform, bellowing and hissing and steaming, but it didn't matter. His tone and expression were enough.

'Safe journey back, Lorraine.' Alec tossed the words over his shoulder as he strode away.

Raine watched Alec join the hundreds of exhausted white-faced soldiers, many looking as though they were putting on a brave face by laughing and shouting and shoving one another as they spilled from the train she was about to board. She stared after Alec's retreating figure, her eyes smarting from the smoke billowing around her from a departing train on the adjacent platform, until he disappeared.

It was only when she managed to find a seat that she felt the tears trickle down her cheek. Hastily, she brushed them away before anyone in the compartment noticed, her father's voice ringing in her ears: 'You don't always think before you speak, Raine, and one day it will get you into trouble . . . or make you regret you'd said it.'

Chapter Fifteen

Ever since they'd moved to Downe, Raine's mother had pulled her up sharply for any disparaging remark she made about the cottage, but this morning as Raine knocked on her parents' front door, she was determined to remain cheerful and positive. She realised how lucky they all were. They hadn't been bombed out of their home like some people she'd met from London or Liverpool. Breathing out a sigh of pure exhaustion as the door opened, she pasted a smile on her face. She couldn't bear the thought of any argument after her thirteen days without a break. But it wasn't her mother who opened the door. She almost didn't recognise her youngest sister.

'Oh, Raine!' Ronnie beamed with delight and twisted her neck to call down the long narrow hallway. 'Maman, it's Raine!'

Raine's smile was wide as her kid sister enveloped her in a hug.

'Hello, Ronnie. What have you done to your beautiful hair?'

Ronnie put her finger to her lips. 'Shhh! Maman is cross enough without you raking it up. My friend is an apprentice hairdresser and she wanted someone to practise on.' She

161

giggled. 'So I let her and her scissors go to work.' She twirled round. 'What do you think?'

Her sister was growing up. Raine smiled and ruffled the short chestnut curls. 'You know, I like you with your short hair, kid. You're looking more grown-up every time I see you.'

'Don't call me a kid,' Ronnie said, pulling away and looking sternly at her older sister. 'Or treat me like one. I'm fifteen and doing my homework like a good little girl . . .' she pulled a face, 'and hating most of it. You were practically learning to fly at my age and I bet you didn't let anyone call *you* a kid.' She pushed out her lower lip. 'If only I could think what to do. Why aren't I clever like you, or musical like Suzanne? Why have I been handed the rotten card?'

'You haven't,' Raine said, looking at her young sister with affection. 'Suzy and I don't know half the stuff you know about nature and animals.'

'But what help is that in a war? If only I'd been born a boy I'd be out there fighting.'

'Not at fifteen, you wouldn't.' Raine smiled. 'Anyway, if you're that keen, and if the war goes on a long time, you could join up. That would take you nearer to fighting the Germans.'

'I shan't, if I can help it.'

'Why not?'

'Because I hate the thought of all that marching. I'd never be able to do it. I'd get the right and left foot muddled the first time someone barked at me. And they might give me a job that didn't suit me. You know how I like being outdoors best of all. But I bet I'd be stuck in some smelly office.'

'Something will turn up when the time is right.' Raine grinned at her sister's vehemence. 'You'll see. And when it does, it will be perfect for you.' She paused. 'Where's Maman?'

'In the kitchen trying out a recipe. She probably didn't hear me call her.' Ronnie lowered her voice. 'She's still a terrible cook. She was so used to having Doreen leave something for supper, and it doesn't help that Dad compliments her all the time on her cooking.'

Raine chuckled. 'I expect she's trying hard.'

'You'd think it would improve with practice, but it doesn't.'

'Why don't you have a go?'

'I've offered, but she refuses to let me. And to be honest, I'm not that interested. I'd rather grow the vegetables, which I'm doing. I dug the plot and I look after them, even though Maman takes all the credit.'

'I'd better go and find her,' Raine said. 'Ask her to put another potato on.'

'Véronique, where—?' Her mother turned as Raine stepped into the kitchen. 'Oh, it's you, Lorraine. We didn't expect you. How long are you staying?'

It's always the same, Raine thought grimly. *No loving greeting like I always hope for.* No, if Maman didn't get her own way, if people didn't act as she told them they ought – and that included her daughters – she'd never properly forgive them.

'You're looking well.' She kissed her mother's raised face, moistened with steam. 'And I'm staying two nights – that is, if it doesn't inconvenience you too much.'

Her mother's eyes bore into hers.

I must stop doing this. It wasn't making her any more endearing to her mother, it annoyed her father and it only gave herself a few seconds of satisfaction before she felt horribly mean.

'Sorry, Maman. That didn't sound very nice.'

'No, it did not.' Her mother raised her hands. 'I worry about you sometimes, Lorraine.'

163

'Believe it or not, I'm a very good pilot,' Raine said defensively, though aware of a flicker of warmth that her mother was actually admitting that she worried about her. 'I wish you could see me—'

'Oh, I don't mean *that*,' Simone cut in. 'I'm sure you are, or they wouldn't allow you to fly such expensive machines.' She paused. 'No, I mean your attitude towards me. I don't think I deserve it.' Her eyes filled with tears.

Raine managed to stop her eyes from rolling towards the ceiling. The theatrical tears. She should have known. It was always about Maman. Always about *her* feelings, with precious little over for her husband and her eldest daughter. She took in a couple of deep breaths.

'Let's not be cross with one another, Maman,' she said. 'I'm only home for a short time and it's not worth it. Not when you hear about such awful things going on everywhere.'

To Raine's surprise her mother gave one of her charming smiles, completely changing her. *She really is a beautiful woman,* Raine thought, not for the first time. No wonder her father had fallen for her all those years ago.

'*D'accord*. Then you may lay the table for dinner.'

'Your father never gets back at dinnertime,' Maman told her when she and Ronnie sat down to corned beef and salad with potatoes. 'But you'll see him this evening.'

'Where's Suzanne?'

'Rehearsing,' chimed in Ronnie. 'She'll be back in time for supper.'

'I can't wait to see her.' Raine smiled. 'It's only been a month but I feel I've been away a year at least.' She leaned forward. 'I'm longing to hear all the news.'

'Well, it's a good job you came today,' Ronnie said, 'because school starts again tomorrow. But if you want *her* news, there's a boy who sounds as though he's soppy over her . . . if that's news of any kind,' she ended with a yawn.

'It certainly *is* news,' Raine said, grinning. 'Suzy's usually so immersed in her music she doesn't even notice when there's a nice boy in the offing. Where did she meet him?'

'Some music thing. She'll tell you.'

'I do wish you would stop using that ridiculous name,' Simone said, lips pursed in disapproval. 'I have given you all beautiful French names and you refuse to use them.'

'If you were teased unmercifully at school with a foreign-sounding name like Véronique . . .' Ronnie rolled her r's with deliberate exaggeration, 'I'm sure you'd have changed yours.'

Their mother's pretty mouth tightened. 'I would not mind so much if you chose *Vera*, but *Ronnie* . . .' she pulled her mouth unattractively, 'is a *man's* name. Why would you want to renounce your femininity?'

'These potatoes are delicious, Maman,' Raine said, knowing *she* would be the next to be admonished if she didn't change the subject.

'They're from my own garden,' her mother said, a note of pride in her voice. 'I'm digging for victory – the way they tell you on the posters . . . although Véronique kindly dug the plot for me.'

'And even sowed the seeds,' Ronnie remarked pointedly.

Her mother then proceeded to tell Raine about the other vegetables she was growing, and how well the tomatoes were doing in the little greenhouse at the bottom of the garden. Remembering Ronnie's words, Raine just said how pleased she was that Maman had found such a worthwhile hobby and was enjoying it.

'*Non*, I am not enjoying it,' her mother snapped. 'It is necessary to do it for the family so we do not starve.'

'Yes, of course,' Raine said, and changed the subject.

After lunch she excused herself, telling her mother she was going to freshen up. Her mother nodded approvingly. After taking off her uniform and spreading it on the only chair, Raine, still in her underclothes, flopped onto her old bed in what was now Suzanne's room. She linked her hands behind her neck, staring at the ceiling, thinking how drastically her life had changed.

Not for the first time did Alec cross her mind. For a split second after she'd told him it would be better if he didn't write he'd looked thoroughly dispirited, but his expression had changed so quickly to his usual couldn't-care-less attitude that she wondered if she'd imagined it. She shook herself. It was no use feeling guilty. She'd said it for the best reasons. Life was precarious these days and she had enough to worry about with Doug fighting the Germans, let alone about someone she barely knew.

Someone she barely knew? Was that really how she viewed Alec? She chewed her lip. Who was she kidding?

Thank goodness in two days' time she'd be back doing the thing she loved best. But it was wonderful to have time to relax with her sisters and Dad . . . and Maman too, of course, she thought with a prick of guilt, before she was due back at the station. Not that she was complaining. But this last fortnight had taken its toll with the amount of advanced training they'd had drummed into them. Her head seemed to be bursting with information.

She closed her eyes. She adored both her sisters but she silently prayed that Suzy wouldn't come back too soon. Two minutes' later she'd drifted off to sleep.

Raine awoke with a start. Who was that downstairs? A man's voice that was definitely not her father's.

She heard a scream then a crash. It sounded like Maman!

Heart thumping in her chest, Raine shot out of bed and grabbed her blouse. Cursing, she fumbled with the buttons, then pulled on her uniform skirt. She sprinted down the stairs, dreading what she would find.

As she burst into the sitting room she found a strange man fussing over her mother whose face was drained of life, her head leant back on the winged chair, her eyes unfocused. The man looked round as Raine flew to her mother's side and took hold of her hand. Maman's fingers were cold. Dear God, she must have had a stroke. But what on earth was this stranger doing in the house?

'Maman, what's the matter? What happened?'

Her mother didn't answer. Just shook her head and squeezed Raine's hand in a vice-like grip.

At least she's conscious.

'I'm afraid I've brought some difficult news,' the man said as he moved politely to one side.

'I'm her daughter, Lorraine Linfoot,' Raine said, looking up at him. He didn't look much older than her now she saw him closer up. 'Please tell me what's happened to my mother.'

'It's not your mother, Miss Linfoot. It's regarding *Mr* Linfoot – he was taken poorly at his workplace approximately an hour ago and they had to call an ambulance.'

'Oh, poor Father. Are you a colleague?'

The man shook his head. 'No, Miss Linfoot. I'm a police officer. PC Riley. I was off duty, but we're so short at the station I was asked to come and see Mrs Linfoot to tell her what happened to her husband.'

She turned to her mother. 'Don't worry, Maman.' She pressed her mother's hand. 'He's in the best place. We'll go and see him right away.'

Her mother remained silent, her eyes now closed.

'Is he in the General Hospital?' Raine asked.

'Yes, he was taken there . . .' The police officer hesitated and she could see him biting the inside of his cheek. 'But I'm afraid it was too late.'

Too late? What is he talking about? An ice-cold sensation took hold of her. She let go her mother's hand and stood up, her limbs trembling.

'Please tell me quickly . . .'

'There was nothing anyone could do,' the officer said. 'The hospital rang and told us it was a brain haemorrhage. The only comfort I can give you is that he wouldn't have known anything about it.'

'How do you know that?' Raine flared. *God, why hadn't they sent someone older – someone more experienced.*

'Well, I don't exactly . . .' he faltered, 'but—'

'Then I would prefer you keep those opinions to yourself.'

Raine's voice was harsh, but tears suddenly welled. She had no right to be so rude to PC Riley. It wasn't his fault and she knew it wasn't right to blame him.

'I apologise, officer,' Raine said with a tremor. 'It must be the shock.'

'Quite understandable in the circumstances.' PC Riley looked relieved. 'Maybe a cup of tea for your mother . . .'

'Of course,' Raine said. 'I'll put the kettle on.' She paused. 'Will you stay for a cup?'

Please say no.

'No, thank you,' he answered. 'I'd best be getting along. I'm on duty shortly.'

She nodded and went with him to the door.

'I'm sorry for your sad loss . . .' he began.

'Thank you, officer. I appreciate you taking the time to come and tell us.'

Her own voice sounded far away. As though another person

168

was speaking. She was parroting the words but had no idea if they were appropriate. A light-headed feeling took over. Her father's smile, his warmth, his love for her. All gone . . .

She swallowed hard to try to remove the lump in her throat, but it stuck there like a piece of concrete. All she wanted was for the policeman to disappear so she could be alone to think what had happened. To try to take it in. But she couldn't. She had to get back to Maman.

'Lorraine, where are you?' her mother's voice called from the front room, stronger now.

'Making you tea, Maman. I'll be there in a minute.'

'I don't want tea.' There came the sound of sobbing.

Raine put the lid on the teapot, her mind whirling with the news. Dad was no longer here. He'd never walk through the door again – smiling as he always did when he was home with his family. Asking how his gorgeous girls were but always going to Maman first. Raine drew in a shaky breath. She'd never be able to talk to him, share a joke, ask his advice. He was the one who usually stuck up for her and occasionally was able to persuade Maman to see *her* side. She gritted her teeth. She mustn't cry. Later, maybe, but for now she had to be strong for her sisters and Maman. She was the eldest, after all. But she worried for Maman who relied on Dad too much. Her mother would be so vulnerable. They would all have to help her.

Hurriedly pouring herself a cup of tea, she gasped as some of the scalding liquid splashed onto the back of her hand. She held it under the cold tap for a few seconds until the worst of the sting subsided, when she heard her mother call out to her again. Squeezing her eyes shut for a brief moment, Raine took her tea into the front room.

'I didn't know where you were,' her mother said, tears pouring down her already swollen face. 'Oh, is that for me?'

She stretched out her arm to take the cup of tea. 'Thank you, *chérie*.'

Raine put it in her hand then turned to go back to the kitchen.

'Where are you going?' her mother sobbed, childlike.

'Getting myself a cup of tea. I asked if you wanted one and you said no, so I gave you mine just now.'

'I don't know what I am saying or not saying.' Simone set the cup and saucer down on a small table and held her face in her hands. She began to cry again.

Raine went over to her and put her arm round her. 'Maman, you've . . . *we've* both had a terrible shock. I can't take it in and I don't suppose you can either.' She paused, aware of the back of her hand stinging from the burn. 'Did you know he had anything wrong with him?'

'If he did, he did not tell me.' Simone sniffed and bent for her handbag close to her feet. She found a handkerchief and blew her nose, then looked up at Raine with an imploring expression. 'What am I going to do without your father?'

'Survive,' Raine answered crisply. 'As Suzanne and Ronnie and I will have to.'

Maman's expression changed to resignation. '*You* will, Lorraine. And so will Véronique. But I think not so much Suzanne. She is very sensitive.'

Raine was about to say something about helping one another when she heard the front door open. Seconds later Ronnie burst into the sitting room.

'I'm home. Is Suzy here yet?'

'Not yet,' Raine said quietly.

Her youngest sister looked at her. 'My, you do look serious.' She flopped into a chair near her mother and looked at her for the first time. 'Maman! You've been crying. What on earth's the matter?'

170

'Your father's d-d-dead.' Simone began to weep uncontrollably.

'What?' Ronnie swung her head round to stare at her sister. 'Raine, what's Maman talking about?'

'I'm afraid it's true, darling,' Raine said, sitting next to her. 'A policeman came round half an hour ago. Dad had a brain haemorrhage at work and by the time the ambulance got him to hospital he was . . . ' Her voice shook and she swallowed hard. 'He was already dead.'

'Oh, no.' Ronnie gave her a horrified stare. 'It can't be true. I said goodbye to him this morning. He was all right then.'

'These things can sometimes happen completely out of the blue.' Raine watched her mother who was whimpering and mumbling to herself.

'What are we going to do?' Ronnie's voice was choked with tears.

'First of all, we need to tell Suzy,' Raine said. 'And then we'll have to have a family gathering.'

Raine stopped herself before she mentioned her father's will. She knew it wasn't really the time to be thinking such things, but she prayed her father had paid off all his debts.

Chapter Sixteen

They waited an hour for Suzanne to return from her rehearsal, but Simone had been so emotionally exhausted that Raine had sent her upstairs to go and lie down. Shortly afterwards, Suzanne arrived home.

'Where's Maman?' was her first question.

'Suzy, Maman's having a rest,' Raine said. 'Come into the sitting room. We need to talk.'

'I'll just put my violin away.'

'Please,' Raine said evenly. 'Just come and sit down now. You, too, Ronnie.'

Although there was less than two years between them, Suzanne always seemed much younger to Raine. It was probably because she was so immersed in her music that she had little time for meeting people and having much adult conversation outside her world of classical music. Raine sighed. It wasn't always easy being the eldest, but she'd had plenty of practice. Her mother had always leaned on Dad for emotional support as well as anything to do with finance. That had obviously been a big mistake. Momentarily, she closed her eyes, dreading how her mother would cope.

Swiftly she told Suzanne what had happened to their father. Her sister kept her eyes fixed on Raine's face.

'You do understand that Dad's never coming back, don't you, Suzy?'

At this, Ronnie leapt up. 'I'm going to my room. I can't stand anymore.' They heard her footsteps pounding up the stairs and a door slam, then a terrible sobbing.

Suzanne made to go after her but Raine held up her hand. 'Let her be, Suzy. She has to deal with this in her own way.'

'Poor Ronnie,' Suzanne said, sinking back into the chair, tears beginning to fall silently down her cheeks. 'She's always felt she's been a disappointment to Maman because she's not as clever as you.'

'Or musical, like you,' Raine added. 'But she shouldn't worry. She's much kinder than I am. Much more thoughtful.'

'That's not true,' Suzanne said softly. 'You just have a different way of showing it, that's all.'

'No, Ronnie's different. The way she's so tuned in to animals and birds. Her love of nature. Maman has never understood her – but Dad did, and she knew it. His death is a real blow to all of us, because he never had a favourite. He treated all of us as if we were his favourite. He loved us all equally and was such a good father—' She broke off, tears blurring her vision. 'He did come unstuck with losing his money, so let's hope Maman has enough of her own so we don't have to move again.'

Suzanne wiped her tears with the back of her hand, just like she did when she was a little girl, Raine thought.

'Do you think we will?' her sister said.

'I hope not. I just don't know what we're going to do about Maman.' Raine sighed. 'She's going to be lost.'

'But I will *not* be lost – I have my daughters near me.'

The two girls swung round towards the door, Raine wondering how much of the conversation their mother had heard. She stood in the doorway in her pink négligée, smiling

173

through her tears, then floated into the sitting room, her arms extended.

'My darling girls. My three wonderful daughters.' She glanced round. 'Where is Véronique?'

'In her room,' Raine said. 'She's very upset and wanted some time to herself.'

Her mother nodded. 'I know you girls will never let me down – never leave me to cope alone. I am so lucky to have you all. I would be lost without you.' She let out a deep sigh. 'Will you call Véronique to come down, Lorraine? I need all of you here.' She sat down on her special armchair and looked directly at Raine.

Raine's stomach turned, making her feel suddenly nauseous. Her mother's insinuation was frightening. Did she really think she and her sisters were never going to leave her side? *There's a war on, for God's sake, Maman*, she wanted to shout. Then her heart practically stopped. Would her mother really make her feel guilty enough to persuade her to leave the ATA? Raine gritted her teeth. Maybe she was reading too much into Maman's words. Her mother was in shock. She didn't know what she was saying. Yes, that was it. Maman wasn't thinking straight. It was too soon, too much to take in. They'd talk about it tomorrow.

'Maman, we all need to eat before we have any family discussion,' she said.

Her mother opened her mouth and then closed it again.

'Let's give Ronnie some time for the shock to settle. And in the meanwhile I'll go and see what I can find for us in the kitchen,' Raine said as she slipped out of the room.

She opened the pantry door. There was a basket of potatoes, the earth still clinging to them. Dad must have dug them up only this morning for lunch. She squeezed her eyes shut and bit her lip so hard she tasted the metallic taste of blood.

174

She mustn't break down. She had to be strong in front of her mother and sisters. She looked along the slate shelves, depressed to see they were almost empty. Maman's organisational abilities were sadly lacking in the food department.

There were a couple of large brown eggs on a saucer, but that wouldn't go far enough to make an omelette for four. Well, she'd have to bulk it up by adding milk and do scrambled eggs on toast.

She was glad to be busy. Dad wouldn't have wanted her to break down. He always told her and her sisters how proud he was of his three daughters. How resilient they all were and must continue to be now the country was at war. He'd said more than once that he wished he was young enough to join up himself.

'You did your bit in the last war,' Raine once told him, 'so you don't need to feel any regrets.'

He'd been an army captain but was too old to fight this time round. Nevertheless, he'd volunteered to be on a night-duty rota as an ARP warden.

'I can't sit and do nothing, leaving it to others,' he'd said at the supper table when his wife had admonished him.

Remembering this conversation, Raine's eyes blurred as she unthinkingly stirred the egg mixture in the saucepan. *Dad.* She'd never be able to give him a hug and a kiss – tell him she loved him. When was the last time she'd told him that? She shook her head to no one. She couldn't remember.

Dear God, what's burning? She glanced down at the saucepan in dismay as smoke hit her nostrils. She snatched the saucepan off the hob, but it was too late. The eggs had been cremated. Furious with herself, and furious with her father for leaving them, her head began to swim. She stumbled over to one of the kitchen chairs and put her head in her hands, desperate to comfort herself. Her shoulders shook. But she didn't cry.

Raine had had to resort to making cheese on toast and

Simone pushed it around her plate, taking two or three dainty bites before putting down her knife and fork together in the English way.

It wasn't an easy supper.

'I feel I am choking,' Simone said. 'And what is the point to eat when I have no hunger?'

'To keep your strength up,' Raine answered. 'We all have to.'

'I would prefer scrambled egg than this cheese I can barely taste,' Simone said petulantly. 'There are two eggs in the pantry. I will have those.'

'I'm afraid I burnt them,' Raine said.

Her mother looked at her in horror. 'You may not realise, but we do not have all the rations here that you are lucky to enjoy at your airfield,' she said, a sharp edge to her tone.

'I'm sorry, Maman, I wasn't concentrating. I was thinking about Dad.'

'Dad loves . . . loved,' Suzanne hurriedly corrected herself, 'cheese on toast. He—'

'I am not ready to discuss him this evening,' Simone said, dabbing her mouth bearing no traces of the morsels of food she'd eaten. 'I shall retire to bed. When you are ready you may come up and say goodnight.'

She rose and made her way slowly from the room, looking to Raine as if Maman had aged ten years since this morning.

'He was her rock,' Suzanne said after the door closed.

'He was a rock for us all,' Ronnie added. 'I'm going to miss him so much.'

'I know Dad's only been gone a few hours,' Raine began, her voice sounding unreal to her ears, 'but I think we need some kind of family meeting – maybe one without and one *with* Maman. Just to voice our opinion on where we go from here.' She looked at each sister in turn. 'As the eldest, I'd better have my say first.'

Suzanne and Ronnie nodded their agreement.

'This is how I see it,' Raine started. 'We've lost Dad and I think we're going to find it very difficult to handle Maman. We always came after Dad in her affections. He was her one and only love. She'll go through all sorts of emotions – feel lonely and angry – and maybe even pretend it didn't happen. Do you remember how she was when Hitler invaded her beloved Paris? It nearly killed her. First she denied it and then she went into that awful depression. And she's likely to slip into another one if we're not careful.

'If you remember, that's the time when she became so dependent. First on Dad, of course, though he never seemed to mind. But now he's gone she'll look to us. So we have to think how to explain to her we're not going to be at her beck and call when there's nothing physically wrong with her.'

'She wouldn't expect us to give up our lives,' Ronnie said.

Raine sent her a pitying look. 'Maman actually said she won't be lost because she has *us* by her side. The meaning was clear. *By her side at all times.*' She heard Ronnie give a gasp of dismay. 'But all of us – and that includes Maman – have to get on with our lives. I love my job – flying's in my bones – and I believe I'm doing something useful and fairly important in this awful war, so I don't intend to devote my life to Maman. We have to be cruel to be kind. She has a strength she doesn't even know she's got because everyone runs around after her all the time.'

'Did she really say that?' Ronnie questioned. 'About us being by her side at all times?'

'Yes, that was the insinuation when you'd rushed upstairs. And if we kow-tow to her we'll be trapped.'

'Well, I'm not cut out for domestic stuff,' Ronnie stated firmly. 'I can see Suzy doing that, not me. And I'm sure Maman will appreciate it as Suzy's her favourite.'

'Of course I'm not,' Suzanne protested. 'She loves us all the same.'

'No,' Raine said. 'It's always been you, Suzy, our musical prodigy. But you're lucky – Ronnie and I happen to love you, too, so we don't get upset.'

'You're making me feel awful. I'm sure it's not true.'

Raine stroked her sister's blonde head. 'Don't be, and it *is*.' She smiled. 'And to make up for it, we both want tickets to your next concert. When will it be?'

'It's scheduled for November,' Suzanne said. 'You know how hard we're rehearsing?' She looked at her two sisters as if waiting for their affirmation. 'Well, they've actually offered me a solo in one of Brahms' sonatas. And the reason they gave it to me was because I'm the only one who's memorised it.' She paused. 'Though I don't know what my playing will be like now Dad's—' She broke off and took a handkerchief from her cardigan pocket.

'It sounds wonderful, Suzy. I just hope I'll manage to get there.' Raine turned to her youngest sister. 'Ronnie? What do *you* have to say about Maman?'

Ronnie pouted. 'She won't want to be cared for by *me*.'

'Why do you say that?' Suzanne said.

'Because I don't have nursing skills. Mother would hate it. And *I'd* hate it. I'd rather be in a factory any day, and that's saying something. No, it will have to be you or Raine.' She looked at her sisters with glistening eyes. 'And delivering planes to fighter pilots is probably more important than playing them a nice tune.'

'You don't understand, Ronnie. Music's just as important for the soul and—'

'Why don't we wait until Maman feels a little better before we make any decision?' Raine cut in. 'We may be worrying for nothing. She may see sense and give us her blessing.'

But she knew her mother would never give in that easily.

Chapter Seventeen

Raine had had a restless night. She hadn't been able to fall asleep with everything whirling through her mind and Suzanne's muffled sobs. She couldn't stop thinking of her father and how he'd had no idea when he'd woken up yesterday that it would be his last day on earth, but she hadn't allowed herself to cry in front of her sisters. She lay motionless in the dark but finally, at half past three, she decided she would telephone the ferry pool in the morning and ask for a few days' compassionate leave. She turned the pillow over to cool her cheek and tried to block out Suzanne's snuffles. Through sheer exhaustion she'd finally fallen asleep.

Now, she tapped on her parents' bedroom door. She swallowed hard as a lump in her throat formed at the thought that it wasn't her parents' bedroom any longer but only her mother's. How could everything have changed in such a short space of time? She heard a muffled, 'Come in,' and opened the door to see her mother sitting up and staring ahead.

'I've brought you a cup of tea, Maman,' Raine said as she put the cup and saucer in her mother's hands. 'Did you get any sleep?'

'*Non*, I did not.'

Raine was about to reply that she'd had very little herself,

179

but she could see it was pointless. Her mother took a sip of tea and grimaced.

'I have never understood why the British think a cuppa – as they call it . . .' the Frenchwoman said the word with a curl of her pale lip, 'is the panacea to all problems. Coffee is so much more civilised and restorative.'

'Coffee's short at the moment,' Raine said, 'unless you've found a supply. And if you have, it'll probably be black market.'

'Please do not use that term in my hearing,' Simone snapped. 'And I do not appreciate these comments.'

'I wasn't being serious, Maman.'

'Then do not say it.'

Raine sighed. This was going to be every bit as difficult as she'd feared.

'We will have to make plans.' Simone suddenly looked more alert as she finished her tea and set her cup down on the bedside table. 'We must call a family meeting with no delay. The first serious discussion without your father.' Large tears rolled down her cheeks. 'You must make the arrangements with your sisters. But first I will have my morning bath.'

She waved Raine from the room.

It was a sombre gathering around the dining room table an hour later.

'This time yesterday your father was alive and well.' Simone's chin trembled. 'Who would imagine we are here to decide what is going to happen now he is no longer with us?' She looked at her daughters. 'He was my 'usband and my dearest friend.' Tears streamed down her cheeks. 'Thank *le bon Dieu* I am not alone. I have my dear girls.' Her gaze fell on Raine, then Suzanne, then Ronnie. She began to weep.

This was too much. Raine swallowed. She was not going

to listen any longer to her mother's plaintive noises. Didn't she understand they were *all* devastated, not just her alone?

Suzanne jumped up and put an arm around her mother's shoulders. 'Please don't cry,' she said. 'You'll start us all off.' She gave her mother a kiss on her cheek. 'Come on, Maman. Dad wouldn't want us to fall apart – especially now.'

Simone sniffed and reached up her sleeve for her handkerchief.

'We all have to keep busy for the war effort,' Raine said firmly.

'And you could be killed any day,' Simone said, her attention now fixed on Raine. 'I never approved of this flying, and you could be the next to die in the family through your own obstinate, selfish desire to prove everyone wrong and think you can do a man's job.'

'It's nothing like that,' Raine said fiercely. 'A woman should be allowed to do the same as a man – if she wants. I don't *think* I can do a man's job – I *know* I can. I'm as good as any male pilot – you can ask anyone at the station.'

'I do not intend to telephone some station to find out that my daughter has sacrificed her life,' Simone said. She gazed intently at Raine. 'Are you already taking the aeroplanes?'

Raine was suddenly alert. Maman wasn't normally that interested. What was behind the innocent-sounding question?

'Yes, and I've finished my training for the fighter aircraft, which is what I'll be delivering the minute I go back,' she said.

'Well, I have had time in the bath to think. Suzanne must go on with her music. It would be a disaster if she missed her rehearsals and her practice. Ronnie is too young to sacrifice her years to look after me. *Non*. The obvious choice is my eldest daughter – *you*, Lorraine.'

Her mother leaned back in her chair as though satisfied

181

she'd got it all worked out, Raine thought, anger rising in her chest.

'I *won't* give up flying, Maman.' Raine caught her mother's eye. 'You're perfectly able to look after yourself, the same as any other widow. This damned war is affecting so many families. Suzanne and Ronnie still live at home so you'll have some company. But I must carry on. Besides,' she added, 'you need the money I send you. And talking of money, did Dad clear all the debts?'

'We can manage without your contribution,' Simone said brusquely, ignoring her daughter's last question. 'I will be in receipt of a widow's pension. Mrs Moore is a widow and she receives ten shillings a week. So I will be given the same.' She fixed her eyes on Raine. 'And please don't swear, Lorraine. It is not ladylike.'

'Who has the time to be a lady, Maman?' Raine said crossly. Was her mother so completely out of touch? 'There is a *war* on, in case you've forgotten.'

'Do you think I am not aware of that?' Simone swung round, her temper flaring. 'When you see what has happened to my beloved Paris.'

The sisters were silent.

'You haven't answered my question, Maman,' Raine tried again. 'Did Dad clear his debts?'

'Not entirely,' her mother admitted, 'but we will not starve.'

'But we still owe money, so that's all the more reason for us to do our bit, Maman,' Raine argued. Would her mother ever understand?

'*Alors*, it will not be possible for me to "do my bit", as you call it. Not even to care for *les légumes*.'

Raine rolled her eyes. It was Ronnie who planted and tended the vegetables. So what excuse *now* was her mother about to trot out?

'You see, you are quite wrong on something, Lorraine. I am *not* able to look after myself.'

'What *are* you talking about? We're all responsible for ourselves.'

There was a hush.

Raine was about to argue again when her mother said, 'I went to the doctor last week.' She stopped and looked at each of her daughters in turn. 'He gave me terrible news.'

Ronnie bolted upright, fear etched on her face. 'What's wrong, Maman?'

'I have had the diagnosis.'

'What for?' Suzanne's voice sounded shaky.

Simone sat silently, staring down at the tablecloth.

'Maman,' Raine started, sudden worry making her voice rise, 'you'd better tell us what's the matter.'

Simone looked at her and gave a sad little smile. 'I have a bad 'eart.' She spread her hands. 'The doctor told me I have to learn to live with it, and the worst thing is for me to have a bad upset. We did not know that I would have the worst upset only a few days later and lose my dear Robert . . .' She choked on his name.

Raine's chest tightened. As far as she was aware, her mother had never shown any signs of a bad heart. But then the first symptoms might only just be manifesting themselves. If her mother really was a sick woman she could end up an invalid. Inwardly, Raine shivered. This news was almost as bad as her father dying. She suddenly had an unwelcome thought.

'Did you tell Dad?'

'*Oui*, your father knows . . . knew,' Simone corrected herself, her eyes wet.

Raine's mind was in turmoil. *Could it have been the shock of hearing this news from his adored wife that caused her father's . . .?* Raine caught herself. No, she mustn't think that.

183

She mustn't blame her mother for something that clearly wasn't her fault. But it was strange he died only a few days after she must have given him the news.

Simone looked steadily at Raine. 'So, *chérie*, I am afraid there is no argument. I have chosen *you*, my eldest and practical one, to come home and look after me. And one day you will thank me for saving your life from one of those death contraptions!'

Raine held her mother's gaze. She couldn't think how to reply. Part of her was frightened with this new condition of her mother's and how they would all cope, but another part of her desperately wanted to be back at Hatfield. She felt she was being torn in two and the only person who would understand was Doug who'd met her father and liked him.

'Maman,' she said, getting up from her chair, 'please excuse me.'

She'd write to Doug this minute.

Chapter Eighteen

Raine woke to the sound of a late summer storm. Sheets of rain were lashing against the bedroom window. She lay there for a few minutes listening to the sound of her sister's breathing. The day of the funeral. She blinked hard. Today of all days she was going to be calm. She was going to take over from her mother who didn't seem capable of doing anything except to pull out a black suit from her wardrobe, more appropriate for winter than the surprising surge of heat they were having during the last fortnight.

At times she could have shaken her mother for leaving everything to her: the funeral arrangements, Dad's favourite hymns, ordering a modest headstone for the burial in the village church cemetery, the flowers for the coffin . . . and then she would feel ashamed when her mother was trying not only to cope with the grief of losing her husband, but also knowing she was never going to be strong. All of them would need time to come to terms with that.

She'd had to telephone Pauline Gower to explain about her mother's situation.

'We all send our sympathy to your mother and sisters,' Pauline had said, 'and certainly as the eldest you must be with your family until after the funeral. But if you can, please come back to us soon. We need every single pilot, particularly as you've finished your second phase of training and would be such a valuable asset now.'

Now, her CO's words rang in Raine's ears. She had one more day to make up her mind.

Well, it was no use lying there staring up at the ceiling. Raine hopped out of bed and threw on a dressing gown.

Ronnie was already up, cups and saucers laid out and the kettle boiling. 'Want one?' she asked, meticulously measuring out two teaspoons of tea for the pot. Minutes later she handed Raine a cup.

'Thanks, Ronnie. Just what I need.' Raine swallowed several mouthfuls quickly, burning her tongue. She glanced at her sister. 'Did you sleep?'

Ronnie shook her head. 'Not much. It's so hard to remember we're never going to see Dad here any more. I keep thinking I hear his footsteps coming down the stairs. I just want to set the clock back to when everything was normal.' She blinked back the tears.

'The trouble is, we forget that Dad was that much older than Maman. But I never noticed it because he was always so full of life.'

Raine drained her cup and set it on its saucer. She didn't feel she had the energy to move. She closed her eyes.

'What are you thinking about?' Ronnie said, making Raine startle.

'I was thinking how upset we were when Nana and Grandpa were killed in that traffic accident. We were only children. It would have broken their hearts to be told their son had died so suddenly at only sixty-two.'

'And now we've got Maman's health to worry about on top of everything else,' Ronnie said.

'I know.' Raine glanced at the kitchen clock. 'I'd better go and get dressed. Thanks for the tea, Ronnie. I'll take one up to Maman and Suzanne. We've got quite a day ahead of us.'

To Raine's relief the storm was easing by the time they entered the church. She shrugged off her raincoat and glanced at her mother who was hiding her face behind a short black veil on her hat. It made her look very aloof and very French, Raine thought. Her sisters had filed in first, followed by Maman and then Raine, who took the aisle seat. She had asked her mother what she wanted to say for the eulogy, but her mother had just shaken her head and said, 'You write it, *chérie*. You know . . .' Her mother's voice shook as she started again, 'You *knew* your father well. I cannot seem to concentrate on anything at the moment.'

Raine felt her legs tremble as she stood behind the lectern. She glanced over her handwritten notes. It would sound false if she just read them out. She knew what she wanted to say, even if it didn't flow as well as her notes would. She stepped to the side and faced the congregation, surprised so many people from the village had packed the pews when they hadn't lived here for very long.

She took a deep breath and spoke from the heart for several minutes.

'. . . and I'd just like to end by saying he was the best father . . .' Her eyes began to sting. She'd left her bag on the seat with her handkerchief. She swallowed. 'The best father we . . .' The words caught in her throat. 'The best father,' she repeated more firmly, 'we three girls could ever have had.'

She walked back to her seat, head erect, where her mother sat like stone. Suzanne was quietly weeping, and she saw Ronnie angrily brush the tears on her cheek with the back of her hand.

We all have to deal with this in our own way, Raine thought.

But as the eldest sister I can't break down. Suzanne and Ronnie always look up to me as the strong one.

But she didn't feel very strong at the moment. If only she could speak to Doug – pour her heart out about her father – but she hadn't heard from him since she'd written to tell him Dad had died. *Please God let Doug keep safe.* She'd write to him again as soon as she had a few minutes to herself.

There was no one else close to them in the church, so after the service the Linfoot family walked home, Raine absorbed in her own thoughts. She couldn't wait to step through the front door and find a spot where she could be on her own for even a few minutes. But to her surprise her mother said, 'We will go in the sitting room. The solicitor gave me a copy of the will and something else your father wrote.' She stared at Raine. 'A letter for *you*, Lorraine, though I am not sure why.'

'Me?'

'Just one for Raine?' Suzanne said, sounding puzzled. 'No letter for the rest of us?'

Simone hesitated. 'No, just a letter for Lorraine.'

'Did you open it?' Raine asked.

'Do you accuse me to open a letter addressed to you?' Her mother's face was lined in hurt.

'I didn't accuse you, I simply asked.'

'Well, I 'ave not, as you will see,' Simone said, putting her hand over her heart.

Immediately, Raine felt guilty. Why hadn't she seen any signs before that her mother was suffering? She said in a softer tone, 'I'm sorry, Maman. May I have my letter?'

Simone took an envelope from her handbag and handed it to her. 'You will read it out so we can all hear what my dear Robert says.'

Raine glanced at the envelope. 'Maman, it's private. I shall read it on my own . . . and tell you and the girls anything I think important.'

Without waiting for an answer she ran up the stairs to Suzanne's room. There must be some reason why her father had written only to her. She took her paperknife from her writing case and perched on the edge of the bed, then slit open the envelope. Unfolding a large sheet of lined paper, which looked as though it had come from a solicitor's yellow foolscap notepad, she noticed the date. He'd written it only months ago.

21st March 1941

My darling Raine,

At only 60 (plus a bit!) I hope to have many more years but lately I've had a few rather bad headaches. It may only mean the worry of work but it could be more serious. Who knows? So just in case the worst happens I want to tell you things I can't when we're together – for various reasons.

You and your mother don't always see eye to eye, but darling girl, please try to be kind to her. Her life wasn't always easy in France, no matter how she insists it was, being brought up by strict Roman Catholic parents. And they made it very difficult for her when she told them we were getting married. I suppose I can't blame them in a way – I was only a few years younger than her father and not of their faith. So I was honoured that she still consented to be my wife and agree to bring up any children we might have as Protestants until they were old enough to choose for themselves. I hope that was the right decision for you three girls.

I've always felt your mother regrets marrying me – well, I am so much older, for a start. Probably not exciting

189

*enough for her. I know I've let her down – let you all
down – by losing my money, and it finally got the better
of me. I admit I was reckless. I can only say I've tried to
make it up to you all by working even harder now, and
that most of the debts are cleared. By the time you read
this I sincerely hope they will all be.*

*I love you, my precious daughter. And contrary to what
you think, she does love you, and also, of course, your
sisters. But she needs you most of all because you're the
most cool-headed. So if anything should happen to me,
darling Raine, I'm asking you to please look after your
mother.*

Your loving father XX

Raine swallowed hard. It was as though her father were
talking to her. His handwriting was his voice, trying to reassure
her that her mother loved her. Raine had never known that she
hadn't had an easy time in France – that was the biggest surprise.
Her mother never stopped making comparisons between France
and England, and France always won. She read the letter again,
this time studying every word. But the last sentence was the
one that sent a shiver of despair down her legs.

He'd always taught her to follow her heart. But now he
was dead. And if she carried out his last wishes, then so was
her flying career.

For the first time since he'd died, she threw herself on her
bed and sobbed.

'Raine.'

It was Suzanne.

'Go away.' Raine's voice was muffled in her pillow.

'I won't.'

Raine felt her sister's hand stroke her hair, the way she'd
tried to comfort Ronnie that morning.

'Was there something in the letter that's upset you?'

'Only that he has specifically asked *me* to look after Maman.' She sat up and looked at her sister. 'He's saying almost the exact words that Maman said. That it would be down to me. I'm sure she's read this letter, Suzy, but I can't accuse her. She's obviously not a well woman. I just don't know what to do.'

'We'll all help,' Suzanne said. 'Don't worry, Raine. Come on. It's not like you to be so downhearted.'

'I'll be all right. It's Maman we have to worry about now. You go down, Suzy.' Raine took her hankerchief from under her pillow and blew her nose. 'I'll be all right,' she repeated.

Raine hated herself for being so weak, lurching from one definite decision to the other in a matter of hours, sometimes minutes. How could she just walk out – go back to the station – and leave her two sisters to take care of Maman? She couldn't leave them to shoulder all the responsibility.

She screwed up her eyes to stop the tears of self-pity. Her head felt as though a block of wood was permanently lodged there. She blinked several times, desperate to clear the odd sensations. She would go mad if she didn't get out of the house. It was beginning to suffocate her. She'd walk to the village in the hope that some fresh air might help.

But warm stale air met her lungs. The weather had suddenly become cloying, doing nothing to soothe Raine's nerves as she wandered down the High Street deep in thought, not noticing the stocky figure of Doctor Hall who was waving to her from across the road. It was only when he tripped up the kerb in front of her, almost losing his balance, that she was aware of him. She put an arm out to steady him.

'Dr Hall, do be careful.'

'Thank you, my dear.' He removed his hat. 'I'm so glad

191

to have spotted you. Please accept my very sincere condol-
ences. I liked your father very much and was sorry I couldn't
get to the funeral. He and I had some good chats in the past,
and even an occasional drink at the pub.' His eyes twinkled
as he looked at her.

'Thank you for saying that, Dr Hall. It's nice to know you
made a friend of him.'

'I wonder . . .' Dr Hall hesitated. 'Do you have a moment
to take tea with me?' He nodded towards a café on the side
of the road he'd just crossed.

I'll have to. I'm sure he's doing his duty by checking how
we all are, especially Maman. But still, it was kind of him.

'Yes, of course.'

'How is your mother bearing up?' Dr Hall began as the
two of them sat on the hard chairs in the café, their tea in
thick white cups.

Surprisingly, the café was almost full. Clouds of cigarette
smoke drifted towards them, trapped as they were in the
corner.

Raine cleared her throat. 'Not very well, as you can
imagine. Maman is in a state. It's been over a week and she
can't seem to stop crying. I hoped she'd calm down a little
when the funeral was over, but I realise it's still very new
and an extra shock on top of everything.'

'Dear, dear me.' Dr Hall removed his glasses and wiped
them on the edge of the tablecloth. 'I must call in and see
her. Perhaps give her a sedative.' He studied his watch as
though it would confirm his words. 'Yes, I shall do that this
week. Day after tomorrow, in fact.' He slipped his glasses
back on his nose. 'And how are you and your sisters coping?'

'I thought Suzanne would be the most affected, but it
seems that Ronnie – Véronique – is feeling the pain terribly.
I suppose it's inevitable as she's the youngest.'

Dr Hall nodded sympathetically. 'And you, my dear?'

'It's bad. I can't believe Dad's no longer here. But we all have to accept it and carry on as he would have wanted.' She leaned forward and said softly, 'Actually, Dr Hall, I'm glad to have the opportunity to talk to you . . . about Maman.'

Dr Hall frowned. 'You mentioned an "extra shock". I take it you're referring to her financial position since your father's difficult time a couple of years back.'

'No, although that's bad enough. I'm talking about her recent diagnosis.'

Dr Hall's expression changed to bewilderment. 'I'm not sure I follow you.'

Raine suddenly felt an overwhelming pity for her mother not having Dad to talk things through. He would have taken charge. Told her he'd always be there for her. But through no fault of his own, he hadn't.

She swallowed and took in a breath, needing to keep calm in front of this nice doctor.

'My mother's heart.'

Dr Hall drew his bushy brows together. 'Her heart?' he repeated, shaking his head. 'What's the matter with it?'

'You don't know?'

Dr Hall shook his head.

This was odd. Raine frowned. 'She's been told she has a weak heart and it could get worse if she has any more upset.' She sent him a sharp look. 'I assumed she'd been to see you.'

'When would this be?'

'Right before Dad had the brain haemorrhage.'

Dr Hall took out his diary and flipped open the pages. 'Ah, yes,' he said. 'Your mother telephoned me with the sad news that same afternoon.' He scribbled a few words.

'And she didn't mention her heart before then?'

'No. And it didn't come up in the conversation either when she told me about your father.' Dr Hall looked her straight in the eye and she knew he was telling her the truth.

'She must have seen a heart specialist then without your knowledge.'

'Hmm.' Dr Hall drained his cup. 'Lorraine, there was something she mentioned about you delivering aeroplanes – you've joined the Air Transport, or something.'

Raine gave a start of surprise at this sudden change of subject. Strange that Maman would even think to discuss her with Dr Hall, especially at that time when she'd telephoned him about Dad.

'That's right – the ATA.'

'She worries about you.'

'I keep telling her not to.' She looked at the kind grey eyes of Dr Hall. Should she confide in him about her situation at work?

'I'm on compassionate leave at the moment but my station expects me back now the funeral's over. But Maman says I must ring them and explain the situation – that I won't be going back.' She bunched up the corner of the tablecloth then let it drop. 'I didn't know she had such a serious health problem. I'm desperate to do my bit in the war, but as the eldest, it's my duty to stay and look after her.'

Dr Hall said nothing. He took out his pipe and gestured to her for permission to light it. She nodded. He took his time lighting up.

'Lorraine, there's a war on,' he said, making little popping sounds with his pipe to get it going. 'You're young. You have your whole life ahead, God willing. And I'm sure they need you at the station even more than your mother needs you at this point.'

'Oh, they do,' Raine said eagerly. 'They've already told me

that and say they hope I'll be back very soon. But how can I leave her?'

'Right.' Dr Hall sucked at the stem of his pipe. 'You explain this to your mother – quietly and calmly tomorrow evening. Unless there is any significant deterioration in her health, you will be going back to the station on Thursday morning. She'll be upset and try to talk you out of it. You must be kind but firm. I will come by Thursday afternoon and talk to her.'

'But if she was to become ill again and—'

Dr Hall held up his hand.

'Don't say another word,' he said. 'You just leave your mother to me.'

Walking back home Raine went over and over Dr Hall's words. Was he holding something back? And then it dawned on her that he'd never said her mother's heart was bad. Surely he would have warned her. He would know if her mother had seen a specialist. In fact, he would have been the one to have arranged it. Was this 'heart condition' simply a pack of lies to keep her at home and stop her from doing the one thing she loved?

But what should she do now? Demand the truth from her mother who most probably would stick to her story? Tell her sisters? They'd taken Maman's news as read. So had she until her conversation with Dr Hall. She gritted her teeth. She wouldn't be able to look her mother in the eye until she had it out with her.

As Raine walked up the path to her home she decided to tackle her mother right away and without her sisters. It wasn't fair to drag Suzanne and Ronnie into her private opinion of her mother.

She was in luck. The front door was unlocked so Maman was probably in. Raine walked into the front room to see her mother sitting on her own having a cup of coffee, the signs of recent crying lingering on her cheeks.

'Maman, can we have a private word?'

Eyebrows raised, her mother put her cup down. 'What do you wish to discuss? If it is to do with your future—'

Raine held up the palm of her hand.

'Maman, please let me speak. I ran into Dr Hall today in the High Street.' She watched her mother closely. Alarm flitted across Simone's face, but she quickly arranged her features in a neutral expression.

'Thank goodness for Dr Hall. He's such a comfort to me. I don't know what I would do without him. I would not have slept a wink without his sleeping pills.'

'Yes, he's a very good doctor,' Raine said, keeping her voice even. 'And he's told me to go back to Hatfield on Thursday and carry on with my job, and that he will be calling in to see you in the afternoon.'

'He said that?' Simone's voice rose.

'Yes, he did. And a few other things as well.'

'Did he mention my condition?'

Raine kept her eyes fixed on her mother's. 'He didn't mention your *heart*, if that's what you mean. But *I* mentioned it to *him*. He didn't seem to know anything about it, so I said you must have seen a specialist.'

'I do not like the idea that you talk to my doctor about me behind my back, Lorraine.' Her eyes flashed. 'It is confidential what I tell my doctor.'

'Maman, he's *my* doctor, too. The whole family's.' She paused. Her mother's forehead was creased in lines of annoyance. 'But it never seems to occur to you that we're *also* terribly upset we've lost Dad.'

'You accuse me of being a selfish mother?' Simone's expression had changed to anger.

196

'I didn't say that. But Dr Hall told me that once you're over the worst of the shock you'll be able to play your part, too, in the war.'

She knew he hadn't said that, but it sounded the sort of thing he would say. She waited. Her mother blinked.

'I will be having a word with Dr Hall,' Simone said, a hard edge to her voice.

Oh, Lord. Her mother was working herself up into a right mood.

'Maman, the station wants to know when I'm returning. They're short of pilots so I *must* go back on Thursday. In case you don't realise, the ferry pilots are doing a vital job in the fight against the Germans. Being French, you should be pleased.' Should she say the next bit? Yes, she had to know the truth. She drew in a breath and plunged in. 'You haven't seen any specialist, have you, Maman? That was all made up, wasn't it, to keep me here?'

Her mother looked at her. The fury had gone from her eyes, but Raine couldn't work out what had taken place.

'Go, Lorraine,' she said in a resigned tone. 'Go and do what you want. You've always done that – had your own way. Tell your station you'll be there this afternoon. There is no need to wait here with your mother until Thursday.'

'Maman, please—'

Simone held up her hand. 'No more, Lorraine. Go and pack your things.'

Chapter Nineteen

As Raine walked into the Hatfield ferry pool she felt it was like coming home. She'd waited until Thursday, her own home stifling her with Maman in tears most of the time and Suzy and Ronnie tiptoeing around her. What on earth would Dad think if he'd known his wife had pulled such a trick. All it had succeeded in doing was to make Raine more alienated than ever from her mother.

Bad heart indeed! Raine snorted. Maman hadn't denied her accusation about not having seen a specialist. But she must have known her lies were bound to be disclosed sooner or later when there was no outward evidence of a dicky heart. But if it hadn't been for pure serendipity – running into Dr Hall yesterday – she would have been stuck, acting as some sort of nurse to her mother. She shuddered at the thought.

Maman had really shown how far she was prepared to go to keep Raine by her side. She'd completely disregarded Raine's part in the war effort. She was unwavering in her effort to exert control over all three daughters' lives. Well, Raine was equally determined that Maman wouldn't control her, and she only hoped her sisters would be strong enough to stand up to her when the time came. Nevertheless, she still wished she hadn't left Maman after a blazing row.

But here she was at last, back at the station with the

blessing of her sisters. They'd been horrified when she'd told them about Maman's perfectly good heart.

'Don't let anything stand in the way of your music, Suzy,' Raine had said as she kissed her goodbye. 'At least Maman wants you to carry on with that. She's so proud of you. So are Ronnie and I. And you know Dad would be, too.'

She turned to Ronnie, who seemed to have lost her boyish humour and energy overnight.

'Don't get sucked into Maman's nonsense, Ronnie.' She ruffled her young sister's new short hair. 'It'll be your turn soon to do something worthwhile.'

'I was thinking about the Land Army,' Ronnie said seriously. 'That way, I'd definitely be outdoors.'

'I've heard it's hard work,' Suzanne said. 'My friend Jane says she's never been so exhausted. I can't believe she mucks out cows and last winter pulled up turnips. I'd hate it. And anyway,' she looked at Ronnie with concern, 'you have to be at least seventeen.'

'Two years too early, then, Ronnie,' Raine said, laughing. 'The war'll be over by then.'

'First of all, I might not be very tall but I'm much stronger than Jane,' Ronnie protested. 'And I could lie about my age. Lots of girls do.'

'I don't want you doing that,' Raine said firmly. 'Something will turn up at the right time that will be perfect, but until then you must continue with your studies.'

Raine had gone in search of her mother to say goodbye but it was as though she were saying it to a stranger. Simone had only offered Raine her cheek, cooler than marble. Something had broken permanently between her and Maman. But the only guilt she'd really felt was to be leaving her sisters. They in turn dismissed such a notion and told her just to get on with her job – and to keep safe. At least the girls have plenty of grit and determination, Raine consoled herself. They wouldn't be cowed under Maman.

'Good to see you back!'

Several of the ferry pilots welcomed her with beaming smiles. Raine felt a lift to her heart. This was where she belonged – with like-minded colleagues who understood her joy of flying and her satisfaction at being part of the team.

She went in search of Pauline to let her know she was back. After telling Raine once again how sorry she was for the loss of her father, Pauline said Lucinda Morris was grounded with a bad cold and could she take over her next delivery immediately.

'Oh, bad luck. Yes, of course I'll do it.'

'And Stephanie's in hospital.'

'Oh, what's the matter with her?'

'We're not sure yet. She was very poorly after her last delivery two days ago. They're running tests. Nausea and headaches seem to be the main problem. But she'll be laid up for a week or so, I'm sure.'

'I'll go and visit her,' Raine said immediately.

'Yes, do,' Pauline said. 'I'm sure she'd appreciate it.'

'This is your chit.' The Ops officer handed her four sheets of paper. 'You know what to do with the copies. You're delivering a Hawker Hart to Silloth but first you have to collect it from White Waltham. One of the air taxis will take you – Audrey's down for the job, I believe. Make sure you read the Pilots Notes thoroughly as I don't believe you're familiar with this one.' He gave Raine a sharp look. 'Are you're sure you're up for it? Tell me now, if not.'

Raine's heart skipped a beat but it was from excitement rather than fear. Her first proper delivery after all the Moths.

And he was right. She'd never flown a Hawker Hart before and she couldn't wait. It would be wonderful to have a change from the Tiger.

'I'm definitely up for it,' she said, smiling at him.

'I was sorry to hear about your father,' Audrey said, as they climbed into the cabin.

'Thank you.' Raine decided to change the subject. 'Have you a busy day ahead?'

She knew Audrey was a far more experienced pilot than herself and was bound to have several deliveries lined up.

'A frightful day, though I shall love every minute. I'm delivering three plus this one – all different. Two I've never flown before. I'll probably be relieved to get back to the station, put my feet up, have a gin and orange and a cigarette.' She laughed. 'I sound like I'm moaning but we all know we wouldn't be doing anything else in the world.'

'You're right,' Raine chuckled. 'And I'll be relieved too, but for different reasons.'

Audrey glanced at Raine. 'What are you taking?'

'A Hawker Hart. I'm rather chuffed and definitely looking forward to it.'

'It's a lot more powerful that the Moth you're probably used to,' Audrey said. 'It's a good plane, but treat it with caution.'

Without warning Alec's face sprang to her mind. Audrey might as well have been talking about *him*. That cocky grin. But he hadn't worn it when she'd last seen him. His expression had been unfathomable and she knew it was entirely because of her. Dear God, how she wished she had someone to talk to now. Even though she'd enjoyed the other girls' company during training, she hadn't so far formed any close friendships at Hatfield. And Stephanie? She shook her head. She'd tried

201

to keep out of her way as much as possible as they had little in common except flying. And what was there to say about Alec? He'd made it clear he was interested in her and she'd made it equally clear that the feeling wasn't mutual.

'You look like you're thinking dark thoughts. It doesn't pay, you know.'

Audrey's deeply husky voice – coated with tobacco, no doubt – jolted her. The woman wouldn't know how close she was to what Raine was thinking. Raine gave a slight smile and a shrug but didn't comment.

'Okay, Raine,' Audrey said, 'I need your help to get the undercarriage up. You've not flown an Anson and they can be tricky.'

We've probably only got our pilot's wings in common, Raine thought as they worked together to retract the under-carriage. That was the trouble. She'd always had difficulty making friends. Too acerbic, Maman told her more than once; too self-important – not an appealing trait. Was that really how others saw her?

'You okay?' Audrey enquired after some minutes.

'I am now,' Raine said. 'Never happier than when I'm in the air – but I had a bit of a row with my mother before I left home.'

'Oh, dear. What about? Coming back to the station?'

'How on earth did you guess?'

'Stands to reason. She's lost her husband. Now she feels she's losing her daughter. She probably thinks there's a good chance you'll be killed on the job and she'll have lost both of you. And she's not a million miles away from the truth, let's face it.'

Raine sat quietly, thinking over Audrey's words. They seemed to make sense. How could a stranger possibly have such insight into a woman she'd never met?

'I'm right, aren't I?'

'I don't know. I hadn't thought of it like that. But I suppose you could be.'

'Is she on her own now?' Audrey asked.

'No, she has my two sisters – eighteen and fifteen.'

'That's good. It's awful to think a brand-new widow is sitting at home alone, still shell-shocked.'

'I shouldn't have left her the way I did,' Raine said, guilt pouring over her.

'Write to her. Sometimes it's better on paper. Then the person can read it over again. Make sure she's understood the sentiment.'

'Thanks, Audrey, I think I'll take your advice.' Raine smiled.

She was still going over Audrey's words about Maman and wondering if Suzanne and Ronnie would cope when Audrey broke in.

'You've gone quiet again.'

'Oh, I was thinking about what you said about my mother. And the family . . . you know.'

'No, I really don't,' Audrey said, a touch of bitterness thinning her mouth. 'My family have washed their hands of me since I told them I'd filed for divorce. I haven't seen them for two years.'

Raine threw her a look of curiosity. This wasn't the kind of discussion she'd ever had with any of the other female ferry pilots.

'Oh, dear. That sounds bad,' she said, although she was more interested in why Audrey had wanted a divorce rather than commiserating with her that her parents had turned their backs on her.

'He was a humbug,' Audrey said with feeling. 'He never told me before we were married that he preferred men.'

Raine gasped. She'd heard, vaguely, of these kinds of men, but she'd never met one, as far as she knew. Hearing that one of them was actually a married man was surprising.

'I had no idea when I first met him because he swept me off my feet. My parents adored him, mainly because he was rich and titled – oh, and very good-looking – and they never stopped telling me how lucky I was to make such a catch. I never told them about his preferences, even when I said I was going to sue him for a divorce. Ugh.' She shuddered. 'And I hated being called Lady Armstrong. I wasn't interested in flower arranging in the local church and raising money for charities through baking cakes and flogging them. So when the war started it was a marvellous excuse to join up.

'I applied to join the WAAFs and Leonard was furious. He wanted me to start a family. No fear. Thank goodness Hitler put paid to that. The only decent thing that megalomaniac did.' She gave a mirthless laugh, then a narrowed glance at Raine. 'Oh, I can tell what you're thinking. I've just told you Leonard was keen to start a family when he preferred men. He could still get it up for me and it was his way of appearing normal – whatever that means.' She broke off and laughed at Raine's sudden flush. 'Oh, don't tell me you've never done it,' she said. 'How old are you?' Without waiting for a reply, she continued, 'Anyway, if I'd had children, it would have convinced the navy that he wasn't "one of those" because he had a wife and two adorable children at home.

'But I wasn't about to stay at home with a couple of snivelling kids while the rest of the world was bombing one another to Timbuktu. I needed to be in on the action.'

Raine listened, fascinated. She could only relate to that last bit.

'But you still wear your wedding ring,' she ventured.

'That's true,' Audrey agreed, glancing down at it. 'I told

204

myself I'd wear it until the divorce came through. It's due in a couple of months, so they say. But the ring has its uses – it stops the men from pestering me.'

Seeing Audrey at close quarters, Raine had to admit she was an extremely attractive woman with her swept-up hair, almost black, and generously painted lips. Yes, the men would like her, all right – and Audrey knew it.

To stop herself from staring, Raine said, 'When did you become a pilot?'

'I began flying rather later than most of the ATA girls,' Audrey said. 'I was in my early twenties. It was a hobby at first until I realised when war was declared that I could be of some use. I tried the ATA, but I'm sure you know they took their time admitting women, though it was bound to happen sooner or later when so many of our boys were being shot down. I kept applying every six months and eventually they gave in, and here I am.' She gave Raine a twisted smile. 'Enough about me. What made *you* decide to be a pilot?'

Raine couldn't help admiring the guts of the woman. Somehow her own story having to move to a smaller house because her father had been foolish with his money didn't sound nearly as dramatic.

'I wanted to learn since I was fourteen,' she answered, 'when my father took me to watch the aerobatics in Cobham's Flying Circus – in Kent,' she added.

'They were marvellous, weren't they?' Audrey said, beaming. 'I'd already got my pilot's licence and was one of the few females who actually took part in it.'

'Really?' Raine was impressed. 'You might have been performing when I was watching that day – in West Malling.'

'I've flown many times at West Malling so I may well have done.' Audrey glanced at her. 'So how did you come to be in the ATA?'

'I had a letter from a pilot – who's become a close friend. He taught me to fly. He joined the RAF as a fighter pilot but he knew flying was my life and told me about the ATA. At that time they were only taking highly experienced women, so I didn't get in. But a few months later I had a letter from Pauline Gower to go and see her if I was still interested. So I did.'

'Do you still hear from your friend?' Audrey asked.

Raine nodded. 'Yes, but only occasionally. I worry about him, though.'

'We might as well face it that we're *all* doing dangerous work,' Audrey said. 'I expect he worries about you just as much.'

Raine smiled. 'I suppose he does. Well, we just have to get on with it. The awful thing is, if there hadn't been a war I wouldn't be doing what I love most, because my father wasn't able to pay for flying lessons for me when I left school.'

'This close friend – are you in love with him?'

Raine pulled up with a start. 'Doug?' Somehow she didn't mind Audrey asking the question. 'He's a few years older than me, although it doesn't seem such a gap now I'm working. I suppose I look upon him as an older brother. And he's always treated me like a kid sister.'

'Hmm. I bet he has a different view from you,' Audrey remarked with a knowing wink. She glanced at the map. 'Right. We should be approaching White Waltham pretty soon now. But I'm enjoying the conversation.' She turned to look at Raine. 'Any other chap in your life?'

There was Alec Marshall, flashing like a beacon in front of her.

'Not really,' Raine replied. She didn't want to discuss Alec with Audrey, or anyone else, for that matter.

'The hesitation means there *is* someone,' Audrey teased.

'Enjoy yourself while you can, is my motto, and that's even more crucial with this war on. You could be here today and gone tomorrow.'

It was a chilling thought.

The Anson began its descent to White Waltham, and with all the banging and clattering of the undercarriage being let down, Raine was saved from having to say more.

'Nice to chat to another woman,' Audrey called, the wind catching her words as they walked together to the admin building. 'The chaps don't always take me seriously.'

I'm not surprised, Raine thought, hiding a smile.

'Well, I'll see you back at Hatfield,' Audrey said. 'I've got a Typhoon to deliver and I'm not much looking forward to it. They haven't got the best reputation in the world.'

'Good luck,' Raine said.

Audrey was a fascinating character. It might be fun to get to know her better.

Raine showed her chit to one of the engineers. He looked at it and shook his head.

'No, we haven't got a Hawker Hart to be delivered,' he said. 'But we *do* have a Hawker Hind that needs to be ferried to Silloth.'

Raine caught her breath. She knew the Hawker Hind had a much more powerful engine than the Hart. That particular plane would already be a big step up from the Moth, but this one would leave them both standing. She swallowed. She could do it. Of course she could, though not only was it a much more powerful plane, it would also be her longest flight by far.

For Lucinda Morris, who had many more flying hours and had flown a variety of aircraft, the Hawker Hind wouldn't have been a problem. But Lucinda was grounded with her cold and it was now up to Raine. She drew in a deep breath. Pauline trusted her to do a good job.

The same engineer accompanied her across the airfield. Her heart beat hard as she approached the biplane. It was a beautiful aircraft and, as she expected, much bigger than the Moth.

'Can you point out anything I need to know?' Raine asked, hoping he hadn't heard her voice wobble.

The engineer showed her how to use the mixture lever for the boost. Then, to her consternation, he looked at her and added, 'You'll find the radiator shutter tricky when you want to raise or lower it. This is the ratchet wheel,' he pointed to it, 'and to move it you have to reach right down and grab a handful and pull it back. Bad design, in my opinion, 'cos not only is it bloody heavy to work – especially for a woman – it's in the wrong position to get hold of in the first place. But at least your feet won't get cold.' He looked at her. 'I take it you've never flown one of these.'

'Well, no, but—'

He nodded as if to confirm her reply. 'That's only one of the reasons why I don't believe in letting women fly these fighters.'

His last comment was enough for Raine. It sparked her into action. She gave him a confident smile.

'Thanks for the warning. I'll certainly look out for the pesky radiator shutter.'

A doubtful expression crossed his face.

'Good luck. You've got reasonable weather now, at least, though I hear it's going to get worse the further north you go.'

Chapter Twenty

Her stomach still in knots from anxiety in trying to cope with the blasted radiator shutter that had behaved just as badly as she'd been warned, Raine pulled off her flying helmet and tore the rubber band from her hair, shaking it loose. After grabbing her flight bag she climbed out of the aircraft, almost slipping on the wet wing. Two ground crew ran towards her, shining thin beams of light from the torches they held against the dense fog.

'Good God, it's a woman!' the taller one exclaimed. 'We're not expecting you, are we, love?' His voice rose in a question. 'Especially in this pea-souper.'

'No, not here.' Raine smiled. 'I was supposed to deliver the Hind to Silloth but visibility was bad after only half an hour or so. I couldn't make out where I was going. I thought if I could see a clear landing spot on any airfield I'd come down . . . wherever it was.'

'Do you know where you are?'

'I haven't a clue.' She smiled at them.

The two men chuckled. 'You've landed at Croughton,' the other man, short and tubby, said.

'No idea where that is.'

'Just north of Oxford.'

Raine tutted. 'Oh, dear. I didn't get very far, did I?'

The men shook their heads, their meaning clear that they weren't at all surprised she'd got lost. Raine could almost hear them thinking, *What do you expect from women pilots.*

'Where's your chute?'

'Damn. I left it in the plane. I'm not thinking straight.' She gave a weak smile. 'The weather wasn't the best.' She made towards the aircraft, thoroughly annoyed with herself.

'Let me.' Tubby ran over to the plane. He was back in no time with the parachute slung over his shoulder.

'Come with us and I'll show you where the office is . . . and the mess. You look like you could do with a drink.'

'I could murder a cup of tea.'

'Nothing stronger?' The taller one winked.

'No need. Everything seems better with a cup of tea,' she laughed. 'But I can find my own way, honestly. I'll just listen for the clanking cups.'

'We wouldn't dream of it, would we, Eddie?' the taller one said. He turned to Raine. 'You go with Eddie and I'll start checking the plane.'

After she'd signed a copy of her chit and filled out the delivery report, making a note of the thick fog being the reason why she hadn't made it to Silloth, Eddie showed her where she could dump her parachute.

'Now I'll show you the officers' mess,' he said.

It had begun to drizzle now but at least the fog looked as though it might be clearing.

Eddie pointed to a low white building. 'Over there,' he said, turning to her. 'And don't even *think* of going up again until this lot lifts.'

'Believe me, I have no intention of doing so.'

Inside the building was the usual rowdy atmosphere, everyone talking at once. She looked over to a small table in the corner. It was actually empty. Keeping her eyes on it, she walked over and dumped her flight bag and parachute on one of the two chairs, out of normal vision unless anyone came closer. If they did, they'd see the table was occupied.

There was a long queue. By the time she got to the counter a full twenty minutes had passed. She glanced under the glass at the food. A sandwich would do the trick.

'What can I get you, luv?' the woman behind the counter asked.

'An egg sandwich, please, and a cup of tea.'

The woman busied herself setting the sandwich on a plate and taking a cup and saucer from the overloaded shelf. She poured a cup of tea from the enormous enamel teapot.

'Thank you.' Raine took the tray and paused a second to take a sip of the stewed-looking tea, then made for her table.

Only it was no longer her table.

To her intense irritation a figure with his back to her was already seated. There was little she could do – the mess was becoming busier by the minute. All she wanted was a bit of peace.

She hadn't been prepared for the surge of power from the Hawker Hind, for a start. And that damned radiator. Thank goodness the flight engineer had warned her. For a few heart-stopping moments she'd struggled, but somehow she'd managed.

She took a steadying breath as she neared the table. The aircraft would be familiar on a second go and if the weather improved she could deliver it to Silloth tomorrow.

As she set her tray on the table in a deliberate fashion, the man seated shot to his feet.

'Oh, I am sorry. I thought the table was empty until I saw the bag . . .' He eyed her for a few seconds. 'And then it was too late. No other seats left.' Impatiently, he used his fingers to flick back a lock of shiny brown hair that had fallen forward. 'Though I am glad this was the only table.' He gave her an appreciative smile, showing strong white teeth.

She glanced at his wings. A fellow pilot in RAF uniform, but he wasn't English. He had a charming accent – Polish? She was too tired to enquire. She didn't feel like talking. All she wanted to do was sit quietly and try to blank out the cacophony going on around her. If only she was back at her own station. She picked up one of the sandwiches, then put it back on the plate untouched. Suddenly the thought of food made her feel nauseous.

'I won't talk, if you prefer?' His voice broke into her thoughts.

She gave a start. She'd almost forgotten him.

'No, no, it's all right. I'm sorry. I must seem awfully rude. It's just that . . .' She stopped and pulled in a deep breath.

'Was it a rough flight?'

'The weather wasn't the only problem.' Raine looked into his brown eyes. He'd laugh if she told him her initial panic with the radiator, thinking – even if he didn't say it – that it was because she was a weak woman with no business to be flying such a machine. She wasn't going to give him that satisfaction.

'It's all right. We all have difficult flights one time or another. Sometimes it helps to talk, and sometimes you just want to forget and be grateful you find your way out of whatever the difficulty . . .' he hesitated, 'or the danger. And if I do not want to talk, I find music helps me more than anything. Unfortunately, I must leave my piano in my country. It is a little too big to carry.'

She smiled. His voice was gentle, soothing even, and he spoke near-perfect English, but the voices around her jangled her eardrums. She had to get out. She jumped up.

'I'm sorry,' she said again. 'I need some air.'

The foreign pilot, wherever he was from, leapt to his feet. 'Maybe we meet again. I'm in 310 Squadron – my name is—'

'No, don't tell me,' Raine broke in quickly. 'I don't want to know people's names. Especially pilots.'

He took a step back, eyebrows raised in surprise.

'I'm really sorry. I'm sounding awfully rude, but—' She broke off. How could she explain to this nice man that knowing another attractive pilot was the last thing she needed?

She bent down for her bag, then turned on her heel, relief – though from what, she wasn't quite sure – overwhelming her as she pushed open the door and stepped outside in the cold damp air, breathing deeply, the fumes of the aerodrome like nectar.

She wondered again what country the pilot was from, then set her chin. Right now she needed to call in at the Met Office to check weather conditions as the Hawker Hind still had to be delivered to Silloth.

Chapter Twenty-One

Ammonia and the smell of floor polish bit into Raine's nostrils as she walked up to the reception desk of Welwyn Garden City General Hospital two days after her successful delivery of the Hind. Although it was one of her precious days off, Raine had decided to stick to her ATA uniform, replacing trousers with a skirt. She wouldn't then be put through answering questions from the nursing staff, and in the end not being a close enough relative or friend to be allowed in.

'Just along the corridor, miss, and you'll see Women's General. Ask for Staff Nurse Quentin.' The hospital porter smiled briefly before he resumed mopping the floor.

'She's in the far bed by the window,' the staff nurse said.

If it hadn't been for Stephanie's blonde hair spread out on the pillow, Raine didn't think she would have recognised her. The girl's face had no more colour than the white sheet tucked around her neck and there were dark shadows under her closed eyelids. She and Stephanie weren't particularly bosom pals, but it was awful seeing one of her fellow pilots looking so ill.

'Stephanie, it's Lorraine,' Raine said softly. Stephanie's large blue eyes flickered open. 'I'm so sorry you're not feeling well.'

'It's nice of you to come.' Stephanie's voice had lost its

usual brightness. 'There's a chair by the bed. Can you prop me up a bit?' She struggled to sit up.

Raine piled the pillows behind her and when Stephanie was comfortable, she said, 'Are you feeling any better?'

Stephanie shook her head. 'No, I'm still feeling absolutely rotten.' She put her hand across her forehead. 'I've got a blinding headache that simply won't go away and I feel sick all the time.'

Raine chewed her lip. It sounded serious.

'What has the doctor said?'

'He thought at first it might be a very bad migraine, but I told him I've never had headaches unless I've had a few too many at the bar.' She tried to smile, but Raine could tell it was an effort.

'Tell me what happened.'

Stephanie sighed. 'I'd felt so happy through the flight as for once it was a fine day – lovely blue cloudless sky . . . you know that marvellous feeling that you're all alone and free from any troubles. Then as I was about to prepare for landing I started to feel ill . . . sort of woozy and nauseous, and my vision was blurred. I actually felt scared, which isn't like me, but I tried to keep calm, as we've been trained.

'Anyway, I managed to land the damned thing, but when I tried to get out of the cockpit I collapsed. Thank goodness one of the ground crew got me out.' She pulled the sheet free from her neck as though it was choking her. 'They just thought I'd had a rough flight and a cup of tea would pull me round. Next thing I knew I woke up in hospital.' She looked at Raine. 'I've been thinking and thinking, lying here. Goodness knows, I've had plenty of time. But you know what, Lorraine. I've come to the conclusion it was the aeroplane and nothing to do with my health.'

Raine startled. 'What were you flying?'

'A Typhoon. And they haven't got the best reputation. Some pilots won't even touch them. I heard of one pilot who died when the bloody floor dropped out.' She winced and Raine couldn't tell if it was from the pain in her head or for the unfortunate pilot.

'Are you saying there was some fault with the plane?'

'Yes.'

'But at least you managed to bring the plane down safely,' Raine said, hoping her words would offer at least a crumb of comfort that Stephanie had been skilled and cool-headed enough not to have gone to pieces.

'At one point I almost thought of baling out,' Stephanie said. 'And now I wish I had. Because I think I've been poisoned!'

Raine's mouth fell open. 'Stephanie, are you serious?'

'Dead serious.' Stephanie looked directly at her. 'I think there was a leak from the exhaust. That's the only place I can think of. And some sort of poisonous gas escaped.'

'I've never heard anything like this happening before with any aircraft.' Raine paused. 'You need to report this to your doctor.'

'Don't worry, I've already told him this morning what I think. It's taken that long to clear my head enough and think what it could be. He said I could be right and he's going to run some tests.' She looked up and Raine's heart turned over at how unfocused the girl's beautiful blue eyes were. 'I just want to get out of here and back to work. But I don't know how long that'll be.'

Raine patted her hand. 'You're going to be all right, Stephanie,' she said. 'I just know it. You just need rest and don't worry about anything.'

'I'll try.' Stephanie leant her head back on the pillow and closed her eyes.

216

'Come back soon,' Raine said, her heart going out to the still figure. 'We all miss you.' She hesitated then added with a sincerity that surprised herself, '*I* miss you, dammit.'

She was rewarded by the hint of a smile on Stephanie's pale lips.

Raine couldn't get Stephanie out of her mind on the way back to the airfield. Something was terribly wrong, she was sure. She felt guilty for ever having had uncharitable thoughts about her. It was very frightening if there really was a mechanical fault with the Typhoon and other pilots were still flying them. She remembered Audrey had mentioned she had to deliver one only yesterday. She closed her eyes, her thoughts barely coherent. *Please God let Stephanie get well. Let her make a full recovery.*

As she stepped off the bus she made up her mind she would talk to Pauline – tell her about Stephanie's fears. It wasn't just the doctors who needed to run tests, it was the flight engineers on the Typhoon itself.

Pauline was the first person Raine spotted as she came through the door, but instead of her usual smile, the CO said, 'Lorraine, can you come to my office right away?'

What was up? Had she done something wrong? She couldn't think of anything. Was it Maman? Had she telephoned to insist her daughter go home to look after her? Well, she'd have a word with Dr Hall first to see whether he'd checked up on her mother as he'd promised. Her heart beat hard against her chest as she took a seat on the other side of the desk. Pauline removed her glasses as she regarded Raine.

'My dear, I'm afraid I have some distressing news.'

Fear squeezed her stomach. *Oh, no. Not Maman. Please don't say that Maman really does have a bad heart—*

'. . . so we don't know any more than that at the moment,' Pauline Gower finished.

What was that? Pauline hasn't mentioned Maman.

Raine looked across at Pauline. 'I'm so sorry, but would you please repeat what you've just said. I didn't quite catch it all.'

'I said that Flight Lieutenant Douglas White, who I believe is a friend of yours, is missing and that we don't know anything further at the moment.'

Not Doug. She gripped the edge of the desk. She mustn't cry . . . wouldn't cry in front of her CO. She was made of firmer stuff. But she wasn't. She sat very still, as though the stillness, her outward calm, would make everything all right. She wouldn't break down. She looked at Pauline with a steady expression, though her heart was bursting with anxiety. She opened her mouth, but no words came out.

'When did you know?' she finally whispered.

'The call from the RAF came about an hour ago. I believe you were at the hospital visiting Stephanie.'

'I was.' She must remember to talk to Pauline about poor Stephanie, as well. But now she needed to know about Doug. She swallowed the bile that had risen in her throat. 'Was Doug . . . was he shot down?'

'We don't know exactly, but they presume so. Most of the other planes returned but his and one other didn't. His CO promised to come back with more details as soon as he knows more.'

'How did they know I was Doug's friend?'

'One of his pals found a letter from you in his locker.'

She blinked back the threatening tears. Doug was her staunchest ally. Her best friend who always listened and encouraged her.

'Missing, presumed dead,' she said flatly.

'They haven't said that.' Pauline put her glasses on as she glanced at the notes she must have made when she took the phone call. 'They've said "missing". Try very hard not to worry until we know more. One step at a time.'

That's what she'd told Alec they must do. And now the words felt hollow.

'Would you like to be by yourself for a while?'

'No,' Raine said emphatically. 'I'll be all right.'

'How did you find Stephanie?' Pauline asked after a few seconds' pause.

Thankful Pauline had reminded her about poor Stephanie, she said, 'She's not at all well. I'm quite worried about her. They're running tests but she thinks it's the plane – the Typhoon – that should be tested.'

Pauline stiffened, suddenly alert. 'What do you mean?'

'She thinks the plane's at fault and nothing to do with her health. That there was some kind of leak of poisonous gases.'

Pauline twiddled her pen, a grim expression on her face. 'Thank you for seeing her and finding this out, Lorraine. I need to get to the bottom of it. But first I'm phoning the hospital to tell them what Stephanie suspects, if she hasn't done so already, so they give her the correct tests.' She made some more notes, then looked up. 'If Stephanie is right and she *was* poisoned, we could so easily have lost her.'

As I believe I've lost Doug. But she didn't say it aloud.

As though reading her thoughts, Pauline said gently, 'Meanwhile, we must hope for the very best for your friend, Douglas.'

'What's up, Raine? You look awful.'

Several of the women pilots, including Audrey, were huddled round a table in the mess, each enjoying a bowl of soup and

219

a hunk of bread, but they all looked at Raine as she squeezed between them. She'd thought she was hungry but now the smell of cabbage curdled her stomach. All she saw was a fight between Doug's Spit and a German plane, then a bang and Doug's Spit nose-diving in a deadly descent, then bursting into flames – burning him alive. She shuddered. She mustn't think like that. He was missing . . . not dead. Not confirmed yet, anyway. She must *not* give up hope until she was told any different. He might have been found by the enemy.

A chill ran down her spine. If he'd been taken prisoner she wouldn't see him until after the war – whenever that would be. And what kind of condition would he be in? It would be the end of his flying career, that was certain.

She didn't feel like telling anyone about him. She didn't want sympathy. She must do as Pauline said – try not to worry until there was more news. But it was easy for anyone to say if they'd never gone through something similar. She let out a trembling sigh. The only thing left was to carry on.

The others sat waiting.

'I've been to the hospital to see Stephanie.' Raine quickly told them what had happened, and Stephanie's suspicions.

No one carried on eating while she was talking. When she'd finished there was a horrified silence.

Then Beth said, 'She was absolutely fine on the day she delivered that plane and full of her usual beans. Couldn't wait to fly her first Typhoon – and it was a glorious day for a change.'

'Well, I've reported to Pauline, so we can only wait and see.'

'I'm bloody well not going to step foot in another Typhoon until they get to the bottom of this,' Audrey said firmly, getting up. 'I've never liked them . . . for one thing, they're frightful to start in cold weather, which we've got coming up. No, I don't think Pauline should make any of us deliver them until she finds out for certain that there's no danger.'

Five days later one of the clerks handed Raine a letter. It was from Doug! Her heart leapt with relief and joy. He was alive and he'd written to her! Luckily, her first delivery wasn't until mid-morning. She rushed off to the crew room which was only occupied by Gwen Masters, one of the small batch of pilots Pauline had initially taken on. Everyone was in awe of Gwen as, like Pauline Gower, she had set up her own flying school before the war. At the moment the older girl was absorbed in a book, but raised her head as Raine crept in.

'How're you doing, kid?' she said, smiling encouragingly.

'So far, so good,' Raine said. *Oh, Gwen, please go back to your book so I can read my letter in peace.*

'Have you delivered a Spit yet?' Gwen asked.

Raine shook her head, the very word sending fear through her limbs.

'Then you're in for a treat.' Gwen snapped her book shut. 'It's a true woman's plane. You're going to love it.'

Raine gulped. 'Gwen, I'm sorry not to be very sociable, but I've just had a letter from my friend who I was told was missing. But he's alive.' A tear trickled down her cheek and she wiped it away with her finger. 'Silly, I know—'

'That's marvellous news, Raine.' Gwen smiled. She got up and put an arm around Raine's shoulders. 'Then I'll leave you to enjoy your letter in peace.'

Raine breathed out. She tore open the envelope and took out the two sheets of paper.

My dear Raine,
  I'm sorry I haven't written lately – Jerry's been busier

221

than usual. But even when you don't hear from me you're always on my mind and I love receiving letters from you, knowing you are enjoying your work.

I was so sorry to hear about your father. I liked him a lot. I always felt he wanted the best for you. Please give my sympathies to your mother and sisters, although I've not yet met them.

Dearest Raine, I know I've always treated you like the kid sister I never had, and it was a delight to teach you to fly and I can't tell you how proud I am that you've been accepted in the ATA. I know it's the perfect place for you, doing what you love and knowing you're doing a damned good job – the same as any man. I know that's important to you! The chaps tease me because I call my Spit 'Raine'. It makes me feel closer to you.

But one day this war has to end. And when it does, and if we both survive – please God that you will – I'm hoping we can be together – in a different way. What I'm trying to say, Raine, is that I'm in love with you.

Raine gasped. *Oh, Doug. Dear Doug.* These were the words she'd once longed to hear when she was too young to understand what love meant or how to recognise it when it came along. She held her hands on either side of her head as she read that last sentence over and over, not able to think straight.

'For heaven's sake, Raine, pull yourself together,' she said aloud after long agonising moments.

She read on.

I think I fell in love the first time I saw you swinging on the gate at Biggin Hill. A lanky sixteen-year-old, with a serious vision of what she wanted in life. I was determined then to help you achieve it. But I had to wait for you to grow up before I could think we might have a future. And now you have. You've grown into a lovely woman who I want to spend

There was a page missing. Raine looked in the envelope again, but there was nothing. She read the two pages again and shook her head, puzzled. This wasn't the letter of someone who'd been shot down. Who'd been missing for nearly a week. She looked at the date at the top of the page which she hadn't really registered: *3rd October*. What was the exact day Pauline had called her in?

She counted back. It was last Wednesday, the eighth. This letter was dated the third, which would have been the Friday. She swallowed hard as realisation almost knocked her sideways. He must have been answering her last letter before the boys had their orders to scramble, then dropped his pen and rushed out with the others and . . .

Dear God, she couldn't think any more. Only the image, again and again . . . Fate had played the cruellest of tricks with the timing.

Desperate not to be sick where she stood, she fled to the lavatory and brought up her breakfast. Sweating and shivering, she rose from the bowl on trembling legs. She glanced in the mirror. A dishevelled, wild-eyed woman stared back at her. Abruptly, she turned away. She would keep this to herself.

But that night she wept hot bitter tears into her pillow. Doug loved her the way she'd dreamed of when she was sixteen. If he was still alive, maybe his love for her would help him to survive . . . she wouldn't think further.

Without warning Alec Marshall's image floated in front of her, making her catch her breath. What if something

223

happened to him, too? If *he* was shot down? It made no difference that he wasn't a fighter pilot. His job was equally dangerous, especially if he was caught. And she'd told him it was best not to write to her. How could she have been so horrible not to have allowed such a little thing, which no doubt would have given him a few minutes' pleasure?

And if she were honest, she would have liked to receive his letters. When they weren't arguing she had to admit he fascinated her. He was a man she wanted to know more about. But she'd treated him as though he didn't matter. No wonder he'd simply walked away. Out of her life. And she'd done nothing to stop him.

She couldn't think further about Alec, either. All her prayers must be for Doug that he might still be alive. And Stephanie's recovery, too, of course.

Chapter Twenty-Two

October 1941

Raine hadn't gone home for several weeks. She thought it best to let things quieten down with her mother. She'd had a note from Dr Hall telling her he'd been to see her and that she was resigned to the fact that Raine needed to help the war effort. She was not to worry – her mother was in good health, and she had Suzanne and Véronique with her. Raine was grateful to receive such reassurance, though it didn't entirely relieve her guilt.

One morning Pauline Gower called her into her office.

'We're very pleased with you, my dear,' she said as soon as Raine had sat down. 'You're becoming a fine pilot.' She looked closely at Raine. 'How are things with your mother now?'

'My sisters tell me she's much calmer and taking more interest in what's going on around her, so I suppose that's some progress.'

'Well, I think she'd be proud of her daughter if she knew what an excellent job she was doing,' Pauline said. 'And I believe it's time for you to deliver a Spitfire. You've done your next phase of training on a single-engine fighter, so we'll make sure you have a delivery next week.'

'Thank you,' Raine murmured.

She couldn't let on to Pauline that it brought her out in a cold sweat just thinking about it. Doug had been in his Spitfire when something had gone terribly wrong. She tried to concentrate on Pauline's words, but it didn't matter that any of the other women who were already delivering them said they were the most beautiful planes to look at, and even more so to fly. She'd still heard no more word from Doug and was trying to brace herself for the worst. And delivering a Spitfire would not be helping how she felt at the moment, even though it had once been her dream to fly one.

'Once you've flown a Spit you'll be reluctant to fly anything else,' Pauline was saying. 'And you automatically become Second Officer Lorraine Linfoot – with an extra stripe.'

The CO was looking for some kind of reaction. Raine forced a smile. 'Yes, I understand that is the case. Thank you.'

'That will be all, my dear.' Pauline rose from her desk. 'Ah, one other thing. Have you heard any further news of your friend, Douglas White?'

'No,' Raine said, the familiar numbness creeping over her.

'Let's hope you hear something soon,' Pauline said. 'We mustn't lose hope.'

Raine had been trying to rest to calm her nerves, but was too strung up to do anything but fidget. She was called to the phone in the crew room only two hours later.

'Am I speaking to Miss Lorraine Linfoot?'

'Yes.'

Please tell me he's been found. He's all right.

'I'm Peter Hilbert, Douglas White's wing commander.' There was a pause. 'I understand you're a close friend of his and I believe you're aware that he's missing.'

Raine gripped the receiver. 'Yes. Have you heard anything?'

She squeezed her eyes shut to concentrate on his answer. 'We have some more details about what might have happened.' She heard him clear his throat. 'One of our planes was shot at just as our chap was about to leave the French coast – he was flying close to another one of ours, who was in the line of fire as well. He baled out and saw this pilot doing the same thing – we can only assume it was White. But he never registered White's parachute opening due to the fact he was concentrating on getting out of the way of the firing double-quick. White's Spitfire would have taken a complete nosedive and there's no way we'd be able to find it – it'd be deeply buried on French soil.'

Nausea rose to her throat. 'But it's still possible he's alive?'

'It's possible, I suppose, but we've heard no sign at all from him.'

'Then there's still a chance . . .'

'A slim chance he's been picked up . . .' Another pause. 'But that might not be so good if it was the Germans.'

'No, it wouldn't.' Raine felt sick. She didn't think she could carry on with the conversation much longer.

'If we hear anything more we'll be sure to let you know, but for the time being, all I can say is how sorry I am. He was one of the best.'

Was one of the best. Peter Hilbert obviously thought there was little hope that he was still alive. Her throat closed. She was choking . . . She began to cough and felt for her hand-kerchief.

'Are you all right?' The voice sounded concerned.

'Yes,' she said flatly, then added, 'Thank you very much for telephoning me.'

Her legs feeling like lead, Raine put the receiver back. So if it really was him baling out and his parachute hadn't opened, it would have been terrifying when he realised he wasn't going to come out of this one. Was she his last thought? She swallowed hard, wishing she smoked. They said it calmed your nerves. It's what Doug used to say. He smoked incessantly and said it was as loyal as any friend. He was only twenty-six. And he'd been waiting all these years for her to become a woman.

But would she have actually married him? She closed her eyes. She didn't know the answer to that one – even if she'd never met Alec.

True to Pauline Gower's word, a week later, Raine collected a chit that up until a few weeks ago would have filled her with joy. She was to deliver her first Spitfire from the factory in Eastleigh in Hampshire to RAF Lyneham. It was only a short hop but the excitement she would normally have felt to be flying one was gone, replaced only with misery that she would be reminded every second of Doug's last flight. She shook herself. She was becoming maudlin. Doug wouldn't want her to be acting like this.

'You're here to do a job, my girl, and do the job you will,' she imagined him saying in an instructor's firm tone. 'You'll earn the respect of every male pilot when you do – and that's been your cherished dream.'

How she wished she was meeting him tonight for a well-deserved drink after a full day. She missed her friend deeply and blinked back the tears. He was right. She had a job to do. But deep down she wished the honour of flying her first Spitfire was going to one of the other girls.

'Wish me luck, then, as it's my first Spit,' Raine said, smiling with a confidence she didn't feel.

The engineer's eyes widened. 'Really? Well, I suppose there has to be a first.' He looked at her with more interest and smiled. 'You might find the plane flies *you* rather than the other way round. Be prepared for a completely different flying experience.'

They all say that, Raine thought. It can't be *that* different.

Once the chocks were pulled out, Raine waved the two men away. Ignoring her fast-beating heart she taxied out, hoping she would make a perfect take-off in the unfamiliar aircraft with the men curiously watching. She mustn't let the side down.

With a roar of the engine she was up! And it was the most glorious feeling in the world. No wonder Doug had loved it so much. For the first time since he'd been posted as 'missing' she felt an exhilaration shoot through her entire being. That was how *he'd* felt. Her body became weightless. Free. Liberated. She and the Spit were flying as one machine.

All it needed was the lightest touch of the control column and it responded almost before she'd even nudged it. She loved its throaty growl and felt happier than she had in a long time. She'd heard that Merlin engine growl when she was on the ground and always admired its elegant flight. And now, here she was, actually part of it, *belonging* to it. And it was like no other feeling in the world. The female pilots all agreed – it was, indeed, a woman's plane.

Skimming the clouds Raine remembered the excitement the first time she'd gone solo in a Tiger Moth. How that evening she'd told her family. The expression on her mother's face and her threat that she would never see the day Raine became a qualified pilot. She'd never forget it. But Dad – he'd been proud of her, she knew. And so were her sisters.

And then the rumours of war had become a reality. Once Neville Chamberlain had declared war on Germany that gruesome day, it had changed everything. Terrible though it was, Raine could never forget it had opened the best door in the world for her.

Peering at the map she thought she should already be close to RAF Lyneham. It had started to rain again and now it lashed against the windscreen, making the airfield itself difficult to spot. Clouds had gathered but she didn't dare fly above them. Those were the rules. She flew on, looking for a break in the clouds.

To her relief, she saw a clearing. Hoping it was the airfield she dropped lower, and thank heavens, she was right. Circling a couple of times, she waited for a plane to take off and a second one to land, looking for a slot before the next plane came in. There was her chance! She eased the throttle and pushed the stick gently away for the descent. Now for the undercarriage. Yes, there were the two green lights showing her it was down.

In spite of the worsening weather the flight had gone as smoothly as though she were in the hands of a professional, which she supposed she was. Any other plane would have buffeted about in the wind, but Raine made a perfect landing.

With reluctance she stepped out, her parachute over her shoulder, beaming. It was raining hard now but she didn't care because she'd done it! The Spitfire was a plane to adore. She was still smiling as she practically ran through the sodden grass and stepped into the office.

A fair-haired man had his back to her, his head bent over a filing cabinet. At her entrance he turned.

'Oh, hello, I was just—' Raine stopped in her tracks, the smile wiped off her face.

'Well, if it isn't Miss Linfoot,' Alec Marshall said. 'I presume you've come to sign in for your delivery.' His eyes glittered as they met hers.

Warmth rushed to her cheeks. It was so unexpected

seeing him again that she couldn't quite believe it *was* him. She hadn't been kind to him when they'd last said goodbye. And by all appearances it didn't seem as though he'd forgotten.

He pushed the book over to her to sign. She scribbled her signature by the delivery. Alec didn't even glance at it.

'Alec, I'm sorry—'

He held up his hand. 'Don't mention it. I perfectly understand.'

'But you don't,' Raine said wildly. 'Is there somewhere we could go for a few minutes?'

'I don't see there's any point.'

'Please, Alec. There's something I want to explain.'

He hesitated, then shrugged. 'Where've you flown in from?'

'Eastleigh.'

'Do you want something to eat? Drink?'

She breathed out. 'I'd love a cup of tea.'

'We'll go to the mess.'

Five minutes later they were sitting on one of the sofas, the space between them enough for a third person not to feel cramped. People were chatting so she felt able to speak without the risk of being overheard. She turned to him.

'Alec, I really am sorry what I said about writing to me. I had quite a bit on my mind at the time. And I wasn't sure about something. You see, Doug—'

'He's the boyfriend, isn't he?'

Her eyes filled with tears. 'He was never my boyfriend, and I didn't realise at the time that he wanted to be more than friends. But now he . . . he . . .' She swallowed.

'Go on.'

'He's missing . . . presumed dead.'

Alec's face clouded. He touched her hand in sympathy. 'I'm sorry, Raine. I mean it. That's rotten luck when you know someone. But people have come back after being reported missing.'

'His wing commander spoke to me a week ago.' She quickly told him what they had pieced together.

'So it looks like he baled out as well as the other chap,' Alec said, 'but you say they've heard no word since.' He sucked in his breath. 'It doesn't sound good, but you shouldn't give up hope. Of course he could have been picked up by someone in the French Resistance.'

She gulped. 'Or the alternative – by a German.' She sent Alec a beseeching look. 'If they found his body at least I'd know. It's terrible being in limbo in this way.'

He nodded and looked at his watch. 'I'm sorry, Raine, I have to go. I have a report I need to do urgently.'

'Oh, I didn't mean to keep you—'

'No. I'm glad we've had a chance to talk, even though it's been slightly rushed.' He held her gaze.

The room suddenly blazed with light, then went dark again, followed by a loud roll of thunder. Alec went to the window. After some moments he turned to her.

'Actually, the weather is looking pretty bad out there. I don't think it would be wise for you to even *think* about going back this evening. Why don't you phone them at the camp and stay over?'

'They're expecting me back,' Raine said, her heart leaping. Was Alec going to stay over as well? 'And because it's not far, I was going by train.'

'It's late and it's dark already. And listen to that storm outside.'

She went over to the window and stood by him. He was right. A train journey would be miserable – if, indeed, trains were running. These days they were sometimes cancelled without any notice, and there were often innumerable delays

232

with no explanations. If you asked, they reminded you there was a war on. Besides, the compartment would be freezing cold and full of smoke. Or she'd end up in a corridor sitting on her chute. No, it didn't sound very appealing.

'What about you?' she said, acutely aware of his presence, his shoulder almost touching hers. 'You're not going up in this, are you?'

'No, I'll go early tomorrow morning. I'm just doing a report at one of the other huts. If you stay we could have supper together.' He suddenly smiled. 'Would that be acceptable to you, Miss Linfoot?'

A warm feeling stole round her heart. She returned the smile. 'Perfectly acceptable, Flight Lieutenant Marshall,' she said.

He grinned. 'I'll order a cab then. Can you be ready by seven?'

'I can. But I've only brought an overnight bag in case I was held up, so I don't have any evening wear to change into.' She looked down ruefully at her trousers. 'I didn't expect to go out for supper. But I have my ATA skirt with me. Will that do?'

'*You'll* very definitely do,' Alec said, his green eyes glinting.

It felt strange to be sitting in the back of a car next to Alec. She was acutely aware of how close he was, their shoulders brushing. If she reached over she could take his hand, curl her fingers around his.

She'd had twinges of anticipation all afternoon thinking about the evening to come and how she could make things right between them. The adjutant at Hatfield had told her she was very wise to stay at RAF Lyneham if they could put her up. If only she had something nice – something more feminine – to change into.

In the small dormitory where she was to spend the night she quickly buttoned the standard blue shirt, tucking it into the dark blue skirt, and neatened her tie. She looked at herself in her small powder compact mirror and frowned. Her eyes had darkened in the dim light. But she'd managed to apply her precious red lipstick and give her chestnut waves a thorough brushing. It was the best she could do.

'Where are we going?' Raine asked, breaking the silence.

'Chippenham,' Alec replied. 'A lovely old market town. They call it Little Bath. It's not far from here and right on the Avon as well. I've booked us into one of the old restaurants overlooking the river.'

'It sounds wonderful.'

For the first time she relaxed in his presence. The interior of the taxi was cold and she pulled her greatcoat more firmly around her. Alec leaned over and tucked a fold of the material at the hem under her knees. It was such an unexpected gesture that she couldn't look at him. She pretended she'd barely noticed. But when she gave him a furtive sideways glance he caught her looking and grinned.

'You'll soon get warm in the restaurant,' he said.

He kept a conversation going, mostly about the history of Chippenham, and she was contented to put her head back on the seat and listen to his voice – warm and melodic. And when she made a comment his gaze didn't falter, as though he was genuinely interested in what she had to say.

His vitality reminded her of Doug. She gulped. Tonight, she would try to think only happy things. There was so much misery and cruelty going on that she wanted to have this one evening without thinking sad thoughts. Without discussing the war.

'The canal and Brunel's Great Western Railway are what

put Chippenham on the map,' he was saying. 'Crucial for communications and sending supplies.'

Although it was dark in the cab she could make out the shape of his face studying her.

'Have you been listening to one word I've been saying?' he chuckled, briefly putting a hand on her arm.

She gave a jolt as a spark of electricity shot up her arm.

'Of course I have,' she said, embarrassed she'd been caught out but keen not to let him see it. 'I've been hanging on your every word.'

'Hmm. I doubt that. I'll test you later. Then we'll see how much you've taken in,' he said, and even though it was dark, Raine could still make out his grin.

Ten minutes later the taxi driver pulled up on the side of the river overlooking a row of Tudor buildings.

'The one second from the right is the White Rose.' The driver pointed. 'This is the nearest I can take you, but if you walk over the bridge it's right there.'

'Thanks.'

Alec paid him and opened his door, putting out his hand to help Raine. He held onto it for a few seconds then abruptly let go.

'Right,' he said crisply. 'Let's get going before we freeze to death.'

The darkness enveloped them. All the buildings and houses opposite had their blackout curtains pulled and the street-lights were covered, providing about as much light as a candle. If only there was a moon. Raine was terrified she would stumble over something and Alec would think she had done it on purpose so he would have to come to her rescue.

For goodness' sake, Raine, she told herself crossly, *you're behaving as though you're a heroine in a fairy story.* But the next moment Alec turned to her.

'Here, take my arm,' he said. 'I don't want you to fall over and twist your ankle. I'd have to carry you in and that wouldn't do at all, would it?' The corner of his mouth twitched.

Damn. He'd read her thoughts exactly.

'No, I'd hate that,' she said lightly as she took his arm.

He flicked on his torch, also covered but allowing a pinprick of light as they made their way carefully towards the restaurant, Alec using the toe of his shoe to feel the edge of the kerb.

Inside, the White Rose was buzzing with chatter. It seemed as though everyone in Chippenham had decided to come out for supper. The owners had put up Christmas decorations to create a festive atmosphere, even though Christmas was still a month away.

'Your name, sir?' a waiter came up to them.

'Marshall.'

He looked at a list. 'Ah, yes. Table for two. I've had to squeeze you into the corner so I hope that will be acceptable to you and the young lady. As you can see, we're extra busy tonight. But at least you'll have some privacy.'

Alec raised an eyebrow to Raine.

'Perfectly acceptable, thank you,' Raine said, her cheeks a little flushed, smiling at the waiter.

Once they'd sat down another waiter brought them a menu.

'I'm afraid it's not the usual variety with the meat rationing,' he said apologetically as he flicked a cigarette lighter and lit the candle. 'But I can recommend the baked cod, if you like fish.'

'Fish sounds lovely,' Raine said, smiling up at the waiter.

'And a bottle of champagne,' Alec said. 'One you recommend for a special celebration.'

'In that case, I'd recommend a bottle of Veuve Clicquot, sir.'

Alec nodded. When the waiter disappeared he looked at Raine. 'I think you'll approve of that.'

'It sounds awfully expensive.'

'We're celebrating.'

Raine looked at him, her eyes wide. 'What are we celebrating, exactly?'

'Thanking you for bringing the Spit. It'll bring me luck, knowing you were the last one to fly it.'

A quiver ran across Raine's shoulders. Trying to appear casual, she said, 'I was only doing my job.'

'But it was your first Spit, wasn't it?'

'How did you know?'

Alec tapped the side of his nose in an annoying manner. 'Not much slips by me.'

'No, I mean it. Who told you?'

'One of the ground crew.'

'Well, they've got no business to . . .' Raine started. She caught Alec's eyes twinkling and burst into laughter. 'Men never believe a mere female should be flying a Spitfire,' she spluttered. 'They think we don't appreciate its beautiful lines, its perfect control . . . What they don't realise is that it's a very feminine plane – a woman's plane.'

Alec grinned. 'The important thing is – did you like it?'

'I absolutely adored it.' She hesitated. 'Just one thing. Did you know it was going to be *me* delivering the plane, or was it just a coincidence?'

Alec's eyelashes flickered. 'I'll have to admit it. I found out you'd be bringing it today and I managed to get a 24-hour pass. I wanted to see you again – simple as that.'

It didn't sound simple at all, the trouble he must have gone to. Did he like her more than a little bit? Perhaps it piqued him that she hadn't been swept off her feet by his attentions. If only she could look into that handsome head of his. See what was going on.

To her relief the waiter interrupted by bringing the champagne in a silver bucket and poured two glasses. He set the bottle back in the ice.

Raine picked up her champagne glass and clinked it with Alec's. 'It's wonderful and very thoughtful of you to celebrate my first flight in a Spit, because it really *is* something special.'

She brushed the image away of her mother's frown and took a swallow of champagne, then laughed as the bubbles fizzed in her throat and up her nostrils. Alec laughed, too, then took his napkin to wipe the droplets from the top of her mouth and dabbed her nose.

'I must look a mess,' Raine said, desperately trying to ignore a tingly feeling she knew was nothing to do with the champagne bubbles.

'You look absolutely charming,' Alec said, his face serious. 'Beautiful, in fact.' His eyes held hers.

There was a silence between them. Raine gave an almost imperceptible sigh. The only movement was the faint flicker of the candle from that tiny puff of air, but she was hardly aware of it. All she could concentrate on was the green of Alec's eyes. She couldn't drag her own away. Dear God, she had to break the spell. If she didn't, he would think things that weren't true . . . like she was falling in love with him.

'Raine . . .' He put his hand over hers. 'Are we friends again?'

She nodded. She couldn't trust herself to speak.

'Are you all right?'

'Yes.' For something to do she eased her hand away and picked up her glass, then took a deep swallow. And another. She needed to calm herself.

'What did you do to your hand?'

Alec's question startled her. She put her flute down and glanced at the back of her hand. There was still a faded mark where she'd scalded it.

'It's nothing. I spilled some boiling water over it, that's all.'

Holding her gaze, he gently raised her hand to his mouth and lightly brushed the scar with a kiss.

She was aware of no one but Alec. She wanted that mouth on hers . . . more than anything in the world at this moment.

For an instant she saw Doug's face. She'd never felt like this with him. Never. She'd had that crush but *this* – now – with Alec – was completely different. It mesmerised her and consumed her. His eyes were still fastened on hers as he released her hand and leant across the table to brush a stray lock of hair from her face.

'You're so beautiful, Raine. I expect you've been told that many times before. But I mustn't get carried away. You love someone else.'

'But Doug—'

'Yes, I know,' Alec said gently. 'He might not be alive. But whether he is or isn't, I think you're still in love with him. And if you're honest, you'll tell me I'm right.'

'Please, Alec. I don't want to talk about him. Not in that way.' Her eyes filled with tears.

'All right,' he said, dropping his hand and finishing his wine. He took the bottle and poured them another glass.

'Is that wise?' she said. 'We both have to work tomorrow.'

'Tomorrow may never come.'

Chapter Twenty-Three

Raine turned over in the narrow bed for the hundredth time. She could hear gentle breathing emanating from the temporary cots of the two other women pilots she'd been told to share the room with, but it wasn't really that keeping her awake – it was Alec. Those green eyes that seemed to read her deepest thoughts and the smile that set them alight, like a mischievous schoolboy. Really, he wasn't cocky at all when you got to know him. That was all bravado.

She stretched out her legs then wished she hadn't when one of her calf muscles hardened into cramp. Practically falling out of bed she put her bare feet on the floor and bent down to rub the offending muscle. For a few moments it seemed her rubbing had relaxed it, but the next moment she screwed her face in agony as the muscle cramped again – this time even harder and tighter, making her feel sick. She paced the room, hoping she wouldn't wake the others, but they looked as though they were deeply asleep. How she envied them.

As suddenly as it came, the cramp vanished, leaving her leg sore but at least mobile again. She was never going to sleep now. She'd tiptoe down the stairs and make herself a cup of tea.

Back in bed she sat up in the dark, sipping her tea and going over the last part of the evening. It was almost impossible to remember their conversation after he'd told her she was still in love with Doug. He'd been attentive but somehow the magic had shifted. She'd enjoyed watching the shape of his mouth as he said the words, but not taken in the words themselves. What on earth was the matter with her?

He'd asked her about Suzanne and Ronnie, and about her parents. She'd told him about her beloved father and he'd squeezed her hand in sympathy. Then she'd asked about his family, at which point a shadow passed over his face.

'My parents are alive, but my mother isn't well,' he said. 'Her nerves are in shreds. They live in London, and of course London has taken the brunt of the bombing.'

'Have you any siblings?'

'A sister. She used to look up to me. "He's my big brother," she'd say to anyone who'd listen. I adored that child.'

'Oh, Alec, you sound as though something awful happened to her.' Without thinking she took hold of his hand and pressed it.

He shook his head. 'She died of flu soon after the First World War. She was only four. I was six. It was a terrible time. I couldn't stop crying and kept asking my mother when she was coming back.' His eyes filled at the memory, as if it had happened just yesterday.

'I'm so sorry,' Raine said, keeping hold of his hand. 'I can't imagine not having my sisters. Oh, we have our ups and downs, but we really love each other and would do anything in the world for one another.'

She hoped she wasn't sounding overly sentimental, but Alec nodded.

'Make sure you always keep it that way,' he said.

The night drew to a close far too soon.

'We should go,' he said. 'It's late.'

'I've enjoyed this evening so much.' Raine swallowed the

last few drops of the creamy vanilla-tasting champagne. 'And thank you for making this evening so . . .' She hesitated, searching for the right word. 'So special.'

'It was already special as soon as I saw you in the office,' Alec said.

Neither of them said a word in the taxi back to the station, but Alec took her hand, pulled off her glove, and kept her hand firmly in his own warm one.

'I'll say goodnight, then,' he said when the taxi disappeared from view.

Would this evening end just like that? Raine lowered her eyelids, not daring to look at him. Her nerves were taut. If they stretched a tiny fraction further she would fall to pieces. She wanted this man in every single way, so much so that the idea of it almost unbalanced her. She needed to get away before he guessed and before she embarrassed them both. Then she felt his finger tilt her chin upwards. He was going to kiss her. She knew it. Her lips parted slightly in anticipation and her eyelids drooped.

'Good night, Raine.'

With shock, her eyelids flew open. He gazed deep into her eyes.

And then he turned abruptly without another word.

Raine set her empty cup on the bedside locker. She put her finger to her lips. Why hadn't he kissed her? Was it his way of taking control of the relationship, flimsy though it was, knowing she'd expected it and refusing to comply? But those last moments when his eyes met hers it was as though he were looking into her very soul. She gave an inward shiver of recognition.

Alec had helped her about Doug without realising it. Not to forget him – she'd never do that – but to believe they were continuing the fight against Hitler's evil that Doug may have given his life for. It gave her a strange feeling, but she felt comforted in spite of it.

She sank back down in the bed and drew the blanket up to her neck, then turned over. It was an hour before she finally drifted off to sleep.

The following evening, after the pilots had made their deliveries, Pauline Gower asked them to gather in the hall as she had an important announcement to make.

'I'm delighted to tell you that Stephanie Lee-Jones has made an excellent recovery and will be coming back to work next Monday.'

Several cheers went up, Raine's the loudest.

'Do we know what was the matter with her?' one of the girls asked.

'I was coming to that.' Pauline wore a serious expression. 'It was nothing to do with her general health. The hospital doctor confirmed she'd had carbon monoxide poisoning which could only have come from the plane she was flying – a Typhoon.'

There was a collective intake of breath.

'I flew one the other day.' Evelyn said, turning pale.

Pauline held up her hand. 'Let me continue, Evelyn. I've received confirmation this morning from the Air Ministry that they've reached the same conclusion.' She put her glasses on and looked at the sheet of paper in her hand. 'Apparently one of the ferry pilots had to bale out recently because he started feeling sick and dizzy. He was lucky to escape as he was on a long flight. He could so easily have died.' Her gaze swept over the women. 'Stephanie was extremely lucky because she was only on a very short flight of no more than twenty minutes – enough to make her ill, certainly, but thank goodness not enough to leave any permanent damage.'

'It sounds to me as though the exhaust stubs were leaking,' Audrey said.

'Exactly,' Pauline said. 'I have to say I put it down to bad design. But the report I've just received assures me that all Typhoons are being fitted with longer exhaust stubs and the port cockpit doors are now being sealed. The Pilots Notes are to be amended today with these words: "Unless the words MOD No 239 have been embodied it is most important that oxygen be used at all times as a precaution against carbon monoxide."' Pauline took her glasses off and glanced around. 'I will send a memo to you all to remind you of this wording. In the meantime, if anyone has a Typhoon to deliver, I want you to use an oxygen mask, whether or not the Typhoon has been modified. That will be our extra precaution.' Her sharp eyes scanned across every individual in the room. 'Is that clear?'

There was a chorus of 'Yes, ma'am.'

Raine's head swam just thinking about poor Stephanie feeling more and more ill, yet knowing she had to keep alert to land. Even though they were not in direct combat they were all risking their lives every time they went up. Only the other day they'd had word that a ferry pilot, Pamela Mason at Hamble, had been killed while trying to land in a storm.

'One more thing,' Pauline said. 'I'll be transferring to White Waltham in ten days' time.'

There were a few audible groans and a couple of boos.

'Well, at least no one has shouted "hurrah",' Pauline said, smiling. Then her expression became serious as her attention fell on her group of pilots. 'You are brave and loyal women – not to mention you're all excellent pilots,' she continued, 'and have done me proud. I know you will carry on doing so.' She paused and suddenly the smile was back, even wider this time. 'I think we can say we've definitely shown the men a thing or two here at Hatfield when they said a female-staffed and female-run ferry pool would have little chance of success.'

There were cheers and laughter. Raine tried to cover her disappointment that Pauline was leaving by feebly attempting to join in. She admired and liked everything about the CO, who she considered a wonderful example and who always did her utmost for each and every one of them, particularly speaking up on their behalf when there were unfair allegations about women pilots.

'I will miss you all very much,' Pauline was saying, 'although the way people move around, I won't be at all surprised to see some of you again. I should alert you that Hatfield might be closing down as a training school, possibly early next year, so you might all start thinking about where you would prefer to be transferred.'

Raine's initial disappointment swiftly dissolved.

There was nothing to stop her putting in for a transfer to White Waltham as well. And there'd be an added bonus – she'd be that bit closer to a certain RAF station.

December 1941

'And now I have some news for those who might not yet have heard it on the wireless,' First Officer Jean Randall told the group of ATA pilots.

There was a hush of expectancy.

'The Japanese have made a surprise military attack on the US Naval Base at Pearl Harbor – that's Hawaiian territory, which, of course belongs to the US.' There was a gasp from the women. 'Bad news for them,' she continued, her face breaking into a grin, 'but marvellous news for Mr Churchill, as the Americans will finally come into the war – no doubt about it.'

There was an excited murmur.

'I'm sure you will all be on your best behaviour when you encounter any US Air Force personnel and show them how professional you all are. That is all.'

She nodded and left the room.

The women looked at one another, then all started talking and cheering at the same time.

'Things are sure to take a different turn now the Yanks will be coming,' Audrey said, and Raine was amused to see her friend's eyes were sparkling with anticipation. 'I can't wait to show them how *professional* we are.' She burst into a peal of laughter.

Christmas was approaching and Raine had drawn the lucky straw for a 48-hour pass over the holiday. She still dreaded going home to face Maman, but she'd have to get it over with sooner or later. Besides, she missed her sisters terribly. Suzanne wrote regularly, but it was mostly asking how Raine was getting on with her aircraft deliveries, a few details about her music rehearsals, and that she'd joined the church choir but maybe it was a mistake. There was a boy in the choir who tried to stand as near to her as the choirmaster would allow, and insisted upon buying her a cup of tea after each practice.

Keith is very sweet but his voice has barely broken,' Suzanne wrote, *though he wants to join up. I should think his mother will have something to say about that. But it makes me think even more that I should be doing something for the war effort as well.*

Raine smiled. As she'd suspected, it didn't sound as though Suzy had found herself a boyfriend at all. She quickly finished reading her sister's letter about Maman keeping occupied with her friends and her knitting and trying out new recipes, all the while grumbling about several food items that weren't rationed but were probably about to be by the scarcity in the shops. Even milk was being controlled, so Maman wrote. Raine had only had two brief notes from Ronnie. She was never a letter writer, being too impatient to sit at the table for half an hour.

After the first month of silence Maman had written regularly and dutifully, but the letters were all about her and how difficult life was without her father. Raine pursed her lips. If only her mother would take up something useful. See how well off she was compared to so many others. But in her last letter her mother had actually said she missed her and hoped she'd be home to spend Christmas, at least, with her family. *Surely there won't be any need to deliver planes over Christmas*, Maman had finished with a huge question mark.

When Raine stepped through the front door, Suzanne and Ronnie ran to meet her. After hugs and kisses, Raine said, 'Where's Maman?'

'You won't believe it!' Suzanne said, laughing. 'She's teaching a group of young women to knit. A weekly class. Apparently they're making scarves but Maman is showing off with her first jumper.'

Raine chuckled. 'Well, at least she's doing something practical to keep her busy.' She paused. 'Has she been keeping well? No symptoms of any heart trouble, I mean?'

'Nothing,' Ronnie said, her cup clattering in the saucer in annoyance. 'That was all a great big fib to keep us here. We all know it, including Maman, and I find it hard to forgive her. I still can't believe she tried to pull such a trick. Whatever would Dad have said?'

'He'd have been horrified.' Suzanne shook her head. 'But Maman must have panicked, thinking she'd never be able to cope on her own. We mustn't forget that she totally depended on Dad. It must have been a terrible shock to have him one day and gone the next. But I think she's improving.'

'You always stick up for her, Suzy,' Ronnie said. 'It was a shock to *all* of us, not just Maman, but she shouldn't have told that lie. It wasn't fair to make us so worried about her when we'd only just lost Dad. Especially trying to stop Raine from flying.'

'I'm sure she only did it because she was terrified something would happen to you.' Suzanne turned to Raine, her eyes filled with concern.

'I suppose that's part of it,' Raine conceded, 'but I think she's desperate to control us, now Dad's gone. She doesn't seem to have enough faith in herself to be able to function without him.'

'*I* think Maman's jealous of you,' Ronnie said, 'because you're doing your dream job.'

'You do come out with some daft things sometimes, Ronnie,' Raine said teasingly, then gave a start. The expression in Maman's eyes when she'd told the family at the supper table that she'd flown solo that day . . . It had crossed her mind at the time there might have been a spark of envy. Maybe Ronnie was right. Maybe Maman hadn't ever fulfilled her own dreams. Raine swallowed, resolving to have more patience with her mother. Maman hadn't had that easy a life – if Dad's hints in his letter to her were anything to go by.

'And if it hadn't been for bumping into Dr Hall, you wouldn't be at Hatfield,' Ronnie went on, warming to her theme.

'I really thought at the time she had something serious,' Raine said soberly, 'and had resigned myself to stay at home – especially with Dad asking me to look after her.' She paused. 'Supposing I'd had a husband? Would she still have tried to drag me away?'

'I'm sure that would have been very different,' Suzanne said. 'But it's turned out all right. Ronnie and I are both still at school, and I'm here most evenings when I'm not rehearsing, though I don't know how much longer Maman will be able to afford my lessons. And she can only take so much of my practising when I'm at home.'

'It's what we all want for you, Suzy,' Raine said. 'Our sister, the musician. You love it more than anything, don't you?'

Suzanne nodded. 'It's my life.'

'You're both doing what you want to do,' Ronnie said, 'and I still don't have a clue.' She worried at her lower lip. 'Though I'm still serious about joining the Land Girls when I'm seventeen . . . if the war's still on.'

'Have you spoken to anyone else about it yet?' Raine said, inwardly hoping Ronnie hadn't, 'because it's backbreaking work. You should speak to someone who's doing it.'

'Well, I'm more or less a Land Girl now,' Ronnie laughed. 'All the veg we're having at Christmas is from yours truly . . . dirty nails and all.' She spread her hands out to show her sisters.

'That's all very well, but when you're mucking out the cowshed, you might just change your mind,' Raine said.

'No, I won't. I like being outside with nature and animals. Just as you like being in the air.' She looked at Raine. 'Do you *really* love flying?'

'I wouldn't do anything else in the world.'

'Have you met any handsome pilots?' Suzanne asked.

'They all look handsome in their uniforms.' Raine smiled, immediately thinking of Alec. Then she remembered someone else who'd made an impression on her for the way in which he'd been so nice to her even when she'd been short with him. 'Actually, I *did* meet a handsome one not long ago. Dark hair and warm brown eyes. He was foreign – maybe Polish, and very well-mannered.'

'He sounds lovely,' Suzanne breathed, looking dreamy as though she was picturing him. 'What was his name?'

'I don't know. He wanted to tell me but I wouldn't let him.'

'Whyever not?' Suzanne demanded.

'Because . . .' Raine swallowed hard. She didn't want to tell them the truth as they'd start worrying about her safety, but they were waiting for her answer. This was the real world. It was no use forever trying to protect them. 'Do you remember me talking about a friend of mine called Doug, who taught me to fly?'

Her sisters nodded.

'I didn't tell you. It didn't seem right in a letter. But he crashed his plane in France. It must have burned him alive.' She swallowed, hardly believing what she was saying.

'Oh, that's so sad,' Suzanne said, her eyes filled with tears. 'What a shock for you.' She got up and put her arms round Raine and gave her a hug. 'We didn't meet him but he sounded so nice. And I'm sure Maman was worried that something like that would happen to you . . . which is not impossible,' she added. 'And if you had a horrible accident—'

'I'm not going to, silly,' Raine broke in swiftly, hugging her back. 'My job's not nearly so dangerous as the ones the boys up there are doing.'

'Promise you'll be careful.' Suzanne's words were coated with anxiety.

'I promise.' Raine's eyes moistened. 'I still can't believe it about Doug,' she said. 'How can anyone die when they love life the way he did?'

Suzanne was silent. 'It's hard to imagine,' she said finally. 'But you'll just have to remember the good moments. He wouldn't want you to be sad.'

'I know you're right, but it's still hard.'

'But now you've told us about Doug, you can't pretend it's not dangerous,' Ronnie chipped in.

'*My* job is not so risky,' Raine said, not wanting to alarm her sisters. 'I don't have to fight anyone.'

Alec's face danced in front of her. Taking photographs of the French coast, she imagined, but she wouldn't be at all surprised to know he flew as far as Germany, though of course he never mentioned it. He'd have to keep a lookout for German fighters and being unarmed, he'd only be able to dodge them and clear out as fast as possible. Luckily, the Spit was designed for that very purpose.

As though Suzanne knew what her sister was thinking, she said, 'Do you ever bump into that fair-haired pilot?' A mischievous expression took over her pretty features. 'The one with incredible green eyes – who you were horrible to at the dance? Alec, wasn't it?'

'Yes,' Raine said reluctantly.

Please don't question me about Alec.

Ronnie was looking at her sisters with curiosity. 'I don't know about any pilot with green eyes . . . or warm brown ones,' she added, her mouth turning down a little peevishly. 'I'm not so young that I can't be part of those sort of discussions.'

'As a matter of fact, I *have* seen him – the green-eyed one,' Raine laughed a little self-consciously, 'a couple of times.'

'You have? Oh, how exciting.' Suzanne clapped her hands in glee. 'Are you going out with him?'

Her sisters were looking at her with wide eyes and Raine couldn't help chuckling.

'No, Suzy, I'm not. I had supper with him once, that's all. He wanted to celebrate that I'd just delivered my first Spitfire. So there's no need to get excited, both of you, because there's nothing serious in it.'

'I bet there is where Alec is concerned,' Suzanne teased.

251

'And who is Alec?'

The three girls turned to see their mother standing in the doorway. Raine's heart fell. Maman was looking straight at her.

She moved to give her mother a kiss.

'Well, it's nice you've been able to get a few hours off to come and see us,' her mother said, allowing Raine's kiss to settle on her cheek.

'I'm here for Christmas,' Raine said, reminding herself not to let her mother needle her.

Her mother gave her a brief kiss. 'That's nice. We'll be a family again.' She became tearful. 'Except for my dear Robert.' She studied Raine. 'But who is Alec? A boyfriend? And if so, why haven't you brought him home to meet us?'

'First, because he's not a boyfriend,' Raine said firmly. 'And second, because I'm sure he has his own family to go home to.'

Immediately she'd uttered the words she remembered about his sister who'd died. And his mother who wasn't well. Her heart going out to him, it struck her that she didn't know if he was able to take any leave to spend Christmas with his parents. She hoped he wouldn't be alone on Christmas Day, at least. Then she berated herself for being soft. Alec hadn't been in touch since that last evening.

'That's a shame,' Maman said. 'I would like to meet him.'

'How are the knitting classes coming along?' Raine asked, hoping to steer her mother off anything too personal.

Her mother elegantly sank into a chair.

'I thought they wanted me as a teacher but they can all knit perfectly well,' she said, her lips pursed with aggravation. 'They have all knitted since children and laughed when I offered to show them how to cast on. They said they didn't do it that way, and it must be because I'm French. I may not go back again.'

'Maman, you always take everything so personally,' Ronnie said. 'I'm sure they didn't mean anything horrid.'

'And I am sure they *did.*' Her mother's eyes sparked. '*Non*, I will never understand the English. But I will find something else to do where I am treated with respect.' Her face softened as she looked at Suzanne. 'And how was your lesson today, *chérie*?'

'My teacher had to cancel because her mother is poorly. She had to catch a train as her mother lives quite a long way away – Bath, I think.'

Her mother leaned back in her chair, her eyes closed. 'She sounds like a very kind daughter,' she said.

Raine rolled her eyes.

'I'll get you a cup of tea, Maman,' Suzanne said, going towards the kitchen.

'Impossible. I cannot drink one more cup of tea today.'

'Well, as we've almost gone through the week's tea ration, maybe that's just as well,' Ronnie said.

After lunch the telephone rang in the hall and Ronnie jumped up to answer it. Raine, who was ironing a blouse on the dining room table, could distinctly hear her sister's voice. She held her breath and cocked her ear.

'Yes, operator?' After a long pause Ronnie said, 'Miss Linfoot? There are three Miss Linfoots and I'm one of them.' Raine heard her sister giggle. Another pause. 'Lorraine? Yes, she's here. Who shall I say it is?'

Raine put the iron on its pad and went into the hall, her heart beating rapidly. Could it be Alec? But he didn't have her telephone number.

'It's a Mr Adamson,' Ronnie mouthed, cupping the receiver and frowning.

Not Alec. Raine's shoulders drooped in disappointment.

'Oh, he's my host at my digs,' she said, adopting a cheerful tone and taking the receiver. Hoping nothing unpleasant had happened to Mrs Adamson, she said, 'Hello, Mr Adamson.'

'Good afternoon, my dear. I'm sorry to disturb you, but I'm very concerned about Stephanie.'

Raine frowned. 'Why? She's been doing so well since she came out of hospital.'

'It's not her health,' came Mr Adamson's hesitant voice. 'But she hasn't come down from her room. It's Christmas Eve and I have the feeling she's not been invited anywhere. She's not mentioned her family or going home. And my wife says her eyes are red and swollen.'

'Is she in her room now?'

'Yes. Would you talk to her?'

'Of course.'

'I won't be a mo,' Mr Adamson said, relief clear in his voice.

Less than a minute later she heard a mumble and then Stephanie came on the phone.

'Lorraine?'

'Yes, it's me. Are you all right?'

'Yes, yes, I'm all right.'

She didn't sound it, Raine thought. 'Mr Adamson seems quite concerned about you.'

'Well, he mustn't. He has enough to cope with looking after Mrs Adamson. She's getting very forgetful.'

'It was Mrs Adamson who first noticed you'd been crying and told him,' Raine said. 'What is it, Stephanie?'

'Oh, the family – I'm . . . well, I'm not going to see them this Christmas.'

'Is this your decision?'

'Not exactly.' Raine heard Stephanie snuffle.

Raine hesitated. Stephanie sounded upset. And she'd been through such a lot with that awful carbon monoxide poisoning. Should she . . .? Before she could change her mind, she said, 'Would you like to spend Christmas here with me and my two sisters . . . and my mother, of course?'

'Oh, would you really have me?' Stephanie's voice lifted. 'Are you sure it wouldn't be too much trouble?' Before Raine had a chance to reply, Stephanie said, 'What about your mother – would she mind?'

Raine grimaced. She had no idea what her mother would have to say about it, but she couldn't let Stephanie be on her own for Christmas.

'Not at all. We'd be delighted to have you.' She quickly gave Stephanie her address. 'Then it's settled,' Raine said. 'We shall see you tomorrow morning. Will you come on the train?'

'I'll see if I can cadge a lift to Biggin Hill and take it from there,' Stephanie said, sounding more like herself.

Raine put the receiver down and set her shoulders as she walked back to the sitting room.

'Who was on the telephone, *chérie*?' her mother asked.

'Stephanie, one of the pilots. She sounds lonely and is having to stay at our digs over Christmas.'

'Why do you not invite her here?' Simone said immediately. 'We have enough food.'

'Actually, I did, hoping you wouldn't mind.'

Her mother frowned. 'Do you think I am such an ogre, Lorraine? It will be a treat to have a new face at the table.'

Privately, Raine thought her mother might regret the invitation, but it was too late now. If she knew Stephanie, the girl would already be packing. And in a strange way Raine was glad she'd have someone from the station to talk to. And glad that she was able to do something nice for Stephanie.

Chapter Twenty-Four

'Put that ruddy light out!'

Cross with herself, Raine flew to the sitting room window and opened the sash. A gust of icy air hit her nostrils as she looked out to see an ARP warden glaring up at her in the fading light.

'Sorry,' she shouted, and he nodded and briskly moved on to catch the next careless person.

She drew the blackout curtains together more firmly and cast a critical eye round the sitting room. It didn't strike her as very Christmassy, with just a few cards on the mantelpiece, although there was a glittery one from Linda who'd enclosed a letter. She'd escaped the clutches of Foxy at Biggin Hill and joined up. She sounded happy with her life in the ATS.

'*They call us the Ack-Ack girls,*' Linda wrote. '*Short for anti-aircraft gunfire. And every time one of our guns go off I imagine it's another bullet in Foxy!*' Raine couldn't help laughing at that one. Curvy, feminine little Linda, out there in the field doing what would once have been called men's work. Linda finished her letter with, '*Did anything more come from his threats to you?*'

She must drop a line to Linda and tell her how she enjoyed hearing her news, and no, thankfully, she'd heard no more of Foxy, and nor did she expect to. Pauline Gower's complaint to his superior, if that's what had happened, had obviously done the trick.

Carelessly placing a sprig of holly over the top of a landscape painting that hung above the fireplace did little to enhance its dull appearance, Raine decided, as she stepped forwards to look at the painting more closely. More than once she'd wondered about it. It showed what looked like part of an old covered bridge over a river.

In her opinion the view was uninspiring – but if she ever passed a remark Maman always reminded her it was a valuable original that she'd brought over from France and was not to be touched by anyone except herself. So what was so special about it? It was competent, but the artist was no genius, she didn't think. For the first time she peered closer and just made out the name of the artist: Pièrre Brunelle. She'd never heard of him. She turned her attention back to the room.

Now Stephanie was coming they should make more effort. She would find the box of baubles and trimmings and get Suzy and Ronnie to help her scatter a few bits around the house and on the dining table. It was too late to buy a Christmas tree but something must be done to bring some sign of the season of goodwill into the house.

The square box containing an assortment of Christmas nonsense, as her father used to call it, was in the attic, so she set up the ladder on the small landing, then climbed up and pushed open the trapdoor. She stuck her head in the space. *Damn.* It was black as night. Down she went again and fetched a torch from one of the kitchen drawers, then climbed back up the ladder.

She wedged the torch between a couple of beams and bending low so as not to smash her head, she made her painstaking way over the boards, skirting round old suitcases and trunks, and boxes of French magazines her mother had collected over the years and refused to throw out. Ah, that was the Christmas box. She put out her hand and managed to knock over several pictures propped against one another. She swore softly as a cloud of dust rose and began to cough as she shoved the box towards the trapdoor with her foot.

The front door bell rang making her jump and bang her head on a beam, causing another cloud of dust.

'Damn, that hurt,' she muttered under her breath.

There were muffled voices. Then she heard Ronnie exclaim, 'Yes, this is the Linfoots'. Do come in.'

Oh, no. It couldn't be Stephanie already, surely.

'Thank you.'

The low sound of a man's voice. It must be Dr Hall. Suzanne said he dropped in every week to make sure Mother was all right and keeping occupied. She needn't worry about her wild appearance – Dr Hall was bound to have seen much worse.

'I just wanted to wish Raine a happy Christmas. Is she in, by any chance?'

Raine froze. Alec! Her mind raced. How had he found her? Why had he come? Oh, if only he hadn't. She glanced down at herself. Dust and cobwebs clung to her old skirt and jumper that she'd planned to change in time for supper.

'Raine!' Ronnie's voice called up the stairs. 'There's a visitor to see you.'

She couldn't answer. Heart beating in her eardrums she listened as Ronnie told him to come into the sitting room.

'I'll go and fetch her,' she heard her sister say.

Good. If she was quick she could rush to the bathroom and wash her face. Tidy her hair and apply a dab of her precious lipstick. She switched off the torch and threw it in the Christmas box. Shoving the box under one arm, she turned to come down the stepladder backwards, holding onto the rail with her free hand.

She was almost down when the box masked the final rung and her foot slipped. Frantically she let the box go to recover her balance, but with a cry she crashed to the landing, falling heavily onto her bottom, the Christmas decorations tumbling around her. She tried to haul herself up but was stopped by a violent pain that shot through her ankle and up her leg.

A door was flung open and a man's footsteps bounded up the stairs, Ronnie and Suzanne behind. In a flash Alec was down on his haunches beside her.

'Raine, what happened? Here, let me help you sit up properly.' Strong arms encircled her as he eased her into a sitting position. 'Are you hurt?'

'Only my pride.' She gave him a weak smile. 'Actually, it's my ankle. Left one.' She leant forward and held onto it with both hands.

'Can I see? I do have some first-aid knowledge.'

Ridiculously, she wished she could sit a few moments longer with his arm around her, without the curious glances of her sisters, but instead she said, 'Be my guest.'

He took off her shoe.

Even under her stocking she could see the swelling. Gentle fingers probed.

'I'm not sure if it's broken or sprained,' he said, 'so you need to go to the hospital and have it X-rayed. I'll order a taxi.'

Raine shook her head. 'No, honestly. I'm all right. Hospital's the last thing I need on Christmas Eve.'

'You should go,' Suzanne said, her white face appearing over the banister. 'You gave us such a fright and at least they'll tell you if it's broken or not.'

'I'm all right,' Raine said more firmly this time, remembering what a sight she must look. 'Just give me five minutes, you two, and I'll be down.'

259

'Are you sure you should stand on it?'

'Quite sure, Suzy.'

She smiled to herself to see Ronnie grab hold of Suzanne and pull her older sister down the stairs.

'Okay, we'll see if you *can* stand on it.' Alec put his arm around her waist again. 'Lean on me, but try to help yourself up so I can judge how bad it is.'

Conscious of his nearness she pushed herself up, muffling her squeal against the shooting pain as he gently pulled her to a standing position.

'How is it?'

She grimaced. 'Painful, but I'm sure it's only sprained.'

'You're probably right,' Alec said. 'If it was broken I don't think you'd be able to bear the weight. But I wish you'd let me take you to get it checked.'

'There's really no need.'

He looked at her, his green eyes unwavering. It was as though he revealed his innermost thoughts and wanted her to understand why he'd come especially to see her. Her eyes suddenly narrowed.

'How did you know where I lived?'

He cleared his throat. 'I bumped into your room-mate.'

'Who, Stephanie?' He nodded. 'You went to the Adamsons'?' she demanded.

'Yes. I thought you might be there. Stephanie told me you'd invited her for Christmas. She was trying to cadge a lift to Biggin Hill. I knew I could get hold of a Maggie so I told her she could come with me. We took a taxi from Biggin Hill. It all worked out perfectly.'

Raine's eyes flew wide. 'You mean Stephanie's here as well?'

'Yes, she's in the sitting room talking to your mother.'

'Alec, I'm not sure about all this tracking me down. I haven't heard from you in weeks since we last met . . .' she hesitated, 'when you acted very strangely that evening. I didn't know what I'd said or done.'

'Do you really not know?' Alec raked his fingers through his hair.

She was close enough to breathe in the scent of him. His warmth. His energy. Her insides fluttered. She wasn't sure she wanted to know the answer. And this wasn't the time or place for any intense discussion.

She took a deep breath. 'I must look a fright so I'll go and freshen up. Will you join the others downstairs?'

She didn't miss the fleeting look of disappointment on his face before he composed himself.

'Let me pick up these baubles first before you have another accident. I'm guessing they're for the tree.'

'We don't have a tree.'

'How can you have Christmas without a tree?' His brow creased comically.

'Easily. I don't think any of us are in the mood for Christmas this year.'

'Do you think two new people at the table might make a difference?' He raised an eyebrow, a hint of laughter hovering over his lips.

'Oh, did my mother—?'

'Yes,' Alec interrupted. 'She invited me to stay for supper, but I said I'd have to clear it with you.'

Raine frowned. *Maman* should have been the one to clear it with her. She wasn't ready to have Alec at the table with everyone scrutinising him and making assumptions. But she'd been rotten to him before and regretted it. And he'd come a long way just to say 'Happy Christmas'. It would be unkind to send him back to the station with no food inside him.

'Then I'd better set another place on the table,' she said.

Alec's mouth turned up a fraction. 'I'll take that as a yes,' he said. 'See you downstairs, then.'

Raine locked herself in the bathroom and glanced in the mirror. No wonder Alec had looked as though he wanted to break into laughter. She could have stood in for Miss Havisham. Cobwebs clung to her hair and eyebrows, the dust had turned her dark hair to a sticky matted grey, and her face was pale as a ghost.

Suddenly she giggled. Poor Miss Havisham didn't have a very good ending, because she refused to believe that her man wouldn't come back for her and marry her. Whereas *she* could simply wash her face, brush her hair and touch up her lipstick and she'd be more or less presentable again. Though whether she could trust Alec any more than Miss Havisham was able to trust her errant fiancé, heaven only knew. The very idea of such a ridiculous connection amused her and she couldn't help chuckling. Maybe the evening would turn out better than she imagined.

A jolly scene met Raine as she limped into the sitting room. Her sisters and Alec were chatting animatedly and Stephanie, who'd been sitting next to Maman, sprang up to greet her like a long-lost cousin, hugging her tightly, then letting her go so abruptly that she almost overbalanced again.

'We heard you fall over,' Stephanie said. 'Are you all right?' Without waiting for a reply, she went on, 'It's so lovely to be here and your mother has made me so welcome, entertaining me with stories of when she used to live in France before she met your father. And isn't her accent charming?'

Raine gazed at Stephanie in astonishment. Usually, you had to prise it out of Maman to utter a few snippets here and there about her life before Dad. Yes, she had an annoying habit of comparing France with Great Britain, nearly always favouring France, even though England had welcomed her immediately after the Great War. But she'd rarely described any actual incidents in her previous life, or said much about her parents who were still in Paris – only that they were strict Catholics with whom she didn't always see eye to eye. They may have been grandparents but they'd had no contact at all with their granddaughters and Maman had never explained why.

Her mother caught her staring and nodded as though to confirm that Stephanie was an easy and willing person to talk to.

'I came to see what happened, Lorraine,' her mother began, 'but there were so many people on the stairs and landing that I think one more person will be in the way. I could see you had not hurt yourself too much, so I thought it best to let your Alec help and I can start the supper.'

Your Alec. Oh, why was her mother always so embarrassing? She really had no tact at all. Raine felt her neck grow warm and stole a glance at Alec, who caught her looking and sent her a huge wink. Furious with him, her mother and herself, she opened her mouth to explain to Maman that Alec wasn't hers at all, but instead she pressed her lips together. It wasn't worth the bother. Her mother wouldn't believe her, anyway. Maman always maintained that a man and a woman could never just be friends. And Alec would just keep that smirk pasted on his face.

Everyone had grown silent, looking at her and then at Alec who was still smiling and watching her.

Raine swallowed, wishing the floor would let her sink through. 'That was thoughtful of you, Maman,' she said, trying hard to keep the sarcastic edge from her voice. She smiled at no one in particular. 'Has everyone had a drink?'

She wished she could have marched out, but her ankle was too painful.

'He's *nice*,' Ronnie said when she appeared at the kitchen door to ask Raine if she needed some help. When Raine didn't answer, her sister tapped her arm. 'And he's very handsome.' She giggled. 'I can see why you like him.'

'Ronnie, will you and everyone else please stop making out Alec is more than he is. He's a friend, that's all, and sometimes a very annoying one. Maman's already embarrassed him and me to death. He'll be gone after supper, and frankly I'll be pleased to see the back of him.'

'Can I do anything?'

Alec. Oh, no. Had he heard her last remark? He must have done. Oh, why had she risen to Ronnie's bait? Why hadn't she kept her mouth shut? Her face flooded with heat as she forced herself to look at him.

'Or should I disappear now?' His mouth was unsmiling.

'Ronnie, please leave,' Raine ordered.

Ronnie looked as though she wanted to say something, but instead took one look at Raine's face and scuttled off.

'Okay, what's all this about?'

Raine sighed. 'I'm sorry. My ankle's throbbing, my mother is her usual tactless self and even Ronnie is getting on my nerves.' She knew she was near tears – the last thing she wanted Alec to see. She heard her mother's voice from the sitting room. A stab of pain shot through her ankle and she winced. 'Actually, Alec, my ankle's hurting like mad.'

'You should put your feet up – rest it,' Alec said, stepping nearer.

Maybe he hadn't heard her crass remark.

'I couldn't help overhearing—'

Her heart sank. 'Alec, I'm so sorry. It wasn't you . . . it's me. I'm in a bad mood . . . angry with myself for falling down the ladder and—'

'Strangely enough, Raine, I understand.' Alec stepped away and pulled out a packet of cigarettes. He lit one and inhaled deeply, then calmly blew out a stream of smoke. 'But now I've seen you and brought your visitor, I think I've overstayed my welcome. Are you on the phone? If so, I can ring for a cab.'

She wouldn't let him see her disappointment.

'Honestly, Alec, you don't have to. It's getting late for you to fly and—'

'Let me remind you – I'm used to night flying. And I need to get back to the camp.' He took another drag of his cigarette. 'I've borrowed the plane so if I don't return it soon, someone's going to notice it's gone and then there'll be hell to pay.'

'Alec, don't go like that.'

He looked at her. 'Like what?'

'You're angry – and it's my fault for allowing my mother to upset me.'

He went to the sink and stubbed out his cigarette. Then he turned round and stepped towards her. He gripped her arms, his eyes burning into hers.

Electricity sparked the air. She gasped as his fingers seemed to sink into her flesh.

'You told your sister you couldn't wait to see the back of me. So I'd better go.' But his grip didn't lessen in its intensity.

'Alec, I've said I'm sor—'

The apology was stifled as Alec's mouth possessed hers, his kiss fierce and demanding. Then just as suddenly he thrust her away and looked at her, his expression unfathomable.

'Lorraine? Where are you?'

Maman! Oh, why do you have to come at this moment?

Raine swung round, her fingers involuntarily touching her tingling lips. Maman was standing at the doorway, a frown spoiling her carefully made-up face.

'It's very rude of you to leave Stephanie, Lorraine.' Her mother's eyes lifted to the ceiling. 'After all, you *did* invite her.'

Stephanie. Oh, no. She'd forgotten everything, everyone – been aware of nothing except the brief strength of Alec's body against hers, his heart beating as fast as her own.

She was conscious of him behind her, pulling on his coat.

'It was a pleasure to meet you, Mrs Linfoot,' he said, 'but I must be on my way.'

'Oh, I did not mean for you to go,' Simone protested. 'A friend of Lorraine is a friend to me, and I invited you to have supper. And do call me Simone.'

Alec nodded. 'I really do have to get back to the airfield, Simone. It was only meant to be a brief call. But thank you for your invitation. Another time, perhaps.' He glanced at Raine as he put his cap on. 'Get that ankle seen to.'

'We have a telephone—' Raine started. But he was halfway out of the door.

Raine knew her mother was watching her, but she couldn't drag her gaze away from Alec's departing figure as he swiftly walked down the path and out of the front gate. If it hadn't been for the interruption she was sure she could have persuaded him to stay. Why did she always let her temper take control?

'Lorraine?'

'Yes, Maman, I'm coming,' Raine said wearily as she limped after her mother into the sitting room and flopped down.

How she wished she was on her own. She needed time to think. Her mouth felt tender. Why had he kissed her like that?

'How's your ankle?' Stephanie said, bouncing up from her chair. 'Oh, where's your lovely Alec?'

'He's *not* my Alec,' Raine snapped.

Stephanie's blue eyes opened wide. 'You two haven't had a row, have you?'

She didn't want to discuss him with anyone, least of all Stephanie.

'Of course not. He's had to leave now to get his plane back to the airfield before anyone reports him, that's all. He asked me to say goodbye to everyone.' Even though he hadn't mentioned it, for some reason she wanted to put him in a good light.

'Taking the plane just to see you for such a short time was a risk,' Stephanie persisted, 'so he must really like you.' She reached over to a side table and picked up a packet wrapped in Christmas paper, then handed it to Raine with a smirk. 'He asked me to give you this and to wish you a merry Christmas.'

He'd brought her a present? She swallowed. She didn't deserve anything after she'd been so nasty to him. How hurtful to say in his hearing that she'd be glad to see the back of him. She hadn't been brought up to be so rude. And she hadn't meant it anyway. She'd just wanted to shut Ronnie up. Raine swallowed the tears that gathered in her throat.

'You *are* going to open it, aren't you?' Ronnie burst out, a grin lighting up her features.

'Yes, Ronnie, I will.' Raine gave her sister a thin smile in return. 'But tomorrow morning . . . and not before.'

In the bedroom she shared with Suzanne that night, Raine sat on the edge of the bed. She had mixed feelings about the gift Alec had left her. Guilty that he'd come all this way in a borrowed plane, against all the regulations; that she hadn't

267

thought to buy *him* a little gift, and that he'd kissed her for the first time, but not in the way she wanted. Once again they hadn't parted on the best of terms.

The last thing she wanted to do was open the present in front of Maman and Stephanie, but knowing her mother, it would look as though Alec meant even more to her if she tried to make a secret of it. Raine sighed and fingered the packet. It was soft. Stockings? Bedsocks? Handkerchiefs? Well, none of those would come amiss.

She cocked an ear for Suzanne. Her sister was still in the bathroom. Why not unwrap it? She could easily put it back together again so no one would suspect.

Curiosity overwhelming her, and her pulse racing, Raine carefully untied the red ribbon and opened the Christmas paper. She held up the material, allowing it to unfold, and gave a sharp intake of breath.

It was a beautiful creamy-white scarf – a pilot's scarf. And white was the colour the men wore. Blue for the women. It was as though he was telling her she was on the same level as the combat pilots, helping them in the only way she could – to fly planes out to them so they could do their job. And that he understood and admired her for it. She gave a wry smile. She was probably reading far too much into his gift.

Her fingers smoothed over the shiny surface to the fringe at the end where there was a label: Pure Silk. Nowadays, silk was difficult to get hold of. She turned the scarf over and found a hand-embroidered letter 'R' in the corner of one end. He must have had that specially embroidered for her. Cursing herself again for being so horrid to him, she wound the scarf around her neck and stepped over to the dressing table mirror. The image was striking – a creamy-white collar glowing against her dark hair. She turned her head this way and that. Being silk, it allowed her perfect freedom of movement.

There'd be no chafing as several male pilots complained of when their girlfriends had knitted them a woolly one.

She laid the scarf on the bed and was just about to fold it back into the wrapping paper when she noticed a slip of paper inside.

Dear Raine,

If all goes well it will be good to see you again and meet your family. This is a small gift for Christmas to keep the cold winds off your neck when you're in those pesky open cockpits!

I know you will look fabulous in it.

Yours,

Alec

Raine closed her eyes. He'd gone to that much trouble for her. She put her head in her hands and sobbed.

Chapter Twenty-Five

January 1942, White Waltham

'A warm welcome to White Waltham, Lorraine.' Pauline Gower smiled at Raine. 'I'm delighted you got your transfer so you're on my team again. You're a real asset to the ATA and I'm very proud of you.'

'Thank you, Pauline. You don't know how much that means to me to hear you say that. And it's wonderful to be back with you, too.'

'You should be joined by a couple of others from Hatfield very soon,' Pauline said.

'Really?' Raine said in some surprise. 'No one's mentioned it.'

Even though she'd been sorry to leave Hatfield, Raine was relieved she'd been given White Waltham. Several of her colleagues had asked for it and been disappointed, particularly as they'd subsequently been scattered across the whole country.

'Well, you know how quickly things change around here.'

There was no point in asking who the two were, Raine decided. As Pauline said, you never knew from one moment to the other where you'd be.

* * *

White Waltham had more than one advantage over Hatfield, Raine was soon to discover. The biggest difference was that it was a mixed unit, which pleased her no end. With her newly found confidence since her training and her experience of already delivering aircraft to front-line squadrons, there should be no question that she couldn't do the job as well as her male colleagues.

But her real joy was the many classes of aircraft to deliver. She never knew from one day to the other what she'd fly. Also, White Waltham was by far the more active aerodrome. It was nothing to do five deliveries in one day, one of the pilots told her. Also, most of the planes for collection and delivery were brand new, although the same pilot warned her about a special mark Raine hadn't yet come across: NEA.

'It's supposed to mean "Not Essentially Airworthy", but we call it "Not Exactly Airworthy".' The red-haired pilot rolled her eyes. 'It's on its last legs and when you fly it you'll soon find out why she's on her last journey.'

Raine fervently hoped she wouldn't be given too many clapped-out planes to deliver. Once again it brought it home to her that the job she was doing was not without its dangers. She drew in a deep breath. There wasn't another job in the world she'd rather do.

Raine had more or less settled into her new digs. Mrs Grayson, her landlady, was a widow who loved talking and gossiped about everyone – people Raine had never heard of and never wanted to. Even though Mrs Grayson was pleasant enough, her face lighting up when Raine handed over her food coupons, Raine told herself not to get caught up with the over-curious woman. And if Mrs G (as she privately called her) started asking questions, she'd have to make it clear that she'd signed the Official Secrets Act. All right, she hadn't been required to sign that particular form, but never theless she was conscious the pilots of the ATA were under the scrutiny and security of the RAF.

How she missed the motherly Mrs Adamson and her kind husband. She shrugged. At least the room here was bigger than the Adamsons' attic space, but even though Mrs G had provided a spare hot-water bottle and an extra blanket, the room felt freezing.

It was her second week at White Waltham and this morning the weather didn't look promising for a delivery. It had rained all through the night and although it had stopped, there was a bank of ominous-looking clouds. The ferry pilots were having a really difficult time with their deliveries with this awful winter. Today, she'd been to the Met Office several times in between too many cups of coffee, waiting for it to lift, but there was still no sign of a break. The rules were that every pilot should make their own decision about whether to fly or not when the weather was poor. It was entirely up to her. And she couldn't make up her mind.

At half past eleven she decided to walk over to Ops and see what the other pilots were saying about the weather. A figure at the noticeboard turned round and beamed.

'Oh, Lorraine, I hoped I'd run into you soon,' Stephanie said, giving her a hug and reminding Raine of the same exuberant welcome she'd given her at Christmas. 'Isn't it jolly that we're both here? I'm so pleased to see you.'

To Raine's surprise she, too, was delighted to see a familiar friendly face. She gave Stephanie a quick hug back. 'Good to see you, as well,' she said. 'When did you arrive?'

'Last night in pouring rain. They gave me a temporary bed because it was so late, but Pauline mentioned I would be in the same digs as you – Mrs Grayson, isn't it?'

'It is,' Raine said.

'What's she like?'

'Her heart's sort of in the right place,' Raine laughed, 'but she likes to know everything.'

Stephanie chuckled. 'I expect I'll meet her later today. For the moment I'm just finding my way around. I want you to tell me all about it – if it's as good as Hatfield. But here, come and look at this notice.'

Raine stepped over to the noticeboard and read:

ALL WOMEN PILOTS WILL REMOVE THEIR
TROUSERS IMMEDIATELY AFTER LANDING.

'What!' Raine turned to Stephanie who was roaring with laughter. 'How perfectly ridiculous.' But she couldn't help laughing, too. 'We should carry out these instructions to the letter, because whatever daft man wrote that deserves a treat from the women.'

'We should all get together and do exactly that,' Stephanie said, still chuckling. 'Are you game?'

'It would definitely give them all the shock of their lives if we did,' Raine said, 'marching into the mess in our blouse and knickers.' She rolled her eyes. 'Whoever wrote it obviously finds women in trousers so threatening they haven't stopped to see what a stupid sentence it is. Well, I shan't be taking any notice of it.' She slipped her arm through Stephanie's. 'Come on, I'll take you to the crew room and we'll see what the others are doing about going up today.'

They were still laughing about the notice when they arrived at the crew room. Stephanie immediately went to the window and groaned.

'Isn't this weather frightful? I've been sitting here simply ages.' Rita Donovan, an experienced pilot, looked up from her book.

'Do you think there's any sign it's lifting?' Raine said.

Rita shook her head. 'None whatsoever.'

'I can't bear it if we have to hang around, wondering whether to go or not.' Stephanie lit a cigarette.

They sat for a few moments chatting, all the while glancing out of the window. Stephanie finished her cigarette and stubbed the end into an ashtray.

'Right, I'm going.' She rose to her feet.

'I don't think that's wise, Stephanie,' Raine said. 'It still looks very hazy.'

Stephanie made a face. 'I actually quite like flying in poor weather. It keeps you on your toes.' She slung her parachute over her shoulder. 'I was always known as Stormy Stephanie when I was first training.' She laughed. 'Are you coming, Raine?'

Raine hesitated. There'd been a challenging note in Stephanie's voice and she didn't want to be seen as a coward. She looked round at the others. Mary was writing a letter to her fiancé and Evelyn was staring out of the window.

'What do the others think?'

Evelyn looked round. 'Much as I want to get my delivery done, I'm not going to risk it until this lot clears. I think anyone going up at the moment would be mad.'

'Mary?' Raine said.

Mary put down her pen and stood by Evelyn at the window.

'I don't like the look of it,' she said. 'It's not actually foggy, but it's not far off. But they did say it should lift around mid-morning, so I'm with Evelyn. I'm going to wait awhile.'

Stephanie rolled her eyes. 'I'm going to give it a go – do a quick circuit and see what it's like. I'll let you know.'

She was back in twenty minutes. 'It's fair visibility,' she said, 'once you get above the cloud.' She grinned as the pilots shook their heads at her for disobeying the rules. 'I can't stand mooching around here so I'm going to do my delivery.'

'Come back if it gets bad,' Raine said. 'We don't need any catastrophes.'

She waited another hour, flicking through the *Aeroplane* magazine, but with her mind on her delivery. Glancing out of the window once more, she decided the thick haze was finally lifting.

'What do you think, girls?' Raine said.

'I think it's time to pick up our chits,' Evelyn said, 'or we'll look proper wimps when Stephanie makes a successful delivery.'

Raine was given a Hurricane – a plane known to be remarkably reliable and one that had distinguished itself in the Battle of Britain. It wasn't a long flight to Birmingham. She'd get a train back to White Waltham before it got dark. With even better luck she might be able to hitch a flight back.

She'd been cruising for half an hour, pleased that she'd decided to beat the haze, dipping in and out of the clouds, enjoying the intoxicating thrill of the plane and the freedom it gave her as she managed to follow the outline of the river. Occasionally she spotted the railway track that she wanted to follow from her map – then it would disappear. Not long now and she should see the aerodrome.

Completely relaxed, her thoughts turned to Alec, wondering if he'd tried to get in touch with her. Had anyone told him she'd been transferred? Would she ever see him again? She fingered the white silk scarf he'd given her. Even though she was enclosed in the cockpit, she'd worn it on every single flight since. It made her feel closer to him somehow.

Was she falling in love?

Irritably, she shook her head as though in answer to her unspoken question. But that kiss. She'd wanted more. In that moment, she'd wanted to fold into him. But he'd been angry with her. She fought down the replay of those last minutes – when she'd told Ronnie she'd be glad to see the back of him. How would she have felt if the situation was reversed? She'd be devastated and would never forgive him. And yet . . . even though his kiss wasn't loving – or tender, even – somehow, by that very act, she was forced to admit that he'd opened up her heart.

But did he feel the same?

She snapped out of her reverie when she realised she was in sight of the aerodrome. Good. She glanced out, hoping to spot a space in between the landings and take-offs of other aircraft. There was still low cloud but thank goodness she could just make out where she was going to come down. Time to start losing height. She took hold of the selector lever to lower the undercarriage.

It didn't move. Frowning, she pulled again. Still nothing. And she was losing height.

Concentrate, Raine. Grab every ounce of muscle and this time you'll do it.

She glanced ahead. She needed to get the damn wheels down within the next minute – two at the most. What on earth was wrong? She yanked it again, her arm feeling as though it would burst from its socket, and gave an almighty pull. Heart pulsing in her throat, her muscles now screaming in protest . . . *Please God let it give.* She drew in a sharp breath and tried pulling the lever again, but the undercarriage of the aircraft refused to budge.

She sucked in another ragged breath and pulled again. *Did it give just a little that time?* Gathering the last remnants of her strength, her lips parted, her breath coming fast, the

276

sweat trickling down her forehead, she could have cried as the lever finally shifted and the two green lights shone brightly, confirming the wheels were in position.

Dear God, that had been a close call.

She forced herself to take some deep breaths, which steadied her heartbeat, but just as she thought she was safe, the clouds dropped lower and she could no longer see the aerodrome. It felt as though she were flying through milk. Glancing at the petrol gauge she swallowed hard. The fuel was running low. She eased the throttle back to start the descent. Running her tongue over her dry lips, she strained to look through the windscreen. Thank the Lord, there was the railway track again so the aerodrome must be close. She felt the tension in her shoulders subside.

But as though waiting for the last possible second to frighten her, the clouds parted just enough to show her she was much nearer to the ground than she'd thought. Thank heavens she could make out the aerodrome again. The sky was eerily quiet. She felt completely alone. No wonder there wasn't anyone else about in this weather, she thought grimly, as she steered the plane towards the runway.

The wheels touched the ground. She let her breath out in relief. But seconds later a terrible jolt threw her back in her seat then knocked her forward. She heard a faraway thud as her head hit the instrument panel.

What the bloody hell's happening?

She was aware of the Hurricane swerving, followed by a thunderous roar as the undercarriage collapsed beneath her. And then she heard a sickening ear-splitting noise as the underbelly of the plane screeched along the concrete runway.

Hold it steady. Don't let it flip over.

Biting her lip hard she switched off the engines, but the plane juddered on. Feeling like minutes, though she knew it must only be seconds, she somehow managed to bring it to a shuddering halt. Sparks flew. She needed to get out fast.

As she struggled to release herself from the cockpit she heard the roar of the fire engines. Firemen jumped down and ran towards her.

'Out!' one of them shouted.

She grabbed her parachute and scrambled onto the wing, her legs like jelly. One of the firemen held out his hand for her to jump down.

'Come on, miss,' he said, his arm firmly round her waist. 'I'm getting you into the ambulance.'

Before she could protest she found herself being half carried into the back of an ambulance and laid out on the narrow bed.

'I'm all right, honestly,' she said to the medic on duty.

'We're going to have you checked over,' he said, 'just in case you're concussed.'

Raine lay quietly, shivering a little. The landing had obviously jolted her more than she'd realised.

'I don't understand what happened just now. The undercarriage suddenly collapsed.'

'Don't you worry about a thing. We all saw what happened.' He put a blanket over her.

'I'm so worried about the plane.'

'They'll deal with the plane, so don't you worry.'

Easy words. But they did nothing to alleviate Raine's anxiety. Major damage would have been caused to the fuselage, but would there be more structural damage in the plane itself? Was it beyond repair? Whatever the condition she knew she would have to give a detailed explanation as to what had happened.

In the sick quarters a brisk doctor examined her and asked her various questions about her job.

'Not much wrong with you,' he said after a while, 'though you might get a rather nasty bruise on your forehead and it's a bit swollen.' He logged a few notes, then looked up. 'Best thing for you is to get a cup of tea and something sweet. Take a couple of aspirins and go to bed early. I'm sure someone will find you a bed at the station. You don't want to be catching any train until tomorrow when you should be right as rain.'

The doctor's prediction was correct. By morning, Raine's forehead had come up in an angry purple bruise but the swelling had already started to go down. Although still a little shaky from yesterday's events, she felt a whole lot better after her fried egg and tinned tomato breakfast.

When she'd finally arrived back at White Waltham Pauline Gower immediately put her under strict instructions to rest for the day. Staying in bed was not at all what Raine had in mind. No, she'd spend her time mooching round the village, though it was soon evident there was very little in the shops since the owners' efforts at Christmas. She bought her mother some fake pearl earrings, wishing she could afford the real thing, and a birthday card.

After a quiet supper on her own at Mrs Grayson's she decided to settle in the sitting room and listen to the wireless; find out what was happening in the news. She'd just tuned in when Stephanie breezed through the door, stopping abruptly when she caught sight of Raine's forehead.

'What on earth happened to *you*?' She plonked into the easy chair opposite.

Raine switched off the wireless and quickly explained.

'I nearly had the same thing happen the other day and *that* was a Hurricane, too,' Stephanie said. 'I was pulling like mad at the undercarriage lever. It gave way after I swore and called it every dirty name I could think of, but at least the undercarriage didn't collapse when I landed.' She stared at Raine. 'It's either a mechanical fault that needs to be sorted right away or something simple like giving it a double blob of lubrication. Anyway, you don't have to worry – it's not your fault.'

'But I bet it won't be the end of the story for me,' Raine said soberly. 'There's bound to be an inquiry, considering the plane is probably too far gone to repair.'

'Well, if I'm around I'll certainly go with you and tell them I had exactly the same problem,' Stephanie said with feeling.

Raine looked directly at her friend. She felt a warmth stronger than friendship between them. A bond.

'Thanks, Stephanie.' She gave her hand a light squeeze. 'I might have to take you up on that offer if you happen to be around.'

'I insist you do.'

Raine hesitated. Stephanie never talked about her family. Never seemed to have a letter from them like she and the other pilots did. As far as she knew, they hadn't even visited her in hospital. Raine was positive there was something wrong there. Should she say anything?

'What's wrong, Lorraine? You're staring. Have I got a smut on my nose?'

'N-no.'

'Well, what is it?'

'It's just that . . .' Stephanie was watching her intently. 'Stephanie, is everything all right with you?'

'What do you mean?' Stephanie's tone was a little on the defensive.

'At home. Your family. You never mention your mother and father.' Raine leaned towards her, uncertain what to say next. 'Please forgive me if I'm speaking out of turn, but I feel something's wrong there.' She spread her hands. 'And if you ever want to talk about it, you know I'd never blab.'

Stephanie blinked. There was a silence. Raine swallowed. Had she gone too far? Would Stephanie think she was being plain nosy?

'I'm sorry, Stephanie,' she began, 'it's just that—'

'It's all right,' Stephanie interrupted. 'If you really want to hear it . . .' Her voice was suddenly dull. 'Two years ago I did something very stupid and ended up pregnant.'

Raine took a sharp intake of breath. 'Oh, no.'

Stephanie stared at the worn patterned rug by her feet. 'Exactly what the parents said. Only they said a lot more. My father said I was no daughter of his and that he would disinherit me. Luckily for me I had a miscarriage.' She looked across at Raine. 'I don't mean lucky because he kept me in his will, after all . . .' Stephanie's bright blue eyes filled with tears, 'but because of the innocent life that came to an end through no fault of his . . . or hers. It was better for the baby that way . . .' Her shoulders began to shake.

'Oh, Stephanie, I'm so sorry.'

Stephanie shook her head and caught her bottom lip between her teeth. She looked Raine full in the face. 'Mummy persuaded Daddy not to do anything so cruel and because I lost the b-baby, he didn't in the end, but I can't forgive him for threatening to disown me and he's treated me differently ever since.'

Stephanie cast her eyes down again. 'Do you know,' she mumbled, and Raine had to strain to hear the words, 'he didn't even come and see me when I had that poisoning, but at least Mummy didn't let him bully her – *she* came. She said Daddy was worried about me being ill but couldn't bring himself to come too.' Stephanie began to cry.

Raine leapt up from her chair and put her arms around the sobbing girl.

'Oh, Stephanie, I'm so sorry. But I'm sure he'll make it up with you one day.' She paused. 'What happened to the baby's father? Did he know you were pregnant?'

'Yes, he knew,' Stephanie said, sniffing. 'He was married, of course. He couldn't wait to get back to his wife – the woman who didn't understand him.' She looked at Raine with swollen eyes. 'Truth is, she understood him only too well.' She burst into a fresh bout of weeping.

'It's all right,' Raine said, patting Stephanie's back, her own eyes pricking. 'Cry as long as you want. I'm here as your friend any time you want to talk. And one day someone will come along who's more deserving – you'll see.'

That night Raine lay in bed trying hard to fall asleep, but the more she tried, the more sleep evaded her. All she could think of was poor Stephanie. Fancy being pregnant and your own father saying you weren't his daughter any longer and threatening to cut you out of his will. Maman was not particularly a motherly person but deep in Raine's heart she knew neither of her parents would ever have disowned her or her sisters, no matter what. And something else. With all the apparent money Stephanie's family had, it didn't seem to make any of them happy.

A feeling of shame stole over her. She'd been so angry with Dad when he'd confessed he'd lost all that money. She'd kicked up such a fuss about moving to a smaller house and worrying about what people would think. But in spite of her tantrums her father's love for her had been unwavering. She squeezed her eyes shut. Dear Dad. How she missed him. But how lucky she was compared to Stephanie.

She hoped she was right about her friend – that Stephanie

would meet someone nice one day who'd appreciate her effervescent personality, respect her as an excellent pilot. With a deep sigh Raine turned over, for once counting her blessings, until finally she fell into a deep sleep.

One morning, five days later, with a feeling of dread weighing heavily, Raine set her chin and walked into the Accidents Committee Room at White Waltham, hoping against hope that Pauline Gower would be on the panel. If so, she would definitely vouch for her. Pauline had been called away several days ago, so Raine hadn't had a chance to talk to her about the accident.

But her hopes were shattered as she saw three men facing her. A flight captain she vaguely knew by sight sat between two other men. The one to the left was in overalls, and he and the flight captain nodded to her in acknowledgement. The one on her right in RAF uniform didn't. She startled at the sight of him. His eyes, grey and hard as steel, bore into her, the triumphant gleam turning her stomach to water. Foxy! Her heart pounded and for a split second she was back at Biggin Hill with Linda. She looked longingly at the water jug on their table and had to force herself not to lick her lips or he'd pounce on the fact she was nervous.

For a few seconds her mind couldn't work out why he was here. Her thoughts flew. She tried to swallow but her mouth had dried up. This was the worst news possible. Why was he on the panel? Had he somehow found out she'd had an accident? Her heart sank as she remembered her breezy letter to Linda, saying someone – without mentioning Pauline Gower – must have stopped him in his tracks. Willing herself to look him directly in the eye, she knew with every fibre of her being that he would do anything it took to get her into serious trouble.

'Sit down, Miss Linfoot,' the flight captain said in a not unkind tone. 'I believe you know me . . . Flight Captain Jones. Here on my right is Mr Browning, one of our mechanics, and on my left is Flight Lieutenant Fox, who's probably spent more hours in a Hurricane than most of us put together.'

She thanked God the flight captain with his three stripes was Foxy's superior. His expression was neutral although the mechanic sent her a sympathetic glance.

'Perhaps you would like to tell us the, um, difficulty you had in the Hurricane last Friday.'

Raine sat on the metal seat opposite the three pairs of eyes. By the way he was staring at her with that smug expression, she could tell Foxy knew she'd recognised him, but she wouldn't give him the satisfaction of thinking he was causing her any distress. She wasn't that same innocent young girl of two years ago. She fixed her gaze instead on the flight captain.

'I was trying to get the undercarriage down, sir,' she began. 'But the lever was very stiff. It wouldn't give. I tried several times and finally I felt it move. I pulled harder and the undercarriage finally dropped into position.' She hesitated. 'You can imagine my relief.'

She caught Foxy rolling his eyes.

'Quite.' Flight Captain Jones scribbled some notes and nodded for her to continue.

Wishing Stephanie had been able to stand with her and vouch for having had the same problem but who was at that moment delivering a plane, Raine continued.

'So at that point, all seemed to be well. The weather wasn't too good so I wasn't surprised there were no planes in sight, but I managed to see where I wanted to land. The wheels touched down – all quite normally – but seconds later they buckled under . . . just collapsed. I certainly wasn't prepared for a belly landing, but that's what happened.'

Jones turned to the mechanic.

'Have we had any problems before with the undercarriage of any Hurricanes, Mr Browning?'

'Not that I know of, sir. They're a robust plane, as you know, but there's always a first.'

'Sir, I think I can throw a light on the problem,' Foxy said, staring straight at Raine.

'Go ahead.' Jones sat with his pen poised, ready to take notes.

'In my opinion, most of the problem is that Miss Linfoot's a woman, and I'm sure this is one of the reasons why the ATA was so reluctant to open it out to female pilots in the first place.' Foxy gave a slight twist of his mouth. 'And of course they'd never allow them in the WAAFs.' He turned to the flight captain. 'It was only recently that the ATA allowed women to fly operational aircraft and I'm sorry, sir, but in my view they should not have been allowed to fly anything heavier or more complicated than a Moth. They just don't have the same physical strength as men. Or mental, if I may say so, particularly at certain times of the month when the hormones go flying.' He smiled at the feeble joke as he looked Raine fully in the eye.

'No offence meant, of course, to present company but Miss Linfoot is of slim build—' Foxy broke off to give her a smile as though he'd just paid her a huge compliment, 'and you can see how difficult it must have been for her to move a lever which might . . .' he paused, 'or might *not* have been a little stiff. And it was obvious she didn't pull the lever hard enough, as would a man, so the undercarriage wasn't ever in position.'

'Sir,' Raine swung her glance back to the flight captain,

'I've delivered Hurricanes before. It's not a heavy plane to handle and I've never had any problem with them or any other aircraft. The green lights were on, confirming the undercarriage was properly down, so with all due respect,' she glared at Foxy, 'I resent your remarks.'

There was a silence.

She waited, her heart hammering against her ribs. She shouldn't have said that. They could easily get rid of her – it wouldn't take much. Tears pricked at the back of her eyes and she had to use all her willpower not to say why Foxy had made such a comment. That he'd had it in for her ever since she'd refused his advances. That this was his revenge.

She felt the flight captain's eyes on her, probably noting her feeble woman's arms, Raine thought, desperate to hide her fury. She sent him a look of appeal.

'Best we stick to the facts, Flight Lieutenant,' he said, glancing at Foxy, 'rather than one's personal views.'

Raine could have hugged him.

'Of course, sir,' Foxy said through gritted teeth, 'but I do believe it remains quite a problem.'

Dear God, he wasn't going to let it go.

'Anything to add, Mr Browning?' Jones turned to the mechanic.

'There is something that might well have been the cause of the lever being difficult to move,' Browning said. 'The mechanic who checked it might not have lubricated it enough. If that was the case, then it would be exceptionally stiff – or, which is not unknown – he might have forgotten to lubricate it in the first place.'

'Was it checked off as lubricated?'

'Yes.'

'Has the lever been checked since the accident?'

'I've not seen a copy of that report yet,' Browning said.

286

'The engineer was hoping for it yesterday ready for today's meeting.'

'I doubt anyone's flown more Hurricanes than I have,' Foxy muttered, though loud enough for Raine to catch his words, 'and I've never known any trouble at all with the lever.'

'Thank you, Flight Lieutenant. As Mr Browning has pointed out, we don't yet know if anything's shown up in the report about the lever.'

Raine took a breath. 'I'd be very grateful, sir, if you would look at my records and see that I haven't had a single accident since I joined the ATA.'

'I've looked.' He tapped a file on his desk. 'You did get into a spot of bother on your ATA test, though.'

Those bloody barrage balloons.

'That incident was cleared up, sir,' Raine protested. 'The instructor hadn't been warned that Welwyn Garden City had barrage balloons. It was poor visibility and I didn't see them until the last minute. But I immediately gained height and got us out of a potentially dangerous situation. The instructor actually complimented me on my quick action and passed me.' She swallowed, waiting.

'Yes, I have the notes in front of me.' Jones looked at her as though assessing whether she was a cautious pilot or a risk-taker. 'Getting back to the accident, Miss Linfoot. Were you injured at all, besides that bruise on your forehead?'

Raine's neck had been painful for days but she'd dosed herself up with aspirin.

Foxy was looking directly at her and smirking. Anything she said he would pounce on – make out she was a delicate female instead of simply a pilot who'd tried to deliver an aircraft with some kind of mechanical fault.

'No, sir.'

'Do you have anything more to add?'

Raine hesitated. Should she mention Stephanie had had the same problem with the undercarriage lever? She decided against it. It wouldn't be fair to involve Stephanie if she didn't have to. But she would make sure Stephanie had reported it on the chit when she'd delivered it. The flight captain was waiting for her reply.

'No, sir, only that I don't know the extent of the damage to the undercarriage, but I'm hoping it can be repaired.'

Jones glanced at what looked like a formal document, and then at Foxy. 'Yes, the undercarriage failure is an entirely different matter. The fuselage was badly damaged, as you might imagine, and the propeller as well. As you know, every aircraft is precious and very costly to replace, and we need every single one of them.'

Raine gulped.

The flight captain gave her a half-smile. 'But you'll be relieved to know it's in the workshop being repaired. Although we haven't seen the report, I shall take it that it's an unfortunate mechanical failure, which we will follow up to make sure it's only happened in that particular plane.' This time he looked her directly in the eyes. 'And that's how it will be logged. No fault of the pilot.'

He made a few more notes, giving Raine a chance to breathe out slowly. Then he looked up and smiled.

'We're only relieved that you weren't injured.' He tapped his pen. 'I'd like to say, Miss Linfoot, you have a first-class record and you're doing a fine job for our fighting chaps, so keep up the good work.'

The dear man.

Raine risked a sidelong glance at Foxy. His mouth was twisted in fury. She immediately concentrated on Flight Captain Jones again.

'Thank you very much, sir.' She hesitated. 'Will that be all?'

'Yes, Miss Linfoot, you may go.'

Raine nodded her thanks. She couldn't wait to get away from the look in Foxy's eyes as she rose to her feet. She felt his eyes boring into her back as she walked out of the door, her head held high. Blinking back tears of utter relief, she shut the door quietly behind her and made her way to the mess for a cup of life-saving tea.

Thankfully, the officers' mess was quiet. She hoped no one would come in and start talking. She needed to think. Although she'd given up sugar as soon as rationing had come in, she felt the need for something sweet. She searched in her bag for her emergency bar of chocolate they were all given each day in case they were too busy to have lunch. Her mind whirled as she tore off the wrapper and bit into the first couple of squares. What could have caused the mechanism to be so stiff as to be near impossible to move? Had Browning been right? That maybe the mechanic hadn't lubricated the lever enough – or at all? If so, it would have been an oversight. A human error, but bad enough to have had deadly consequences.

If only Pauline had been here. A sudden thought flashed through her mind. Could Pauline have reported Foxy for lying about the minimum amount of flying hours required in any pilot interested in joining the ATA? She'd certainly indicated that she would take it further.

Before Raine could think any more, a voice interrupted her. She knew that voice. She looked up.

'May I take this seat, Miss Linfoot?'

Her heart somersaulted. The last person she expected to see, Alec Marshall was looking down at her, but she couldn't read his expression. She felt awkward remembering how they'd parted the last time. Come to think of it, they never did seem to part on good terms. And now, in her mind, reliving that kiss that had knocked her senseless, her face warmed. Another thing – she'd never written to thank him for the beautiful silk scarf. He must think her abominably rude.

'How did you know I was here?' she asked, trying to cover her embarrassment.

'I phoned Hatfield. They told me you'd been transferred.'

She looked at him. 'Do you know where I've just been?'

'No. Tell me.' He sat down and lit a cigarette.

Certain she could trust him not to judge her, she poured out her story but left Foxy out of it. If she was honest, she was a little afraid of Foxy. He could ruin her career if he put his mind to it and she didn't think she'd heard the last of him.

Alec listened without interrupting.

'Thank God you weren't hurt,' he said when she'd finished. A shadow passed over his face. 'One of the chaps bought it yesterday with engine failure . . . in his Spit, of all planes. Apparently, he glided in perfectly okay, but didn't see a ditch and turned a somersault. Poor sod was trapped in the cockpit and there was an explosion.' He sighed out a jagged breath.

Raine gasped.

Alec spread his hands. 'It's not unheard of for even the most reliable planes to let you down occasionally.' He took a final drag on his cigarette. 'Benny Benson. Super bloke. We were good mates. We all miss him but we have to get on with it.' He stubbed the cigarette violently in the ashtray.

Without thinking Raine put her hand out and covered his. 'I'm so sorry, Alec. It's awful to lose a friend.'

He looked at her. 'Yes, you lost your friend, didn't you?' He turned his palm up and curled his fingers round her hand, gently squeezing it. 'The only thing you can do is to think about something nice. Spending some time with me, for instance.' He smiled.

All she was aware of was the touch of his skin.

Reluctantly, she started to extract her hand, but his enclosed hers ever more tightly.

'I've got a couple of days' leave at the end of the week and wondered if you were due any time off. I think we need to talk . . . in private.' He glanced around. 'There are always people whenever I see you. So I was thinking about a trip to London now the bombing's eased off quite a bit. Mind you, it's bound to be chock-a-block with Americans now they've *finally* come in with us.' He turned to her. 'What do you think? Maybe even stay the night,' he added.

Her eyes widened a fraction.

'I want to spend time with you, Raine.' He ran his hand through the front of his hair, causing it to spring up comically before it fell back into place. 'The question is, do you want to spend time with *me*?'

Chapter Twenty-Six

'No problem at all, Lorraine,' the adjutant said. 'It'll do you good.' He glanced at her. 'You look a bit peaky, if you don't mind my saying so.'

'I'm a bit tired, that's all.'

'I see you've done eighteen days on the trot, and while we're grateful you stepped in for Gwen, it's even more important you get away from here – have a complete change of scenery so you come back refreshed.' His gaze was steady. 'Will you be going home to see your family?'

Immediately she felt her face flush. 'Er, no. I haven't made a decision what I'm going to do.'

'You're going to give yourself a surprise, eh?' He looked up after making a note of her name and when she was due back on the leave sheet. 'Well, enjoy yourself wherever you end up,' he said, giving her a knowing wink as he handed her a slip of paper with his permission.

She managed to bite back a retort. Nothing must upset her precious 48-hour leave.

In the officers' mess she hadn't known how to answer Alec. Every part of her wanted to say yes, longed to say yes, she'd love to spend her two days with him, but Maman's face swam in front of her, accusing her of preferring to be with her boyfriend (though Alec could hardly be called that), instead of going home to see how her mother was. Raine battled with the usual feeling of guilt where Maman was concerned for several seconds while Alec waited for her answer.

'You don't have to worry about anything when you're with me,' he said firmly while she searched for the right words to thank him nicely, but say it just wasn't possible. 'All we'll do is enjoy being together. No arguments, no questions, no complications – just you and me having fun. An oasis in this damnable war.' His glance was penetrating. 'We could even pretend we're in love.'

'What?' Raine's voice rose.

'Yes. I know we're not, but wouldn't it be fun to act as though we are?'

'Why would we do that?' Raine wished her heart would stop pounding.

'To stop us from squabbling.'

Raine opened her mouth to protest but he continued.

'That way it will be more romantic. We can forget – just for a short time – we're not living through this frightful war and instead we're like a normal couple.'

'Pretend, the way you did in that café in London? That was just a silly joke in front of that nice couple. But this time I'm not sure at all that I like the idea of play-acting for that long.'

'Why not?'

'Because . . . because what about if one of us . . . one of us . . .' She faltered, looking anywhere but at that intense green gaze.

'*Really* falls in love with the other?' he finished with a chuckle. 'Well, that wouldn't be such a bad thing, would it?'

'It would if the other one didn't reciprocate.'

'Let's take that risk.'

'Don't we take enough risks every day without adding to

293

them?' Raine said, forcing a smile, trying desperately to make light of it, not wanting him to see how hurt she was by his crazy suggestion. But worryingly, she felt she was fast losing her battle with herself.

'This is different. Falling in love with you would be far more risky than fighting off the Luftwaffe.' He grinned at her, such a wicked grin that she couldn't help responding. 'So what do you think?'

She picked up her cup of tea and swallowed the last mouthful. It was stone cold. 'We don't even have a relationship.'

'Are you sure about that?' Alec said, still smiling. 'We'll see. But you haven't answered my first question yet. Shall we plan our escape?'

'All right.' The words sprang from her lips almost without her realising. She'd actually agreed! A frisson of excitement raced through her at the thought of spending a whole day with him. 'But I'd really prefer somewhere other than London. Somewhere the war hasn't touched.' Did she sound ungrateful when he'd invited her to London as a treat? But London at the moment didn't really appeal. 'Would you mind?'

'No, I don't mind at all not going to London – but some-where that's escaped Jerry? It's a tall order.' He frowned. 'Leave it with me.' He broke into a smile. 'I'll just have to surprise you. But you, in turn, will have to trust me.' He held her gaze. 'Can you?'

'I'm not so sure about that.'

'I'll take that as a yes,' he said, a triumphant smile playing about his mouth. 'Are your digs very far from here?'

'Not far. I usually cycle in but if the weather's bad I can get a bus. It'll be easier to meet you here.' The last thing she wanted was Mrs Grayson's prying eyes on her.

'You don't want to do that with a case to carry. And the forecast is not too good. Possibly snow. I'll cadge a lift here and take a cab to your place – say, ten o'clock. Okay with you?' She nodded. 'Good,' he said, and took a small notepad and a pencil from his pocket. 'Write down your address.'

He glanced at the slip of paper she handed him.

'I can't wait,' he said, grinning. 'Especially now I know we're going to fall in love.'

'Don't hold your breath.'

She turned to leave, his chuckle sounding in her ears.

Although the Met Office at White Waltham warned everyone that the weather was extra cold for February, they hadn't predicted any real difficulties for the ferry pilots, despite the icy roads first thing. Raine hoped it would stay that way for a few days longer.

Even though there was no one around when she collected her chit the following day and studied the map, her face warmed at the idea of staying with Alec overnight. She had to admit she didn't know whether she could trust herself – let alone him – to keep him at arm's length. Part of her had to admit how easy it would be to fall in love with him. He had a presence she'd never felt before with anyone. It was as though she was drawn to him, magnetised, and the power of it so overwhelmed her she couldn't think straight.

Thankfully, her three deliveries were short and without incident, so she could wrestle with her conscience as to whether or not she would pack an overnight case that evening. It was obvious what Alec implied. In return, every fibre of her being longed to spend the night with him.

But Maman had brought her and her sisters up not to even think of sleeping with a man if she wasn't married to him. Raine grimaced. It sounded so old-fashioned nowadays, particularly with a war on and you never knew when would be your last day, last hour alive. She'd be twenty-one in June.

At this rate she'd end up the last virgin in Britain, she thought grimly, if she couldn't make up her mind soon.

She couldn't bear the thought of dying and never being made love to, but she didn't want Alec to think she was the kind of girl who slept around. Although if she had a choice as to who her first lover would be, it would be Alec – every time. She sighed. Come what may, she'd have to make a decision this evening.

The next morning Raine awoke and lay quietly for a few moments, letting her mind wander, then jolted up. She cocked an ear. Something felt odd. An abnormal silence. She couldn't hear a thing. No footsteps, no cars going by, no clopping of horses and shouts from their owners . . . nothing.

She padded over to the window and pulled back the blackout curtains. She gasped. Wherever she looked was white. Every rooftop, the telephone box and the pillar box opposite, was covered in a blanket of snow. There were footprints on the pavement below but the roads looked untouched. It flashed through her head that the planes would be grounded. And even if Alec managed to get a lift on an Anson to White Waltham, the roads would be impassable.

So that's the end of our trip, she thought. All the worrying about making a decision had come to nothing. *Hell and damnation.* Tears of disappointment stung her eyes. She wanted to be with Alec now more than ever, see his face that fascinated her so, hear his voice, feel his touch, his lips . . .

She was being ridiculous. She wouldn't give up that easily. The sun could come out and thaw the snow and she wouldn't be ready. She glanced behind her at the small overnight bag she'd begun packing yesterday evening. She shook herself. Alec wouldn't allow a layer of snow to come between them.

Turning from the window with a shiver, she quickly washed

at the sink, then scrambled into her underwear. She was just securing her second stocking when there was a tap on her door.

'Shan't be a minute,' she called.

Quickly, Raine finished dressing in her uniform skirt and blouse and opened her door to see Stephanie, fully made up and still in evening dress, grinning at her.

'Going somewhere nice?' Without asking, Stephanie sat on the edge of the bed, settling the folds of her dress around her. She nodded towards the overnight bag. 'You don't have to answer,' she went on annoyingly. 'I can see you are by the way you're oh-so-carefully folding up that lovely red dress.'

'Sorry, I can't tell you,' Raine said, wishing Stephanie to be a million miles up in the sky. 'I don't even know myself.'

'Oh?' Stephanie narrowed her eyes. 'You have a weekend pass and you don't know where you're going? Hmm.' She looked Raine full in the face. 'So assuming it's not your very nice family – as you'd know that – I suspect a man. Any chance it would be that lovely green-eyed pilot of yours?'

Warmth sprang to Raine's cheeks.

'A*ha*!' Stephanie said. 'You're blushing, so it *is* him. Thank the Lord you're *finally* going to have a dirty weekend.' She gave Raine a horrible wink.

'It's going to be nothing of the kind,' Raine protested. 'You are awful thinking such a thing.'

'I'm only awful because I'm right.' Stephanie snorted with laughter. 'But I can see I'm not going to get any sense out of you at the moment, so you can tell me all the gory details when you're back.' She studied Raine with narrowed eyes. 'So why are you going to meet him in your uniform? Surely you're sick of navy blue, and he must be as well.'

Raine shrugged and looked down at her skirt. 'I hadn't really thought about it. It seems automatic now not to have to wonder what to wear.'

Stephanie threw her hands in the air, then leapt up and opened Raine's wardrobe. Swishing the few coat hangers for a few moments, she brought out a straight black wool skirt and a cream blouse tied on one shoulder with a bow.

'This will look a whole lot nicer . . . and sexier.' She winked. 'Now your shoes.'

'It's cold. I'll have to wear my boots. I've got some shoes for the evening.'

Stephanie nodded. 'Thank goodness I was here,' she said, 'so I could get you sorted out.'

'Don't know what I would have done without you.' Raine couldn't help smiling. Trust Stephanie to focus on what ought to be the right outfit for a rendezvous with a man. 'So why are you still in your evening wear?' She nodded at Stephanie's dress.

'I haven't had a chance to change.' Stephanie gave a wide yawn. 'Bit of a late night. I only came to ask if by any chance I could borrow your shampoo. I've completely run out.'

'There's a small bottle of Silvikrin on my shelf in the bathroom cabinet. But please be sparing. I read in a magazine the other day that they're going to have to restrict it.'

'Whatever else are they going to restrict?' Stephanie said. 'They keep telling us that "beauty is your duty" but don't give us the tools to carry it out. Thanks, anyway, Lorraine. I promise only to take the smallest blob.' She paused and sent Raine a mischievous grin. 'Give my love to him, won't you?' She shut the door behind her with a loud click.

Stephanie was annoying sometimes, Raine thought, as she quickly changed her clothes, but even though they were very different, she felt they were now true friends. She hoped Stephanie felt the same, because in spite of her bravado, Raine suspected the girl was often lonely. That father of hers sounded horrible. Raine sighed. Whenever you looked more deeply into a person's life there always seemed to be something upsetting. She realised how lucky she was to have her two dearest sisters . . . and difficult though she often was, even Maman.

But for now she could only think of Alec.

Opening her window and letting a blast of icy air in, Raine stuck her head out and cast an anxious glance at the sky. It had that strange yellowish look as if the sky was full of more snow to come.

'A piece of toast is not enough breakfast for you,' Mrs Grayson admonished when she collected Raine's plate and cup and saucer.

'I can't manage anything more,' Raine said, 'but I did have some of your delicious plum jam.'

The sweet jam seemed to have soothed her nerves which this morning felt jangled. Maybe it would all be fine when she saw Alec. At the thought, her heart did a somersault. She couldn't wait to see him again. Feast her eyes on him. Would he kiss her again? If he did, she was sure this time the kiss would be loving, tender, passionate. And she would kiss him back. She shivered, but she didn't know if it was the coldness or the anticipation of seeing Alec.

She was waiting for him at exactly ten o'clock. Twenty minutes later she donned her coat and went outside to check on the weather again, tutting with irritation as the cloud was still low. Raine tilted her head to the sky, hoping to hear the hum of a plane, but there was nothing in sight. Damn. All aircraft must be grounded. Her heart dipped with disappointment as she said a little prayer that the sun would come out to melt the snow. The cold wind whipped her cheeks and feeling self-conscious in case anyone saw her gazing longingly at the sky, she shot back inside.

Listlessly, she picked up one of Mrs Grayson's magazines and began to flip the pages over. Another half an hour. When she'd almost given up she thought she heard a motorcar engine. Rushing to the window she saw a taxi draw up and Alec leap out. She threw on her coat and grabbed her case, then rushed to the door before Mrs Grayson had a chance to size him up.

He stood there, a grin plastered across his face.

'Sorry I'm late. We had to wait until the runway was cleared.' He pecked her on the cheek. 'You're wearing the scarf even though you're not on duty.' He made it sound like an intimate garment.

'Yes. I love it.' Raine fingered the silk, wishing she could stop the pounding in her chest. At this rate he'd be able to hear it. 'My neck feels bare without it.' She smiled, willing her heart to calm down. 'It feels so soft and comfortable when I'm in an open cockpit – just as you said. But I wear it on every flight – almost for luck,' she added without thinking, hoping he wouldn't mock her for being superstitious.

But he simply nodded. 'I'm glad.' He glanced towards her bag. 'Ready?'

'Ready.' She nodded, resisting the urge to pull him into her arms.

As if he knew exactly what she was wishing, he said, 'We'll do the romance bit later,' and chuckled when she blushed. 'For now, we need to get going.' He picked up her bag.

'Where to?'

'Well, most of the trains aren't running,' he said, 'so London would have been out of the question anyway. I thought we might go somewhere more local to you. Come on, let's not keep the cab waiting.'

Raine followed Alec outside where the driver of a battered old Austin 12 was trying to park closer to Mrs Grayson's door.

'You just jump in, miss,' the driver said, raising his hat, then taking her bag. 'It's too cold to be hanging around.'

Raine stepped into the cab and Alec followed. Huddling into

the back with Alec, Raine was aware of how intimate it was. Just like it had felt when he'd taken her to supper near Lyneham. But this time there was something different between them – something had shifted. As though he realised it as well, he took her right hand and removed her glove. Then he entwined his fingers through hers and little shocks buzzed up her arm.

She sent him a sideways glance, wondering if he'd felt it, too. He was looking out of the window. She liked the shape of his head and one of his ears that was not quite so flat against it. His hair was cut in crisp military style, but there were a few stray locks that refused to lie down in the nape of his neck.

He turned to her. 'You were staring at me,' he accused, but his green eyes shone with mischief.

'I only had a view of the back of your head.'

She liked the shape of his nose, just a tiny bit crooked. *Had he broken it when he was young?* She liked the way his fair hair was brushed from his forehead. She liked how his mouth curved at the corners as though he found life amusing.

He grinned. 'Well, you're staring now.'

She smiled. 'Do you mind?'

'Not a bit.' He looked down at their linked hands. 'Are you warm enough?'

'This hand is,' she said, giving his a tiny squeeze, knowing she was flirting a little, 'but the other hand is freezing.'

'Give it to me.'

She held it across her body towards him. He massaged it between both of his hands until the blood warmed and her skin tingled.

'That's better,' she said.

'Then you may have it back.' He laid it carefully on her lap but took up her other hand again.

'I wish you'd tell me where we're going,' she said, more

for something to fill the silence because, frankly, she didn't care where he was taking her.

'We're going somewhere I hope you've never visited.' Alec looked out of the window. 'It's only a few miles away, but the clue is that there's a special castle on a hill overlooking the town.'

'Windsor?'

'You've guessed. Does that mean you've been there before?'

'No, but I've always wanted to.'

Alec grinned. 'That's exactly what I hoped to hear.'

Raine had seen pictures of Windsor Castle in newsreels, papers – everywhere – but nothing prepared her for her first sight of the real thing. It was straight out of a child's picture book of fairy tales. She caught her breath at the sheer elegance, the size and the overpowering strength of the mighty walls. A fortress that could defend itself but was now a perfect castle under a thick dusting of snow that glittered in some unexpected sunshine.

Her face was alight as she turned to him. 'I can't wait to see it closer up . . . it's so beautiful.'

'Yes, isn't it?' Alec said. But he wasn't looking at the castle.

Embarrassed by his gaze, Raine turned away and made a pretence of looking out of the cab window, so that Alec would think it was the castle that was holding her attention. But the vision in front of her wasn't Windsor Castle: it was Alec. His eyes challenging her, questioning her. She didn't think she would ever forget those brief moments when his gaze fixed on hers. The expression in those incredible eyes didn't strike her as false. Weren't your eyes supposed to be the mirror of your soul? She was probably making something out of nothing and shook away the thought. They were here to enjoy themselves and take a break from the war. Dare to have fun. There was no need to go any deeper than that.

But really, she knew she was deceiving herself.

'We're here.' Alec broke into her thoughts as the cab pulled up outside a hotel, built in traditional warm red brick.

What had he done about the room? She prayed he'd booked two. Or maybe he hadn't made any booking at all. Maybe he was going to ask her what she preferred. Or try to persuade her to share a double room.

Her nerves now at breaking point she took his hand as he helped her from the cab then paid the fare. The driver tipped his cap and gave Alec a wink.

If he winks back I'll insist upon going home, she thought crossly. And that will be the end of it. But he didn't. Instead, he nodded his thanks and picked up the bags.

'I hope you like it,' he said to her. 'It's not the top one in Windsor, but it has character.'

She wondered how he knew so much about hotels in Windsor. And this one, the Riverside Hotel, in particular. How many women had he taken here? She mustn't think like this or she'd spoil the time they had together. Forget everything except the moment, she told herself. He was looking at her a little strangely, so she forced a smile.

'If the outside is anything to go by, then it's lovely,' she said, her heart thumping in her eardrums as she followed him to the polished reception desk where a man and a woman were smiling at them.

'Good morning, sir . . . madam.' The man, sporting a dark moustache and Brylcreemed hair, stepped forward. 'Have you booked a room?'

He looked across at Raine as though to say, *Oh, yes. Don't try to tell me you two are married.* Raine stared back at him, unblinking, and he dropped his eyes.

'Yes,' Alec said, 'two, in the names of Marshall and Linfoot.'

Raine felt her shoulders relax but she couldn't ward off a flicker of disappointment as Alec asked her to sign the register.

Alec unlocked her bedroom door and handed her the key.

'May I take a look?' he asked.

Feeling self-conscious she nodded and went ahead, setting her bag on a rack and slipping off her coat and scarf. She moved over to the window to orientate herself, all the while aware of his presence.

She gasped. The Thames stretched in front of her. She watched as boats bobbed in the current and ducks skimmed the surface of what must be freezing-cold water.

'Oh, Alec, how lovely.'

She felt his breath on her neck as he stood behind her, looking out over her shoulder. The masculine scent of him. She closed her eyes. If she turned she'd be in his arms.

'Good. They did what I asked and gave you the river view. I thought you'd like it.'

'I love it.'

There was a silence. She felt awkward. Ripples of excitement flooded her. He mustn't suspect what she was feeling. Her stomach muscles tensed.

'And where's *your* room?' She managed to sound quite normal.

'Opposite you.'

'No river view then?'

'No. But I don't mind. However,' he took her by the shoulders and lightly turned her to face him, 'if *you* mind that I have a lousy view over a car park, then you might take pity on me and invite me in to look at the stars over the Thames tonight.'

'And if I don't . . .'

'You don't have to make a decision right now,' Alec said, 'but this might help make up your mind.'

He lowered his head and the next moment his lips touched hers, softly, gently. His kiss traced the outline of her mouth and then he kissed her again, deeper this time, and it was even more magical than she'd dreamed.

She gave herself up to him. Kissed him back with a passion that startled her. She heard him groan, and then he drew away and took her face between his hands.

'You're very lovely,' he said, his voice husky, then took a step back to admire her. 'You know I haven't seen you in civvies before, except for that first night we met when you made it so obvious how much you disliked me.' His mouth twitched.

'No more than you deserved,' she teased.

'I'm not so sure about that.' He looked her up and down. 'Mmm. Very chic. Love the blouse.' He kissed her lightly on the lips, making them tingle. 'But I think we should get some fresh air before I get completely carried away.'

'I'll just hang up my things,' she said, aware that her voice now sounded shaky and far away to her ears.

'Yes, of course. I'll do the same. Shall we meet downstairs in ten minutes? That be long enough?'

'Plenty,' she said.

'Good, because I can't wait any longer before I see you again.'

He shut the door behind him and immediately the room lost some of its charm.

Chiding herself for being so fanciful, Raine hung up her red dress for the evening. She was glad she'd brought it. Her vampire's dress, he'd called it, that first night they'd met at the Palais when she'd been so horrible to him. This time would be different. She couldn't help smiling as she took another hanger for a spare blouse for tomorrow, then went into the bathroom to tidy her hair. The girl in the mirror looked different. Her lipstick was smeared but her eyes glowed. What was happening to her?

Chapter Twenty-Seven

The snow was already melting on the pavements and the sun, weak though it was, made the air feel less chilly by the time the two of them walked out of the hotel a quarter of an hour later. Raine's long legs easily fell into step beside Alec's strides.

'It's such a relief to walk round a town without any noticeable bomb damage,' Raine said as Alec tucked her hand in the crook of his arm.

'They did have a couple of bombs drop a year or so ago,' Alec said. 'A pub was totally obliterated but it was late at night so I don't recall there being any injuries. And a Messerschmitt actually made a forced landing in Great Park during the Blitz!'

Raine's jaw dropped. 'Good Lord! What happened to the pilot?'

'He was rescued and I'm sure dealt with appropriately. I'm not certain of all the ins and outs but I did go with some pals to see the same plane they put on display a few weeks later. You could go and look at it for sixpence a time.' He grinned at her. 'Apparently, they raised quite a bit of cash for the Hurricane Fighter Fund – a nice ironic twist, don't you think?'

Raine couldn't help a chuckle. 'But couldn't you have looked without paying sixpence if it was out there for everyone to see?'

'No, they had it behind a tall canvas screen. It was quite something. And would have been a disaster if it hadn't landed in the park.'

Raine imagined the scene. 'It could so easily have crashed into the castle,' she said with an inward shiver, 'killing all the royal family.'

'No, I think the castle is reasonably safe. The pilot would have avoided that at all costs.' Alec glanced at her. 'You may not know, but it's rumoured that if there's ever an invasion – and they won't rule it out yet – dear Mr Hitler has his sights set on Windsor for his own ends. He probably sees himself and his henchmen lording it up in the castle. So it's likely he's forbidden them to bomb it, let alone crash into it.'

Raine shuddered. 'What a horrible thought to have that monster in place of our royal family.' At such an image she gripped Alec's arm. He glanced at her and smiled.

'I don't mind at all that you find the idea repulsive if it makes you hang on to me – it's probably only propaganda anyway.'

She made a play of snatching her hand away, but he put it firmly back in place.

'There's some icy patches around,' he said. 'The last thing you want to do is slip and wreck the other ankle. Next time you might not get away with it so lightly and be plastered for several weeks. That would certainly put you out of action, Miss Linfoot.'

'I don't see any icy patches,' she chuckled, 'but thank you for the warning, sir.'

She nudged him with her elbow and they both laughed.

'Shall we proceed then, madam?'

They walked along in companionable silence, keeping the castle to their left. It was so surreal-looking she couldn't help glancing at it every few steps.

'I do wish we could have a peep inside,' she said, stopping yet again to admire its sweeping lines. 'I'd love to see all those plush interiors. Maybe get some ideas for when I ever set up house,' she laughed, then wished she hadn't said something so crass. He might think she was hinting at something more from him.

'It would hardly be "royal" if every Tom, Dick and Harry were let in,' Alec said, 'and somehow I don't think even *you* would be able to wangle an invitation, although the royals do seem to be spending most of the war here.' He turned to her, looking unusually serious. 'Do you think one day you'll have a home of your own, Raine?'

The question caught her off-guard.

'One day, perhaps.' Raine was annoyed with herself for having started this line of conversation. 'But not yet. I can't imagine anything like that with this war on. Everything – everyone – seems so fragile and vulnerable. It's hard to imagine anything steady and stable any more. Putting down roots.'

'It's what this war is about,' Alec said. 'To make a more stable world. Somewhere that's tolerant and just, which Hitler has deliberately forfeited under his Nazi regime. But it's certainly a bloody awful way of retaining our democracy when even the French have given it up . . .' He glanced at her. 'Sorry, Raine, I shouldn't be swearing in front of a lady.'

'Don't worry. I have several curse words I use – mostly in my head,' Raine said soberly. 'Being brought up by a strict French mother who's a Catholic doesn't allow me to say them aloud – though you should hear me when I'm on my own.' She laughed.

'I'd like to.' Alec put the arm she was holding on to round her waist.

Even through her greatcoat she could feel the outline of

308

his body, closer now. She gave a sigh of pure contentment and he scanned her face.

'You sound happy.'

'I am,' she said and realised it was the truth. She steeled herself and said, 'Are you?'

There was an expression in his eyes that she couldn't fathom. 'Yes, sweet Raine, I'm happy, too.'

They strolled a minute or two without speaking, Raine simply aware of his presence beside her, his hand on her waist as she breathed in the crisp air. Squeezing her eyes shut she tilted her face upwards towards the thin rays of the sun, almost hearing waves crashing as they surfaced on a golden beach.

'Do you like the sea?' Alec asked suddenly.

Raine startled. He had that habit of knowing what she was thinking. It unnerved her.

'Yes,' she said truthfully. 'Just now, with the sun on my face, I was imagining I was walking on golden sand . . . instead of this slush,' she added ruefully, then realised it might have sounded ungrateful. 'Oh, I didn't mean—'

'I know you didn't.' Alec stopped and turned to face her. 'One day, Raine, we'll go to the seaside for the day – pretend we're on holiday.'

'You do a lot of pretending,' Raine said seriously.

'Sometimes it's the only way to keep one sane in this war.' He gave her a quick kiss on her forehead. They smiled at one another.

'This is a beautiful little Edwardian theatre,' Alec remarked a few minutes later when they'd passed a few shops. He stopped in front of an elegant building with Theatre Royal emblazoned on the Art Deco façade. 'I wonder what's playing tonight. Shall we go in and find out? It's bound to be good as the plays go on to the West End – unless they're flops.'

Without waiting for her reply Alec opened the door and they joined a short queue in the foyer.

'*Blithe Spirit* – the new Noël Coward – is on this week,' the man behind the ticket counter said. 'They say it's excellent – well, all his plays are.' He smiled, showing a gap between his front teeth. 'Does that interest you?'

'What do you think, Raine? It'll be a comedy.'

'I'd love to see it.'

'Then two tickets for tonight, please,' Alec said, pushing a pound note through the slot. 'Do you have a preference where to sit?' he asked Raine.

'I'm afraid we're completely sold out this evening,' the man interrupted before Raine could answer. His smile was apologetic. 'There's a matinée this afternoon at half past two, though we only have a box available at twenty-five shillings.'

'We'll take it,' Alec said immediately, taking another note from his wallet.

'Thank you, sir. I'm sure you'll enjoy it.' He handed the tickets and two half crowns through the slot.

'I'm sure we will.' Alec turned to Raine with a wicked grin.

When they were outside Raine said, 'Alec, they're terribly expensive. I think we should have said no, or at least thought about it. But anyway, I insist upon paying my half.'

'No chance,' Alec said, taking her elbow. 'I rarely go anywhere to spend my money, so this is a treat for me. And I don't want to hear another word about it.'

'All right,' she answered, 'but only if you let me pay for supper.'

'We'll see.' He looked at his watch. 'Are you ready for coffee?'

'Definitely.'

After coffee they strolled by the Thames, their breath coming out in visible little puffs as it met the cold air. There were few young people about, as was to be expected, but several harassed-looking housewives were pushing prams, the pram hoods up against the chill. Raine couldn't help glancing in to see the babies as they passed by. They were swaddled in blankets, some fast asleep, some howling, their mothers, or maybe they were nannies, bending over their prams, trying to soothe them.

Sulky children hung on to their mothers' hands. Raine saw one little boy, who seemed to be on his own, bend to grab a handful of snow and make it into a ball. He looked hard at Alec then hurled it, hitting him on the nose. Raine doubled up with laughter at the shock on Alec's face.

'Little monkey,' Alec said, stooping down, then chucking a snowball back at the boy, to his screams of delight.

'Come on,' Raine said.

The next second she was slipping on a patch of ice. She grabbed Alec's coat sleeve.

He put his arm firmly round her. 'Careful.'

'Whoops,' he said the second time she skidded on her boots.

The pavements had become slippery and Raine would have fallen this time if she hadn't been clutching Alec's arm.

'Lucky you saved me again,' she laughed, beginning for the first time to feel completely comfortable with him.

'I promise always to save you,' he said seriously. 'Always remember that.'

She didn't know how to answer, so she just nodded and gave him a quick smile.

They walked for another hour or so, mostly along the old High Street with its higgledy-piggledy Tudor buildings, many of them having been converted to shops, and two or three pubs. They turned down a small side road and stopped to admire a row of Georgian houses.

'I love these houses,' Raine said. 'And what lucky people live here – and in such a beautiful town.'

'Yes, they're very elegant . . . and probably cost a fortune to keep up, I don't doubt.' He turned to her. 'Are you getting ready for a snack? Maybe a bowl of soup to warm you up?'

'I'm not cold,' Raine said, 'but a bowl of soup sounds very appealing.'

'Right, then, let's try this one.'

He pushed open the entrance door of the nearest café. The room was packed.

Alec grimaced. 'Is it too smoky for you?'

'All the cafés will be the same,' Raine answered. 'But if we can grab that table by the window, at least it's near the door so we'll have a bit of air every time people come and go.'

The table had recently been occupied, judging by the state of the cups and saucers, dinner plates and an overflowing ashtray.

It was several minutes before Alec managed to catch the eye of one of the waitresses, but as soon as she came over with a tray she cleared the dirty dishes.

'I'll be back in a jiffy,' she said.

Once they'd ordered leek and potato soup and some bread, Raine smiled at Alec.

'I'm so looking forward to the play this afternoon, but I need to go back to the hotel after our lunch so I can change.'

'You don't need sequins for the theatre,' he said. 'But just in case our dear King and Queen decide to attend, then by all means . . .'

'You don't *really* think they will.'

'I'm told they attend quite regularly,' Alec said. 'We may even share the same box!'

'At the price of those boxes, I wouldn't be at all surprised,' Raine said, laughing.

* * *

In the end there hadn't been time to go back to the hotel and change. Raine consoled herself that the red dress was not really appropriate for afternoons, but thankful that Stephanie had made her change out of her uniform and into the black skirt and cream blouse, though she kept her boots on. By the time they entered the theatre it had started to snow again, but only lightly. Alec bought a programme and handed it to her as they mounted the stairs.

'Your box is the second on the right,' the smiling usherette gestured.

Raine walked ahead and opened the door to find a tiny room decked in red velvet. There were four seats, two at the front and two behind. Alec looked at the ticket numbers and checked the ones on the seats.

'We're supposed to be in the back row,' he said. 'Well, we'll take the front seats and if anyone comes in we'll have to move.' He glanced over at a small table laid out with a plate of tiny sandwiches and a silver-covered teapot, surrounded by several cups and saucers and a bottle of champagne with a set of champagne glasses.

'Good gracious, Alec, did you order this?' Raine asked.

'No, but I would have if I'd known they could provide it. It must be part of the ticket price. Well, we won't let it go to waste, especially as we didn't stop for a cup of tea.'

He helped her off with her coat and removed his, piling them on the seats behind.

'Are you ready for tea, madam?' he said in a voice like a butler.

'Thank you, Marshall. That will be lovely.'

He grinned and poured her a cup. 'A sandwich for madam?'

'Just the one, Marshall. I've only just eaten a short time ago. I had a huge bowl of soup.'

'You've such a beautiful figure, madam, if I may say so,

313

and I don't think two small sandwiches would be at all out of order.'

'You're most kind, Marshall, though I don't believe you should be making such personal comments.'

They both fell into laughter as Alec popped the champagne cork and poured out two glasses. He took the seat next to her and clinked her glass.

'To us,' he said. 'I can't imagine anything more perfect than to be sitting here with you in this charming theatre, in our cosy box, drinking champagne. I just hope no one else comes in.'

'So do I,' Raine said emphatically.

Minutes later the lights dimmed. Just as the red velvet curtains on the stage slowly parted she felt Alec's fingertips on her chin, gently turning her face towards him. Her breath came quickly as his mouth found hers. Wonderful as his kiss was, she wished they weren't seated. She wanted to fold herself into him. Feel his arms fully around her.

The warmth and intimacy of the box and the champagne made her bold. She put a hand inside his jacket and stroked his chest, smoothing the crisp cotton shirt under her fingers.

'Ah, Raine.' Alec groaned as he kissed her more passionately.

Her lips parted and she felt the tip of his tongue. She put both arms around his neck. The next moment she startled as she remembered where she was. In the dark she saw the flash of Alec's teeth as he grinned and squeezed her hand. The actors sounded a long way away although she clearly heard their next words, wondering how much the two of them had missed of the opening lines. She opened her eyes.

'And when you're serving dinner, Edith, try to remember to do it calmly and methodically.'

'Yes'm.'

'As you're not in the navy, it is unnecessary to do everything at the double.'

There was a roll of laughter from the audience.

'I hope I may continue serving you calmly and method-ically, madam,' Alec whispered then kissed the tip of her ear.

She giggled and at that moment the door behind them opened. Raine immediately pulled away.

'Sorry to disturb,' came a nasal voice as a thin young man carrying a large canvas grip guided an even thinner girl in front of him.

'Here, you're in our seats,' the girl said in a surprisingly strident voice, hanging over them.

'Damn,' Raine heard Alec mutter as they got to their feet.

'I'm sorry,' Raine whispered to the couple who were hardly allowing them to move away before they claimed their seats.

The smell of cheap perfume invaded Raine's nostrils as the girl stripped off her outer clothes.

'I'm dying for a cup of tea,' she said, 'and some of them sandwiches. D'ya want me to pour yours, Len?' She went over to the table.

'Aw-right.'

The girl swung round and glared at Raine and Alec. 'Here, look at this mess. Have you been at the afternoon tea we ordered? We've paid extra for that high tea.'

'Shhh. The play's already started,' Raine said in hushed tones, annoyed that the couple were making such a song and dance. All right, she admitted, she and Alec were at fault, but really . . .

'We thought it was for all of us because there were more than two cups and glasses.' Alec's voice was equally quiet, though firm. 'But I'll be more than happy to reimburse you.'

'Forget it, mate,' the young man said with a cocky shrug. 'I can easily order another.'

After much tutting from the girl, they plonked themselves down in the front row and after a few more mutterings were thankfully silent. The young man lit a cigarette but made a big point of blowing the smoke over the edge of the balcony rail. Her view now slightly masked, Raine had to move her head closer to Alec's to see between the shoulders of the couple in front. If only they could have had the box to themselves. Then she reprimanded herself. She was being selfish, just as Maman always accused her of.

'I want to make love to you,' Alec whispered in her ear, sending quivers of excitement through her.

Her heart beat hard and she found it difficult to concentrate on the play.

She drew in a deep breath, but it came back out in a sigh.

But there was another sound . . . a mewing. She caught Alec looking at her with raised eyebrows.

'Did you hear that, Raine?' he whispered.

'Yes. It sounded like a kitten . . .' Raine started.

The girl in front bent down and brought up a bundle of shawl, jigging it up and down on her lap and shushing it. The mewing turned into a full-lunged howl. A baby!

People began turning round in their seats and looking up towards the boxes. A man at the box next to them stood up.

'Will the person who has brought in a baby please take it outside. It's disturbing everyone. We've come to see a play, in case you hadn't noticed.'

There was a chorus of 'Hear, hear' and 'Call the manager!'

So that's what was in that large bag. The war was making people do all kinds of things they probably wouldn't normally think to do. Raine was sure it wasn't allowed to bring a baby into the theatre, but maybe they hadn't been able to find a babysitter and might have saved hard to get these tickets. But it wasn't fair spoiling other people's pleasure either.

The girl put a dummy in the baby's mouth and immediately there was a glorious silence except for the actors.

Raine settled down and found herself thoroughly enjoying the play. It was heaven to laugh and have Alec by the side of her, laughing with her. That's what he needed in this war, knowing the danger he was in every time he went up to face the Luftwaffe. The train of thought led her to thinking of Doug. She couldn't help a shiver of fear. If something happened to Alec now they seemed to have reached a truce at last . . .

He put his arm round her shoulder and drew her to him. 'You're not cold, are you?'

She shook her head and mouthed 'no'. On the contrary, the box was beautifully warm, permeating her bones and loosening her muscles. Or maybe it was the champagne. She closed her eyes in contentment.

The screech of the air-raid siren shocked her from her chair. Her heartbeat quickened. Oh, God, not Windsor. Alec had been so sure they'd be safe here.

He looked up at her. 'What do you want to do?' he asked in a low voice.

She bit down on her lip. 'People often stay in the cinema when the warning goes, but . . .' She glanced over the banister and saw several people already leaving. She turned to him. 'I'm not so sure, being this high up. Maybe we should go.'

Alec immediately stood and picked up their coats. The young man in front twisted round to them.

'Not letting Jerry beat you, are you?' he said in a challenging manner. 'Nothing will prise *us* away. We've got the last act to come yet and we won these seats fair and square.'

'Come on, Raine. Here's your coat,' Alec said, giving the boy a curt nod.

She slipped her arms in the sleeves and grabbed her bag. They joined a small crowd of people swiftly moving down the stairs and into the foyer. She was surprised when she looked over to the bar to see people still ordering drinks.

317

'They're obviously not bothering about any warning,' she said, gesturing towards them.

The minute they left the building and crossed the road there came an ear-splitting bang behind them followed by an explosion. The ground shook. A flash of brilliant light showed Alec's face, pale and eerie-looking. Raine looked back at the theatre. In the darkness she could see a handful of people running from the entrance. There was another flash. Dust swirled around them in the acrid smell.

Alec grabbed Raine's arm. 'Come on. Hold on to me and run!'

'That couple—'

'What couple?' Alec shouted.

She jerked her head back. 'The ones in our box. We have to help them.'

'Are you mad?' He stopped, a look of disbelief crossing his face as she pointed to the upper part of the building they'd just left seconds before.

Smoke was curling around the roof.

'The theatre must have been hit. We *have* to do something.'

'They're not our responsibility, Raine. Come on.'

'Alec,' she implored, 'there's a *baby* inside. We can't leave them there without knowing if they're all right.'

'All right, *I'll* go.' Alec's tone was an order. 'Just don't follow me, Raine, do you hear? It might be a one-off, but you never know – it could be a raid.' He looked up, an ear cocked, listening for the sound of planes, but there was nothing. 'Go with all the others.' He gestured to the crowd that was moving swiftly away from the theatre. 'They might know of a shelter. If not, run like mad and go to the hotel. They'll have a basement or something.' He pointed. 'I'll join you as soon as I can.'

He turned and tore back to the theatre. Raine stood for thirty seconds, frozen with fear and shock. Then as though a wild animal was chasing her, she flew after him. But as she got to the door one of the theatre staff put his arm out in front of her, barring her way.

'Sorry, miss. No one's allowed in until we find out the damage.'

'My friend's gone in to help.' Raine's voice was frantic.

She tried to push past but he was too quick for her.

'Can't let you go in, miss. But don't worry – we've called the fire brigade. They'll be along in a jiffy.'

Some people demanding to know where the bomb had struck diverted his attention. Raine took her chance. She ducked and ran inside, at the same time fumbling for the torch she always kept in her greatcoat pocket.

Seconds later she'd climbed the first flight of stairs, the thin light barely showing the way through the swirling dust and dark. Her heart beat painfully against her ribs. To think she and Alec had left only minutes ago . . .

Smoke filled the air and she began to cough. There was no sign of any explosion or fire, so where was the smoke coming from? One more flight and she'd be on the same floor as the theatre boxes. Then she heard a terrible moaning like some animal in pain.

Scared but resolute, she picked her way up the stairs.

She reached the second floor and stumbled towards the box. The moaning grew louder. She opened the door, dreading the worst. Clouds of dust swirled to meet her and she coughed again as she shone her thin beam inside. To her horror the girl who'd shared their box was standing, leaning with her back to the balcony, her arm raised to the still-seated young man as though about to strike him. The balcony was creaking.

Raine swung her torch at them. '*Stop!*'

The girl's arm froze in mid-air.

'Come away from that balcony,' Raine ordered. 'It's not safe.'

The girl stared at her, then blinked.

The young man looked round, his eyes wide with anguish. 'Wasn't you sitting behind us with your bloke?'

'Yes,' Raine said.

Where the hell was Alec?

She made her voice as stern as one of her teachers. 'Didn't you hear the explosion? A bomb's gone off. There may be more. We need to get out *now*!'

'I keep telling Evie. But she won't come with me.'

Even in the weak torchlight Raine could see the girl's eyes were swollen. Tears streamed down her cheeks.

'She won't move. I've tried to tell her.' The young man began to cry and turned to the girl. 'Please, Evie.' He wiped his face with the back of his sleeve.

Raine walked slowly towards her, terrified that if she made a sudden movement, Evie could step backwards and topple over the rail to her death. The girl seemed mesmerised, watching every step Raine took without flinching. Cautiously, Raine put a hand on her arm and very gently pulled her away from the balcony.

'Come and sit down, love.' Raine put her hands on the girl's narrow shoulders and eased her onto the seat. She took the seat next to her and felt for Evie's hand. 'Are you hurt?'

But as soon as she'd said the words Raine knew something terrible had happened.

'Where's the baby?' she asked. A feeling of dread crawled over her body.

'My baby's dead!' Evie whispered.

'It's all right, Evie,' the boy said, putting his hand out to her.

Evie smacked his hand away, her chest heaving in her agitation.

'You've killed our baby! My little girl. Little Christine.' Her eyes blazing she began to shout. 'I *told* you we shouldn't take her. But would you listen? No. You wouldn't miss the stupid play. Not you, Lenny. Think yourself better than everyone when you start bragging that you've seen a lousy bleedin' play, and stayed in the middle of an air raid. Not that you understood any of it. And now you've killed her.'

Dear God. Lenny killed the baby? What on earth was Evie on about?

'Oh, Evie, tell me what happened,' Raine said, forcing herself to stay calm.

Evie shook her head.

'When we heard all them bangs,' Lenny started, 'I went to pick the baby up to comfort her and get us all out of here. Her dummy had dropped out but she didn't look right. And then . . . then,' his voice faltered.

'Then what, Lenny?' Raine asked softly.

'I could tell she were dead – but I don't understand why . . . or how. I never killed her. Why would I do that? I'm her father. I loved her.'

'I'm sure you did,' Raine soothed. 'And I'm so very sorry. But are you certain . . .?' She couldn't finish the sentence. Instead, she said, 'Would you allow me to look at her?'

'Would that be all right, Evie, if the lady has a look at Christine?'

'Is she a nurse?' Evie's tone was scathing.

'No, but I have some first-aid knowledge.'

Evie said nothing. Lenny nodded to Raine to go ahead. She squatted down and gently pulled back the blanket that was half covering the baby's face. The child was on her back, her dark hair stuck to her head with perspiration, the dummy fallen to the side. But what frightened her most were the baby's eyes, blankly staring up at the ceiling. Raine bit her lip.

Her hand shook as she reached for her handbag and found her powder compact. She undid the catch and pointed the mirror close to the baby's nose, where a trickle of blood had escaped, then lowered it slightly to the baby's mouth for some seconds. She brought the mirror close up and shone her torch on the small piece of glass. She peered at it. There was no misting on the mirror . . . no sign of any life.

She felt the baby's arm. It was much too cool and smooth to her touch. She bent her head to the little chest. Nothing. No movement; no sound. The baby was as lifeless as a doll.

With the tip of one finger Raine gently closed the baby's eyes then pulled the blanket up. She stood.

'I'm afraid you're right . . . I'm so sorry, but she's gone.'

Evie began to sob again, but the noise was immediately drowned out by another explosion. *Oh, God,* Raine thought. *The whole bloody place is going to come down.*

A shower of plaster fell on the small group and Raine quickly bent to pull the baby's blanket further round the small dark head, then rose.

'Go!' she commanded. 'Lenny, take the torch.' She thrust it in his hands. 'Keep hold of Evie. I'll bring the baby.'

Galvanised into action Lenny dragged Evie out of the door, Raine following close behind, hoping to get a little benefit from the torch.

'Come on, Evie,' Raine heard Lenny say. 'It's not safe here.'

Somehow the three clambered down the two flights of steps and into the foyer which looked untouched. A handful of people stood at the exit door but seemed in no hurry to leave. Two other men were in staff uniform, one the same stocky man who'd barred her way.

'I thought I told you not . . .' He stopped when Raine held out the bag. He peered inside, then looked at her, a deep frown bringing his bushy ginger eyebrows together. 'You're not allowed—'

Raine raised her hand to stop him from saying more.

She nodded towards the couple, Lenny still trying to calm Evie.

'Their baby's dead,' Raine said as she stepped outside, out of earshot. 'We need to call an ambulance.'

'Poor little blighter.' He looked towards the bag again. 'We've got an ambulance but it's picking up some injured folk round the corner. The theatre was hardly touched, thank God, but several of the old houses nearby have had it.' He raised his fist and shook it at the starless sky. 'Bloody Jerries.'

Can't he see this is urgent?

'Is there a doctor nearby?' Raine could feel her voice rising.

'Not that I know of. Best thing is for the baby to be taken to the hospital. Leave it to me and I'll see what I can do.'

He turned away to talk to his colleague. She saw the second man go to his ticket booth and pick up the phone.

A few people were hanging around in the bar talking animatedly and Raine spotted some vacant chairs.

'Lenny, take Evie to the bar so she can sit down while we wait for the ambulance. They've already called for one so Christine can be examined at the hospital, and I think you should insist they look at Evie as well.'

Lenny nodded. Evie was silent but she allowed him to put his arm round her, though her legs were bent in an odd manner as they would buckle under at any moment. Raine was relieved to see that at least Evie had quietened down and wasn't fending Lenny off. The two of them obviously loved their baby but they looked heartbreakingly young to be parents.

Raine's arm was beginning to ache as she took the bag holding Christine to the bar. She set it down gently near Evie's feet.

'How long will they be?' Evie muttered.

'Soon,' Raine assured her. 'They're on alert all the time, but I've just been told it was the building behind us that got hit. I don't know any more than that.'

'We want to thank you for everything, don't we, Evie?' Lenny said.

Raine's eyes filled with tears. 'I didn't do anything,' she said. 'I wish I could've done more. I just can't tell you how sorry I am about little Christine.' She touched Evie's arm. 'Where will you go after the hospital?' she said.

Evie shook her head.

'Back to my parents,' Lenny answered. 'They've given us a room and Christine has the b-boxroom.' He broke down. 'Whatever will they say when we don't come back with her?'

He sniffed and Raine handed him a handkerchief. He blew his nose with a loud trumpeting noise and gave her a tearful smile.

'Well, I know what Evie's mum and dad will say – they'll say, "Good riddance." Their own granddaughter.' He curled his lip. 'Do y'know, they put Evie out as soon as she told them she was expecting.'

Raine swallowed. She could just imagine the scene.

'I shan't ever forgive them for that,' Evie whispered. 'And now Christine's gone, I won't go back – *ever*.'

Thankfully, at that moment Raine heard what sounded like the ambulance. She shot up from her seat and ran across the foyer just as it drew up outside. She opened the theatre door to see one of the crew, a hefty chap, jump down from the vehicle. She smell of smoke hit her again. The fire must be taking hold somewhere near. And then she heard a roaring sound and men's shouts. The noise was coming from the street behind the theatre. A building must be on fire! What was it the man had said? 'The theatre's not been hit. But some old houses took it.'

Please God, don't let Alec be there. But where the hell is *he?*

She wished with all her heart that she could look for him right away, but first she had to see Evie and Lenny and little Christine safely on their way to the hospital.

'Did you call for an ambulance, love?' the ambulance man said as soon as he set foot in the foyer.

'Yes, it's for a couple who were watching the play.' She quickly explained what had happened. 'But it's not just the baby. Her mother is very young and in deep shock. I think she needs attention as well.'

'We'll make sure she gets it,' he said as he hurried to where Evie sat, quiet now.

'Evie, the ambulance men are going to take you and Christine to hospital. They'll look after you. I promise.'

The ambulance man held his hand out to Evie. 'Come on, love. I'll bring the baby. You take my other arm.'

'No,' Lenny said. 'I'll bring Christine and Evie. We're a family, aren't we?' He picked up the bag holding Christine. 'Hold on to me, Evie. Everything's going to be all right.'

'What about you, love?' The man turned to Raine. 'Do you live in Windsor?'

'No. I was visiting with a friend and we were watching the play near them.' She nodded towards Lenny and Evie. 'My friend ran back to the theatre to see if they needed any help, but he's disappeared and I'm really worried now.'

'All the drama is going on in River Street,' he said grimly. 'So if I were you, I'd go back to your hotel. He's probably there already, wondering where *you* are.'

Chapter Twenty-Eight

Raine followed the couple out to the ambulance. When the driver started the engine she breathed a sigh of relief. Ignoring the ambulance man's advice to go back to the hotel she immediately dashed round the corner to River Street where the full scene of the destruction from incendiary bombs, eerily lit by the moon, knocked her back. Three firemen were training their hoses on a building where flames poured out of every window, making that same fearful roar she'd heard outside the theatre while waiting for the ambulance. Now it filled her head, stopping her from thinking straight.

Men's voices shouting. Cursing. A stench like she had never smelt before. Her stomach heaved. She swallowed several times, fighting the nausea in the back of her throat. Even though she'd never smelt it in her life, she knew without doubt what it was. Burning flesh. Her skin crawled as she spotted two men carrying a stretcher to a waiting ambulance.

Alec, where are you? Please don't be the body on the stretcher.

She twisted her neck this way and that, but it was too dark to pick out anyone from the crowd that had already gathered. Two more firemen called out to the people to make way so they could get to the buildings. One of them bent down and picked up something small and black from the debris. Raine peered through the darkness. It was moving.

She crept nearer and saw it was a kitten. She could hear the tiniest of mews, so plaintive against the mayhem all around. The fireman held out the little ball to the crowd and said something. One lady held out her arms. The man put the kitten into her hands and she tucked it inside her coat, shaking her head as she walked away.

Raine tilted her head to look up at the burning building, where a man was dangling like a piece of meat from a rope fixed to a massive steel structure at the height of the top floor. The firemen below were shouting upwards. *Alec.* Maybe he was trapped. Her breathing came fast. Almost without thinking she stepped forward but immediately felt a hand on her shoulder, firmly pushing her back.

'Don't go any nearer,' one of the firemen warned. 'Leave us to get on with our job.'

'I'm looking for someone,' she panted. 'My boyfriend. He came to help. I have to find him. You'd know him if you saw him. He's tall, fair hair . . .' Her mind suddenly went blank and she couldn't think of anything else to describe him.

'Sorry, miss,' he said, his voice softening a fraction. 'We've had many people volunteering to help but we've had to send them away. More trouble than they're worth unless they're experienced – or a medical person. And in the dark, all the smoke, I wouldn't recognise my own mother.' He looked at her. 'My advice to you, miss, is to get home before Jerry gives us another swipe.'

'I can't leave. He may be injured . . . or . . .' She couldn't bring herself to say the dreaded word. Her voice had sunk to a whimper.

'If there's anyone injured, we'll find them, love, don't you worry.'

He put an arm round her, and although she realised he was being kind, his grip was as strong as if he were arresting her. She had no choice but to allow him to lead her back to Theatre Street.

'Will you take my name . . . just in case?'

He removed a small notebook and pencil from his inside jacket pocket.

'It's Lorraine Linfoot.'

'All right, Miss Linfoot. And your friend's name?'

'Alec Marshall.' She gulped. *Where on earth* is *he?*

'Right you are.' He scribbled in his book, then looked up. 'Do you live here?'

'No. We're staying at Riverside Hotel for a couple of days.' She blushed as he gave her a sharp look.

He snapped the notebook shut and put it back in his jacket. 'My advice to you, miss, is to go back to your hotel and have a nice quiet cup of tea. And at least we'll know where you are if we come across him.'

He gave her a sympathetic pat on the arm and disappeared.

Sick at heart because she could think of nothing better to do, she slowly walked back to the hotel. She tightened her silk scarf round her head to muffle her against the biting cold. What else could she have done?

A feeling of dread stole through her body as she unlocked her bedroom door. It had started out as such a wonderful day. Now, nothing was the same. A baby had died . . . Her eyes stung, but whether it was for the baby or from the smoke – or Alec – she couldn't tell. She sat on the edge of the bed, her legs trembling, her throat sore. There was a small glass of water on the bedside table. She swallowed it all in one long rhythm of gulps. She was just putting the glass back on the table, when she heard footsteps treading heavily up the stairs. Heart pounding against her ribs, she jumped up and ran to open the door. It might only be one of the maids but . . .

Alec was standing outside, almost unrecognisable. He looked exhausted. Showers of ash had turned his hair grey and his face was smeared with soot. He smelt of fire. And that terrible stench. His brows were drawn together and his eyes were dark with anger.

She recoiled.

'Well, that's a relief, at least, to know you're still alive,' he said, fury coating his words.

'What on earth are you talking about? It's *me*,' Raine thumped herself on the chest, 'who's been worried sick about *you*.' When he didn't say anything, she said, 'Where *were* you?'

'More to the point, where the hell were *you*?'

'Don't you dare swear at me!' Raine flashed.

He suddenly looked contrite, then said, 'Are you going to leave me outside and let all the residents hear us having a row?'

Feeling ashamed, Raine opened the door wider and stepped aside. He immediately flopped into the only chair. She sat on the bed, hardly able to look at him.

'Bloody hell, Raine, you really had me worried. I've been looking everywhere for you.' He threw her a suspicious look. 'Did you follow me?'

'Yes.'

'I thought so. But I told you not to.'

'No, you *ordered* me not to.'

'And you don't take orders, is that it?' Alec brought out a packet of cigarettes. He flicked his lighter and lit one.

'It's not that. I was so worried about that couple and the baby . . .' Tears gathered in her throat and she swallowed.

'Did you find them?'

'Yes. They were exactly where we left them, so why weren't you there?'

'As soon as I ran back to the theatre, one of the staff told me it hadn't been damaged very much, though there'd been some vibration. Bit of plaster fallen but no one was injured. He said the smoke was from some idiot in the balcony who hadn't put his cigarette out properly and that the buildings on River Street were the ones that were blasted. So I went to see what I could do to help.

'Those three beautiful Georgian houses were almost totally destroyed – do you remember how we admired them when we had our walk?'

She nodded dumbly.

'Two shops with flats were just a pile of bricks. One of the firemen told me two people had already died. And you and I had only just said how lucky they were to live in such beautiful houses. One youth was asking everyone if they'd seen his parents. He said they were all sitting in the dining room together. But he couldn't find them . . . he was sobbing. Dear God . . . who knows? There were bits of bodies every-where. It was a dreadful sight.' His voice broke and he put his head in his hands. 'I couldn't do much because I could see I was in the way.'

'I went there after I got the couple and their baby into an ambulance,' Raine said, her voice shaking.

He looked at her in surprise. 'What time was that?'

'Maybe twenty minutes after you left. Maybe half an hour. I don't really know. So much was happening.'

'You said that couple had to go in an ambulance. Why? Were they hurt?'

'The baby.' She looked at him, her eyes tear-filled. 'The baby . . . when I got there . . . in the box . . . the baby – oh, Alec, it was horrible – the baby was already dead.'

His head jerked up. 'Dead? How?'

'They don't know. I think it must have been the shock from the noise of the explosions. Oh, Alec, she was just a little mite – they named her Christine. She had her eyes open

330

but there was no sign of life. It was so sad. And the poor mother was hysterical.'

She broke down, sobbing. Seconds later she was aware of him on the bed beside her, a pair of strong arms enfolding her. She felt his hand in her hair, stroking, soothing.

'Don't get upset, Raine,' he murmured. 'Tell me everything later when you're feeling better. Don't cry. Please don't cry. I'm here now.'

'I'd better go back to my room and clean up a bit,' Alec said after a few minutes when she'd poured it all out. 'I must look a wreck – and I certainly feel it. But do I risk not being allowed in again?' He held up her tear-stained face and kissed both eyelids. Then he gave her a tender smile.

'You'll have to take a chance,' Raine said, giving a wan smile back.

He brushed his lips to hers and disappeared.

Slowly, she stood and stepped into her bathroom, thinking she must look a sight as well. In the mirror she barely recognised herself. Bloodshot eyes stared back at her as though in dismay from what she'd subjected them to. Her white face was smeared with soot and her hair, covered in bits of plaster dust, was falling out of its pins and kirby grips. She looked ten years older. She grimaced at her reflection which seemed to be mocking her.

Raine washed the soot off her face and with a comb smoothed a few wisps of hair out of the way with more pins. There was no time to redo it properly. She lightly swept lipstick over her mouth and went back to her room, then sat on the bed where he'd left her and waited.

There was a light tap at the door.

Alec was smiling and there was no mistaking the warmth in his eyes.

'Come in,' she said, catching her breath.

'Before half the hotel knows I'm entering your boudoir?'

he grinned, sweeping her into his arms. 'Are you feeling better?'

'Yes,' she said, 'I am.'

He bent his head and kissed her. She wound her arms round his neck, running her fingers through the short fair hair, kissing him back, over and over, until they were breathless.

'I don't know what I would have done if something had happened to you,' he said thickly.

She felt exactly the same, but she couldn't bring herself to say the words.

'I love you, Raine.'

Something twisted deep inside. They were words she had dreamed of hearing. But did he really mean them?

'You're not saying anything. It's that other chap, isn't it? Doug. You haven't stopped loving him, have you? Even though we said we'd love one another this weekend and not let anyone or anything interfere.' He kept hold of her arms as she drew away.

'You said you wanted us to *pretend* to be in love,' Raine flashed. 'That's a whole lot different from the real thing. I've told you before, it's not Doug.' She blinked as the tears threatened to flow again. 'And I don't want to play any silly games.' Whatever she said, however much she explained, it was obvious he wouldn't believe she was not in love with Doug. 'My head aches and I want to be left on my own for a while. Maybe I'll feel better if I have a nap.' She held his gaze. 'Do you understand?'

'It's probably from ingesting all the smoke, and the strain of what you've just been through, so of course I understand.' He hesitated. 'But if you need me, you know where I am. Just across the hall.'

He kissed her forehead lightly, and then he was gone.

* * *

332

It was impossible to sleep. Raine looked at her watch for the tenth time in the last hour. Coming up to half past eight. It felt like midnight, she was so tired. It was no use. She couldn't lie there a moment longer, thinking of Alec. Thinking of Doug. Thinking of the couple with the baby – except they no longer had a baby. Poor little soul. If it hadn't been for the couple bringing her in against all the rules, the child might still be alive . . . Raine blinked furiously as she sat up. Surely there were no more tears left in her.

But what of Alec? Where was he? Still in his room? Sleeping? Why did it always end like this when they were together? And why had he told her he loved her? Right out of the blue. Was it only because he so badly wanted to share his precious leave with her as an escape from the war? She sighed. As usual she'd gone and spoilt it. What must he be thinking? Did he wish he'd never set eyes on her?

She remembered his tired expression when he'd stood at her door, the tiredness suddenly changing to anger. She'd felt angry, too, but when she'd thought about it, it was only because she was so relieved. Maybe it had been the same for him. He risked his life every day and all he wanted were two perfect days – and she couldn't even give him that. A flicker of shame pulled her up. She had to spoil something good between them because she couldn't stand anyone telling her what to do. Well, if this was love she felt for Alec, then she was certainly doing a good job to disguise it. Had she ruined everything that might have been?

She splashed her face again, this time with cold water, and cleaned her teeth. Her hair was beyond repair. She needed to start from the beginning. The pins were digging into her scalp anyway. She removed them all and shook the waves free. That was heaps better. Her stomach rumbled and she wondered if Alec might feel hungry. Maybe they could put such difficult questions and answers to one side for the time being and simply enjoy a quiet supper somewhere in each other's company.

Without thinking further she opened her door and knocked on the one opposite. It opened immediately. The bedside lamp was on and the counterpane was creased and dented. A book was on the floor, face down.

'Raine.' He seized both her hands and brought her inside. 'Are you feeling better? Did you sleep?'

'Yes to the first, and no to the second,' she said, smiling.

'I'm sorry—'

'I'm sorry—'

They spoke at the same time.

'I shouldn't have sworn at you . . .' Alec started.

Raine put a finger to his lips. 'Please, Alec, will you kiss me?'

He pulled her to him. His mouth was warm on hers and her lips parted. He took his mouth away and kissed her neck, then the curve where it joined her collarbone. Her whole body tingled and her breath came quickly as he gently unbuttoned her blouse. Then he slid his hand under the silky fabric. She didn't want him to stop. Her head spun. She leant even further into him.

'Raine, I meant it. I love you. There's no pretence.' He held her away and looked deep into her eyes. 'You're so beautiful and I want you more than I've ever wanted any woman. But I won't do anything you don't want me to.'

'I want you, too.' Her voice sounded weak and shaky to her ears.

'You do?'

'Yes, I do.'

He drew her over to the bed.

He finished unbuttoning her blouse. She dragged her arms

from the sleeves and tossed the garment on the chair, then took off her skirt and threw it on top, not caring about creasing it.

'Sit on the bed, darling.'

She kept her hand on his bent head as he removed her stockings. He kissed the tops of her legs, then the bare skin between her French knickers and lacy brassière. Then he laid her on the bed, quickly removing his shirt and undoing his trousers. Lying half on top of her he kissed her again.

She stroked the contour of his face. Ran a fingertip over his mouth. 'I want you to make love to me, Alec.'

'Are you absolutely sure, darling?'

'More sure than I've ever been of anything in my life.' She was quiet for a few moments. 'Today made me realise how we're all living from day to day, minute by minute, never knowing when we might be blown to smithereens. The little baby . . .' She gulped. 'It seems so pointless to hang on to my virginity as if it's something precious. I want to experience love. And I want that person to be you.'

'So I'm the first,' he said softly.

'Yes.'

'Then it's even more precious to me. And I want it to be precious for both of us. I'll try not to hurt you, Raine. It might hurt for a few seconds and there might be some blood afterwards, but don't worry . . . it's normal.'

She sat up and fumbled with the fastenings of her brassière.

'Allow me, madam,' he said, making her smile.

He did it with one deft movement, then he carefully pulled her French knickers down and let them fall to the floor.

'Well, well,' he said, smiling, admiration and desire written all over his face. Somehow his expression took away her embarrassment. 'Don't *you* look absolutely gorgeous!'

335

He quickly undressed.

'And *you* look like one of those Greek gods I ogled in the British Museum on a school outing when I was fifteen,' she said, laughing. Oh, how good it felt to laugh. 'Our teacher had to drag me away, saying it was shocking for a young girl to gawp at a man's nudity . . . or "extremities", I think she called it. I remember thinking at the time that she'd probably never been married.'

'Well, not to someone like me,' Alec said, joining in her laughter. 'But perhaps *you* should be the judge of that, my love.'

Then it was only Alec who occupied the space in her head. Alec who was holding her hands as he entered her – a searing sting of pain – and then she was floating with him above the clouds.

Afterwards, Raine lay with her legs entangled with his, her hand on his chest, stroking and gently tugging the soft golden hairs, her breathing at last slowing with his. She looked at him and laughed.

'That's not the reaction you're supposed to have,' Alec said, grinning.

'I can't help it. I'm no longer a virgin.' She squeezed her eyes shut in delight. 'I could shout it from the rooftops. "Listen, everyone. You know what? I'm twenty years of age and I've finally done it!"'

'Is that all you wanted me for – to deflower you, as they used to call it? Turn you into a woman?' His mouth quirked at the corner.

'Course it was,' she said, and laughed again. Then she kissed him soundly on the cheek. 'I'm teasing.'

'I should hope so.' Then he became serious. 'Raine, do you love me? Because if you do, you've never said.'

'Are we pretending now?' she asked, half teasing, half serious.

'What do you think?'

'I never know with you,' she answered. 'But I think there's a good chance I might be falling in love.'

'Only *might*?' His green eyes widened.

'Maybe if you make love to me again, I'll know for sure.'

'Then come here. I'd better help you to make up your mind.'

He swept her up in his arms and this time there was no pain at all. Only the wonder of having Alec inside her again.

Chapter Twenty-Nine

Raine didn't regret being with Alec, giving herself to him, body and soul, for one second. She only knew he must survive this war. She couldn't lose him as she had Doug. It would truly break her heart. She only hoped he might not be in quite such a dangerous position as the fighter pilots, though his job was bad enough, even if he did always make light of it.

When the cab driver dropped them off at White Waltham after a hurried lunch, it was nearly impossible to tear herself away from him.

'Will you write, darling?' he asked, kissing the tip of her nose.

'Yes, of course.'

'You promise?'

'I promise.'

'I love you. Don't you ever forget it.' He kissed her long and hard as he held her against his heart, then quickly strode out to the other pilots waiting for a lift in the Anson.

She shielded her eyes as she watched the aircraft carry him upwards until it was a tiny speck. She looked around the airfield and it was as though she'd dreamed what had turned out to be only thirty-six hours together. But it felt as though she'd known him all her life. He was her only love, no matter what the war threw at them.

As soon as she walked into the station one of the clerks waylaid her.

'Oh, Lorraine, you're back nice and early. Well done. Can you do an urgent delivery?'

She followed him into the office where he handed her a chit.

'For delivery as soon as you arrive, so the powers that be requested,' he continued. 'You should enjoy this one. It's your first Lizzie, isn't it?' He looked at her and grinned.

She nodded.

'It's not a long trip so you'll easily be back this evening.'

'I thought they'd let me have my full two days off,' she grumbled.

'Sorry, Lorraine. We're a bit busy at the moment. If you can't do it—'

'No, no,' Raine said quickly as she glanced at the delivery details. Pick up a Lysander from the manufacturers at Westland in Yeovil and deliver it to Tangmere.

'Is there an Anson going from here to Yeovil?' she asked the clerk.

He glanced at the board showing the flights going out that day.

'Doesn't look like it,' he said. 'You'll have to go by train. But you should be able to get a lift from Chichester as we have one of the pilots delivering there about the time you'll be coming back.'

Yes, she'd be back this evening, but only if she managed to get a lift. If not, heaven knew how long another train would take. But whatever time she arrived back she would find time to write to Alec, as she'd promised. Even if she had to stay up all night.

'I can drop you off in Yeovil,' Audrey said as she came into the office. 'I've got a couple of pilots to deliver south of here.'

'Wonderful,' Raine said. That would knock two hours off, that was certain.

* * *

She enjoyed flying the Lysander. It was an easy plane to handle; the undercarriage was fixed so she didn't even have to worry about that aspect. And the weather had improved at last. It had given her time to let Alec drift into her thoughts when she wasn't reading her map or trying to spot landmarks to confirm she was approaching Tangmere. For all his outward casualness she felt Alec was quite a complex character. Maybe we've all become like it with this war, she thought. Things we've always taken for granted can't be any more. Things like planning your future. People you love might one day not be here. Not just Doug, but all the other boyfriends and fiancés and husbands she'd heard of who'd been shot down, killed or taken prisoner to be bullied and tortured. She shook herself. She mustn't get into that depressing train of thought. She set her jaw. She had a job to do and she was bloody well going to do it.

Disappointingly, she'd had to catch a train back to White Waltham. Although the train was cold, for once there'd been no delays and Raine had found a seat in a compartment with no one standing. By the time she reached what she now thought of as home, it was coming up to eight and her stomach was gurgling. For all her chattering, Mrs Grayson was a kind-hearted woman and an excellent cook. Raine prayed there were some leftovers.

'Ah, there you are, dear,' Mrs Grayson said when Raine stepped through the front door. 'Your friend's had her supper but she's still in the dining room. I'll go and heat yours up. I think I'd better put it over a saucepan of boiling water so it don't dry up like it would in the oven. You just go in and chat to Stephanie while I get cracking. She said she enjoyed hers, so I hope you like it. I had to queue for an hour to get the meat and even then—'

'Thank you for saving me supper, Mrs Grayson,' Raine broke in. All she longed for now was to sit down at Mrs Grayson's table and tuck into whatever dish the landlady had created. 'I'm really hungry.'

'You go on in, dear, and I'll bring it to you in two shakes of a lamb's tail.'

Stephanie was still at the dining room table when Raine walked in.

'I tried to wait for you,' she said, giving Raine a beaming smile, 'but the smells from the kitchen were too good. I had to have a small seconds and you're lucky I didn't finish off the whole dish.'

Raine laughed. 'I'd be pretty fed up if you had.' She took the seat opposite.

'Well, come on,' Stephanie said, her blue eyes agog. 'We need some good news after what was in the newspaper today.'

Raine blinked. She'd been so full of thoughts of Alec that she hadn't even glanced at any newspaper.

'Not more bad news?'

''Fraid so,' Stephanie said. 'Singapore has fallen to the Japs.'

Both women were silent for a few moments.

'And it seems Jerry is having all his own way at the moment here,' Stephanie said. 'But it *will* change. It's got to. We have right on our side.'

'Let's hope so,' Raine said grimly.

'Let's talk about nicer things.' Stephanie's face was pure mischief. 'You were about to tell me all about the weekend with your pilot. Did you have a good time . . . or need I ask?' she added with a knowing wink.

'It didn't turn out quite as expected,' Raine said, reluctant to go into any details, but she might have known that Stephanie would jump on it right away.

'Oh?' Stephanie's face fell. 'You mean there was no romance?'

'Some bombs exploded when we were watching a play in the theatre.' She bit her lip.

'How awful,' Stephanie said, looking contrite. 'Did anyone get hurt?'

The baby.

'At least two people died. We never knew the full story.' That was true at any rate.

'Was this in London?'

'No, Windsor.'

Stephanie gasped. 'How shocking. Were the King and Queen in residence?'

'More than likely,' Raine answered. 'But you don't see them wandering about, although I'm told the princesses are often doing their "Dig for Victory" bit in the vegetable garden.'

'*Really* mucking in,' Stephanie chuckled. Then she sobered. 'Sorry, Raine, I don't mean to be flippant about your frightful experience. What happened, exactly?'

Raine gave a shortened version with no mention of the baby. That was somehow too painful.

'How terrifying.' Stephanie puffed out her cheeks. Then she threw Raine a wicked grin. 'But I hope you didn't let it interfere with your special weekend with Mr Green Eyes.'

Raine's face grew hot under Stephanie's scrutiny.

'Or did it?' Stephanie said. 'You're blushing, Lorraine. Did something happen you're not letting on?'

'It's warm in here, that's all.'

'Not that warm. Not enough to set your face on fire.'

Please stop badgering, Stephanie.

Raine heard footsteps coming along the passage and to her relief Mrs Grayson came into the room bearing a tray. She put a plate in front of Raine.

'You just get that inside you, dear. I expect you've had a

long day so it should perk you up. It's what my Albert used to say when he was tired. He always felt like a better man when he'd eaten.'

'It smells wonderful,' Raine said, looking at the generous slice of meat pie and vegetables.

'I'll leave you two to have a girls' natter then.' Mrs Grayson turned to go, then swung round. 'Oh, I almost forgot. There was a phone call for you about half an hour ago, Lorraine. A young man asking for you. I said you were due home this evening but you'd want some supper. He said he'll telephone again about nine if that wasn't too late. He sounded a very polite young man – well, they're all young to me at my age.' She broke off, giggling like a girl.

Alec certainly knew how to get on the right side of everyone. Raine smiled to herself. He must be checking to see she'd arrived back safely. It gave her a warm glow to know he cared.

'Thank you very much for the message, Mrs Grayson.'

'That's all right, dear. I'm never the one to stand in the way of true love.' She gave a throaty laugh as she disappeared.

'Alec!' Stephanie grinned when Mrs Grayson was out of earshot. 'I knew it when she told me some chap had phoned asking for you.'

'Please don't make a big thing of it,' Raine protested. 'There's nothing serious between us. We've become better friends, that's all, which is pleasant after all our sniping at one another. And that's the way I want it to stay.'

'Mmm. I wonder . . .' was all Stephanie remarked.

Supper passed quietly. Stephanie for once allowed Raine to enjoy her meal without her usual patter by moving to one of the pair of shabby but comfortable chairs by the fire and picking up one of Mrs Grayson's romance magazines.

Raine savoured every bite of their host's delicious pie,

even though the meat was difficult to find, and finished with a bowl of tapioca topped by a teaspoonful of Mrs G's home-made strawberry jam.

'Mmm. That was delicious.' Raine let out a contented sigh and joined Stephanie on the chair opposite. She stretched her legs out towards the fire, which was dying down.

'Do you think we should put a bit more coal on it?' Stephanie said wistfully, throwing down the magazine. 'I don't think I've ever been warm in this house.'

'Let's risk Mrs G's wrath.' Raine chucked a few pieces on. 'My feet are still cold from the train.'

'What's the time?' Stephanie said.

Raine glanced at her watch. The minute hand had hardly moved. 'Twenty minutes to nine.'

They chatted about work and Stephanie told her about a new pilot who had arrived the day before. Her name was Dolores, a lively American girl who'd joined the ATA via Montreal and been sent straight to White Waltham.

'She came with this huge food parcel,' Stephanie said, her eyes wide as she recounted all the items of food Dolores had pulled out. 'Cookies and candy, as she called them – biscuits and chocolate to you and me, Lorraine,' Stephanie said with a wink. 'And there were tins of peaches and pears, a pound cake, she called it – all sorts of lovely things we haven't seen for a long time. Oh, and American ciggies.' Stephanie pulled a face. 'Actually, they're not that good, but she was so generous the way she shared everything with us. That's how to make friends, I reckon.'

'She sounds lovely,' Raine said. 'I'm looking forward to meeting her. And enjoying some of her lovely food parcel – that is, if you haven't already cleaned her out.'

The minutes crept by and at last, a couple of minutes after nine, Raine heard the shrill of the telephone.

'Give my love to him,' Stephanie teased as Raine jumped from her seat.

She shut the door behind her as she hurried out to the hall, hoping Mrs Grayson would be far enough away not to overhear. Raine let it ring one more time, enjoying the feeling of anticipation shooting through her body before she finally picked up the receiver.

'Miss Linfoot?' the operator said.

'Yes,' Raine answered with a wide smile.

'I have a call for you. One moment, please. I'm putting you through.'

'Hello, Alec,' Raine said a little breathlessly. 'It's me.'

There was a long pause.

Was he still there? Had they been cut off?

'Raine?' the voice said, sounding puzzled. 'It's Doug.'

It was as though someone had squeezed every ounce of blood from her. Her hand shook as she tried to hold on to the receiver, but it slipped from her fingers and dangled on its wire. Her head whirled. She was going to faint.

Don't be silly. Of course it's not him – you're imagining things.

'Hello. Hello, Raine. Are you there?'

She licked her lips. She opened her mouth to speak. And then she slumped against the wall. She put out her arms to stop herself from falling. Her head buzzed and she groaned as she crumpled to the floor.

Someone was bending down. She flickered open her eyelids.

'Lorraine. Are you all right? Speak to me.'

Raine tried to raise herself to stand but her legs wouldn't obey her. Stephanie peered down at her, alarm on her face. Hadn't Stephanie told her Alec had phoned? Then surely it was Alec who'd rung. She couldn't think straight. Because it couldn't have been Doug. He was dead. They'd told her he'd never have survived that crash. His body would have burned to cinders in the fire.

She tried to shake the nightmare image away and pull herself up, but her legs wouldn't obey her.

'Here, let me help you,' Stephanie said, putting an arm round her.

Was someone playing a cruel prank? But if it *was* him . . . Raine's eye went to the receiver which was still twirling slowly on its wire. She remembered now that she'd let it slip from her fingers.

'Stephanie, could you see if he's still on the phone?'

'Of course.' Her friend picked up the receiver. 'Hello, anyone there?' She waited a few seconds. 'Hello, hello.' She hung it back up. 'Sorry, Lorraine, it's just the dialling tone. Don't worry – I'm sure Mr Green Eyes will call back.'

Raine shook her head.

'Did you finish your conversation?' Stephanie asked.

'No,' Raine mumbled. 'We didn't even start it.'

'Come and sit in the room, darling,' Stephanie said, her arm surprisingly strong as she steadied Raine. 'You look as though you've seen a ghost.'

That's exactly what it had felt like – a ghost. Dumbly, she allowed Stephanie to lead her into the sitting room. Thankfully, she could hear Mrs Grayson clattering in the kitchen. She couldn't face her – or anyone. Even though Stephanie was being so kind.

'What did he say to make you so upset?' Stephanie said when she'd joined her on the sofa.

Raine shook her head. She was dumbfounded. It couldn't be true. Doug couldn't be alive. But if it really *was* him, and not someone playing a hideous joke, then it was the most wonderful news. And now he must think she'd simply put the phone down on him, not wanting to talk to him. If it was really him, he must have had a terrible time . . . and miraculously come through it.

'Did he say he didn't want to see you again, the cad?' Stephanie's eyes were wide with sympathy.

'No, nothing like that,' Raine said, her voice hardly recognisable to herself. It was more like a croak.

'Take your time.' Stephanie took one of Raine's cold hands in her own and rubbed it.

'You see, it wasn't Alec,' Raine whispered.

'What? Another admirer? Well, that shouldn't have put you in such a state.'

'It was Doug.'

There was a silence. Then Stephanie said, 'Do you mean your friend who was shot down in his Spit?'

Raine nodded. Her mouth was dry. She tried to swallow and couldn't. She licked her lips. She was in a dream. She'd prayed that Doug would be alive so many times, but in the end she'd forced herself to accept he couldn't possibly have survived. That's what they'd said. That's what she'd had to believe.

Stephanie sprang up. 'I'm going to ask Mrs G if she would make us a cup of tea.'

'Oh, don't mention anything to her—' Raine started.

'No, I won't . . . I promise.'

Raine leaned her head on the back of the sofa. If it really was him, maybe he wouldn't phone again, thinking she wanted him out of her life. She didn't know his number or even where he was stationed now he was back in England. If it really *was* him. Which it couldn't have been. She smacked her hand against her head. Was she going mad?

Stephanie was back with a tea tray and some digestives in a matter of minutes.

'What did he say?' she said once Raine had taken a few sips.

Raine closed her eyes, recalling his voice. 'I thought it was

347

Alec.' She took in a deep breath and turned to Stephanie. 'So I said, "Hello, Alec, it's me." And there was a long pause. I thought we'd been cut off. And then he said, "Raine? It's Doug."'

'My goodness. What a surprise – shock, I suppose. But you should be thrilled. I always thought you had a soft spot for him.'

'Oh, I do,' Raine said. 'And I know he does for me.'

Stephanie's eyes held hers. 'But you're not in love with him, are you?'

Raine shook her head. 'I love him, but as a dear friend. Almost like the brother I always wanted.'

'Is he in love with *you*?'

Raine stared at her as though Stephanie had the answer, not herself. Why was she feeling so shaken up? This was her dream that Doug was still alive. Stephanie must be right – she must still be in shock.

'He said as much in the last letter he was writing to me and hadn't finished it before . . .' She cleared her throat as tears pricked the back of her eyes. 'Before they were all called to scramble.'

'And could you imagine now he's back – if it really *is* him – that you might care for him in the same way?'

'No,' Raine said emphatically. 'I cared for him deeply and when I was young – sixteen – I thought it was love. But then . . .' She broke off.

'Then Alec came along and this time you knew the difference.' Stephanie said it as a statement.

Raine nodded miserably, her eyes downcast. 'Yes. I knew the difference,' she said, repeating her friend's words, 'although I didn't realise it at the time. But now I feel so guilty. It *was* Doug on the phone. I know his voice.' She caught her friend's hand and burst into tears. 'Oh, Stephanie, I don't know what to do.'

Chapter Thirty

That night Raine's dreams tormented her. Alec had come to take her out, but when he turned up his face changed in front of her to Doug. And it was an angry and hurt Doug who told her she had to choose between him and her 'new boyfriend', the one called Alec. When she properly awoke in the morning she lay there, hot and perspiring, feeling thoroughly ashamed of herself.

Stephanie was right. She should be so happy, so relieved that Doug was alive and safe and back in England. If only Mrs Grayson had asked who was calling. But Doug had probably, with the best intentions, wanted to surprise her and wouldn't have told Mrs Grayson anyway. He must have wondered what on earth had happened when he'd told her who was ringing and there was no answer. And if he'd tried the number again it would have been engaged.

He was her dearest friend and she'd mourned him deeply, but she'd never told him she loved him. But had she led him on without realising? Or had he assumed more than she could give him? No, that would be the meanest of tricks to blame him.

She sighed. She didn't have a clue how to contact him so there was little she could do except wait for him to ring again. But when two days passed with no telephone call she felt sick at heart. Doug would be hurt by her lack of response. She didn't know what condition he was in, or if he'd been injured. How had he managed to escape death? So many questions that required answers.

All she could do was concentrate on her job and pray that he would give her a second chance and telephone again.

'Post, everyone.' Beryl, one of the clerks, began handing round envelopes the following morning.

'Anything for me?' Stephanie asked, her face tilted up in anticipation.

Beryl flicked through the pile. 'Sorry, Steph, nothing.'

Stephanie turned away, but not before Raine saw the hurt look in her eyes. She was about to give her a comforting word when Beryl came up.

'Three for you, Raine,' she said, handing Raine the envelopes.

Practically grabbing them from Beryl's hand, Raine glanced at the top one. Maman's handwriting. She'd read it later. The second address was typed, postmarked Wolverhampton, and 'Confidential' typed in the top left-hand corner and underlined twice in blue ink. Then her heart leapt. The third was Doug's unmistakable large scrawl.

She rushed to the crew room and was disappointed to find three male pilots chatting. They looked up as she entered. She knew them by sight and said, 'Good morning,' but luckily they merely nodded and carried on with their conversation. She found an easy chair as far from them as possible and ripped open Doug's letter with trembling fingers.

19th February 1942
Dearest Raine,
I don't know quite what was going on when I phoned. At first I thought you'd put the receiver down on me, not

wanting to have me back in your life, and then I thought that couldn't possibly be true and that you must have somehow been interrupted. I realised you couldn't phone me back because you wouldn't have known where I was speaking from. I'm actually back at Biggin Hill in their sick quarters. Anyway I decided it was easier to write you a letter. I wanted you to know what happened to me as I imagine they had me down as 'missing, presumed dead' and I like to think you were a bit sad by that news!

You probably heard I was shot down and my plane caught fire. That bit was true but I managed to bale out. Thank God I landed in France and not in the Channel! But I couldn't get up. I'd broken a bone in my leg! I was spotted by a lovely young girl out for a walk with her dog – certainly my lucky day! – and she rushed home to tell her family. Her father and brother arrived and carried me back to their house. Thankfully they all loathe Hitler and his vile regime or I would have been done for!

At the time I was hardly aware of what was happening, as I banged my head on impact. They got a doctor to set my leg, but I couldn't remember anything except my name. Brigitte, who rescued me, talked to me every day, jolting my memory, and eventually things started coming back. Your face especially.

Raine swallowed hard as she read on.

This all took several weeks. I only have very rusty schoolboy French so it was difficult to communicate, but when I could walk without help, somehow that brave family managed to get me onto the first leg (no pun intended!) of the escape route and after several weeks I eventually got back to Blighty.

I thought it had healed on its own but it played up a stink on the way back from France – partly what took me so long – so they are re-doing it. But it's my head that is having the hardest time to heal, though not in the physical sense. For those few moments when I was all alone in the Spit, somersaulting down, my last thoughts were for you, my darling. I do hope you don't mind my calling you that, but it feels right and natural to me. The old saying that 'life's too short' certainly rings true after what I've been through, so I don't want to stifle my feelings for you any longer. You must know what I'm trying to say but I'll wait until I see you before I say the words.

I do hope you can come and visit me – maybe when you next see your family – though I shouldn't be in here too much longer. Don't worry if it's too difficult as I know you're very busy with deliveries, but a letter would be wonderful.

Am longing to hear from you.

All my love,

Doug xx

It was hard to take it all in. Raine read through the letter again, more slowly this time, her tears trickling onto the paper. What a brave family they'd been to help him get home. The French were well aware that if they were caught by the Gestapo helping one of the Allies they would face certain death – and not only themselves, she'd heard, but their entire family.

Her stomach curdling at the thought, she wiped her eyes and rose to her feet. She'd go to the cloakroom and splash her face with cold water. Peering in the mirror above the sink she saw her eyes and nose were red as though she had a cold coming. If only it was just a cold. She could put up with being grounded for a few days, as pilots had to do if they caught one, but this was worse. Lack of sleep and being worried out of her mind.

Alec was constantly in her thoughts but now she must push his image away. Doug, her dear, long-standing friend, needed her attention. But how was she going to answer the last part of his letter where he'd made it as plain as if he'd told her to her face that he'd fallen in love with her. He'd called her his darling, but instead of the endearment making her thrill she felt vaguely uncomfortable. She took a deep breath and let it out in a long sigh. Why must life be so complicated? But it was the war; it had changed everything.

And as Stephanie had so neatly put it . . . she'd met Alec.

She didn't even have time to look at her other two letters. It was already nine o'clock and she needed to collect her chits for the day's deliveries.

Going by the chits, she had a full day ahead of her. The first plane was a Mosquito. As it was built for speed, Raine couldn't help flying a little faster than she was supposed to and enjoying every moment. Next was a Miles Magister and then finally, a Hurricane. Thank goodness the ATA kept her busy.

She'd had to eat her emergency chocolate bar as there'd been no time to stop even for a sandwich. She was pathetically grateful she'd been able to grab a lift in an Anson from the furthest delivery and was back home, having her supper at Mrs Grayson's table, exactly eight hours later.

This evening Mrs Grayson chose to join her for supper. She said Stephanie was out for the evening and was being most mysterious about where she was going. Raine smiled. Stephanie ought to be an actress – she certainly loved a bit of drama.

She suddenly remembered Maman's letter and the typed one. The minute she put her knife and fork together she excused herself, saying she was tired out and was going to read in her room and have an early night.

Her mother's letter was full of the usual descriptions of

the frumpy WVS ladies who she couldn't deny worked hard every day.

If I could just get my hands on a few of them, Maman wrote, *I could turn them into feminine women instead of carthorses. Some of them are not bad-looking but they have no idea how to make the best of themselves. . .*

Raine couldn't help a wry smile. Maman would never change, war or no war. Her mother briefly mentioned Suzanne, that she'd started playing the piano again, and that Véronique hadn't given up the idea of being a Land Girl when she was old enough. *But it is the last thing I want for my baby,* Maman wrote. *Rough red hands and dirty broken nails.* She ended the letter, *Your loving Maman.*

If only . . .

Raine sighed as she opened the typed envelope. She glanced at the signature: Pauline. Curious as to why Pauline should be writing to her in confidence, she began to read.

Dear Lorraine,

I wanted to drop you a quick note as I'm not sure how long I'll be here at Cosford. I have received a full report from Flt. Capt. Jones on the Hurricane accident and can only say how pleased and relieved I was with the outcome. I wish I had been at WW at the time and on the panel, especially when I found out the person who had been brought in to testify on the performance of the aircraft was none other than Flt. Lt. Fox, whom I understand did everything in his power to put you in a bad light.

Raine's heart beat a little faster at seeing Foxy's name. Was that nasty little man going to haunt her all her life? Taking a deep breath, she continued to read.

354

*Thank goodness Flt. Capt. Jones is a fair-minded and
sensible person.*

*Now for the good news – well, it is as far as you're
concerned. Fox has been caught red-handed! Yes, another
typist at Biggin Hill. I won't go into the gory details but
it was serious enough for him to have been demoted. I
don't think he will dare bother you again.*

*I wanted you to know, Lorraine, so you can rest assured
that he got his comeuppance.*

I hope to be back shortly at WW.

Yours most sincerely,

Pauline Gower (Director of Women Personnel)

*P.S. I know I don't have to remind you that this letter
is confidential and the contents must not be discussed.*

Raine placed the letter back in its envelope, a thoughtful
expression crossing her face. What a perfectly stupid man Foxy
was. He had so much to give with his experience in instructing
young pilots, and instead had made an absolute fool of himself.
But she was glad he was no longer able to continue such
abominable behaviour – at least, not in the RAF.

Funny that Linda had asked in her last letter if she'd heard
any more about him. It was a pity she wasn't allowed to tell her
that he'd been caught red-handed and demoted. Linda would
have loved that. But she could certainly tell her about Foxy on
the panel after the Hurricane accident – and for all his efforts
he hadn't managed to persuade the flight captain that it had
been her fault. And she could tell Linda how the flight captain
told him to keep his opinions to himself in more or less those
words. She gave a rueful smile. That would have to suffice.

White Waltham was particularly busy right now and Raine
found herself doing another double shift, all the time hoping

to squeeze in some time to see Doug. She'd written to him that same evening explaining it was the shock of hearing his voice when he'd phoned and she'd dropped the receiver. A fellow pilot had assumed she was just hanging up after her conversation and had set it back on its cradle. It sounded feeble even as she penned the words, but it was more or less the truth.

She described how happy she was to know he was safe, and that she'd come and see him as soon as the CO could let her off. She deliberately didn't mention anything about his changed feelings towards her. She needed more time to think how to answer that letter.

She received a quick note in reply saying of course he understood and to come whenever she had a chance.

That same day she'd heard from Alec. Thankful the postman had come early this morning, she was able to read it before going to the station.

Raine, my darling, my dearest,

I can't stop thinking of you. And remembering our time in Windsor. I know it was terrible about the bombing, but nothing – not even that – could take away my joy that we were together as we were meant to be. I felt so close to you in every way and I think you felt the same.

Raine, I love you and I'm not pretending. You do believe me, don't you, my love?

I wish I'd never asked you to play such a stupid game as it almost backfired. I just wanted to let you think we could have a nice relaxing break from this bloody awful war, and that if we were in love it would be even more magical. In my mind I thought if we played at it – pretended – we would actually feel it for real – although I always did. I just had to convince you!

We've been extra busy in the department but soon I should get a day or two's leave and hope it might coincide with yours. Let me know and I'll work things out. Where would you like to go? I don't mind, so long as I have this gorgeous woman holding my arm and looking at me with those fascinating eyes! That's all it takes to make me happy.

Well, darling, I have a long day ahead of me so I will close now and wait for your letter.

Sending you love,

Alec

XXX

A lump settled in the back of Raine's throat. She swallowed hard, but it wouldn't shift. She knew he loved her as well as she loved him, even though she still hadn't said the three magic words she knew he wanted to hear. But now things had taken a new turn and he didn't know it. He wouldn't love her when he heard that Doug was back. But how could she face Alec and explain? And how could she face Doug?

She hadn't mentioned anything about Alec in her letter to Doug. It would have been cowardly just to have written it, and she prided herself on always meeting trouble or any difficulty head on. She needed to see both of them face to face. But her insides quaked at the thought.

This was another one of those times she wished she smoked. A cigarette would have helped, been a comfort – that's what every smoker told her anyway. If only the weather would pick up. It was almost March and the first daffodils were in bud. Soon, she hoped, they'd be making a splash of colour. She shivered. Yes, the room was cold. But that was not the reason why she suddenly wanted to crawl back into bed and pull the bedclothes over her head.

Chapter Thirty-One

'We have a new chap joining us today,' one of the adjutants announced in the crew room one morning. 'He's a Czech. Maximillian Janda – Max for short.' He paused to take a drag of his cigarette. 'He's one of the RAF's best pilots. Utterly fearless.'

Why is he here then? Raine thought.

'Afraid he had a bit of bad luck last year,' the adjutant continued. 'Shot down by our own side. Bloody unfortunate. His right arm took the brunt as well as his Hurricane.' His eyes swept the room. 'So give him the usual welcome. Make him feel at home. Well, when I say "at home" I don't mean that literally – it's a bit of a trek to go.' There was a ripple of polite laughter. 'He'll be one of our senior pilots and will also act as an instructor as and when.' He looked towards the door. 'Ah, here's the chap himself.'

All eyes turned to the figure in the doorway. Something flickered in Raine's mind. She'd seen him before but it took her a moment to place exactly where. Of course. He was the foreign chap who'd tried to be kind to her that time when she'd had a rotten flight, but she'd refused to let him tell her his name. She'd thought afterwards his accent might have been Polish.

And then she noticed the right sleeve of his tunic and

gave a sharp intake of breath. It simply hung flat, empty. Poor bloke. His arm hadn't just taken the brunt, it had been amputated. So how on earth . . .?

'Let me introduce you to some of your fellow pilots, Max, old chap,' the adjutant said, gesturing him to join them.

Max walked in. He stopped and hesitated. He was an attractive man, craggy-featured, with his very dark hair and brown eyes. Although he smiled politely at everyone, he wasn't smiling with his eyes at all, though Raine was sure he was taking everything in. His glance fell on her with a look of recognition.

A few people stared at the empty sleeve, but there was a warm murmuring of approval. Doubtless he'd been tested on his ability to still be able to fly, but Raine knew nothing would be commented on in public. Audrey sent Raine a wink and held up her thumb. Raine hid a smile. She knew enough about Audrey to know that she had already set her sights on him.

Max Janda proved a popular figure around White Waltham. It was a little embarrassing for Raine at first when she remembered how she'd treated him so curtly that first time in the NAAFI, but he didn't seem the least bit put out when Raine stopped and introduced herself, breaking the ice between them.

'Nice to know your name, after all,' he said, smiling. That same smile that didn't light up his eyes the way it should.

Probably not hearing from his family at home, Raine thought. It must be terribly worrying for him. She resolved to have a proper chat with him soon.

'Douglas White is in the visitors' room – probably having a sneaky cigarette.' A smiling nurse pointed along the corridor Raine had just walked along. 'First on the right.'

'Thank you.'

Raine's heart hammered. She could feel it throb in her ears. She took a deep breath and knocked and opened the door.

Three men were sitting at a small table drinking tea and smoking. They turned towards the door as she entered.

'Raine!' Doug jerked up, then half lost his balance and clutched the edge of the table.

The man sitting next to him caught his arm. 'Steady, mate.' He eased Doug back into his seat.

Doug raised his eyes to her. 'Sorry, love, I can't move as fast as I'd like.' He looked at the other two men. 'This is Lorraine who I've told you about.' He turned to her, laughing. 'Probably bored the pants off them.' He held out his hand. 'Come and sit down, Raine, and let me introduce you to Fred Simpson and Johnny Burton. Bertie, as we call him, is from my old squadron.'

The one called Bertie got to his feet and gestured to her to take his chair. He slid an empty one over to the other side of her and sat.

'So you're the beautiful girl he left behind,' Bertie said, turning his head and giving her a wink. 'I can see why he was anxious to get back to you.' The admiration in his eyes was plain.

This was worse than she'd feared. It seemed Doug had already told other people about their relationship – how he saw it – before she'd had a chance to speak to him.

'Nice to meet you both,' she said, briefly glancing at the two of them and removing her forage cap.

'We'll be getting along, I think,' Simpson said, standing up. 'Come on, Bertie, time to leave the two lovebirds alone for their romantic reunion.'

Bertie seemed reluctant to follow. His gaze fell on Raine. 'Shame. Just as I was getting to know her.'

'I'm sure you'll get to know her,' Doug cut in, grinning, 'but not as an available woman, if I have my way.'

'What a spoilsport,' Bertie laughed, his eyes roving over her. 'Well, Raine, it's very nice to put a face to the name.'

Politely, Raine held out her hand to him, annoyed he was using her diminutive name without asking, and annoyed with Doug's presumptuous remarks. Keeping his eyes locked with hers Bertie took it and raised it to his lips. With a wink at Doug this time he followed Simpson out of the door and shut it with a click.

'Don't take any notice of him,' Doug chuckled as he took Raine's hand. 'He's a bit of a womaniser. Can't resist a pretty girl. And I don't blame him. Who could resist you?' He paused. 'What's wrong, love? Bertie didn't mean any harm. He's just a charmer, that's all.'

'It's not that,' Raine said, biting her lip, 'although to be honest, I didn't find your friend charming at all.'

She watched Doug's brow crease. She probably shouldn't have said that about one of his mates.

To her relief he broke into a smile. 'You're probably right. He can be a bit of a devil sometimes.' He tapped his thigh. 'So if it's not Bertie, what is it?'

How could she say the words that would destroy his happiness and his love for her? He was holding her hand and smiling at her.

'This must all have been quite a shock for you to find out I'm alive and kicking.' He glanced at his leg and chuckled. 'Well, not exactly kicking, but you know what I mean.' He gently pulled her round to face him.

'Doug—'

'I'm sorry I'm not much good at standing at the moment, but I will be. It's all healing properly this time. I want to take you in my arms and thoroughly kiss you – the way we never have before.'

'Doug, I—'

Clumsily, he put his arms round her and took her chin in his hand. 'Oh, Raine, this is what I've been dreaming of.'

'I don't think this is the right place,' Raine said, averting her face, her eyes drawn to the door. 'Anyone could come in at any moment.'

He took the still burning cigarette from the ashtray and stubbed it out. 'Raine, you did realise in that letter I wrote that I'm in love with you?'

She realised she was holding her breath. She looked at him. His dear face. His clear blue eyes.

'Doug, you've taken me completely by surprise. I never dreamed you felt like that about me. You were always my big brother.'

'That's the way I thought of myself, too,' Doug chuckled. 'No one was more surprised than me when I realised how crazy I was about you.'

He'd lost weight and looked older, but when he laughed she could see the old Doug shining through. Her dearest friend. She swallowed hard. She'd rehearsed her words so many times for this moment but nothing felt right. It all sounded so false to her ears.

'Dare I hope you feel the same about *me*?' He squeezed her hand gently.

When she said nothing he looked at her, his expression anxious.

'I don't know what to say,' Raine said truthfully.

'I expect it's a shock, but that's what war does. It makes you realise what's important and do something about it before it's too late.' Doug patted his dressing gown pocket. 'Drat. That was my last cigarette. They keep count in here and you're only allowed five a day.' He gave her a rueful smile.

Say something, Raine. You've got to tell him. It isn't fair on him . . . or Alec.

362

As though he'd read her thoughts he suddenly said, 'By the way, Raine, I've been meaning to ask who this Alec is that you mentioned? You thought I was him on the phone.'

Dear God.

There was a tentative knock at the door. Desperately grateful for the interruption, Raine jumped up and opened it. A white-faced girl stumbled in, sobbing her heart out.

'What is it?' Raine put her arm around the shaking shoulders. 'Come and sit down a minute – here.' She patted her chair and frowned to Doug, nodding her head towards the door for him to leave them.

'We need to finish this conversation, Raine,' he said over his shoulder.

'Yes, I know. I'll catch up with you in a bit.' She turned to the girl sitting beside her. 'What's the matter, love? Is there anything I can do?'

'N-n-nothing.'

'Would it help to tell me?'

The girl looked at her with tears still streaming down her cheeks. 'I'm trying to find the chapel. I need to say a prayer for someone.' She brushed away her tears with the back of her hand.

'For someone you love?' Raine said softly.

'Yes,' the girl whispered. 'My boyfriend. I didn't get here in time.' She broke down again and held her hands to her face.

Raine's heart turned over.

'What is his name?' Somehow Raine needed to know this was a real person who had lost his life and not just 'another one'.

'Ken.' The girl's voice cracked as she said his name through her trembling wet fingers.

'And *your* name?' Raine asked gently.

'Pat,' the girl said thickly. 'We were to be married next

363

month. And now he's d-d-dead. I don't know what I'm going to do.' She looked at Raine for the first time. 'You see, I'm going to have a baby.'

Raine stroked Pat's hair. 'I don't know where the chapel is, love, but I'll ask someone. Where are your parents?'

'I haven't told them about the baby,' she said. 'They'll probably throw me out.'

'I'm sure they won't. They love you and they'll be thrilled to be grandparents – once they get used to the idea.'

Pat didn't look convinced.

'I'm going to find out where the chapel is,' Raine said, standing up. 'Will you promise to stay here? I'll be back in a jiffy.'

'Yes, all right,' Pat sniffed.

Raine walked swiftly back to Doug's ward. He saw her and waved her to come over, but she shook her head and spoke to the sister.

Sister nodded. 'Leave her to me,' she said. 'I'll show her where it is and stay with her. She shot off as soon as we told her, poor girl.'

'I'll tell her so she knows I haven't abandoned her,' Raine said.

Sister opened the visitors' room door and Pat looked up.

'Sister is going with you to the chapel,' Raine said. 'I have to say goodbye now to the person I was visiting.' She patted the girl's thin arm. 'But I'm thinking of you and will say a prayer for you.'

'Thank you.' Pat gave her a watery smile.

Sister briskly took hold of her. 'Come on, my dear. After your visit to the chapel we're going to make you a nice cup of tea and you can tell me where you live. We'll make sure you get home safely, so don't you worry.'

'Thank you, Sister,' Raine said. 'I'd better get back to Doug.'

Doug was sitting on a chair beside his bed. He looked up at her approach and her heart lurched at his serious expression. She grabbed another chair and set it down opposite him.

'Sorry about that,' she said, 'but I had to do something. Her boyfriend died before she could say goodbye to him. It's so sad.'

'Yes, it is,' Doug said, an impatient edge to his tone. He caught her eye. 'Now, where were we?'

This was it. But how could she say anything in a ward full of people?

A nurse suddenly appeared. 'Sorry, visiting hours are over. Mr White is due for an X-ray, so please say your goodbyes.' She began to swish the curtains together.

Saved again, Raine stood, despising herself for being so cowardly.

'But we haven't had any time to—' Doug began.

'You know the rules.' The nurse gave him a disarming smile. 'Your girlfriend will come and see you soon, I'm sure. Anyway, you're due for discharge in a few days so you'll have plenty of time together.'

'If only.' Doug looked like a bad-tempered schoolboy.

Everything seemed stacked against her telling Doug the truth, but it was no good. The hospital just wasn't the right place to have such a personal conversation. Even the nurse assumed she was his girlfriend. It would be a rotten trick to spill out her love for another man in front of other patients and nursing staff, as though she'd picked such a place on purpose so he couldn't give a natural reaction. And afterwards, he'd be left on his own to absorb the shock. Then there'd be all the questions he'd want to ask.

Raine picked up her coat and leant down to say goodbye. He tried to kiss her mouth, but she turned her head a fraction and his kiss landed on her cheek.

'I'll see you soon, Doug,' she said, putting on her coat and collecting her cap and handbag.

'All right, love,' Doug said. 'Take good care of yourself.'

'You, too,' she said.

'Raine, just one more thing.'

She turned.

'I love you,' he said. 'Don't forget it, will you?'

'I won't.'

Tears sprung to her eyes she walked away, along the corridor and out of the entrance door. She couldn't wait to get back to White Waltham where the only turbulence was in the air.

Chapter Thirty-Two

It wouldn't have taken more than a minute or two to have explained to Doug who Alec was – and it would have stopped him having any further illusions – but the nurse had glared at Raine, putting her in a difficult position. Raine tried to convince herself that the dreaded moment had been put off by no fault of her own, but a little voice inside her head insisted that if she'd really wanted to tell Doug, she would have asked a passing nurse to direct that poor sobbing girl to the chapel.

But it had been impossible while he was in hospital, she argued with herself. She needed to meet him somewhere where no one was liable to burst in at any moment. She'd have to make do with writing him a letter, but not make a big thing of it. Simply tell him to let her know when he was to be discharged and they could then have a proper talk.

She received his reply in a short note saying they were discharging him in exactly a week and where could they meet. And how much he was looking forward to seeing her again now his leg had improved, and they could talk things through and make their future plans.

Happy though she was that his leg was so much better, and he'd be coming out of hospital soon, she was once again exasperated that he was jumping ahead with no hint from her that this was what she wanted.

She desperately needed to talk to Alec. She missed him with such an ache it hurt. But when should she tell *him*? He deserved to know about Doug right away. She closed her eyes for a few seconds as though her own instinct would give her the answer. But she was disappointed.

As usual, when something played on Raine's mind, it was her work that saved her. She was simply too busy to deal with anything emotional as she'd had to cover for yet another pilot, working several ten- and twelve-hour days, one after the other. She sent a note to Doug telling him she'd let him know as soon as she got a few spare hours off. Doug wrote a disgruntled note in return.

'Four of you will be flying in a gaggle tomorrow from Scotland delivering the four Tiger Moths – it's the most efficient way to get them to the same place at the same time.' Pauline Gower's eyes swept round the group of pilots waiting to pick up their day's chits. 'Stephanie, Dolores and Audrey . . .' She paused. 'Audrey, you can take over from the other taxi pilot on the outward journey when necessary.'

It was going to be a long trip.

Pauline's eyes landed on Raine. 'Lorraine, you'll make up the fourth.'

Raine had heard about gaggles and the difficulty of keeping in formation and she didn't like the sound of it one bit. They had enough to do navigating their own routes without instruments, let alone making sure three other planes stayed in sight, but if that was the instruction, then they would carry it out.

'Any questions?'

'Our route?' Stephanie enquired.

'Ah, yes. You'll be leaving here in an Anson heading for

368

Perth where you'll stay the night and next morning pick up the Tigers – that's when you'll be flying in a gaggle – and deliver them to Hawarden near Chester. From there you'll separate and make any deliveries they have you down for. With a bit of luck you might even get off lightly and not have another one.

'The main thing is to contact us when you reach Hawarden and let us know where you're heading next, or whether you're coming straight back to the station. That could mean a long train journey unless any other pilot is going your direction.'

Raine knew the others, like her, were trying to imagine flying from Scotland to Chester in an open cockpit in cold, windy British March. And more than likely a long miserable train journey back to London.

'You've all flown in formation, I take it?'

'Actually, I haven't,' Raine confessed.

'Nor have I,' Dolores admitted.

The CO regarded them with raised eyebrows.

'It's not difficult. All you have to do is keep each other in sight. If you do that you'll be fine.'

'Any chance, darling, of getting off for a few hours the day after tomorrow?'

It was Alec. It had been more than a month since their time in Windsor that she'd seen him.

'No chance at all, I'm afraid,' she said. 'Four of us are off to Perth tomorrow. We'll have to stay the night and then we're delivering four Tigers to Hawarden. From there I might, if I'm really lucky, be able to cadge a lift back. If not, I'll have to take the train and goodness knows what time I'll arrive. And I'll be so exhausted I won't want to see anyone.' She paused. 'That's assuming I don't have to make another delivery from Hawarden. Pauline wasn't sure. It's all a bit flexible at the moment.'

369

'Damn. It's the only free time I have,' Alec said. 'The day after tomorrow evening and maybe a few hours Wednesday evening.'

She squashed the disappointment.

'Look,' he went on, 'I'll come to White Waltham the day after tomorrow evening and wait for you. I don't care how long. I just want to set eyes on you again. I might forget what you look like if I go on much longer.'

'It's too chancy. Why don't I telephone you when I'm back in case I'm laid up with bad weather somewhere or sent to another far-flung station.'

There was a pause.

'I suppose that's sensible, though I'm not feeling very sensible at this moment.' Alec's voice softened to an intimacy that made her quiver. 'Oh, Raine, I miss you so terribly. I want to feast my eyes on you. Kiss those luscious lips again. I can't wait.'

'Nor can I,' Raine said, her heart giving a little skip of excitement. 'But I'll be home before we know it, and if it's not too late I'll ring you. If that's the case, I'll phone first thing Wednesday morning.'

'Then I'd better say goodnight, my love.'

'Goodnight, Alec.' She let seconds tick by on purpose. 'By the way, don't get too cocky,' she grinned to herself, 'but I miss you, too.'

She heard him chuckle. 'Good. That's how I want it to stay.' Then he added, 'Don't forget I love you.'

'I won't.'

'You promise?'

'I promise.'

She put the receiver down and hugged herself. She'd be seeing him soon. Very soon.

* * *

370

To Raine's surprise it was the Czech pilot, Max Janda, casually leaning against the fuselage of the taxi, who was taking them to Perth. A long way, she would have thought, with only one arm, though he'd have Audrey to take over every so often. Audrey was already standing by his side, her head close to his as he spread the map out on the wing and showed her the route he'd marked with a red pencil. A delighted grin smattered Audrey's strong features as she nodded her approval.

'Good morning, ladies,' he said, looking up and smiling. 'I hope you will have a comfortable flight. There is some wind but we should be okay. Audrey will be my co-pilot as it is a long flight. We will break it up, of course. So if you take your place, we will prepare for take-off.'

Raine took a seat with Stephanie and Dolores in the cabin. While Max was going through the checklist with Audrey, Raine glanced at Stephanie, remembering how hurt the girl had looked when Beryl told her she had no letters for her. Today Stephanie looked pale underneath her powder and lipstick. It was strange. She hadn't liked Stephanie much when she'd first met her, but she'd grown very fond of her. Stephanie had proved herself a loyal friend.

Bit like Alec, Raine thought ruefully. She hadn't liked him either at first – too self-assured for his own good – but he'd turned out to be her love. It just showed that first impressions weren't always the truest. And that one should be careful not to jump to the wrong conclusions. A feeling like a warm blanket wrapped around her. She was so lucky. Glancing sideways, Raine noticed Stephanie was staring straight ahead, her expression set. She gave Stephanie's hand a fond squeeze.

'Are you okay, Stephanie?' she asked, when Stephanie turned and gave her a look of surprise.

'Yes, fine.' Stephanie lowered her voice even though Max had already started up the engines. 'Though I'm rather

371

worried about the one-handed flight. These Ansons are heavy beasts to fly. I did it once and felt it was in control of *me*, rather than the other way round. But I suppose I'd get used to it soon enough if I had another go.'

'Max will manage perfectly. They say he's one of the best pilots. And anyway, he's got Audrey with him.'

'I hope you're right,' Stephanie said. 'Well, nothing we can do. We're in his hands, so to speak.' But her smile was stilted.

'We'll be landing at Burtonwood in a few minutes for a refuel and a leg-stretch,' Audrey announced.

They were back in the Anson in no time. Carlisle was the next stop where they refuelled again. The weather had been better than expected and Max had made two smooth landings for the refuelling. But now they were approaching Perth, Raine could see that it was changing. The soft blue sky that had accompanied them most of the way on this six-hour journey had gradually changed to a dingy grey, and clouds were gathering in worrying formations.

Raine's heart sank. This weather seemed set. Although Chester wasn't considered a long journey at just under three hundred miles to make their deliveries, it was long enough to freeze in a much smaller, less powerful plane, and in an open cockpit. She didn't relish it at all, but there was a job to do and she'd just have to get on with it. Alec's scarf would simply have to work extra hard!

Max had taken the now poor visibility in his stride and made his third perfect landing. Looking over his shoulder Raine realised he was using instruments. Not for the first time she wished they'd been given instrument training which would have come into its own with this long winter weather, but the ATA were adamant that their pilots always keep below the clouds, whatever happened. She shrugged. They'd given

372

all the pilots superb training so they obviously knew what they were doing.

After signing in, Max ordered a cab to take them into the town to a small guesthouse where they were booked for the night.

'I am staying at the camp,' he said, while they waited for the cab, 'so we will see each other tomorrow morning at nine o'clock here.'

The two twin rooms in the guesthouse were clean but bitterly cold. Raine had thought her room at Mrs Grayson's was freezing but this was twice as bad.

'Haven't they heard of electric fires?' Dolores said, coming into the room Raine was to share with Stephanie. 'It's like the Dark Ages.'

'I'm going to demand that we have a bath and go to bed with a cup of cocoa and hot-water bottles,' Stephanie said. 'We won't be fit to fly planes if we don't get warmed up soon.'

'We'll come with you for moral support,' Raine said.

'There's no hot water after five o'clock,' Mrs McCloud, the landlady, asserted.

Her smug expression told them clearly she was not going to put herself out for four silly women who fancied themselves by taking men's jobs.

'We've been flying for hours and need to wash properly,' Raine said. If there was any chance of seeing Alec tomorrow evening, she wanted to wash her hair. 'Could you bend the rule this once? We've come such a long way – from near London.'

'Well, I knew you weren't a Scot with those fancy accents.' Mrs McCloud stood with one hand on her hip. 'No, I'm sorry but you're much too late. You can have a kettle of water and wash in the sink in your room.' She looked at each of them. 'And I've only two stone water bottles, so you'll have to take them in turns.'

'I see,' Audrey said, staring at the woman. 'Well, we'd all appreciate cocoa to warm us . . . and some biscuits.'

'No biscuits,' Mrs McCloud said firmly, 'but you can make yourselves cocoa in the kitchen so long as you clean up after yourselves. I won't have my kitchen left like the last lot,' she went on, not stopping to draw breath.

Raine sighed. Mrs McCloud obviously ignored the popular feeling at the moment that they were 'all in it together'. Thank goodness she and the other pilots were only stopping for one night.

Although Stephanie was already snoring by the time she crept into bed, Raine slept well, dreaming she was flying by using her own wings attached to her back. She flew straight into Alec's arms. She smiled when she woke, enjoying the sensation and not wanting to break it. But she knew she was being silly – and she couldn't lie here all day – so she hopped out of bed and washed her face. To her surprise, there was hot water in the tap. She looked up to the mirror. Her hair wasn't looking its best, but it would have to do because it was too late to start washing it now.

She was the first downstairs and looking forward to some real porridge she'd heard the Scots were famous for. Mrs McCloud plonked a bowl of what looked like gruel in front of her. It didn't look anything like she'd imagined. She glanced round the table for some sugar or treacle but couldn't see anything that would do – she'd have to eat it as it was. She took a spoonful and almost spat it out. Ugh. Where there should have been sugar, it tasted of salt. Had Mrs McCloud added salt instead of sugar by mistake? She took another tentative mouthful. It was no good. She laid down her spoon.

Mrs McCloud pursed her lips when she saw Raine had left her porridge.

'What is the matter with it?' she demanded.

'It's rather salty,' Raine murmured.

'It's how it should be.'

'I suppose I'm not used to it.'

'No, I don't suppose you are.' Mrs McCloud looked down her broad nose. 'You English girls are so delicate, you don't know what's good for you.'

Raine was thankful to be given a cheese roll which she tucked into her bag for later. She looked at her watch. Already eight o'clock. She'd better go and wake the others.

'We'll refuel the Tigers in Carlisle again,' Audrey said that afternoon, automatically taking charge of the little group. 'Then when we get to Hawarden and sign our deliveries we'll go straight to wherever they give out the chits and see if they have any more for us.' She grimaced. 'I hope not. I think we're all going to feel really tired from yesterday and today's flights.'

Max had stood waving to them as the four women started their engines and took off.

What a nice man, Raine thought. A real gentleman, but a very sad one. She only hoped he heard from his family now and again, although there were whispers of terrible stories of the Nazis' treatment of Czechoslovakians and Poles since the Germans had invaded those countries.

Clear your head, Raine. Concentrate on keeping in the gaggle.

Audrey was ahead, and Stephanie and Dolores were behind to the left and right, while Raine was bringing up the rear in a diamond formation. They'd hardly been in the air for half an hour before she admitted she wasn't really

375

enjoying it. Having to keep close to the others felt less liberating. Not only that, but in spite of her layers of clothing and her fur-lined flying jacket she was already feeling thoroughly cold.

She scrunched and released her toes in her boots, trying to keep her circulation going. How she longed to be in a Spitfire or a Hurricane . . . or anything that had a closed cockpit. But it was no use moaning – there was no one to hear her.

She glanced from left to right, noticing the clouds becoming lower. Sometimes she could only just make out Audrey in the front and the others disappeared from her peripheral view every so often and then came back again. She hoped they weren't having too much trouble keeping Audrey in sight from their different angles. Immediately this thought crossed her mind she realised she couldn't now see any of them.

Peering through her goggles she could see nothing. No speck in front. Well, she hadn't relished this formation flying and she was right to do so. She checked her compass to make sure she wasn't off course. No. She should be approaching Chester at any moment. Thank God, a space. She peered down and there it was – a large airfield. Dodging through the clouds, she prepared her descent.

Just as she approached the aerodrome she saw Audrey still in front and Dolores to her right. She watched both women land and waited for Stephanie's plane to come into view. She couldn't see any plane approaching. After circling a couple of times she decided she should land. Stephanie would no doubt be behind her and would come in shortly.

Audrey and Dolores climbed from their planes and waited for her to join them.

'Where the hell is Stephanie?' Audrey said.

376

Raine shook her head. 'It was pretty thick cloud and you all appeared to dip in and out. One minute I could follow you and the next you'd all disappeared.' She looked up at the sky. 'I'm sure she'll be here in a few minutes. She may have gone slightly off course. We shouldn't worry because she says she's known for flying in bad weather.'

'You're right,' Dolores said, banging her gloved hands together. 'She said they even called her Stormy Stephanie at her flying school! So I think we ought to go in and wait for her. She'll know we've gone to the mess to get warmed up after signing in.'

'Good idea,' Raine said. 'She may even be in the mess. She could've beaten us and have her hands warming round a mug of tea, giving us one of her triumphant grins.'

But she knew she was saying this to comfort herself as well as the others as she followed them across the damp grass and into the heated building.

Raine's fingers were so numb she could hardly hold the pen to sign in.

'Stephanie Lee-Jones hasn't arrived yet, has she?' she asked hopefully.

The adjutant glanced at the signing-in book.

'Not yet,' he said. 'We're expecting her soon.' He looked up. 'Wasn't she with you in a gaggle?'

'Yes,' Raine said. 'But we hit cloud coming in and we lost sight of her.'

'Right. I'll get on to that straightaway.' He picked up the telephone and delivered the message, then looked up. 'I'm sure she'll arrive soon.'

'Do you know if we have any more deliveries to make?' Raine asked, crossing her fingers and praying they didn't.

He nodded. 'Yes, we do need you ladies this afternoon, but go and have something to eat first and we'll sort them out.' He looked at his watch. 'Why don't you report back at two. Gives you ninety minutes to have a proper break.'

Raine stood in the queue behind Audrey and Dolores in the NAAFI. She didn't really fancy anything even though she hadn't eaten for several hours. Her stomach felt too het up worrying about Stephanie. The smell of sliced Spam and the mush of overcooked vegetables made her feel queasy. If only Stephanie would appear.

She looked on the counter at the various offerings. Something sweet – a bar of chocolate with her tea might do the trick.

'Do you have any Kit-Kat?' she asked the woman behind the till.

'You what, love?' The woman put her hand behind her ear to drown out the noise of the clattering and chatter.

'Kit-Kat,' Raine repeated loudly.

'In that box on your left.' The woman pointed.

'I didn't recognise them,' Raine said, tossing a couple of bars on her tray.

'Nor did we. When I asked the rep why they'd changed the wrapper to blue he said there's a war on.' The woman curled her lip. 'As if I'd forgotten. He said it reminds people they've had to change the recipe because of the rationing. As if anybody cared. All they want is to get some chocolate down their necks. Waste of money, I told him.' The woman rolled her eyes as she rang the till.

There were mutterings behind her to stop yakking so everyone could please get served. Raine mouthed 'sorry' to the people behind her, thanked the woman at the till, and joined the others at a table giving a clear view of the airfield.

'We can keep a lookout for her from here,' Audrey said. 'I must say I'm now getting slightly concerned.' She bit into

378

her Spam sandwich and pulled a face. 'Have you tried our delicious Spam, Dolly?'

'Yes, and I never want it again, thank you. I think I'd rather starve.'

The three of them chattered about rationing, every so often glancing over to the window, hoping to see Stephanie.

'It happened to me once when the fog was so thick I couldn't even see to land,' Raine said. 'That must be what's happened to Stephanie – and then there's the worry about the fuel.' She looked round at them. 'But she's a good pilot. I'm sure she's all right and will soon be here.'

'But if there's no clear spot, what then?' Dolores said anxiously.

'She'll find one,' Audrey said. 'We must try not to worry until we hear something definite.'

Dolores took a sip of coffee and made a face. 'I can't believe they serve this up as coffee. It tastes nothing like it.'

'It's Camp, I expect,' Raine said, smiling although she didn't feel like it. 'You know coffee and tea is rationed here. Has been for quite a while. Same as sugar and butter and chocolate and loads of other things we took for granted and now miss like mad. You don't know how lucky you Americans are.'

She knew she was gabbling but she was beginning to become alarmed. For something to do she stood up and wandered over to the window, peering out. A bank of low dark cloud did little to reassure her of Stephanie's fate. Fearing something really bad must have happened, she turned from the window and at that moment, to her huge relief, she saw her friend walk through the door.

'Stephanie!' What happened?' Raine hurried over to her and gave her a quick hug. 'We were all getting worried.'

Dolores and Audrey leapt up and also hugged her. Raine

379

noticed the pleasure on Stephanie's face as though she was surprised they should be so demonstrative.

'I was getting nervy myself, I can tell you. I must have strayed further than I realised and couldn't see a damn thing with all that cloud. I completely lost sight of you all – and worse, the ground, so I had no landmarks to go by. I was still peering at the map as I was trying to actually land.'

'Come and sit down and tell us what happened.' Dolores sat at the table again and patted the empty seat beside her.

'I'll get you something to eat and a cup of tea,' Raine said. 'I shan't be a tick. Don't start without me.'

She was back in time to hear most of Stephanie's story.

'It got so bad where I was that I actually flew above the clouds for a bit trying to see if there was a clear space between them. But there was nothing, so I set the compass and just kept flying straight, coming down every so often for a dekko. I knew it wouldn't be long before I ran out of fuel, so that didn't help. And then when I saw the Mersey I nearly had a heart attack. I'd been about to approach *Liverpool*.' She bit her lip at the memory. 'I was so worried about the fuel I almost decided to land at Speke, but I chanced it and flew on, and . . . well, here I am, safe and sound, but with no more fuel than would fill a teapot.' She grinned. 'When I landed I felt like kneeling down and kissing the ground.'

After Stephanie had eaten a sandwich and drunk her tea she breathed out a long sigh.

'That's better. It wouldn't have been good to have spoiled my nickname of Stormy Stephanie,' she chuckled.

'I'm surprised you can fly at all with the length of those nails,' Audrey said drily. 'Don't know how you press the booster coil and the starter coil in a Spit, for instance.'

'That's easy,' Stephanie giggled. 'Those little buttons are quite tricky to press at the same time with long nails, so I just use the top of my lipstick case for one and the bottom of the lipstick case for the other. It works a treat.'

'You're incorrigible, Stephanie,' Raine said, laughing with the others.

The four women chatted about ways of dealing with the idiosyncratic nature of the various types of aircraft until it was time to report to the office at two.

'Apparently we all have another delivery,' Raine said, rising to her feet, 'so we ought to go.'

Please give me a station that's not too far from White Waltham. Raine crossed her fingers as she and the other girls stepped into the office.

Chapter Thirty-Three

Raine could hardly bear to look at her chit. Her face fell. She was to deliver a Blenheim – that bit was good – but to Silloth, which wasn't.

Audrey looked at her chit. 'I've got an Oxford to go to Desford. I'm happy with anything if it's got a closed cockpit.' She looked at Raine. 'You don't seem very enthusiastic about yours.'

'I never mind where I'm sent normally,' Raine said, hating to moan about a job she loved, 'but I'm off in the opposite direction – a Blenheim to Silloth . . . more or less where we've just come from. I was hoping for something to take me nearer to home.'

'Oh. Any reason?'

Raine blushed. 'I'm supposed to be meeting someone this evening.'

'Rotten luck,' Audrey said. 'He'll have to wait a bit longer for you.' She chuckled. 'Makes them more keen.' She winked. 'I like the Blenheim. It's a good rugged one.' She turned to the American girl. 'What about you, Dolores? You look very happy. Where are you headed?'

'They must know I'm from the States,' Dolores said, all smiles. 'I'm taking a Harvard trainer to Lakenheath. Apparently it's an American base in Norfolk, so I'm gonna feel right at home. With luck I'll stay overnight and stock up at the PX—'

'What's the PX?' Audrey interrupted.

'It's an abbreviation for Post Exchange,' Dolores said, 'and the biggest retailer in the US military.' Her gaze swept over the little group. 'Like I said, I'll stock up on items I've not seen over here . . . for the benefit of *all* of us,' she added, grinning.

What a smashing girl, Raine thought as Audrey let out a cry of delight and patted Dolores on her arm.

'What about you, Stephanie?' Raine said. 'You've gone very quiet. Are they sending you even further than me?'

'Hate to brag but it's the best one of all,' Stephanie answered.

Raine looked at her curiously. 'Well, you don't seem that chuffed about it.'

Stephanie stared at Raine. 'I'm not quite sure how to tell you this, Lorraine, but it's to take a Spit to RAF Benson!'

Raine startled. 'What! But that's where—'

'Yes, I'm well aware that's where Mr Green Eyes is stationed,' Stephanie said, her own big blue eyes now gleaming. 'And I'm sure I won't cause half the sensation *you* would when I turn up.'

Raine forced a smile. What bad luck to think it had been given to Stephanie. But that was the name of the game and there was a war on. You had to get on with whatever you were dished out.

'Is this green-eyed pilot your boyfriend?' Dolores asked, her dark eyebrows raised.

Raine hesitated. She was torn between spilling out everything and not saying a word. The others looked at her.

'Well,' Audrey said, 'you might as well tell her. Stephanie and I know how desperately in love you are.'

Heat rose at the back of Raine's neck.

'He can't be known only as Mr Green Eyes,' Dolores chuckled, 'although that's mighty intriguing. But I assume he has a name.'

'Alec,' Raine said. Just saying his name was a relief. It made him feel closer somehow. 'His name is Alec Marshall. And yes,' she said, smiling at the little group, 'I know I'll never hear the last of it if I don't tell you I'm madly in love with him.'

'Does he know that?' Stephanie demanded. 'If he does, you've not told *me*.'

Raine hesitated before saying, 'I haven't exactly told him.'

'Why not?' Stephanie snapped out.

'Um . . .'

'I suppose she must have her reasons,' Audrey broke in, rolling her eyes. She turned to Raine. 'And Alec?'

'What about him?' Raine said.

'You know full well,' Audrey said impatiently. 'Is *he* in love with *you*?'

'So he says. I want to believe him.'

'Any reason why you shouldn't?' Stephanie said. 'Because from where I sat at your place last Christmas he was besotted – and even though you had a row with him, anyone could tell you felt exactly the same.'

Had it really been that obvious? Raine wouldn't tell them about the 'pretending' business. It was something that still niggled her.

'Let's hope he keeps that way,' she said lightly, wanting to change the subject.

'Hmm. These men can be slippery characters,' Audrey said with feeling. 'And I should know.'

'I've never thought of Alec in quite that way.' Raine couldn't help laughing. She glanced at Stephanie. 'Stephanie, would you take him a note from me? Then he'll know I'm not going to make it back this evening?'

'I can do better than that,' Stephanie said, looking pleased with herself. 'I'll swap you – but only because you have a Blenheim.'

Dolores let out a cheer. Audrey's smile cracked her face in two.

Raine stood transfixed. Silloth was as far as Carlisle.

'Stephanie, that's so kind of you,' she said. 'Are you sure?'

'Course I'm sure,' Stephanie said, looking almost embarrassed by her good turn. 'We're friends, aren't we? That's what friends are for. And I haven't forgotten how you threw me a lifeline when I was pretty low after that poisoning business and you invited me to your home.' She slipped her arm through Raine's. 'But we don't know yet whether a swap is even on the cards, so you and I need to go and talk to someone.'

'I'm sorry,' Mrs James, Hawarden's ATA commander, told the two women. 'We can't allow swaps. It's against the rules.' She looked up at them. 'Why would you want to do it anyway?'

Stephanie looked at Raine. 'Shall I say?'

Raine nodded. Maybe the woman would be sympathetic although it was hard to tell. Mrs James looked all business and low on romance.

'All in the name of love,' Stephanie said.

Mrs James raised her brows.

'Lorraine has a boyfriend at the station,' Stephanie continued, 'who she hasn't seen for several weeks. And he only has a few hours spare this evening before he has to go off again. I wouldn't want to be responsible for standing in love's way.'

Was Stephanie going too far? Raine almost wished she'd kept it more practical, but you couldn't stop Stephanie once she got started.

'I'm really sorry, Miss Linfoot, but that wouldn't be an acceptable reason to swap,' Mrs James said, looking at Raine over the top of her glasses. 'The reason why it's against the rules is that pilots are experienced in different classes of aircraft and it would be far too dangerous to be swapping and maybe flying something you may not have even been trained for.'

'But we've been trained to fly both aircraft,' Raine argued. 'And we're highly experienced on them.'

'If you telephoned White Waltham and spoke to one of the adjutants, she'd confirm it.' Stephanie persisted.

The CO shook her head. 'I'm really sorry,' she said. 'Break the rules for one and it will open the floodgates.' She rose from behind her desk to indicate the meeting was over.

'Thanks anyway, Stephanie,' Raine said when they were out of earshot. 'At least we tried.'

'You're not giving up?' Stephanie's eyes were wide.

'You heard what she said – it's against the rules.'

'So what can they do to us?' Stephanie said. Her eyes gleamed as she grabbed Raine's arm. 'They need us more than we need them. So what do you say? Are you game to be a rebel with me?'

Raine thought for all of two seconds then broke into a huge grin. 'All right, Stephanie, I'm game!'

It had been easy. She and Stephanie signed their chits and picked up their parachutes and harnesses from the store. After saying goodbye to Audrey and Dolores, they strolled over the grassy airfield towards the two planes that sat side by side. Raine gave a start. She'd never seen a sky-blue painted Spitfire before. It was the most beautiful sight, its glorious curves glistening with raindrops from the last downpour, making the aircraft shimmer even on such a dull day.

'You're a lucky girl, love,' one of the ground crew said. 'Especially flying this model. It's even lighter to handle because it doesn't carry any armament.'

Raine frowned. 'Oh?'

'It's used for photographic reconnaissance,' he explained. 'That's why it's painted the same colour as an English sky on a sunny day – as camouflage.' He tilted his head up. 'Not that we'll be likely to have one of those rarities today,' he chuckled.

Yes, of course. Alec had mentioned it. Her heart lifted. It would be a personal journey from her to him. It might even be the very plane he'd fly on one of his missions. Her pulse quickened at the thought.

'Those clouds look a bit dodgy,' the other said, peering up at the sky. 'Think you can handle it, ladies?'

His expression told her he couldn't believe these women had been let loose on the two expensive planes.

'I'm sure we can,' Raine said, annoyed at his tone.

'Good luck then, Raine.' Stephanie turned to her. 'Hope the reunion is as romantic as you dream. Meanwhile, think of me in my first Blenheim.'

Raine was just about to leap onto the wing when she stopped abruptly.

'What did you say?'

'About the reunion? That I hoped—'

'No, not that,' Raine said impatiently. 'You know jolly well – about it being your first Blenheim.'

'Oh, that.' Stephanie beamed. 'Didn't I tell you? I've never flown one. But if I can fly an Oxford and a Whitley I daresay I can fly a Blenheim. It's only another twin engine. There can't be a lot in it. And I've always wanted to get my hands on one.'

'Read the Pilots Notes very carefully – *twice*,' Raine

shouted, but Stephanie had already disappeared into the aircraft.

Raine set her parachute on the seat as a cushion and clipped on her harness. She glanced through the Pilots Notes and went through her checklist. In the tight space she already felt as one with this beautiful little plane and was certain the blue Spitfire felt the same. Grinning at the absurdity, she started the engine.

She was up! Together, they were flying at one thousand eight hundred feet, keeping just below the cloud. She kept it steady for the next hour or so until visibility became a little difficult. She'd go above the clouds like she had before, breaking not one but two rules in a day, but she might as well be hanged for a sheep as a lamb.

She pulled the control stick gently towards her and the Spit practically sailed through a bank of clouds where a welcoming sun greeted her. Raine laughed aloud. She was all on her own, loving every single moment. It was just her and her Spit and the sky. She'd give herself half an hour and then go back below the two thousand feet as regulations required.

Thoroughly enjoying herself she began to hum one of the latest Andrews Sisters songs that Suzy sometimes played on the piano and they'd sing together. Raine sang out the words, tapping the beat with her finger on the control board: 'You've got to laugh a little, cry a little, until the clouds roll by a little . . .'

She shouted with laughter at that last bit, then broke off as a plane suddenly appeared from the right. She turned her head and squinted, trying to make out the model. It flew closer and she side-slipped, not wanting to endanger them both. But the plane side-slipped with her.

She grinned. It must be one of the boys having fun. All right – she'd show him she was up for a tussle as well as any man. Adjusting the strap of her flying helmet and bracing herself, she gently moved the control stick to the right as she flew towards him. And then her blood curdled. A black-and-white cross on the side of the fuselage. A Focke-Wulf. *Dear God.*

Panicking, she jerked back the control stick to gain height, but it was too late. There was a burst of fire and to her horror she saw a stream of tracer bullets whizz past her windscreen.

Sweat broke out over her forehead and above her lip. He was following her. She dropped through the clouds, hoping against hope that the thick haze would shield her from his sight, but she knew he would have another go. He was just above her now, looking down at her. So near she could see his face. My God, he was bent on killing her. Without thinking she tore off her helmet, shook out her hair and waved to him.

She almost laughed as his expression changed to one of shock. And then a miracle happened. He nodded and gave a stiff wave in return before thundering away – to become an innocent speck in the sky.

Raine blew out her cheeks. *Bloody blimey, that was close.* If she hadn't shown him she was a woman he would have shot both her and her plane into oblivion – no doubt about that. And she'd had no defence. The back of her blouse stuck to her skin. She licked her lips, almost tasting the fear. This is what Alec potentially faced every time he went up – and to think he had no ammunition . . . She shuddered. The sooner she arrived at Benson, the better. See Alec and explain.

And then her resolve wavered as she imagined Alec's anger and hurt when she told him about Doug. The plane gave a sudden jerk and she rapidly began to lose height.

Stop it, Raine. Concentrate. You were bloody lucky with that German pilot and you might not be so lucky the next time. You've got a long journey ahead of you, so bloody well concentrate.

Keeping a grim eye on the horizon she righted the aircraft and kept it steady for the next hour. More relaxed now after her fright and noting where she was on the map, her father's image unexpectedly came to her. His crisp grey hair, the twinkling hazel eyes, his mouth thinner since he'd aged, but smiling his special smile, just for her.

'When you're confused and searching for an answer, Raine, no matter what's troubling you, remember what I've taught you – listen to your heart. It will never let you down. All you have to do is to follow it.'

Yes. She smiled to herself as she held the control stick steady. That was it. It was so simple. She needed to see Alec . . . hold him . . . and tell him for the first time that she loved him.

Chapter Thirty-Four

The officers' mess was crowded on this particular night. Alec managed to find a quiet corner at a table with only one other officer who was reading a book.

'Sorry to disturb you,' Alec said. 'I know what it's like when you're trying to read.'

'Go ahead. You won't disturb me.' The man put his book down. 'It's not that gripping anyway.'

Alec sighed inwardly. He didn't really feel up to chatting this evening. He'd put in a long day and instead of being able to relax, he found himself on edge worrying about Raine. Yes, he was sure she was an excellent pilot but it wasn't the best weather for flying, and even if she didn't have another delivery she'd be on a long journey home at this minute in a bitterly cold train that could be delayed with no explanation at any time. Either way wasn't pleasant.

He couldn't keep her out of his thoughts. If she telephoned in the next couple of hours, he was determined to somehow get a lift to White Waltham. The thought cheered him a little. He found himself yawning and glanced at his watch, which showed it to be only six o'clock. With the best will in the world she wouldn't be back for another hour or two at least.

He'd had little sleep the night before. He couldn't go on like this as it would start to affect his job. He should eat something but he wasn't hungry. If this was what being in love was like . . . he had to smile to himself.

A steward came over and spoke to Alec's table companion. 'Sorry to have kept you waiting, sir. What can I get you?'

'I'll have a beer.'

The steward turned to Alec. 'And for you, sir?'

'Coffee, please. Black.' He needed to keep awake. God knew how late Raine might be.

'Excuse me.' The officer stood. 'I'll be back in a moment.'

Alec nodded and watched as the man walked a little unevenly towards the Gents'. When he came back to the table Alec looked at him curiously.

'I haven't seen you here before.'

'No. I just got transferred. I'm in . . . or *was* . . .' the officer sounded bitter as he emphasised the past tense, 'in Coastal Command. Well, I suppose I still am, though it doesn't feel like it now I'm doing admin and bored out of my head.'

'Oh, I sympathise,' Alec said, feeling genuinely sorry for him, imagining how he'd feel if he couldn't fly his beloved Spit.

They chatted some more and the time passed until Alec stood up and said, 'I need to make a phone call, but it was good to meet you.' He put out his hand and the man shook it. 'I don't know your name,' Alec said, 'but I'm Alec Marshall – photographic reconnaissance.'

'Pleased to meet you, Marshall.' He jerked his thumb towards himself. 'Doug White – was a fighter pilot but now I'm pushing a bloody pen around.'

Doug? Alec stared at the officer. It was a common enough name. Had she told him his surname? He couldn't remember. And anyway, Raine's friend had been shot down. True, they'd never found his body. But people did sometimes turn up after a 'missing, presumed dead' report, shocking the life out of everyone.

'Hope you don't mind my asking, but being a pilot myself, I know I'd hate it as well if I couldn't fly. So why have you been relegated to office work?'

'Bit of a long story,' Doug said with a rueful smile. 'I don't want to keep you if you have a phone call to make . . .'

'It can wait,' Alec said without hesitating, glad for the opportunity to talk to someone. It might take his mind off worrying about Raine. Besides, he needed to be completely clear in his mind that this couldn't possibly be the same Doug. Even thinking it was insane.

Doug leaned forward as though eager to tell his story.

'I was shot down by a Messerschmitt,' he began. 'The plane caught fire and I baled out. Broke my leg on impact and pretty much lost my memory. Thankfully, a delightful French girl discovered me . . .'

He went on talking but Alec was hardly listening because the dreadful realisation that this was the same Doug filled his head. Did Raine know he was alive? If she did, she hadn't trusted him enough to tell him Doug had survived the crash. Did she think he was someone who wouldn't understand she'd once had feelings for another man before he came on the scene? Or was she playing a game – keeping her options open? Or worse – she didn't know how to tell him that she still loved Doug, and now he'd come back from the dead, so to speak, the two of them could resume their love affair.

But she'd already told him she didn't love Doug in that way. Dear God, was he about to lose her? He had to speak to her now.

He remembered the scent of her hair when they had lain together after the most joyous lovemaking he had ever imagined. The feel of her fingers through his hair, tracing the outline of his shoulders, kissing him with those tempting lips . . . They couldn't possibly be the actions of a woman in love with another man – *could they*? Surely he would have sensed something.

He swallowed hard and looked at Doug with guarded interest. He was a good-looking chap, Alec had to admit, with that dark hair and bright blue eyes. Just the sort of man he could see Raine going for.

Something made him glance towards the door.

Raine was standing in the doorway, staring straight at him.

Chapter Thirty-Five

Raine's heart beat fast with anticipation. Any minute now she would see her love. She'd signed in that she'd delivered the Spitfire, and someone told her Alec Marshall was probably in the officers' mess having a bite to eat. She smiled to herself as she thought how surprised he'd be to see her at his station.

As her hand went to the door handle, she paused. She'd nipped into the Ladies' to tidy her hair – the hair that had probably saved her life! – and touch up her powder and lipstick. She knew without any particular conceit that she looked good.

Someone came from behind her. 'Here, let me hold the door for you,' the officer said. She smiled at him as he held it wide.

'Thank you.' Her eyes swiftly took in the room.

'Are you looking for someone in particular?' he asked.

'Yes, I . . .'

She froze. Sitting at the same table, talking to Alec, was Doug.

Alec was facing her. Their eyes locked. He didn't smile.

She could tell in that instant that he knew. He knew who Doug was. There was no other explanation.

There were people coming up behind her. She had to decide whether to walk into the room or turn and run.

Every step towards their table felt like a mile. Alec was still watching her but he remained seated. Doug glanced over to where Alec was looking and immediately got up, a beaming smile plastered over his face.

'Raine!' He hurried towards the door as fast as his bad leg would allow and swept her into his arms. 'Goodness, what a coincidence to see you. I was only transferred here yesterday. I was going to telephone you this evening.' He kissed her cheek.

Raine felt Alec's eyes glued to her.

'Come and sit with us,' Doug said, getting hold of her arm and leading her to the table where Alec sat. 'I've been having a good conversation with Marshall – a fellow pilot.' He turned to Alec. 'Let me introduce you to my gorgeous Lorraine.'

Raine wished the floor could swallow her up.

'No need to,' Alec said, slowly rising to his feet, keeping his eyes fixed on Raine. 'I know the lady.' He looked at her. 'Hello, Raine. What a surprise to see you here.'

'I've just delivered a Spit,' she stuttered.

Alec raised his eyebrows. 'A blue one?'

She nodded and swallowed.

'That's the one I've been waiting for,' he said. 'Mine's gone in for a repair.'

He sounded friendly enough to anyone who didn't know him, but Raine knew different.

'Well, now you have a new one.' She was aware that Doug was eyeing the pair of them with frank curiosity.

'So you two already know each other?' he said.

Think, Raine. Think what to do. How do I get out of this? Doug doesn't know who Alec really is, but Alec has cottoned on already – I can see the hard look in his eyes, hear the tone of his voice.

Before she could say a word, Alec said, 'Well, I'll leave you and your friend in private. You've probably got plenty to say.' He turned to Doug. 'Good to meet you, White.'

'Alec . . .' Raine started, but he was already striding towards the door.

She let out a long sigh and took the chair Alec had occupied.

'Smashing chap,' Doug said, staring after him. He turned to Raine. 'Jolly nice of him to be so tactful.'

Raine bit her lip.

'What's the matter, Raine? You don't seem that happy.'

'Tired, that's all,' she said.

'I'll order you some tea.'

She could have cheerfully downed a double whisky right now.

'I don't want anything,' she said flatly.

'Aren't you hungry?'

She shook her head. She had been. She'd imagined having supper with Alec. But any hunger pangs had vanished.

'I'll find a steward. He was here a few minutes ago.' He got up.

At least it would give her a few moments to pull herself together. Try to work out how to tell Doug she was in love with someone else and that he just happened to be the 'smashing chap' Doug had been chatting to this evening. Well, she'd got her wish to see them both face to face – it was just that she hadn't pictured them being in the same room at the same table, that was all.

Doug was back before she'd had time to gather her thoughts. She blinked and tried to concentrate on something he was saying.

'He'll be with us in a moment in case you change your mind. You should have something after a long flight.' He paused and looked at her. 'Raine, I know you pretty well by now. Something's up. I can tell by your face and I think I know the reason.'

Raine averted her eyes. So he *had* guessed who Alec was.

'You think I'm rushing you, don't you, love?'

She looked at him, barely making him out, her eyes were so full of tears. *Dearest Doug. He'd got it all so wrong.* She hated the thought of hurting him, but it had to be said.

'It's this bloody war that makes you aware how precious time is,' he said, taking her hand. 'None of us knows if we'll come out of this in reasonable shape – or at all. Look at what happened to me. One moment I was doing my job, the next I was being shot at. Most terrifying moment of my life when I thought I was going to die.'

Raine squeezed his hand. 'You can't know how upset I was. They told me you were missing, presumed dead.' Her voice shook.

'It must have been awful for you. But I'm here now. Unless, of course, you've already replaced me.' He winked at her and grinned.

'Doug, they told me you were dead.'

Doug's smile instantly vanished. He stared at her. 'My God, you *have* replaced me.'

'I haven't replaced you – how could I replace *you*? It would be impossible.' She gulped. 'But I *have* met someone else,' she added quickly before she changed her mind.

'When was that?'

For a few seconds she couldn't remember when she *had* met him, because it seemed as though she'd known Alec forever.

'When I worked at Biggin Hill.'

'The job I got for you,' Doug said, frowning. 'Is he another pilot?'

'Yes.'

Doug kept his eyes glued to hers. 'In Fighter Command?'

'No.'

'Bomber Command?'

'No.'

'What, then?'

'He's in photographic reconnaissance.'

'You never told me at the time about him.'

'I didn't actually *meet* him then,' Raine said unhappily. 'It was a few months later – at a dance. Suzy and I went to the Palais in Bromley. You'd already joined up.'

'Have you been seeing him all this time I've been in France?'

'We've bumped into each other occasionally.'

She was beginning to feel sick with her deceit. But it hadn't been deceit. She and Doug had never promised their hearts to each other. She felt a flicker of anger. This was Doug's fault as well as her own. He'd assumed too much without a discussion of any kind as to her feelings for him.

'On purpose, no doubt.' He gave her a thin smile. 'I'm not sure I want to know what's coming next, but I think I deserve to be told the truth.' He sat back and lit a cigarette.

'Yes, you do,' Raine said, wishing they were somewhere completely private. At least there was plenty of background chatter and no one was taking any notice of them. She cleared her throat. 'This is the hardest thing I've ever had to tell anyone, but you see I didn't mean to.'

Doug frowned. 'Didn't mean to what? Come on, Raine, say it.'

'What I'm trying to say is that I've fallen in love with him. So you and I can only ever be friends . . . very dear friends,' she added.

Doug's head jerked up. 'Who's this lucky bloke?' His question was tinged with bitterness.

'The chap you were talking to when I came in – Alec Marshall.'

There. She'd said it.

Doug momentarily closed his eyes. When he opened them, she saw by their expression it had all fallen into place as far as he was concerned. He clicked his tongue and shook his head.

'Alec Marshall! Of course! When I phoned you and you thought it was Alec. You said his name. I didn't take a lot of notice at the time. What a bloody fool I am.' He tapped the side of his head with his forefinger. 'And an even more prize fool to think you could love me with my gammy leg.'

'Doug, it's nothing to do with your leg,' she said indignantly. 'I'm not like that – you know I'm not.' She looked him straight in the eye. 'I think as much of you now as I did before the accident.' She *had* to make him believe her. 'The thing is, if Alec lost *both* legs I'd still love him just the same.'

'I see.' Doug took in a deep drag of his cigarette then stubbed it out. 'Then you'd better go to him.'

'Please don't be like that,' Raine said, her eyes imploring. 'I can't bear it if we're no longer friends.'

'It'll take me a while to get used to this bombshell.' He looked directly at her. 'Oh, Raine, if only I'd told you sooner that I loved you, maybe this wouldn't have happened. We would've got married—'

'I'm sorry, Doug,' Raine interrupted. 'I wouldn't have married you anyway. It would have been like marrying my brother. I admit I had a schoolgirl crush on you when I was only sixteen because you seemed so sophisticated, and you had your pilot's licence . . . something I wanted more than anything. By giving me lessons you made my dream come true. No one else could have done that. And I'll never forget

400

it. But please say we'll always be friends. If you love me the way you say you do, you'll want me to be happy.'

'If he promises to make you happy, I suppose I'll have to go along with it,' Doug said. 'But if he hurts you in any way, shape or form, he'll have *me* to deal with.' He tapped his chest and she noticed his blue eyes were moist. 'You'd better go to him, Raine.'

'Thank you, dear Doug, my dearest friend.' Raine stood. She kissed him briefly on his mouth. 'One day you'll meet the right girl. And she won't care tuppence about gammy legs.'

'I only have the one gammy leg,' he said, giving her a wry smile. 'The other one's perfectly fine.' Then he put his hand to her face and traced its outline with his fingertips so tenderly she had to stop herself from bursting into tears for hurting him so.

'Go to him,' he repeated softly.

No one had seen Alec Marshall.

'You could try the crew room,' one officer told her, his glance taking in the wings on her tunic. 'I'll show you where it is.'

A minute later he opened the door and gestured her in. There was only one pilot, his back to her, bending down to open one of the metal lockers on the end wall. A dim light from a desk lamp fell on the back of his head and lit the outline of his broad shoulders in a distorted circle as he removed something from the locker, then shut the door. She heard a faint click as he locked it.

'Alec.' Her voice was almost a whisper.

But he'd heard. He jerked upright and swung round, a pair of goggles in his hand.

'Raine! Why aren't you with your boyfriend?'

'Don't speak of him in that tone,' she retorted. 'I won't have it.'

He gave a deep sigh and carefully laid the goggles on one of the nearby tables.

'I guess I'm not feeling myself at the moment. Probably lack of food after a tough day.'

'You should eat something. You need all your energy for the job you do.'

He held her eyes. 'Raine, you haven't come to talk about my health. So why are you here?'

Raine blinked. 'Why do you think?'

'I really don't know,' Alec said, moving towards her. 'But I imagine I'm to congratulate you.' His eyes were hard as emeralds.

'What for?'

'Your engagement to White, of course.' Alec's tone was impatient.

The only thing that stopped her from walking out in fury was the hurt in his eyes that had replaced the bitterness. He was doing his best to be nonchalant, but it wasn't working.

'Can I talk without you jumping down my throat?'

'Go on, then. It's all the same to me.' He pulled up a chair by the dying embers of the fire. 'You'd better come and sit down. At least we'll have some privacy in here.'

Raine perched on the edge of one of the easy chairs, longing to sink her aching back into the upholstery, but not daring to relax until she'd had her say. He studied her.

'So your Doug's come back from the dead,' he said when she didn't say anything. 'And I'm genuinely pleased about that, Raine, even if you don't believe me. No pilot wants to see or hear about another pilot – whether they know them or not – going down.'

'Whatever you think—' Raine began.

402

'It doesn't matter a jot what *I* think,' Alec interrupted. 'It's what *you* think . . . but you might have told me about him out of common decency.'

'I told you about Doug when he was missing. I didn't hide the fact that he was a dear friend and that I was devastated when they told me he was now presumed dead. And I remember you were so understanding.'

'That was when I didn't suspect any love affair,' Alec said sharply.

'There's never been a love affair, nor even the hint of one with Doug.' Raine's tone was equally sharp.

'Hmm. As if I can believe that.'

'If you don't, there's no hope for us,' Raine said. 'Doug jumped to all sorts of conclusions – just like you're doing now. He thought we could slide from a friendship to a romance in one easy step without asking me how *I* felt. I've told him I look upon him as a brother and couldn't possibly contemplate marrying him for that reason alone.'

'What did he say?' Alec was suddenly sounding more alert.

'I think he realised in the end the mistake he'd made,' Raine said. 'He'd simply taken everything for granted. And then when I turned him down he said it must be to do with his gammy leg. So I said, "No, that isn't true. If Alec had *two* gammy legs or even *lost* them, I'd still love him just as much," so it's got nothing to do with—'

Alec shot up and practically dragged her to her feet. He held on to her arms.

'What did you say?' he demanded, those green eyes boring into hers.

'I said I wouldn't care if you lost both legs.' Raine turned her head away. She'd blurted out something she'd wanted to tell him only if he believed her and still loved her.

'You didn't say that,' Alec said, pulling her so tightly against his chest she could feel the strong, steady beat of his heart. 'What were your *exact* words?'

'I've already told you.'

He pulled her close again. 'No, you haven't. Not the exact ones. And I'm not letting you go until you tell me,' he said. 'Now, for the last time, what did you say – word by word?'

She gave a theatrical sigh. 'I said I'd still love you just as much even if you had no legs.'

'Yes, that's what I thought I'd heard,' Alex said, a glimmer of a smile touching his mouth, 'but I wanted to be absolutely sure. So perhaps to confirm after such a shaky start, you can say it again – slower this time – and put some feeling into it. Or do you need me to kiss you to remind you how being in love feels?'

Without waiting for her answer, he kissed her.

'I've missed you so much, Raine,' he murmured against her lips. 'It's been far too long. All I keep thinking about is you and me in Windsor.'

He kissed her closed eyelids, her neck, the tip of her ear. Then he cupped the back of her head in his hand and kissed her lips again, this time with such passion she had to hold on to him or she would have sunk to the floor.

'All right, you've reminded me,' Raine said, leaning back a little as his arms held her safely, thankful he'd never given up on her, though she'd never tell him that. Her lips parted as she tried to catch her breath.

'I'm still waiting.' Alec lightly pressed her.

She hesitated. This was more difficult than she'd thought to say the words he wanted to hear. She'd never said them to anyone before. But Alec was her love. So what was the matter with her? Her father would be the first to tell her to hang on to such a good chap. Not let him slip through her fingers. She could see his smiling face now, giving her a wink of approval. She blinked back a tear. If only the two of them had met she was sure they would have got on well together.

Wishing she could hug her father for the last time, she realised there was no need to play games or hold back anything more from Alec – this wonderful man who just happened to be her heart's desire and who she'd follow to the ends of the earth. She pulled in a deep breath.

'I . . . love . . . you.' She looked at Alec, a mischievous sparkle in her eyes. 'Was that slow enough, and said with enough feeling, to satisfy you?'

'It will have to do for the time being,' he said, chuckling, 'but I insist you take a lifetime to keep practising – until you *really* get it right.'

She'd do all the practising it needed and adore every moment, Raine thought, beaming up at him. But in the meantime there was a war on and she had a job to do. And nothing – not even her darling Alec – was going to stop her from completing it . . . however long it took before Mr Churchill sent his instructions for the church bells to peal out victoriously from every belfry in Great Britain.

Acknowledgements

If an author ever tells you what a lonely life they have writing in their garret, don't believe them. Being a writer opens up the most wonderful world of other authors who truly root for you, and during the research you are privy to so much that the general public are not. As soon as I say I'm an author, doors are swung wide open for me to step through. Strangely enough, I'm never asked to show any evidence that I really *am* a published writer!

Writing this latest novel, *A Sister's Courage*, has been really special.

I'm so grateful to all the female ferry pilots who wrote their memoirs of their time in the ATA (Air Transport Auxiliary). Their stories were a joy to read. I felt I was with them every moment of their flights, and it was nail-biting when they ran into serious technical difficulties and bad weather. I could almost smell their fear as they tried to work out how to get out of dangerous situations.

But of course I still didn't *really* understand how it *actually* felt to fly a fighter plane, and as practically everyone who's ever flown a Spitfire waxes lyrical over the machine, it seems the Spit gave them their greatest experience. So what was its magic?

Surfing the net one day when I was about halfway through a very rough first draft, I came across the Maidenhead

Heritage Centre – described as a small museum but packed with the best collection of ATA memorabilia in the country. A gift to this author who was struggling in unknown territory. (Why can't I keep to the rule: write what you know?) After an initial enquiry and making a definite date when I would show up so the right people would be there to help me, I arrived one morning by train. I was met by a team of volunteers, all enthusiastic mature men who were most interested that I was writing a novel where my heroine is an ATA pilot. They couldn't have been more helpful.

Peter Rogers, the computer whizz, showed me how to download various female ATA pilots who'd given audio interviews some decades ago of their experiences. The interviewer would often ask how they felt working in a man's world and how they were received by the male pilots.

'We were all there to do a job,' they said with one voice, 'and so we didn't even think about it.'

One of the ladies laughed. 'Mind you, you'd sometimes get a comment about being a woman, but you learnt to ignore it. You just got on with it.'

Then in the next breath these intrepid ladies would mention the ways in which they retained their femininity. 'Beauty is your duty,' was the government's motto to the female pilots. It was considered to be a morale booster, not only that the women should keep up their appearance for the fighter boys, but also in demonstrating their ability to fly all kinds of aircraft without the benefit of instruments, they were showing an example to the 'green' male pilots, fresh from training.

These remarkable women certainly gave me a rare insight into their world.

I was encouraged to peer into cabinets and take photographs of mannequins in uniforms, see exactly what a chit looked like, and read pilots' diaries. I was in heaven. Then I watched as a boy of about eleven climbed into what looked like half a Spitfire and with the help of an instructor took off!

I'm not keen on flying but I felt I owed it to my readers (and my heroine!) to take a turn. It was only a simulator, for goodness' sake, I told myself sternly. The instructor helped me fold into the cramped space of the cockpit. It smelt unfamiliar. Kind of metallic, and musty. He pointed out so many things I had to do when I started up before I was allowed to take off, that my mind went completely blank. But from outside the cockpit he guided me through all the various steps and eventually I was airborne. What a thrill! The lightest touch of the control stick and we moved gently in another direction or up through the clouds, then down again. And when the instructor said, 'Good, you're holding it nice and steady,' I felt a huge sense of achievement. After twenty minutes or so, he said, 'I want you to land over by that lighthouse.' But no matter how hard I tried I simply could not get my Spit down. With a deep feeling of humiliation I had to allow the instructor to take over.

But I absolutely adored my first flying lesson and can't wait to go back and see if I can improve on a few very dodgy manoeuvres and have another go at landing.

Richard Poad, an ex-pilot, is the founder of this gem of a museum. What he doesn't know about the ATA is truly not worth knowing. He answered loads of questions which I noted, and when he said, 'I'd be happy to read your novel before you send it to the publishers to make sure there aren't any howlers,' I practically threw myself at him in gratitude. What a generous offer.

When I finally finished draft number 17 (or thereabouts) I sent it to him. Only days later he emailed that he'd completed it and found it 'very entertaining'. A list of corrections followed that same evening, mostly ATA inaccuracies which he suggested how to rectify. I am eternally grateful to him, and without his congratulations that I'd done a thorough research job and hadn't over-glamorised life in the ATA, I'm not sure I would have had the confidence to send this one to the publishers.

I do hope you, the reader, will enjoy the story as much as I have enjoyed writing it, safe in the knowledge that almost all the flying incidents my heroine and her friends encounter actually happened in real life to those brave women pilots of the ATA.

I mustn't forget all the other people who helped bring this novel to fruition. There's my dear wise agent, Heather Holden-Brown, of HHB, and the fabulously creative team at Avon HarperCollins, especially Katie Loughnane, my talented editor, who understands my characters – sometimes more than I do myself! My book is all the better for your shrewd observations and gentle suggestions, Katie.

And where would I be without my fabulous writing pals? There are the Diamonds, all published authors: Terri Fleming, Sue Mackender and Joanne Walsh. We have such fun at our monthly all-day meetings, particularly when we brainstorm plots.

The same applies to another small group, the Vestas, that I treasure being part of, although we only manage to meet a couple of times a year on weekly retreats in their second homes: Gail Aldwin, Suzanne Goldring and Carol McGrath – again, all published authors.

Then there's Alison Morton, thriller novelist with a strong alternate history 'Roma Nova' series behind her and more books in the wings; she's a good friend and the best critique writing partner I could wish for. We read everything of each other's with red pen firmly in hand, even though we write in completely different genres. It works like magic.

My husband, Edward Stanton, always gets the last mention, but he reads my novels mainly to check for any anachronisms and historical errors. He particularly enjoyed reading *A Sister's Courage* as he was in the RAF in the late fifties in wireless maintenance working on aeroplanes and is obsessed with all vintage aircraft. He found plenty of mistakes to satisfy his superiority in this field!

Reading List

I can recommend every single one of these books, all non-fiction, many of which are actual memoirs of the incredible ATA women:

Lettice Curtis: Her Autobiography (2004)

The Female Few: Spitfire Heroines by Jacky Hyams (2012)

The Spitfire Girl: My Life in the Sky by Jackie Moggridge (1957)

Contact Britain! by Nancy Miller Livingston Stratford (2010) (American pilot)

Naomi the Aviatrix by Nick Thomas (2011) (American pilot)

Spreading My Wings by Diana Barnato Walker (2003)

The Hurricane Girls by Jo Wheeler (2018)

Spitfire Women of World War II by Giles Whittell (2007)

Read on for an exclusive extract
from the next Molly Green novel . . .

A Sister's Song

Coming May 2020

Chapter One

Downne, Near Bromley
Easter 1943

Suzanne stood at the open door of a side room leading into the main area of the village hall, ready to take her place by the other musicians. She couldn't stop shivering. Although it was mild outside, the hall was always cold – but it wasn't that. She had never before performed the solo in the finale of her favourite violin concerto in front of a real audience.

There was her cue.

You'll be all right, she told herself sternly, holding her violin tight to her chest. Despite shaking legs she walked up the three steps to the wooden platform they called a stage. The eight other musicians turned their heads towards her as she nodded to them, then at the modest audience. She sat down, her fingers instinctively tracing the familiar curving outline of her instrument.

Even though Suzanne couldn't see that well in the gloom of the badly lit hall, she couldn't mistake Maman. Swathed in her fur coat which she refused to discard until May, her mother sat in the front row on one of the hard chairs, no doubt on the cushion she always brought with her. But where was her sister Ronnie? She should be by Maman's side. But

415

this was no time to start asking questions. The conductor looked at her with raised eyebrows. Suzanne settled her violin under her chin, took up her bow, and nodded.

As soon as she played the first notes she relaxed, now sure of herself. Barely aware of her surroundings, she closed her eyes, the music filling her brain, her heart, and flowing through to the tips of her elegant fingers as the bow caressed the strings of her beloved violin.

Her whole being was immersed in Mendelssohn's wonderful concerto when suddenly the high-pitched, blood-curdling wail of an air-raid siren, rising and falling over and over again, stopped her in mid-stroke. Her heart jumped with fright. She'd never heard one so close. Dear God. The Luftwaffe must be heading for Bromley. Or even Downe! Blood pounded through her temples. Her fingers fluttered. Would the hall be struck? Why weren't people rushing out of the door?

Everyone on the platform stopped. Suzanne hesitated and looked over to the audience. One tall man at the back immediately sprang up, caught her eye for a brief moment and nodded, then shoved his hat on and quickly left. *He* certainly wasn't going to risk it by staying, and she couldn't really blame him. Oh dear, there was Maman on her feet. Should she go to her? No one else moved. They sat quietly on the hard seats, faces upturned, as though eager to hear the rest of the piece. To her relief she saw her mother look round at the others and quickly sit down again. Suzanne glanced at the conductor who tapped on his stand and said:

'Back to the beginning of the solo, please, ladies and gentlemen.'

There was nothing for it but to carry on. She nodded, her hand shaking as she took up her bow, waiting a few moments for her introduction.

416

A minute later a droning sound, and then a high-pitched whine – different from the siren – sounded overhead. *BOOM!* The sound of an explosion rattled her eardrums as the very platform she sat on shook with the vibration. She was frozen to the chair. Then another explosion. Her heart thudded against her ribs waiting for the next one. This time the noise was deafening when one of the windows shattered. A few heads briefly turned, then looked towards the small orchestra again. Still no one got up to leave. The conductor gestured once again for her to continue.

Somehow the bravery of her audience transferred itself to her and she played the last section, her fear replaced by her love of the joyous music. Although still trembling, she poured her heart and soul out to the audience, letting the music flow and comfort them. She played the final notes and sat, beads of perspiration gathering on her forehead, completely spent.

There was a hush for what felt like minutes but must have only been seconds. And then the sound of applause echoed round the draughty hall.

Her cheeks flushed with embarrassment at such an enthusiastic response, Suzanne faced the audience who were still applauding. She could see Maman clapping louder than anyone else but it was strange that Ronnie hadn't appeared. Suzanne knew her younger sister didn't much care for classical music, but she'd said only this morning she'd be coming with Maman.

Dear God, please don't let something have happened to Ronnie in the air raid.

A feeling of unease crept over her but she pasted a smile on her face for Maman, and was rewarded by the little hat bobbing up and down as her mother waved and blew kisses in her daughter's direction.

417

Mr Rubenstein, the elderly conductor, bowed and gestured to Suzanne to stand and take a bow for her solo performance. Still shaken from the noise of the bombs, she briefly lowered her head and bent forward. Next, the other musicians stood, looking towards her, softly clapping and smiling.

Before she could respond, the whine of another siren filled the hall, but this time it built to a high crescendo and stayed there for more than a minute. Suzanne breathed out slowly and smiled back at the musicians and then the audience. It was the welcome sound of the All Clear, now practically swallowed up by another enthusiastic burst of clapping from the concert-goers and shouts of 'Hurrah!'

'That was close,' Mr Rubenstein said, addressing the audience. 'And we would have completely understood if you'd left for the shelter, so I want to thank you for having such faith that we would all come through this latest attack together.'

'It was a bit like the *Titanic*,' someone at the back called out. 'The band kept playing even when it was going down, so we thought we'd better stay on, too.'

There was laughter and cheers and more clapping, until the musicians sat down again and began to play the first notes of the National Anthem. Immediately, the audience sprang to its feet and sang with even more gusto than usual.

The concert was deemed a great success – everyone said so as they trooped out of the village hall into the cool early April night.

'Wasn't that lovely?' Suzanne heard Mrs Holmes, one of their neighbours, say to her friend. 'Something beautiful to listen to . . . and almost spoilt by those dreadful Nazis. But they have us all wrong if they think we're scared of them.'

'Yes, I'm glad we stayed till the end,' Mrs Holmes's friend agreed, 'but I wonder where those bombs dropped. What damage they've done. It'll be more misery, that's for certain.'

'Maman' – Suzanne turned to her mother who was gripping her arm – 'Constable Peters is over by the door. I'm going to have a word with him.'

'I would prefer to go straight home.'

'I want to ask if he's seen Ronnie, so just wait a moment – please, Maman.'

She broke from her mother's grasp and hurried over.

'Constable Peters, was anyone hurt in that raid just now? I'm so worried about Ronnie – you know, my young sister.'

'No one hurt, miss, as far as I know. They all got safely into the shelter – except all of you in the village hall,' he added. 'You want to think yourselves lucky you didn't come to no 'arm.'

'Did you see Ronnie?' Suzanne said anxiously.

'Not that I remember.' PC Peters stroked his chin, making a rasping noise. 'Mind you, they was all packed in tight so I might have overlooked her. She's shorter than you and your other sister, isn't she?'

Suzanne nodded. 'I can't help being worried because she was supposed to have come to the concert this evening.'

'I 'aven't 'eard nothing to the contrary,' the constable said. 'Fortunately, the bombs all dropped in the field, so no real damage, thank the Lord. Even the cows and horses were spared, so I shouldn't worry too much.'

Suzanne thanked him and turned to see Maman hovering behind her, impatiently tapping her foot.

'What did he say?' Simone demanded. 'Has he seen Véronique?'

'No, but he said everyone got into the shelter and no one was hurt.'

As far as I know, PC Peters had added. Suzanne swallowed. She wouldn't alarm her mother, but she wouldn't feel happy until she saw her sister, unharmed, with her own eyes.

'That is a relief.' Maman dabbed her eyes with a pristine

handkerchief. 'You made me worry for a moment. Let us go home and put the kettle on.'

'You sound like a real Englishwoman,' Suzanne said, smiling, as she tucked her arm through her mother's for the short walk.

'That is not a compliment for me,' Simone admonished, somehow making the cloth bag holding her cushion look elegant as it dangled from her wrist. She stepped along the pavement, her high heels making a rhythmic tap.

'Just teasing, Maman. You're French through and through, and could never pretend otherwise.'

Her mother flashed her a smile of forgiveness. 'I do not understand teasing, as you well know, Suzanne, but if you say it was only a joke, I will believe you.'

Oh, dear. Maman was so touchy these days.

'Ronnie told me she was coming with you.' Suzanne couldn't push down that niggling feeling that all was not right with her sister. That something had happened.

'She told me the same.' Simone pursed her mouth. 'And I do wish you would call her by her proper name, Suzanne. How many times do I ask you?'

'She hates being called Véronique,' Suzanne said. 'You know what a tomboy she is, and she doesn't feel it suits her. In a way, she's right, but she'll change when she's a bit older and starts to notice the boys.'

'She should be proud of her name,' Simone said. 'I gave you all beautiful French names and she and Lorraine refuse to use them.' She flicked a glance at Suzanne. 'At least you do not call yourself Suzy like your sisters do. If you did, I would be very upset.'

'Did you see her before you left?' Suzanne asked, wanting to change the subject about their names that Maman brought up time and time again, and trying to work out what could have happened to Ronnie.

'She came in from a walk. I told her to wash her face and change into something presentable, but that I must leave so I am not late.' She threw a glance at Suzanne. 'Sometimes I cannot believe she is my own daughter, that it is so hard for her to find anything suitable. I expect she decided to remain at home.'

'I don't think so,' Suzanne said worriedly. 'She doesn't really care about whether she's dressed appropriately or not.'

'Well, she ought.' Simone's tone was non-compromising when it came to fashion and appearances.

'I do hope she found somewhere safe in the air raid.' Suzanne bit her lip. 'But if she'd started out for the village hall and heard the siren, she didn't go into the shelter – at least, Constable Peters couldn't remember seeing her there.'

'She knows to go under the dining table,' her mother said firmly. 'That is where we will find her.'

Suzanne gripped her violin case closer to her side and, unable to ignore the knot of anxiety growing in her stomach, prayed silently that her mother was right.

If you loved *A Sister's Courage*, why not curl up with another heart-warming story from Molly Green?

War rages on, but the women and children of
Liverpool's Dr Barnardo's Home cannot give up
hope…

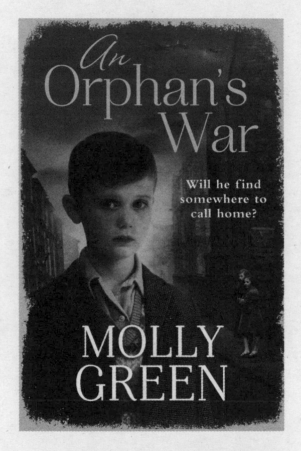

Available in paperback and ebook now.

Even when all seems lost at Dr Barnardo's
orphanage, there is always a glimmer of hope to
be found…

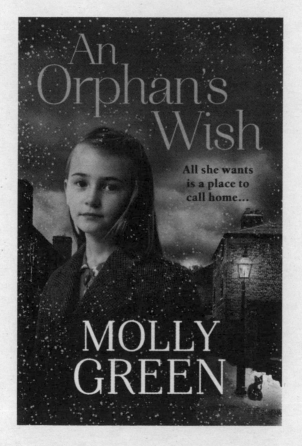

Available in paperback and ebook now.